THE BURNING MAN

A GRIPPING SERIAL KILLER WITH A SHOCKING TWIST

DI STEPHANIE BROADBENT SURREY HILLS CRIME THRILLERS

BOOK 3

JACK PROBYN

CLIFF EDGE PRESS

eBook ISBN: 978-1-80520-193-9
Paperback ISBN: 978-1-80520-194-6
First Edition

Visit Jack Probyn's website at www.jackprobynbooks.com.

ABOUT THE BOOK

When the charred remains of a body are found in the quaint Surrey Hills, the trauma of DI Stephanie Broadbent's past is reignited.

The victim has been burned alive. No clues. No witnesses. Soon every lead turns to ash.

When another body appears, Stephanie uncovers a connection that threatens to set the world — and more bodies — alight.

If she is to catch the killer, she must step into the flames and face her fear.

CHAPTER
ONE

When Nigel Hadlow first opened his eyes, a sharp burst of pain detonated behind his skull, flashing like a thunderstorm and leaving him dazed and disoriented. As he opened them again and his vision began to clear, he took in his surroundings and realised he was enclosed by four wooden walls that felt as though they were closing in on him.

The mid-November air was cold and sharp, damp with the scent of hay and decaying manure from outside, soon overpowered by a chemical smell that clung to the back of his throat like splinters and made his stomach twist.

He tried to move.

Nothing happened.

He tried again, straining his arms and legs, and that's when he realised his hands were stretched wide beside him, bound tightly at the wrists with what felt like rope, anchored to something in the concrete floor. He craned his neck down the length of his body and, in the weak light, saw his ankles bound together, also encased in rope and fixed to something cold and hard.

He was in a horror movie.

Panic bloomed in his chest.

He tried to shout, but his voice came out weak and broken, as if he had been screaming for some time without realising it.

What the hell was happening? How had he ended up here?

He closed his eyes and tried to remember.

He'd pulled over on the side of the road after hearing a strange noise from the tyres. He'd left the engine running and hopped out, making his way round to the front of the car to inspect them. Then another car had pulled over, awkwardly and at an angle, its tyres skidding as if the driver were in a rush. A figure had emerged and started towards him. It was dark – after seven o'clock – and so visibility had been low, except for the headlights briefly illuminating the figure's features. Yet there'd been something familiar about the face, hadn't there?

Yes.

Except he couldn't place it. A face lost long ago. Lost to time, lost until it had become less than a memory.

And then darkness.

He hadn't noticed the Taser being drawn from the figure's pocket. His brain had shut off completely. And now here he was, in the middle of a cold, dark place, tied to the floor like he was on a cross.

The sound of the Taser echoed in his ears again, furious and electric.

It was quickly replaced by another noise. Something nearby. More repetitive. Harsher.

Moving closer. Getting louder.

He caught a glimpse out of the corner of his eye. A flash of orange, red, yellow. Small at first, but unmistakable. A flame, poking its head beneath the wooden wall.

As soon as it registered in his delirious state, Nigel's body trembled against the ropes. He yanked with all his strength, but the bindings didn't yield. The more he struggled, the more the fibres bit into his skin, carving lines into his wrists and ankles. Blood trickled, warm and useless.

Within seconds, a line of fire crawled along the bottom of one of the walls, greedily consuming straw and wooden debris like dry paper, spitting hot embers into the air. The wooden beams above groaned and popped, their frames blistering under the heat.

Nigel screamed.

Pure, animalistic terror.

The fire surged forward, creeping along the floor towards him. The dense smoke thickened, wrapping around his face and filling his lungs. He coughed and gagged, his throat seizing as the oxygen was pulled from his body.

His chest heaved, each inhale agony like glass shards slicing down his windpipe.

'Help!' he rasped, his voice failing. It was barely louder than a whisper.

The flames continued their approach, like a predator slowly stalking its prey. He could feel the heat, blistering, searing, singeing the hair on his body. His back arched instinctively, trying to break free from his restraints, but the ropes held fast.

He writhed. His skin prickled. Then boiled.

The fire kissed his boots first, melting the soles. Flames burst around his ankles, then curled into the crooks of his knees, swallowing the ropes until they charred and split. The pain came quickly. Great swathes of agony erupted within him. Soon after, his flesh blistered, then burst. The agony was white-hot, crawling up his legs like molten lead. He screamed again, but the smoke stole the sound from his throat, just as it was about to steal his life.

His body convulsed.

Then came the worst part. The realisation that he wasn't going to die instantly.

That it would be slow and deliberate, designed to make him suffer, to make him feel every excruciating second.

The fire climbed his stomach, flaring over his chest and curling under his arms. His shirt caught – a whoosh of flame like a match to dry twigs. His skin peeled. His eyes bulged. His lips parted, but he could no longer scream. Just the sound of choking. Suffocating in smoke.

Above him, the building's structure groaned again.

He turned his head in one last act of instinct, straining towards the door that would never open. Towards the air he'd never breathe. Towards the light that would never come.

And then darkness, and the pain stopped.

CHAPTER
TWO

The egg bobbed violently in the simmering water, bouncing off the walls of the new Tefal pan she had bought at the weekend like it was trying to escape. Stephanie leaned against the kitchen counter, arms folded, watching the bubbles burst and leap like they were at a concert. She became mesmerised, lost in the bubbles, her eyes struggling to keep up with the egg as it ricocheted and danced. Leaning forward, she hovered her face over the water. The heat was intense, and she quickly retreated as droplets of water splashed onto her arm. Pain flared on her bare skin, and she rinsed it under the tap. A few moments later, the pain subsided, replaced by a dull, numbing sensation. She switched off the tap and stared at the tiny red welt blooming on her forearm. A pinprick of pain.

She stood there for a moment, leaning against the sink, looking outside. A light drizzle had begun to fall that morning, pattering against the window.

Then the water in the pan began to spill over and sizzle on the electric hob, distracting her. She sprang into action, carefully removing the heavy pan by the handle with both hands. Steam curled up from the pot, rising in ghostly fingers. Keeping one hand on the handle, she switched off the hob with the other. Just as she started to drain the water into the colander she'd found lurking at the back of one of her cupboards, her phone began to ring, vibrating angrily on the surface. Her eyes flicked towards the screen, and in that brief second, she tilted the water too quickly, splashing some onto her forearm.

'Bugger!'

She dropped the pan clanging into the sink. A wave of pain welled on her skin, and she swore repeatedly under her breath while keeping her eyes fixed on the screen.

She recognised the number immediately.

He was calling again. The twentieth time in the last five weeks. Or was it more? She'd lost count.

Not to mention lost interest.

She had no desire to speak with him. He had come into her life recently, and already she felt as though he was trying to impose himself on her, moving at his own pace when, in her mind, it should have been the other way around. Sure, he was the one whose father had just died, and he had also just discovered he had two half-sisters he knew nothing about. Sure, he was the one who'd just found out that his dad was actually his uncle and that his real father had given him away at birth. And yes, he had grown up an only child while Stephanie had her sister, Kimberley. But so what? Where was the consideration for what *she'd* gone through? She had spent the past thirty years trying to free herself from the stranglehold her father had over her. She was the one who'd been abused and maltreated by him. Not Kimberley. And certainly not Jordan. By all accounts, he'd had a loving childhood that had only soured in recent years. But still, there was no consideration for her.

Finally, the call ended. Her jaw clenched as the missed call notification appeared on the screen. She continued staring at it, waiting for the voicemail notification to show up.

A moment later, it did.

Another one. No doubt similar to the rest.

Hey Steph, it's me. Just wanted to see if you were free this weekend for some coffee maybe? I know Kim mentioned there's a place she likes, and I think she wanted to come as well. Would be good to see you and finally have a chat. Anyway, you know where to find me...

As the screen turned black, his face appeared in the reflection. She grimaced, her body flushing cold. It was frightening how much Jordan looked like him – like their father. The dark, leering look in his eyes. The sharp, angular face. Even the way his hair was beginning to recede at the temples.

She couldn't shake the creepy sensation that coursed up and down her body.

Mercifully, her brain reminded her that there was something else she needed to tend to: the pain in her wrist that felt like it was beginning to spread to her upper arm. She turned on the cold tap again, allowing the icy water to flow over her forearm, offering some relief as it cascaded over her skin. For a moment, she closed her eyes and focused solely on the running water splashing against the stainless steel sink, and the distant patter of rain against the glass.

Once the pain dulled, she reached for a tea towel and gently patted the burn dry. She absently peeled the egg, the shell cracking like dry bark beneath her fingertips, and dumped it onto a plate with a handful of wilted salad leaves, a drizzle of olive oil, and a dash of Maldon sea salt.

Hardly the breakfast of champions, but it would be enough to get her through the litany of meetings she had that morning.

She sat at the table, pulled the plate towards her, and speared the egg with a fork. Just as she was about to take a bite, her phone began to ring again.

Not Jordan this time.

Control.

She groaned and wiped her mouth with the back of her hand, her thumb hovering over the green icon before she swiped to answer.

'Broadbent.'

The voice on the other end was professional, calm.

'Detective Inspector, sorry to disturb you. We've had a call from Guildford Fire and Rescue. They received reports this morning of a barn that may have been set on fire overnight.'

'Right. Are the fire teams on it?'

'Yes, ma'am.'

'So why are you calling for the Major Investigation Team?'

'Because they believe they've found human remains in the wreckage, ma'am.'

CHAPTER
THREE

The charred remains of the barn were located in the middle of farmland in Chilworth, a short drive from Guildford, accessible only by a narrow, single-lane country road. Stephanie spotted the burnt-out structure half a mile away, a blotch of blackness against the patchwork of green and brown hills surrounding it. She pulled the car to a stop a few hundred yards away, joining the back of a long line of police cars and fire engines, before making her way along the path to the crime scene.

She was certain it was psychological, but she could feel the temperature rising, the residual heat from the building warming her cheeks and forehead, as if she were stepping closer to a fire that was no longer there. Then she inhaled; the acrid scent of combustion, burned timber, and scorched rubber filled her nostrils.

As she reached the end of the path and the remains came into view, she slowed to a stop, shielding her eyes from the low early autumn sun.

Then the world tilted.

The smell. The sight. Burning plastic, charred wood, and something almost sweet rotting beneath it. The same bitter scent had lingered in her hair, on her skin, and on her pillowcases for weeks during her childhood.

She removed her hand from her eyes, and soon the sun faded. She was no longer in Chilworth, no longer standing in front of a crime scene with uniformed officers and firefighters. She was five years old again, back in that semi-detached house, outside in the garden with the rusted climbing frame and decaying plants.

And he was there.

Her father.

It was early spring, and Stephanie had been sitting outside on the patio, playing with her favourite Barbie doll, Jenny. Jenny with the curly blonde hair and the happy smile. Jenny, who never got angry or shouted. Jenny, who she could talk to and always laugh with.

One moment, she was holding her. The next, she was gone, snatched away by her father.

'Watch,' he said, his voice slurred with alcohol. 'Watch what happens when you don't listen.'

She remembered saying no. Begging. Pleading with him not to.

But he grinned – that insidious, yellow-toothed grin – and set Jenny on the ground before igniting his lighter and holding the flame beneath the doll's hand. The reaction was slow at first: a blackened finger, a slight curl of the plastic. Then, a sudden *poof*. The arm flared bright orange, twisting and melting like wax. The strands of hair caught next, singeing and shrivelling into nothing. Stephanie screamed and lunged forward, but he backhanded her without looking, hard enough to slam her against the side of the house.

Then he grabbed her, holding her face close to the flames. The heat. The stench. It felt as if death itself were breathing on her. She watched as Jenny's body slowly melted away, her head becoming dizzy from the fumes. She remembered the warmth against her face, the ends of her loose hair singeing along with Jenny's as she watched her closest friend's leg curl into a blackened spiral.

Her father's evil, insipid laugh echoed in her mind as the scene faded and the barn came into focus again.

She blinked hard, once, twice, grounding herself.

The fire was gone, but the burn was still there.

She shuffled forward a few steps, taking in her surroundings. What had once been a two-storey agricultural storehouse now stood as a collapsed, skeletal shell. Its beams were blackened to brittle charcoal, like broken ribs. A mass of ash, blackened and damp, clung to the ground. A cordon of blue-and-white tape flapped softly at the edge of the field. Two uniformed constables stood at the entrance. Within the cordon, people moved with quiet urgency. Fire officers in high-visibility jackets clustered near the barn's southern wall, while crime scene investigators, already suited in white paper suits, photographed every blackened inch of the interior.

Stephanie signed in at the cordon, changed into a suit of her own, and then ducked beneath the tape. She was unable to move any farther; her legs had turned to lead, and she didn't have the strength to bring herself closer to the wreckage. She had experienced something similar only a few months before when a university student had been burnt alive in her car. Stephanie had hung back then too, standing at a safe distance, unable to get closer.

'First crime scene?' a man asked, stopping beside her.

Stephanie turned her head towards the voice and did a double-take.

The man standing beside her was tall and broad-shouldered beneath his red firefighter top. On his lower half were his fire-retardant trousers, their high-visibility strips glinting in the sun. A tapestry of scars marked his skin, running up and down his muscular arms, as well as across his neck and face, remnants of a fire incident that had left him severely burned. He noticed her gaze linger on his scars but didn't flinch, didn't say anything, and didn't attempt to hide them. Instead he accepted the stares as if he were used to them.

'My... my first crime scene?' she repeated, mumbling. She knew it was impolite to stare, but there was something both alluring and remarkable about his wounds that held her gaze. 'I've attended quite a few in my time.'

He smiled warmly at her, chuckling softly. 'Me too.'

'This is my first fire scene in a while though. Especially one like this.'

'Not a fan?'

She shook her head. 'Possibly my least favourite.'

'Fear of fire?'

She shrugged. 'You could say that.'

'I did for a while...' he began.

She studied his arms and neck, trying to do it without drawing attention. 'Because of your...? Your...?' She couldn't finish the sentence.

The man glanced down at his wounds. 'Car caught fire when I was a kid. My dad was driving; we hit the central reservation on the motorway, and then the thing went up in flames. All I remember is someone pulling me from the wreckage while it was ablaze.'

'Christ. How old were you?'

'Thirteen. The doctors said I was lucky to be alive. But they worked wonders on me in the end.'

'And you thought, what better career than the one that nearly killed you?'

'I could have spent my life being bitter about it, but instead, I chose not to let it define me. The best way to face your fear is to jump into it head-on.'

Stephanie pondered on that a moment, taking it in and considering it.

'I'm Elias, by the way.' He extended his hand for her. 'Elias Thorne. I'm the watch manager at Guildford fire station.'

'Detective Inspector Stephanie Broadbent,' she replied.

'I guess you need to know what sort of crime scene we're dealing with here.'

'Good place to start.'

He smiled at her, displaying a set of white teeth, and she found him strangely charming. 'Are you all right to come and have a look?'

She glanced at the barn, inhaled deeply, then exhaled slowly.

'What's the worst that could happen?' he asked, gesturing to his forearms.

'That's the spirit.'

As they stepped forward, Elias spoke in a low, calm, and measured voice. She'd used the same matter-of-fact manner when she was relaying information. 'This place hasn't seen anyone in years, I don't think. The call came in this morning at eight o'clock, when a mountain biker spotted the smoke.'

'Nobody saw it beforehand?'

'No.'

'What about the flames?'

He shook his head. 'The fire started in the middle of the night. Just before midnight.'

'How do you know?'

'We can tell by how burnt the wood is. At least, it gives us an estimate.'

'How accurate is it?'

'As accurate as an estimate can be,' Elias said with a shrug. 'We'll have to analyse the matter more closely, but I'm confident in that time frame.'

'The person from Control said there was a body inside.'

They came to a stop just outside what had presumably been the front of the barn, but was now reduced to a heap of scorched wood. Elias pointed to a spot in the centre of the barn's footprint.

'That's where the body was found. From what's left of the victim, we assume it's a male. Middle aged, possibly. Somewhere between thirties and sixties. I know it doesn't narrow it down much, but... there's not much of him left. He's mostly carbonised. The fire consumed most of the soft tissue.' Elias spoke clinically, respectfully. 'We believe he was lying down when the fire reached flashover. Based on the charring patterns, it likely happened fast. Minutes, maybe less.'

They moved amongst the debris, stepping carefully until they reached the body. Elias crouched beside what remained: a blackened outline, limbs curled inwards, one arm angled above the skull like a grotesque dance pose. Stephanie stood beside him, her paper suit already clinging damply to her arms with sweat.

'The body's in what's called the pugilistic pose; see how the arms and legs are flexed like that?' He gestured with a gloved hand. 'That's caused by muscle contraction during exposure to intense heat. The heat dehydrates the muscles, shrinks them, and pulls the limbs into this defensive shape. It's sometimes called the "boxer's pose".'

Stephanie crouched beside him, careful not to disturb the footprint markings laid out by the CSI team. Her body trembled with fear, but somehow she maintained her composure.

'The skin's completely gone,' she said quietly.

Elias nodded. 'Yes. Most of the epidermis and dermis layers have been entirely incinerated. What you're looking at now is carbonised tissue and bone. In some areas, the outer surface of the bones has actually split due to the heat; this is known as heat fracture.' He gently pointed at the torso, or what remained of it. 'The clothing fibres have burned away, but the remnants have fused with the skin and muscle, creating this charred mass. Synthetic materials, especially nylon and polyester, don't just burn; they melt and they stick. Almost like napalm.'

Stephanie swallowed against the rising nausea, but it had little effect.

Elias continued. 'If he was alive when the fire started, he would've gone through several stages of trauma. First, smoke inhalation: the lungs fill with superheated gases, causing swelling in the airways. Breathing becomes impossible. The smoke itself leads to disorientation, confusion, and even unconsciousness.' He gestured towards the chest cavity. 'We won't know for certain until the post-mortem, but if there's soot in the trachea or lungs, it will indicate he was still breathing when it happened. If there's no soot, he may have been unconscious, or dead, before the ignition.'

Stephanie stared at the blackened skull. 'Is there any indication that he was tied, bound, or pinned to the ground somehow?'

Elias shook his head, then paused to look at the body before responding. 'Nothing that we can clearly see yet. Other than some melted nails and a few hinges, which you might find anyway in a place like this, there's nothing resembling cuffs or brackets. What's there could have been part of the barn's original structure.'

'So it's possible he came here voluntarily?' Stephanie asked. 'Suicide?'

'Maybe. His positioning doesn't scream struggle, but that doesn't mean to say there wasn't one. We won't know until we've had plenty of time to assess the scene.'

Stephanie paused and surveyed the charred interior of the barn, taking in the devastation around her. Her gaze fell to the victim's skeleton, focusing on the soot-covered teeth in his jaw.

Elias's words echoed in her mind: No better way to face your fears than to jump into them head-on.

Had this man literally been confronting his fears, or was he fleeing from them? Either way, his actions had led to his death.

'How long until we can get him out of here?'

'By midday at the latest.'

That gave them some time to try and find out who he was, and why he was there.

CHAPTER
FOUR

It was times like this that he was grateful for the face mask, for the thin layer of material keeping out most of the toxins and stench that threatened to poison his lungs and leave a black residue in his nostrils.

Derry Oscar was picking his way through the blackened skeleton of what had once been a barn, carefully navigating along the eastern wall. The ground was a grim carpet of ash and debris, with scorched timber, twisted metal, and the occasional unidentifiable lump that might have once been farm equipment or something more worrying.

Derry sifted through the wreckage methodically, his movements practised and patient. Twenty-three years on the job had taught him that crime scenes gave up their secrets slowly, reluctantly. All you had to do was flirt with them a little bit, and they would eventually give it up.

Shame the same ethos had never translated into his personal life.

Reaching the end of the wall, he moved into the corner where it met another wall and shifted a piece of charred wood when a glint of metal caught his eye. There, half-buried beneath a collapsed beam and covered in a thick layer of soot, was a small rectangular tin. Derry's pulse quickened as he carefully brushed away the debris. He had always loved discovering little trinkets, fragments of victims' lives that offered clues about who they were and what type of people they had been.

He hadn't expected to find anything at this crime scene.

Until now.

The tin was old-fashioned, the sort typically used for storing tobacco or sweets, and remarkably intact despite the inferno that had consumed everything around it.

He lifted it with both hands, surprised by its weight, and carefully opened it, easing the hinges with extreme caution. Inside, shielded from the flames by the metal casing, he found a photograph depicting the face and shoulders of a teenage boy, no more than thirteen or fourteen, smiling faintly with youthful innocence. It was a snapshot of a happy moment in time. Derry pulled it out for a closer look. The photograph appeared to have been hastily cut, suggesting it was part of a larger, more complete image.

A miracle it hadn't perished in the blaze.

As he turned it over to examine the back, Derry noticed an inscription on the bottom of the tin, a message that had been etched into the metal with something sharp.

He wiped away a layer of dust and dirt, revealing a short message:

The day that is coming shall set them ablaze, says the Lord of hosts. - Malachi 4:1

Derry stared at the verse, his mind racing. He had seen many things in his time – a lot of things, in fact – but this one, above all else, was certainly beyond his pay grade.

CHAPTER
FIVE

Half an hour later, after navigating the early morning traffic through Guildford town centre, Stephanie arrived outside the station and parked in her designated spot. She didn't know who'd given it to her, but she was sure it had been done as a practical joke, because it was as far away from the entrance as possible and the only designated space not under the shelter of trees or the shade of the building. She was not looking forward to the intense summer heat beating down on her dashboard in six months' time.

Just as she climbed out of her car, her phone began ringing.

Kimberley.

She answered the call, wedging the phone between her ear and neck as she traversed the car park.

'Morning, sis.'

'Oh, so your phone *is* working!'

Stephanie let out a heavy sigh. 'I told you, I'm not ready.'

'Doesn't mean you can keep ignoring him, though. He's our half-brother, Stephanie.'

'*Your* half-brother. You've been quite happy to let him into your family. But I'm not there yet.'

'Why not?'

She paused outside the entrance, stepping out of the way of the small steps that led to the double doors.

'Because he's part of Dad,' she replied.

'So are we.'

'But we have Mum in us as well. And that balances things out. He has a mum who didn't want him and gave him up, and a dad who didn't want him either.'

Kimberley scoffed, clearly upset by the comment. 'We're not always the product of our parents,' she said. 'He hasn't let that define him. He's had a tough upbringing.'

'Tougher than ours?'

Kimberley mumbled, unable to respond.

'That's what I thought.' She made her way to the entrance and placed her hand on the door to the building. 'I have to go. I'm at work. And you can tell him to stop calling or messaging me. I've seen them, and I don't want to reply. If that ever changes, *I'll* be the one to let *him* know. I've got his mobile number.'

Stephanie hung up before her sister could respond, then entered Mount Browne, Surrey Police headquarters, heading upstairs to the Major Investigation Team's office on the first floor. She pushed the door open and was greeted by the familiar glow of fluorescent lights, the quiet clatter of keyboards, and the soft murmur of early morning conversations. The space was large but cramped, lined with cluttered desks and overstuffed filing cabinets that hadn't been emptied in years. To the left, a bank of desks sat beside windows overlooking the car park and greenery in the distance. On the right was their major incident room, a space that occupied half of the office. Hanging from the walls were multiple whiteboards, each detailing different investigations at varying levels of completion. She searched for a clear whiteboard and found it in the far corner of the room.

'Morning, everyone,' she called, her voice cutting through the noise like a whip crack. 'Meeting in about two minutes, please.'

. . .

A few minutes later, like an average version of the Avengers – without the fancy suits, chiselled abs, or superpowers – the team had assembled, dragging their desk chairs into the space. The first to arrive was DS Noah Mackenzie, who looked like a misplaced extra from a 1970s sci-fi convention, dressed in a deep aubergine velvet coat, a light pink buttoned shirt, a rust-coloured waistcoat, and mustard trousers. His haunted expression suggested he hadn't slept since the seventies as he nursed a coffee cup to his mouth.

Beside him sat DS Devon Lafferty, who had changed the angle of his thick, dark hair so that it now fell to the left. Immediately before her was DC Giles Swinger, finishing the last of his croissant, the crumbs of which were sitting neatly on his chest. To her right were the other women in the team, DC Fiona Singleton and DC Olivia "Wellard" Willard, the latter of whom Stephanie noticed was sitting so far at the back of the meeting that she had almost missed her. Fiona sat in front, fiddling with her lanyard – a countermeasure to stop herself from biting her nails.

Stephanie moved to the clean whiteboard, placed her hands in her pockets, and looked each of them in the eye. She immediately noticed Olivia averting her gaze, staring at the carpet.

'This morning, a body was discovered in a burnt-out barn in Chilworth,' Stephanie said. 'Male. Unknown identity. Between thirty and sixty years old. The body was found in the centre.'

Noah scribbled something on his pad. Giles made a noise like a hum.

Stephanie continued. 'So far, it's being treated as an undetermined cause. No obvious accelerants. And the bindings, if they existed, were destroyed in the fire. So officially, there's no evidence yet of third-party involvement.'

'Arson?' Giles asked.

'You've suggested that about every fire incident we've had this year,' Fiona retorted.

'Only because he's still after the people who started that fire outside his garage,' commented Devon.

'That cost me a fortune! The bloody bastards knew it was my garage as well.' Giles folded his arms across his chest and let out a heavy puff of air that blew the croissant crumbs onto the floor.

'Maybe they did it *because* they knew it was your garage,' Fiona muttered, just loud enough for the others to hear. 'I know I would.'

Noah didn't look up from his notepad. 'Do we know how long the body had been there, ma'am?'

Stephanie shook her head. 'The preliminary estimate from the watch manager is that the fire started around midnight. A mountain biker spotted the smoke around eight this morning. The fire brigade arrived shortly after. The body and barn would've burned for at least eight hours before anybody found him.'

'Any ID at all?' Devon asked, leaning back in his chair, one ankle crossed over the other knee, looking like he was watching a box set rather than discussing a charred corpse.

'Not yet,' Stephanie answered. 'But we'll chase it through dental records and DNA. CSI are hoping to get something usable from the remains.'

'Clothing?' Fiona asked. 'Brand tags, stitching, anything like that?'

'Burned beyond recognition, I'm afraid. What's left of the body is... well, it's mostly gone.'

'Could it have been suicide?' Noah asked, finally glancing up. 'Or someone wanting us to think it was?'

'Exactly,' Stephanie said, pointing a finger at him. 'We need to keep an open mind. Until we know otherwise, it could go either way.'

She turned and scribbled *SUICIDE/MURDER?* across the whiteboard in thick black marker. Then added *VICTIM?* beneath it.

'Any CCTV?' Giles asked, brushing the last of the croissant flakes from his chest, then inspecting his fingertips for the final few crumbs.

'Not much in the way of coverage out there,' Stephanie said. 'It's farmland. Nearest house is almost half a mile away.'

'Do we know who owns the barn?' Devon asked.

'No. You'll need to find that out. From the look of the place, it's been abandoned for a while. All the surrounding pathway and concrete was overgrown with weeds. You'll need to find someone who owns the land or knows it, maybe one of the neighbours, old tenants, or locals who've used the footpaths around it.'

'Could be a good place for addicts or teenagers looking to drink where no one can see them,' Fiona added. 'That kind of space gets used a lot.'

'Sounds like you're talking from experience,' Giles quipped.

Stephanie ignored the comment. 'Usually, I'd agree with you. But I didn't see any signs of recent activity. No rubbish. No beer cans. No syringes. It didn't look like anyone had been there for a while.'

They all sat with that for a moment.

Except Olivia, who hadn't said a word.

Stephanie's eyes lingered on her. 'You all right, Wellard?'

The constable blinked, startled by the attention. 'Yes, ma'am. Just listening.'

'You've been very quiet,' Noah said gently. 'Unusual for you.'

She offered a brittle smile. 'Sorry. I'm all good. Just taking it in, staying in my box.'

Fiona gave her a sideways glance but said nothing.

Stephanie let the silence stretch, then moved on. 'We'll set up a timeline next. Noah, you chase the land ownership and check with the council about the building's history. Fiona, I want you to canvas the area. Nearest properties, find out if anyone heard or saw anything last night. Giles, find CCTV, and see if anyone nearby saw or heard anything. And, Devon, I want you in charge of social media and the press.'

Noah raised a hand as if in class. 'And what are you doing, boss?'

'Waiting for something interesting to land in my inbox. I got a call from the crime scene manager saying that one of the CSIs pulled a metal container out of the rubble. There might be something in that. Won't know more until we get the evidence log come through. Everyone understand?'

The team replied with an almost football-team-like grunt, then rolled back to their desks and set to work. Just as Olivia started to rise from hers, Stephanie called out to her.

'Wellard, you got a minute? My office? Or do you fancy a walk outside?'

CHAPTER
SIX

Olivia entered Stephanie's office with the reluctance of a child being told to put their clothes in the washing basket. She carefully shut the door behind her, as if any loud noise or sudden movement might cause the room to collapse. Standing with her hands behind her back, she surveyed the space that had, in recent weeks, transformed from a neutral room into something more personal, inviting, and welcoming. There were now plants in the corners, purifying the air for Stephanie, along with photographs of her fondest memories from her police service and a few colourful ornaments she'd bought from the shopping centre in town to brighten up the place a bit.

Stephanie pulled out her desk chair and settled into it, gesturing for Olivia to sit opposite her. The constable moved across reluctantly. Olivia was like the mother of the office. Caring, considerate; she was always checking in on the rest of the team and asking if they needed anything. She always put the needs of the team over everyone else. But Stephanie wondered how many times people did the same for her. Whether they questioned if she was okay or if anything was keeping her awake at night.

Stephanie rested her forearms on the desk and leaned forward slightly.

'So,' she said softly, 'what's happening?'

'What do you mean?' Olivia asked, hiding behind a small smirk that carried no conviction. She lowered her gaze to her hands.

'Something's up. I can sense it. It's my job. You were really quiet just now. You're usually throwing comments around before suggesting you get back in your box.'

'Am I?'

'Come on, Wellard. Is everything all right?'

Olivia offered a shrug in response. Then, quietly, she replied, 'I'm just... just having one of those days.'

Stephanie remained silent for a moment, allowing the silence to fill the room in a way that felt safe rather than awkward.

'Nothing else going on? Home? The kids?'

Olivia sighed, her cheeks puffing slightly. 'They're giving me a hard time at the moment. They're at that age where they talk back, think they're the bee's knees, and give me loads of aggro just for trying to look out for them. Harry thinks he's too cool for everything, and Josh has been acting out recently. Got a call from the school yesterday because he told his maths teacher to... well, you know, f-off, basically.'

Stephanie winced. 'Charming.'

'And they only talk to me when they want something,' Olivia said with a weary chuckle. 'Teenage boys are like flatmates who don't pay rent and treat you like a vending machine. It's just... relentless sometimes.'

'Sounds exhausting.'

'It is. And here... I love this job, I really do. But lately, I've been feeling like I'm... fading into the background a bit. Just logging statements and updating HOLMES, day in, day out. It's mind-numbing. I want to feel useful again. I want to do more than data entry and fixing people's typos.'

Stephanie studied her. It wasn't a complaint; it was a confession, a cry for help. Stephanie wanted nothing more than to elevate her entire team. That was what leaders did. If one person thrived, they all did. If one person fell behind, they all rallied to support them.

'You've been solid since the day I got here,' Stephanie said. 'You keep things moving, keep us sane, and we'd be in a deep mess without you.

But if you want more – *really* want more – I'll back you. Are you interested in taking on a bigger role in this one?'

Olivia blinked. 'Like what?'

'Like Giles did previously. You saw the change in him?'

'It went to his head. Wouldn't shut up about it.'

'Well, now it can be your turn. What do you say?'

'I don't know… I don't know what I'm doing.'

Stephanie smirked. 'That's the beauty of it. None of us do. But we find a way to make it work.' She glanced at her screen. 'First thing on the list would be the post-mortem. Liaise with the fire team and Leanna, find out how long our victim's been dead, and see if you can get his identity.'

Olivia hesitated, then straightened slightly. 'You want *me* to go?'

Stephanie nodded. 'I think you're more than capable. And if you want to progress, you'll need exposure to every part of the process. You up for it?'

'Yeah,' Olivia said, a small but growing sense of determination emerging. 'Yeah, I think I am.'

'Good. And you can still log stuff into HOLMES if it soothes your soul.'

Olivia let out a genuine laugh, the tension easing from her shoulders. 'It really doesn't.'

Stephanie grinned. 'Welcome to the next level, then.'

'Lucky me.'

'Some people dream of a morning surrounded by the smell of formaldehyde.'

'Those people need a holiday.'

Stephanie stood. 'Right. I'll forward you the details and make sure Leanna knows you're attending. And if the school calls again, put them through to me. I'd be more than happy to take that burden off your shoulders.'

They both chuckled, the moment lingering until Olivia stood and reached for the door.

'Thanks, ma'am.'

'Anytime,' Stephanie replied. 'And Olivia…?'

She paused, halfway out.

'Don't doubt yourself again, please. You and I wouldn't be having this conversation if I didn't think you were not only capable but deserving of it. You work hard for the team, and I want to work hard for you in return. But if your head gets as big as Giles's – or bigger – then I will have to put you back in your box.'

CHAPTER
SEVEN

The moment Olivia stepped out of Stephanie's office, she felt it. A shift. Like something inside her had realigned. She wasn't floating or beaming, but there was a subtle lift in her chest, a quiet surge of energy in her bones. Her step had a bounce it hadn't had in weeks, months. And the world had taken on a brighter, warmer tint as she exited the building. For the first time in a long time, she noticed the colours of the cars, the trees, the leaves. Even the sky turned a little bluer, a little more inviting.

And for the first time in an even longer time, she felt useful. Vital.

Outside, she had a spring in her step as she traversed the car park, arrived at her Peugeot 208 that was costing her too much money a month, and unlocked the door with the fob. As she slid into the car, the smell of the lavender car freshener she'd bought herself in an attempt to calm her down hit her. The aroma seemed more intense than usual, swimming around her head.

She placed her mobile in the dashboard holder, and started her engine. Just as she was about to pull out of the car park, her phone began ringing. An image of Josh, pulling a funny face at a restaurant during their family holiday in Menorca appeared on the screen. She answered the call.

'Josh? Everything all right?'

'I need money.'

Blunt. Straight to the point. No, hello. No how are you? Not even a please. When did she lose control of her kids so that they became the little brats they were?

'What are you talking about?' she asked.

'I need money for lunch today.'

'What happened to the money I gave you at the start of the week?'

There was a pause. 'I... I had to buy a new calculator from the shop.'

'Why? What happened to your old one?'

'It broke.'

'How?'

'It just broke.'

'Calculators don't just break, Josh.'

'I threw it to someone yesterday in maths and it broke.'

She sighed heavily. The colours of the car park dampened slightly.

'That money I gave you was for food. You promised me it would last.'

'I know, but—'

'No, Josh. You're not getting more. I'm at work and I can't keep sending money every time you run out. You need to find that tenner or go without today. Or see if you can return the calculator. Maybe next time you'll think about how you look after things and remember that money doesn't grow on trees.'

There was silence on the other end. She could practically hear the sulking through the microphone.

'Fine,' he muttered.

'Love you,' she said automatically.

He hung up without replying.

Olivia stared at the screen for a second, as the image of his face was replaced with a family photo on her lock screen. She sighed. Told herself not to let it get to her.

Let him sulk. Let him deal with it himself. She was allowed this. A win. A moment. Something for her.

And for the first time in a long time, she didn't feel like just a mum trying to survive the job. She felt like a detective.

CHAPTER
EIGHT

Olivia glanced up at the grey-brick rear entrance of the mortuary, clutching her warrant card in one hand and her phone in the other. She pushed the door open and stepped into a clinically cold corridor. The smell of disinfectant was so strong that it made her nostrils sting. Her shoes squeaked on the linoleum as she made her way down the corridor, her eyes searching for the right room. It quickly became apparent that she had absolutely no idea what she was doing or where she was going. Stephanie had told her the room number to look for, but Olivia was the type of person who could get lost even in a straight line and had no sense of direction. She wandered through the place, up and down the corridors, cautiously opening swinging doors until, eventually, a voice called out behind her.

'You lost?'

Olivia turned towards the voice and saw a tall woman in surgical scrubs leaning against a set of double doors at the far end of the hall. It was Leanna Moore, the pathologist. Her dark hair was pulled into a high ponytail, and she wore black-rimmed glasses perched halfway down her nose.

'I'm DC Olivia Willard,' she said, holding out her ID. 'I'm here for the post-mortem on the Chilworth barn victim.'

'Ah, yes. The firecracker. Come on, we're mid-toast.'

'Mid... what?'

Leanna pushed open the doors. 'You'll see,' she said, disappearing through the doors. Olivia hurried down the corridor and entered the room. Inside, the temperature dropped even further. Stainless steel dominated the space, with two gurneys lined up in the middle; one bore a body covered with a sheet. On the far side of the room was a workstation equipped with instruments, weighing scales, and a digital monitor.

'This one's crispy,' Leanna said brightly, pulling the sheet back with a flourish. 'Meet our John Doe. Or what's left of him.'

The body was blackened and curled inward. Arms bent at the elbows, fists clenched, and knees drawn up slightly. Olivia froze at the sight of it, only vaguely aware that her mouth had fallen open.

'You all right?' Leanna asked, tilting her head. 'You're not going to faint on me, are you? I had a DC faint once. He hit his head on my fridge. I had to stitch him up before I even touched the body.'

'I'm good,' Olivia said, forcing a thin smile as she stepped into the sterile space, letting the door close behind her with a quiet hiss.

The body was worse than she had imagined. What remained was little more than a set of limbs curled into a foetal shape, the skin charcoal, cracked, and fragmented, with facial features melted beyond recognition.

'Male, probably between forty-five and sixty,' Leanna began, pointing at various parts of the victim's body. 'Medium build, five-nine to six foot. We'll know more once we rehydrate the tissue and measure the long bones. We've got over ninety-five percent burn coverage. Skin, soft tissue, muscle – all gone. What you're looking at here is, well, a big piece of man charcoal.'

Olivia jotted down a note, trying to keep her eyes on her notebook rather than the scorched, cracked body.

'Anything external of note?' she asked.

Leanna nodded, peeling back a melted scrap of what might have once been clothing. 'Burned synthetic material here on the thighs. Probably trousers. The rest is fused to the body. We've no intact skin, no distinguishing marks, and certainly no tattoos. However...' She gestured to the wrists and ankles. 'See these areas? Slightly smoother. Less carbonisation. This suggests there was possibly something wrapped around them: ropes, cuffs, maybe cable ties. It shielded the skin from direct contact with the flames for a time.'

'So... he was restrained?'

'Possibly. Or possibly not. It's not conclusive, I'm afraid. If it was rope, it would've gone up faster than a Christmas pudding soaked in petrol. Without residual fibres or ligature impressions, we're firmly in inference territory, and that's not a place I like to be.'

Olivia scribbled quickly. 'Any signs of trauma before the fire?'

'Nothing visible. No sharp injuries. No blunt force ones either. And get this...' Leanna stepped back and picked up a printed report from the tray beside her. 'His lungs were full of soot. Trachea, bronchi, even some mild pulmonary congestion. Carboxyhaemoglobin levels are at sixty-two percent.'

'Which means?'

'That he was alive when the fire started. He was breathing in the smoke like a chain smoker. He likely passed out within minutes from the heat and carbon dioxide exposure, then died soon after. It was relatively quick, but not painless. Definitely, definitely not painless.'

Olivia's face paled.

Leanna softened slightly. 'I know. It's awful. There's no easy way to describe what fire does to the body, I'm afraid. We think of it as dramatic – boom, engulfed. But it's slow, consuming. Everything soft burns away first. The body contracts. Organs shrink. The brain basically cooks. And depending on what he was wearing, the fabric could have melted into his skin and kept burning long after he passed out.'

'Christ,' Olivia muttered.

'There's also a delightful scent of burnt pork during the process, in case you're wondering.'

'I wasn't,' Olivia replied automatically. 'What about his stomach contents?'

'Good spot,' Leanna said. 'He'd eaten. There's partially digested food in the stomach, though it's particularly tricky to discern what. I'm estimating he ate several hours before death, but it was only a light meal.

So, perhaps lunchtime. And' – she raised a finger – 'there's fluid in the stomach too. We'll know more when tox comes back, but it could be anything from beer to Fanta to water.'

Olivia chewed the inside of her cheek, taking in what had once been a face. 'So if we can't ID him visually... where do we start?'

Leanna peeled off her gloves and walked towards a small steel bench, pulling out a clipboard with several documents clipped to it. 'There are a few options.'

'Hit me,' Olivia said, not quite sure she meant it.

Leanna ticked off items on her fingers. 'First: fingerprints, but in this case, they're a no-go. Too much thermal damage. The ridges are gone. Even if we tried, it's unlikely we'd get a print worth running. Second: dental. That's our best shot. We recovered several teeth. Some are fractured from the heat, but a few molars survived intact. I'll get them cleaned up and arrange for some radiographs to be done, but they're not much use unless we can find something to match with. If this guy's ever seen a dentist in the UK and they've filed records, we might be in luck.'

'How long does that take?'

'Anywhere from a few days to a couple of weeks. Depends on how fast we can access records and whether there's even a file to match. Lots of variables. If he had private dental care or changed practices a few times, that can slow things down.'

Olivia nodded, scribbling furiously in her notebook.

'We'll also run DNA,' Leanna continued. 'We can extract a sample from the femur or molars. Again, turnaround is slow – could be up to a couple of weeks, especially if there's no match to compare it to. But it'll go into the national database. Missing Persons might pick something up if someone's been reported recently.'

Olivia let out a breath. 'So basically... we wait.'

'That's forensics for you. We play the long game round here, baby. But like I said, if certain information comes in ahead of that, it could speed things up. I'll email you the full report as soon as it's done. If you've got any other questions, you know where to find me.'

CHAPTER
NINE

Stephanie knocked on the door and entered without waiting for approval. DCI Clive McGowan was in the middle of removing his glasses when she opened the door.

'Busy, sir?'

'Not anymore, it would appear. Come in.'

The chief inspector locked his computer screen and moved the keyboard aside, as if to eliminate the temptation to log in and check his emails while they spoke.

'What's troubling you, Inspector?'

'Wellard,' she replied, sitting down.

'Oh?'

'I noticed something different about her this morning. She was quieter than usual, didn't have too much to say. Looking down, looking like she didn't want to be there. I pulled her into my office, and she mentioned she was feeling a bit lost and tired of the same old job.'

'Right,' Clive responded, nodding thoughtfully.

'She's also got some trouble going on at home with the kids. They're at that teenage boy age where everything they do becomes difficult.'

'Hormones.'

'And then some. I think she'll be okay on the whole, but I've got her working closely with me on this fire incident – Operation Windbreaker. That might give her a renewed sense of purpose, maybe cheer her up a bit.'

More thoughtful nodding. 'Good thinking. Does anyone have an issue with it?'

Stephanie pursed her lips and shook her head. 'Not to my knowledge. But if they do, I'll remind them we're all part of the same team.'

'Good idea. Is there anything you need me to do?'

Another shake of the head. 'Not right now, sir. I just wanted to flag it with you in case you notice something I don't.'

And for her own validation. A little pat on the back to remind herself she was doing a good job.

'I like your thinking,' he said, as if reading her thoughts. 'It's good to give the team more responsibility outside of their usual roles.'

'It raises everyone's level,' she added.

'Precisely.' The chief inspector moved his hands back to the keyboard. 'Anything else? How's the operation coming along?'

'We've only just started, sir. We're still trying to identify the victim. However, one of the CSIs found a small tin with a photograph and a religious inscription on it. The team is looking into both right now, but we can't do much until we ID the victim.'

Before McGowan could respond, there was a knock on the door. They both turned to face it.

'Come in,' Clive beckoned, his voice deep.

A moment later, a tentative Fiona poked her head into the office, looking awkward as if she'd just interrupted a disagreement between parents.

'Sorry to interrupt. I... It's about Operation Windbreaker, ma'am.'

'Go on,' Stephanie said.

'It's come from missing persons, actually. They received a report this morning from a woman in Bracknell. Apparently, her husband was due home last night from a work conference, but he never made it.'

Stephanie straightened instantly. 'How long's he been gone?'

'About eighteen hours or so, I reckon.'

She was already rising from her chair. 'And his description?'

'Vaguely matches that of our victim. Same sort of age, same sort of height, though I know it isn't much to go on in the first place.'

'Great work. Get me the wife's address, and I'll go down there now. Where's Olivia? I want her to come with me.'

CHAPTER
TEN

Jennifer Hadlow led them into the living room with an air of restrained composure, her lips pressed into a polite but tight smile. Stephanie stepped in first, with Olivia just behind, and the warmth of the house enveloped them instantly. The room was immaculate, arranged with the precision of someone who took pride in appearances, as though they entertained on an almost daily basis. A deep navy sofa and two matching armchairs formed a neat horseshoe around a glass coffee table that held a stack of *Country Living* magazines and a carefully trimmed plant. On the mantle above the electric fire sat framed photographs: a young couple at a wedding, two small boys in school uniforms, and a dog now long gone. Everything in the room had its place; it was the kind of home where shoes were never allowed past the front door, and empty mugs were never allowed to linger in the sink.

Jennifer perched on the edge of the sofa, her hands resting neatly in her lap, sitting bolt upright. Her hair, dyed a soft blonde, framed her face with subtle elegance. Stephanie guessed she was in her mid- to late-fifties, and she carried herself with an energy that belied her age.

Stephanie and Olivia sat in the matching armchairs, their notepads balanced on their laps. Jennifer's fingers twisted around each other as she looked between the two detectives, her posture rigid, shoulders held high.

'Thank you for allowing us into your home,' Stephanie began, her voice gentle and soft. 'We understand this is a very distressing time for you. My colleague and I are with the Major Investigations Team.'

'Major Investigations? I dealt with missing persons on the phone...' There was a catch in Jennifer's voice, accompanied by a hint of accusation.

'That's because we're dealing with another incident that took place last night.'

'What incident?'

'There was a fire in Chilworth. Some remains were found. Now, of course, I don't want to jump the gun and assume your husband was involved; however, we are having difficulty identifying the body at this moment. So we need to ascertain the likelihood of your husband's involvement.'

Jennifer put her hand to her mouth. 'A fire? You think Nigel was involved in a fire?'

'We hope not,' Olivia responded. Her tone was softer, gentler than Stephanie's. Mother to mother. 'Ultimately, we hope to rule him out of our investigation and we hope that he turns up safely. But we have to ask...'

Without saying anything, Jennifer leapt off the sofa, disappeared into the kitchen, and returned a moment later with a box of tissues, gently dabbing one in the corner of her eye. She sank back down onto the sofa, her calm and demure composure rapidly crumbling.

'What can you tell us about your husband's movements yesterday?'

Jennifer glanced at the clock on the mantelpiece, then back at Stephanie. 'He was supposed to be at a conference all day,' she said, her voice clearer now. 'In Farnborough. Some big property developer show he goes to every year. He texted me at ten to six to say he was on his way.'

'Did he drive or take the train?'

'Drove. He can't stand commuting.'

Stephanie made a note. 'When were you expecting him home?'

'About an hour after that. By that time, the traffic would have been bad.'

'And when did you suspect something was wrong?'

'It got to about nine o'clock, and I hadn't heard anything from him. I tried messaging and calling, but he didn't respond. He usually uses his phone to let me know he's in traffic. But nothing. So then I thought he'd been in an accident. I checked the news and traffic sites, but couldn't find anything.' Jennifer began to play with the tissue in her fingers. 'I kept ringing around to friends who live nearby, just in case he'd broken down and gone to them for help, but they hadn't seen or heard anything either. They all told me not to worry, that he was probably stuck or lost somewhere, and that he would get home eventually. I didn't sleep at all last night. I was too worried about him. And when there was still no word from him this morning, that's when I reported him as missing.'

Stephanie made another note. She briefly glanced at Olivia, then back to Jennifer. She leaned forward slightly. 'Mrs Hadlow, can I ask: in the past few days or weeks, have you noticed anything unusual about your husband's behaviour? Has he seemed different at all?'

Jennifer exhaled slowly, then nodded. 'He's been stressed, yes. Snappy, sometimes. Off in his own world. But he's got a massive project awaiting approval at the moment – they're still waiting on the contracts for a new development in an abandoned church – and he's had to deal with the investors, the council, everyone. I've seen some stuff about it being on hold or delayed. I think that's got on top of him a bit, but he just... he just gets on with it.'

'Did he say anything specific was troubling him or keeping him up at night?'

'No. He never does.' She gave a small, bitter laugh, as if remembering a previous conversation they'd had. 'He's a typical bloke like that. Keeps everything bottled up, never talks about what's actually going on in his head. I'd ask him, but he'd always brush it off. Nothing's changed in the twenty-five years we've been together.'

'Has he done anything recently that was out of routine?' Olivia asked. 'Changes to his schedule? Meetings he didn't usually go to, perhaps?'

Jennifer rubbed her temples. 'I don't know. I suppose he did have a couple of late nights, but he kept it vague. He was a vague man, really. Only told me stuff when I forced it out of him.'

Stephanie noted the quiet sadness in her tone, gave a gentle nod, then glanced at her notes before continuing. 'Was your husband religious at all, Mrs Hadlow?'

Jennifer looked up, frowning. 'Nigel? No. Not at all. Never went to church as far as I'm aware, unless it was a wedding or a funeral.' She shook her head with certainty. 'Why?'

Stephanie hesitated for a moment, then reached into her folder and withdrew a clear plastic sleeve. Inside it was a copy of the photograph that had been found in the tin at the crime scene.

'We found this,' Stephanie said carefully, 'at the scene of the fire.' She passed it over to Jennifer. 'Do you recognise the boy in this photo? Do you think it could be your husband?'

Jennifer took the sleeve with trembling hands and studied the picture closely. She narrowed her eyes, then brought it closer to her face. 'I... I'm not sure,' she admitted after a long pause. 'I don't think it's Nigel. The nose looks different. And the hair. But I never really saw pictures of him as a boy. You said this was found at the fire?'

Stephanie nodded.

Something shifted in Jennifer's expression, as sadness gave way to a glimmer of hope. 'Then maybe it wasn't him! Maybe he wasn't there. I mean... this doesn't look like him. Not to me. And why would he have something like this?'

Stephanie didn't answer immediately. She wanted to be careful not to offer false reassurance, but at the same time, she recognised the emotional lifeline Jennifer had just latched onto.

'We're exploring every possibility,' she said gently. 'In the meantime, would it be possible to collect a few personal items that might help us with identification? A toothbrush, perhaps, or a razor?'

Jennifer nodded immediately, standing. 'Yes, yes of course. There's one in the upstairs bathroom.'

'And if you could provide the name of his dentist too,' Olivia added, 'it would help us obtain dental records to compare with the remains. Just as a precaution.'

Jennifer paused at the bottom of the stairs, glancing back. 'Just routine enquiries, right?'

'Yes,' Stephanie responded, noticing the rising hope in Jennifer's voice. 'Just routine enquiries.'

CHAPTER
ELEVEN

As soon as the car doors thudded shut, Stephanie leaned her head back against the headrest and exhaled. The interior was cold, despite the afternoon sun streaming across the dashboard. Olivia clicked her seatbelt into place.

'Well,' she murmured, 'that could've gone worse.'

'She's betting everything on that photo being of someone else,' Stephanie replied as she started the engine.

'Do *you* think it's him?'

'Potentially. But we need to confirm it before we can do anything.'

'Very diplomatic,' Olivia commented.

'Perhaps I should have been a politician.'

'No. They're good at lying. You're not.'

Olivia offered Stephanie a knowing smile as Stephanie pulled out her phone and scrolled through her address book. She found Leanna's number, called it, and asked the pathologist for the name and contact information of a forensic odontologist. After receiving the details, Stephanie set the phone on the dashboard and dialled the number.

The phone rang twice before a brisk voice answered. 'Forensic Odontology Unit, Dr Sam Heaney speaking.'

'Dr Heaney, DI Stephanie Broadbent from Major Investigations,

Surrey. We have a suspected ID on the Chilworth remains and need a dental comparison run urgently.'

There was a brief pause, followed by, 'Understood. Do you have the dental records yet?'

'We'll have them by the end of the day. His wife just provided us with the name of his dentist – Winnaker Dental Practice in Bracknell. We'll request the records directly.'

'And the body?'

'It's already in your department's queue. You should've received a call from the pathologist, Leanna Moore, this afternoon.'

'That's correct,' Heaney confirmed. 'A post-mortem dental assessment was conducted, but no ID was requested until now.'

'Well, consider this official. Subject's name is Nigel Hadlow. We'll send the dental file as soon as we have it. Can you prioritise it?'

A pause. 'I *can*, but I'll need written authority.'

'I'll send an email as soon I get to the office, within the next hour or so.'

'Then I'll ensure the comparison is done by tomorrow morning at the latest. Possibly sooner, if there's a strong match.'

'Thanks, Dr Heaney.'

The line went dead. Stephanie tapped the screen to hang up the call. Olivia adjusted the folders on her lap, revealing the image of the boy at the top.

'Think that's him?'

Stephanie didn't answer immediately. Looked at it a while. 'I'm more concerned about *why* it's there, rather than *who* it is.'

CHAPTER
TWELVE

There was little to do for the rest of the day except wait; the worst part of the job, the part Stephanie hated most. As promised, she and Olivia had sent Nigel Hadlow's dental records to the forensic odontologist upon their return to the station, and Dr Heaney had confirmed once again that the results would be with them as fast as possible.

Now it was just a waiting game. So, to save herself from the temptation of calling Heaney's work number every hour, on the hour, Stephanie said her goodbyes, got in the car, and headed home.

It was pitch dark by the time she arrived. Early November. One of her least favourite months. In fact, all of late autumn and winter were her least favourites. Spring, that was when she felt happiness, the season of rejuvenation, rebirth and regrowth. A time when it wasn't too hot or too cold; to her, it was just right. The Goldilocks season.

A light rain descended from the sky, gently spotting her raincoat as she climbed out of the car and opened the rear passenger door to grab a handful of case files and her laptop bag.

As she swung it over her shoulder, her neighbour's front door opened. A thin sliver of light cut their shared driveway in two, and out stepped Jimmy, dressed in a smart shirt and a pair of Levi's jeans. In his hand, he held a black bin bag. He froze when he laid eyes on Stephanie.

'Evening, Detective,' he said, setting the bag in the wheelie bin in front of his house.

Stephanie smirked, slamming the car door shut. 'We're going to have to stop meeting like this. People will start to talk.'

Jimmy cackled in the darkness. 'I stopped caring what people thought of me back in the eighties, dear. More important things to worry about.'

Wasn't that the truth, Stephanie thought. Though she knew, from experience, it was much easier said than done. She had yet to meet someone who could switch off their thoughts as if they were a button.

'Busy day at the office?' Jimmy asked, continuing before she could respond. 'I saw on social media about the fire that took place.'

'Social media?' Stephanie raised an eyebrow. 'I didn't think you used it.'

'I'm as surprised as you are, but I can just about manage the basics. Dreadful what happened, though. I used to visit that barn and some of the other ones nearby as a child. A couple of my friends and I would go out on our push bikes around that area and throw stones across the field to see who could throw the farthest.' His face brightened with the memory. 'Still, like a lot of places now, I guess it just became abandoned and neglected. Do you know if it was arson?'

Steph relaxed her shoulders a little; he knew about the fire, but not about the body that had been found inside it. She and the team had yet to release that information to the public.

'We're not sure yet,' she responded.

'Horrible, horrible stuff. Why do people feel the need to do that?'

She shrugged. 'Your guess is as good as mine.'

'I hope the person responsible gets what they deserve.'

'If I have anything to say about it, they will.' She paused. 'Don't suppose you've seen any suspicious men loitering around my front door or hanging out in the street again, have you?' she asked. 'Seems like every time I see you, there's something suspicious going on outside.'

Jimmy raised a finger in the air. 'Now that you mention it...'

Her expression fell, body tensed.

'Now that you mention it, I haven't seen a thing,' he said jokingly.

Stephanie let out a short, sharp breath that released the tension in her body. Her immediate thought had been Jordan, her half-brother, hanging around outside her house, trying in more ways than one to wedge himself into her life.

'Maybe next time,' she joked. 'And if you do, be sure to take a picture. It makes my life much easier when trying to track them down.'

She started towards the front door, fumbled for her keys in her bag, then bid him farewell. She waited until Jimmy had gone inside before entering her home. As the door swung across the floor mat, it nudged a small pile of post aside. Juggling her folders and laptop bag, she crouched to pick it up, flipping absently through a credit card offer, a takeaway menu, and a letter from the local estate agent asking whether she'd considered selling her property. Then...

Her fingers paused on the final envelope. A letter addressed to her. Handwritten. Second-class stamp. Her stomach twisted. She dropped the bag from her shoulder, kicked the door shut, and took the post to the kitchen. Rain tapped gently against the windows. The house was silent except for the whirring of the fridge and the faint ticking sound it made intermittently.

She ripped open the envelope. Inside was a single folded sheet of lined paper, ragged on one side, as though ripped from a notepad.

Steph,

Hope you don't mind the intrusion, but I've now exhausted all possible modes of contacting you, except I guess for a letter in a bottle that you might find on a holiday one year or sending you something in Morse code.

I just wanted to reach out. If you're ever up for a chat or getting to know me, then you know how to reach me. I'm usually available any time, so you don't have to worry about disturbing me.

I'm just as shocked as you are about this whole thing. I've spoken with Kim, and from the sounds of it, we don't have the best family connection – I'm sorry for what Colin put you through – but I just want to say that I'm nothing like him, and I never will be.

I know it's difficult for you. But it's difficult for me too. Perhaps we could deal with it together?
Hope to hear from you.
Jord x

Stephanie read the note twice, then a third time. An overwhelming mixture of concern and frustration swelled within her, tainted by a scintilla of guilt. It was all very confusing. On the one hand, he'd taken the time to sit down, write, and post the letter to her address – an action that required thought, time, and effort. But on the other hand, it was weird and wrong. The long and short of it was that she didn't want to meet him again, didn't want to get to know him. He hadn't been a part of her life for the last forty years, so why did he think he could be part of the next forty?

And then she remembered the voicemail he'd left that morning; he was right, he really had used all available methods of contacting her. Would there come a point where it was too much? Had they already surpassed that?

Would she eventually break and let him in, or would her concern continue to grow?

At that moment, there was only one thing on her mind.

'How the bloody hell did he get my address?' she asked aloud.

She pulled out her mobile and scrolled to her favourites. Her thumb hovered. Then she pressed Kimberley's name.

The phone rang twice before being answered with an exhausted, 'Steph?'

'Hey. Sorry to bother you,' Stephanie said, trying to keep her voice steady. 'I just got home and found a letter on my doormat.'

'A letter?'

'Yeah. From *him*.'

A pause. Stephanie could hear background noise: the rhythmic washing of the dishwasher, the muffled rumble of the telly, a clatter of cutlery.

'Oh... right,' Kimberley said, already sounding guilty.

Stephanie frowned. 'He had my address, Kim. How do you think that happened?'

Kimberley didn't respond straight away. Then came a sigh. 'He asked me for it. I thought... I don't know. I thought it would help.'

'Help what? Help him barge into my life?'

'He's our brother, Steph.'

'He's a stranger,' Stephanie snapped. 'He's a stranger with our blood, that's it. That doesn't give him the right to know where I live. That's a line you don't get to cross for me.'

'I didn't think it'd be such a big deal—'

'That's the problem, Kim. You didn't think.'

Kimberley's voice cracked, tired and tight. 'I was trying to do the right thing.'

Stephanie paced the kitchen, dragging a hand through her hair. 'Well, it wasn't. I don't want him writing to me, texting me, or calling me. And I don't want him on my doorstep.'

'He's not a threat—'

'He's unwanted. That should be enough.' Stephanie drew a breath, trying to reel in the anger clawing at her throat. 'I'm asking you, as my sister, not to give out my information again. Not to anyone.'

Kimberley went quiet, then finally said, softly, 'Okay. I'm sorry.'

Stephanie hung up before her voice could betray her.

She stood in the kitchen, staring down at the letter on the counter, the rain still tapping gently at the windows. For a moment, the silence in the house felt suffocating. Then, with one decisive motion, she folded the letter in half, shoved it into the drawer beside the fridge, and closed it.

CHAPTER
THIRTEEN

The smell of coffee hung thick in the air, wrapping around Stephanie like a warm wool blanket. Coffee Culture, nestled down the quaint, cobbled alleyway connecting Guildford high street with the busier North Street, was one of those perfect little spots: vintage light fittings dangled low over wooden tables, exposed brick walls provided character, and a series of patterned tiles, each more unique than the last, adorned the floor. Ambient indie music murmured in the background, occasionally drowned out by the hiss of steam from the barista's machine, the scrape of cutlery on ceramic, and quiet conversation.

It was a mid-morning crowd. A group of women in their sixties occupied the table by the front window, nursing cappuccinos. Their handbags sat neatly on the spare chairs, while coats were folded gracefully over their knees. One of them punctuated her story with a loud cackle that turned a few heads. Near the back, a couple of mums with pushchairs chatted quietly, sipping flat whites as their toddlers gnawed on bits of banana. Two university students in oversized hoodies and earbuds sat over their laptops, focused on their coursework. At the counter, a man in Lycra kept one eye on his bike stationed outside while waiting for a matcha latte to go.

Stephanie sat alone at a corner table with her back against the wall, and a clear view of the room. The rustic brown plate in front of her was artfully arranged with smashed avocado, a poached egg, and a sprinkle of chilli flakes on toasted sourdough. It looked delicious, yet she hadn't touched it, save for slicing the egg in half and watching the yolk bleed out.

She toyed with a forkful of avocado, twirling it absentmindedly before setting it down again. Her stomach growled, but her mind told her no. She wasn't in the mood for a battle, but it was happening anyway. She pressed her knee hard against the underside of the table in an attempt to distract herself, but her thoughts wouldn't leave her alone.

The letter was still folded in the drawer at home. Her half-brother, a man she'd only just learned existed, had invaded her life like a slow leak in the ceiling. She couldn't stop thinking about it. About him. What he wanted. What she wanted. Sometimes she wished she didn't have a family; that way, all of the stress and pain in her life would vanish. But then she remembered that she wouldn't have any of the beauty, the warmth, the happiness, the memories she shared with her sister.

Except that Kimberley had given out her address, betrayed her like that. Let her down.

Stephanie exhaled sharply through her nose and finally took a bite, chewing slowly, as if testing her body's reaction. So far, so good.

Then her phone rang, vibrating loudly on the table. Startled, she snatched the device and answered.

It was Olivia.

'You got a minute?'

'I'm on lunch. What is it?'

'We've got a match on the remains from the fire. The odontologist confirmed it ten minutes ago. It's him. It's Nigel Hadlow.'

Stephanie pinched the bridge of her nose. The name echoed in her mind. The missing husband. The man whose wife thought he'd just been stuck in traffic.

'You sure?'

'Positive.'

Steph leaned back in her chair, her appetite dissolving like sugar in hot tea. They had a victim. A name to match their John Doe. Much faster than anticipated.

'What shall we do next, ma'am?'

Stephanie looked down. 'Hold that thought,' she said, rising from the table and chair. 'I'm coming back to the station.'

She grabbed her coat and headed towards the exit, leaving the plate of food almost untouched.

CHAPTER
FOURTEEN

The moment Stephanie stepped through the doors of the incident room, the atmosphere shifted. Conversations died, heads turned, and a few chairs scraped as the team straightened up.

It was all systems go now.

Stephanie strode to her office, shrugged off her coat, and slung her bag under the desk before returning to the incident room.

'Right,' she said, clapping her hands once to get everyone's attention. 'We've had confirmation that the body recovered from the fire in Chilworth has been identified as Nigel Hadlow. That doesn't mean we know what happened yet, so I want every angle covered.' She pointed to Giles and Noah. 'You two, Hadlow drove to the conference that day, so let's start there. Find his car. Trace his route from the conference centre to the barn. CCTV, traffic cams, petrol stations; I want every piece of footage from the moment he left to the moment he went off-grid. Find out if he met up with anyone or if he pulled over on the side of the road to take a piss, or let someone in. We want to know every inch of his route. Got it?'

Noah scribbled furiously in his notepad. 'Aye, aye, captain.'

From Giles: 'Sounds delicious, ma'am.'

'Good.' She turned to Fiona. 'I want you to speak to his wife again. Break the news. Be honest, but don't overload her. We need a clear timeline of Nigel's movements, anything out of the ordinary, anyone he mentioned, anything at all that might explain why he ended up in that barn.'

Fiona gave a tight nod and placed the tip of her pinkie finger in her mouth. 'Understood.'

'And see what you can uncover about any issues in their marriage as well. Affairs, financial problems… that sort of thing. If there's a crack in the surface, we need to find it.'

She looked around the room, her eyes moving from one team member to the next, landing on Devon.

'Look through his mobile and financial records. See if there's anything in there that might indicate someone came after him or if things got so bad that he did this to himself.'

'You still think it might be suicide, ma'am?' Devon asked softly, confidence missing from his voice.

'Until we get the full fire report and evidence to the contrary, I want us to keep an open mind.'

'That report should be with us soon,' Giles said, lifting his hand. 'Last I heard, Elias and his team were compiling it this morning.'

Stephanie nodded and checked her watch. She could feel the adrenaline beginning to coil tightly in her muscles. All she needed to do now was channel it. 'Chase it up,' she said. 'See if they can get it to us before Olivia and I return.'

'Return?' Olivia asked.

'You and I are going to speak with the last person to see him alive: his employer.'

'What do you want to do about the press, ma'am?'

The question came from Devon. She turned to him, studied him for a moment, then replied, 'I'll leave that up to you. But wait until his family has been notified first. Keep it to the facts. Nothing more.'

'Ma'am,' Devon replied with a nod.

'All right. Let's get to it. Let's find out what the hell happened to Nigel Hadlow.'

. . .

The traffic thickened as they rolled into the heart of Guildford and Stephanie slowed to a crawl behind a bus. Rain glistened on the tarmac like glitter. Ahead of them, scaffolding climbed up the skeleton of a half-built high-rise, and a towering crane loomed above the town like a bird of prey waiting.

'That used to be a car park,' Olivia muttered, her arms crossed tightly over her chest. 'A popular and convenient one too. Nobody complained about it, but someone somewhere had the bright idea to dig it up and put another block of overpriced flats on top of it. Genius.'

Stephanie gave a small, noncommittal grunt, her attention on a cyclist weaving too close to her wing mirror.

They passed the old Debenhams site next, or what remained of it. The former department store had been replaced by slick glass panels and a giant banner promising luxury apartments for as little as £500,000. Half a million pounds to live next to a busy road in a lively student town. Stephanie could think of better ways to spend her money, assuming she had an extra five hundred grand lying about the place, which she didn't.

'And there's *another one*,' Olivia muttered, her voice heavy with disgust.

Stephanie snorted. Because she hadn't lived in the area for long and still felt like an outsider in some respects, she had no reason to be as aggrieved as Olivia. 'You sound about a hundred years old.'

'I feel it. It's just a shame, you know. They just hand the keys over to these developer people who don't give a shit about anyone else but themselves and say, do what you want with it, we don't care.'

In the distance, two newer residential blocks rose behind the train station. Clean, sharp, modern.

'And it's spreading,' Olivia added, jerking her thumb towards the windscreen. 'Have you seen Woking recently?'

Stephanie smirked. 'Hard to miss it. I can see it from Chantries Ridge. Looks like someone dropped a stack of IKEA boxes in the middle of Surrey. But people need houses, Liv.'

'Yeah, yeah. But do you know how they get them? I saw on social media the other day that a lot of these old buildings that are being eyed up by developers, well... suddenly they catch fire and burn down.'

'A conspiracy, you mean?'

Olivia shrugged. 'All I'm saying is, it makes you think, doesn't it?'

All it did was make Stephanie wonder whether the barn where Nigel Hadlow had died had been earmarked for a potential property deal, but she realised it was highly unlikely given the remoteness of its location. She couldn't imagine anyone wanting to live in a block of flats several miles from local amenities.

'Give it another ten years,' Olivia said with a sigh. 'I bet we'll all be living in places with QR codes for doors.'

'And robots for neighbours.'

'Can't be worse than the ones I've got now.'

Stephanie chuckled and turned into a narrow side road as they headed out of Guildford towards Basingstoke. It was time to stop moaning about the skyline and start digging into the life of a man who may or may not have burned himself to death.

CHAPTER
FIFTEEN

Only one thought occupied her mind: Stephanie. Despite the physical pain she was feeling in her stomach and the rest of her body, she could only think about the one thing that was causing her the emotional pain, emotional suffering. Her relationship with her older sister hadn't been the same since the revelation that had shattered her entire worldview. She couldn't trust Stephanie anymore, couldn't believe a word that came out of her mouth. Stephanie had lied to her for her entire life, and she sensed there was more that she wasn't being told – a premonition, a sisterly intuition.

They had once been as inseparable as the filling in a sandwich, bonded by their shared history, but that bond had been built on lies. For thirty-three years, Kimberley had believed they would always be together, sisters for life. She had imagined Stephanie as the first person she would call in an emergency, possibly even before her husband, Jason. Yet, when she needed them most, neither had picked up the phone. Both were likely too busy with work to care about her, to drop everything and support her.

Funny, her husband and sister, the people she had once entrusted her life with, were nowhere to be seen. They had abandoned her, revealing their true colours.

A wave of nausea washed over her as a figure moved from one side of the waiting room to the other, pulling her from her thoughts. She shifted uncomfortably in the hard-backed chair, adjusted her coat that lay folded across her lap, and clutched her handbag against her baby bump as if it were a lifejacket. Across the room, a toddler shrieked, tugging at his mother's sleeve while she whispered something stern through clenched teeth. Another pregnant woman flicked through a pregnancy leaflet without reading a word, her expression glazed and distracted.

Kim stared at the pale blue wall ahead, which displayed leaflets about different stages of pregnancy and safe cleaning products. Yet, she didn't see any of it. Her mind drifted back to the smear of blood she had seen that morning. Faint, yes. But unmistakable. The ache in her lower belly hadn't gone away either. Not quite pain but a tightness that made her worry.

The figure beside her shifted in his seat. She turned to face him.

Jordan. The person who had answered her call immediately. The one who had dropped everything to come with her.

Jordan sat calmly, legs spread in a way that suggested he owned the place, his elbows resting lightly on the arms of the chair. He wore a black hoodie beneath a denim jacket, the sleeves rolled halfway up to reveal thin wrists and pale, freckled skin. His dark blond hair was swept back messily, as if he had been running his fingers through it all morning. There was a softness to his face that looked almost boyish, yet his jawline and the shape of his mouth mirrored the one man neither of them wanted to talk about

Their father.

Kim disliked how much Jordan resembled him just as much as her sister did. But while their father had always appeared cruel, Jordan seemed... normal. Tired. Like an adult nearing forty, trying to make sense of his life.

She had felt hope, excitement at the discovery of a new sibling. Not just because she had someone new in her life, but because Jordan felt like a second chance. A clean slate. Someone who could understand the complexities of their childhood without judging her for how she had handled it, or failed to handle it recently. They'd already completed the DNA test, mailed it off, and received the results only a few days earlier: a

99.97% accurate match. Half-siblings. There was something oddly emotional about it. Scientific proof that the stranger beside her was flesh and blood, that he belonged to her and she to him, in some strange, tangled way.

So, in her hour of need, she had called him. And he had answered.

Stephanie's absence ached in her chest like a bruise she kept pressing.

'You good?' Jordan asked, breaking the silence as he placed a hand on her upper arm.

She feigned a confident smile. 'Nervous.'

'I'm sure everything will be fine.'

She forced another smile. 'Thank you for coming, by the way.'

'Don't mention it. That's what families do.' He nodded at her bump. 'I never thought I'd have a brother or sister. And I never thought I'd become an uncle. Now I get to treat the little one like the sibling I never had growing up.'

She chuckled, then massaged her stomach as it gave a small twist. She nodded but said nothing, afraid her voice would crack if she tried.

A midwife in navy scrubs stepped out of a side door and called her name: 'Kimberley Taylor?'

Tentatively, she stood, clutching her coat and bag in one hand, her other instinctively covering her bump. She hesitated for a long moment.

Then she turned to Jordan.

'Can you come in with me?'

'Of course.'

Together, they followed the nurse through the double doors and into the Maternity Unit.

CHAPTER
SIXTEEN

Hadlow & Templeton's offices were located on the first floor of a small high-rise in Basingstoke. The building was exactly as Stephanie had anticipated – modern, spacious, and drenched in white. Something that had been picked up from London and dropped in the middle of Hampshire. Over the last two decades, the company had built its reputation by transforming unused land into profitable housing developments across the South of England, with Nigel and his business associate, Vinnie, at the helm.

A receptionist wearing a headset guided them down a glass-panelled corridor and into a long, high-ceilinged meeting room. The table was oversized, accompanied by angular chairs that were more stylish than comfortable. One wall was entirely glass, providing a panoramic view of Basingstoke and the new-build estates beyond, which made the town resemble a Lego set. At the far end of the room sat Vinnie Templeton, rising as they entered. Tall, in his early fifties, same as Nigel, with neatly combed silver hair, he had a deep tan that suggested a timeshare in Spain and regular golfing trips abroad. He wore a navy, Italian-cut suit paired with a pale pink shirt left open at the collar. Everything about him, from the Tag Heuer on his wrist to his expensive leather loafers, exuded wealth of the pretentious kind.

Stephanie introduced herself and Olivia.

'I understand you spoke to my colleague on the phone, Mr Templeton,' she said.

Vinnie nodded. 'I did. It's terrible, terrible news. I haven't been able to focus on anything since. Please, take a seat.'

Stephanie and Olivia complied, pulling out their chairs at the opposite end of the table.

'Can I get you a coffee? Water?'

'We're fine,' Stephanie said. 'Thank you. And we appreciate you making the time to see us.'

'Of course, don't be silly. Anything you guys need, we are at your disposal.' He ran his fingers through his hair. 'I just... I just can't... And you're sure it's Nigel?'

Stephanie responded with a subtle but firm nod. 'DNA evidence has proved it beyond reasonable doubt.'

Vinnie let out a lengthy sigh and snorted several times, as if holding back tears, or perhaps pretending to. 'A part of me hoped it was someone else, you know. That it was a joke. I know it's a horrible thing to say, but... do you know what happened to him yet?'

'That's why we're here,' Olivia replied, setting her notepad and pen on the desk. 'We're trying to piece together his movements on the night he died.'

'Of course. Of course.'

Olivia allowed a moment to pass before speaking. 'What was Nigel's role in the company?'

Vinnie leaned back, arms folded. 'Nigel oversaw strategic development. He was the one who dealt with local authorities, lobbied council planners, handled land acquisition, planning negotiations, and legal hurdles – the kind of work most developers try to avoid. He was good at it. Charming when he needed to be, and less so when it mattered.' He gestured towards the cityscape beyond the glass. 'Half the developments you see from here wouldn't exist without him.'

'So he had relationships with government officials?'

'Relationships?' Templeton gave a short laugh. 'He practically lived in council offices. He knew every chief planner south of the M25 by name. He was always on the phone, arranging lunch meetings, site visits, coffee catch-ups. A lot of people liked him, and a lot of people didn't. Just part of the process. But he had that... that sense of calm even when things were going sideways, you know?'

Olivia glanced at Stephanie, then back at Vinnie. 'Were things going sideways recently?'

A pause. Vinnie rubbed a thumb across his chin. 'Not dramatically. But we've hit a snag with one of our upcoming sites – a development up near Guildford. It's a conversion of an old church on disused land just outside the town. A beautiful spot. Would have made a lot of young people happy living there. But the site became a sticking point in the community. Nigel was dealing with it. There were a couple of teething issues and some concerns raised internally, but whenever I approached him about it, he told me it was taken care of and not to worry.'

'Did you worry?'

'Hundred per cent,' he admitted. 'It's my job to worry. But I trusted him. The last I heard was that we've stalled.'

'Would he have been under pressure?' Olivia asked.

Vinnie looked up, letting out a chuckle. 'Of course he was. We both are. We have shareholders and investors to answer to at the end of the day. But it never affected him. He could handle pressure.' Vincent paused, deep in thought. 'But... now that you ask, he *had* started smoking again. I caught him outside two or three times in the last fortnight, puffing away like he was twenty-five again. He'd been clean for years. I asked him about it, but he just waved it off.'

'Was that unusual behaviour for him?' Stephanie enquired.

Vinnie shifted in his seat. 'Yes. And no. Nigel internalised stress. That was his thing.'

'What can you tell us about the conference on the night he died?'

'The Southeast Infrastructure and Regeneration Forum? It's only the hottest ticket in town. Myself and Nigel went for the two days, speaking with council reps, other developers, legal advisers, a couple of finance people to see what they were saying about the industry and how things were going.'

'What time did the show finish?'

'Officially, four in the afternoon. But we didn't end up leaving until about six.'

'You went separate ways?'

'Yes.'

'And how did he seem when you left him?'

Vinnie stuck his lips out. 'Perfectly normal. Relaxed, even. Certainly not in any kind of distress.'

'Did he mention any plans for after the show?'

'No.' Vinnie shook his head slowly. 'Just said he'd see me in the office the following day.'

Stephanie leaned back slightly. 'Would you say you two were close?'

'As close as you can be with a business partner after twenty years.'

'Did he ever mention anything that troubled him? Calls? Messages?'

Templeton's smile flattened. 'Not particularly. We've had problems over the years. Residents, environmentalists, the press, protestors camping outside our sites, that sort of thing. Even a few death threats – all par for the course. But he hadn't told me about anything recently.'

'And what about *within* the company?' Olivia asked. 'Any tensions there? Anyone unhappy with him?'

'Not that I was aware of. He and I had disagreements, naturally. You don't build a business together without butting heads from time to time. But there was nothing out of the ordinary.' He hesitated. 'Otherwise I'm confident he would have mentioned it. We were partners. What affected him affected me.'

Stephanie nodded. 'We'd like access to his calendar, company phone, and emails.'

'I can authorise that,' Vinnie said. 'I'll have IT get it ready. Some of it might require a formal request, but if it helps you find out what happened...'

Stephanie thanked him, handed over a business card, and then made to leave. As they moved towards the door, Vinnie called after them. 'Do you think it was murder?'

Stephanie paused, one hand on the door handle.

'We're keeping an open mind,' she replied.

Then she stepped out, leaving Vinnie Templeton alone at the end of the table, staring out at the life-sized Monopoly board he and Nigel had built.

CHAPTER
SEVENTEEN

As Stephanie climbed into the driver's seat, she slammed the door shut against the rising wind and slumped back with a sigh. The sky over Basingstoke had darkened, heavy with rainclouds, and the early evening traffic was already beginning to build on the roads. Olivia buckled in beside her, busy scribbling something into her notes. Just as she was about to speak with her constable, her phone buzzed in her coat pocket. She fished it out and saw Giles's name on the screen.

'Mr Swinger,' she said, placing the phone on the dashboard.

A sigh came through the microphone. 'Please don't say my name like that.'

'But that *is* your name, isn't it?'

'Yes, but I hate it. The amount of grief I got at school, you wouldn't believe.'

'Oh, I can believe it. I know how mean kids can be.'

She recalled a scene from her childhood: a cold February afternoon on the school playground. She had been twelve, dressed in second-hand shoes and her school uniform, standing by the climbing frame, clinging to her paperback for comfort while a group of girls circled around her, pointing at her and laughing at something funny Ellie McFadden had said. She had stood frozen, cheeks burning, hands tight around the book until her knuckles turned white. And then...

'Ma'am?' Olivia's voice pulled her back.

She blinked, realising she was gripping the steering wheel tighter than necessary, then glanced at the detective, who wore a look of maternal concern.

'Sorry. What were you saying, Giles?'

'Nothing. I thought you'd hung up on me.'

'My mind wandered off. What can we help you with?'

'Elias's report. It's just come through.'

'And?'

Giles inhaled slightly, as if preparing for a big speech. 'He asked after you, he did. You, specifically.'

'Right.'

'Said he wanted to hand-deliver the report. He looked quite sad when I told him you weren't here, actually.'

She sensed his tone and immediately disapproved.

'He loitered around for a while afterwards, just in case you might turn up. What's that all about, ma'am? Is there anything going on?'

She felt her throat tighten. 'No. And that's the last time you will mention anything like that ever again. My love life is *my* love life, and right now it's as non-existent as our leads in this investigation, so I'd rather you focus your efforts on getting those before you even think about sticking your nose into my personal life, which will always remain outside of your reach.'

She could sense him smiling through the phone. 'Well, what do you want me to do with the documents he left for you then?'

'Documents?'

'Yeah. He gave me some leaflets and materials about overcoming fears of fire.'

She glanced at Olivia awkwardly. 'Leave them on my desk. I'll look at them when we return. Now, can we get back to the topic? What did his report have to say?'

Giles cleared his throat. 'So, the origin point has been confirmed in the front right-hand corner of the barn on the floor. Elias says the ignition source was consistent with a dropped cigarette or similar item.'

'Cigarette?'

Stephanie and Olivia exchanged a glance.

'Or similar,' Giles confirmed. 'Based on the burn pattern and residue match. He's almost certain it was a lit cigarette. He also mentioned that the fire spread incredibly fast. The barn was full of dry straw, old paint cans, and some old timber. Once it caught, the place went up like a tinderbox. He reckons from ignition to full blaze took less than three minutes.'

Stephanie winced.

'Elias also said they found traces of accelerant on the ground.'

'Where?'

'On the ground, ma'am.'

'Yes. I know that. But where *exactly*? All over? In a small spot? In a pattern? Be specific.'

There was a pause as Giles consulted the notes. 'It doesn't say.'

'Can you find out?'

'What difference does it make, ma'am? Surely the presence of accelerant suggests someone did this to him?'

'Not necessarily,' she replied slowly. 'If the accelerant was all over the barn, it would indicate to me that he took himself there, doused the place in petrol, then sat in the middle and had one final cigarette. If it was only in one corner of the barn, then perhaps someone moved him into the middle and ignited the corner, giving them enough time to escape. Lastly, if it was in a certain pattern – like a circle around his body, perhaps – then it would also indicate someone else was present. Either way, nothing is concrete. The presence of accelerant does *not* determine whether he killed himself or was killed.'

'Understood,' Giles said. 'I'll ask for clarification.'

Stephanie nodded to herself. 'Good. We need to be thorough on this one.'

'Yummy. I'll update you as soon as I hear back.'

The line went dead.

For a moment, neither woman spoke. Outside the car, traffic crawled by. Windshield wipers thudded into life as the first raindrops began to fall.

'So,' Olivia said, glancing sideways at Stephanie. 'Still think it could be suicide?'

Stephanie exhaled through her nose. 'I don't know. Maybe. Maybe not. But either way, this man was silenced. And I want to know why.'

As she inserted the keys into the ignition and turned it on, Stephanie sensed Olivia looking at her with a wry grin. Her expression conveyed a thousand words.

'Don't even say it. Nothing's going on. It's just Giles being stupid.'

'Come on, ma'am. You don't have to lie to me. I think he's a good-looking guy. And he's a firefighter, which makes him even more sexy.'

'Really?'

The grin on Olivia's face deepened. 'I love a man in uniform, me. If you're not interested, I might be.'

CHAPTER
EIGHTEEN

Since they'd been gone, the incident board for Operation Windbreaker had been filled with photographs of the crime scene, images of Nigel Hadlow's smiling face taken from the company website, numerous notes and witness statements, and a map highlighting key locations: the conference centre in Farnborough, the fire site, and Nigel's home address.

The team had already assembled in the incident room when they returned, having received a heads-up from Stephanie. She strode to the front, leaving Olivia to take a seat beside Fiona.

'Right,' she began, slapping a file onto the desk. 'I just had a call from Giles; Elias's report confirms that the fire was started by what appears to be a cigarette dropped onto a highly flammable area of the floor, but this doesn't necessarily indicate foul play. There is also evidence of an accelerant, which raises serious questions about how the fire started and who was present at the time.'

Devon straightened. 'So we're thinking arson?'

'We're keeping both possibilities open until we have more information. It could be suicide or someone covering their tracks. Either way, I want every angle pursued as if it were a murder investigation. Where are we on the land ownership?'

'I've checked the Land Registry and found that the land belongs to the owners of the farm where the barn is located,' Devon replied.

'Have you spoken with them?'

'Yes.'

'And?'

'They're concerned but are not suspects.'

'Why not?'

'Because they're currently out of the country.'

Stephanie nodded, absorbing the information. She then turned to Noah. 'What's the status of Nigel's car?'

'Still hasn't turned up,' he replied. 'Though we received a ping from ANPR at around six twenty pm heading north on the A31, but nothing after that. Either the plates were switched, or it was dumped somewhere without a camera in sight.'

'Get a full ANPR sweep within a thirty-mile radius of the conference venue,' she instructed. 'And cross-reference with petrol station CCTV. Someone's got to have seen it. What car does he drive?'

'A Jaguar F-Pace.'

'I don't know anything about cars. Is that fairly modern and sophisticated?'

'Yes.'

'Then will it not have some sort of tracking or GPS monitoring system? Could they not locate where the car is or has been?'

Noah looked as if he had just woken up. 'I'll find out.'

'Thanks. What about Nigel's phone? His messages, calls? Tracking information on that?'

Devon leaned forward, clutching a stack of printouts. 'I've reviewed his last few weeks' texts, calls, emails, and messages across various platforms. I found a series of messages from an unlisted number that started about three weeks ago. They became more frequent the closer you get to his death. Last message came through at eight minutes past five on the night he disappeared.'

He passed the papers to Stephanie. She skimmed through them quickly:

You think you can just do what you want, don't you?

The public are going to really want to know how you got it through, won't they. Corruption of the highest order.

I've got the emails, Nigel. The bank transfers. The photos. You make me sick.

You shouldn't be allowed to get away with this.

Either this stops, or I go public. Tick tock.

Stephanie felt the hairs on her arms rise. 'Blackmail?'

'Looks like it,' Devon confirmed. 'But there's no name, no contact information. No indication of what they're referring to. And the messages were sent from a burner. No call records from that number, either. Just these texts. I've put in a request to the network provider to see what we can retrieve from the number. After seeing these, I asked the financial crimes team to investigate Nigel's personal and company accounts, and they've flagged two unusual payments to a private offshore account. One went to a private consultancy that doesn't seem to exist, and the other... well, we're still tracking that down.'

'How much are we talking about?'

'High five figures. Both transactions occurred within the last six months. They've not been expensed by the company, and they're not reported on his personal taxes either.'

'Hush money,' Stephanie muttered. 'Does anyone know the current status of the church development?'

Fiona glanced at her screen. 'Hadlow and Templeton applied for permission to redevelop St Clement's, a deconsecrated church in Chertsey, last autumn. The application faced resistance from conservation groups, local residents, and the MP. However, it was approved unusually quickly – within six weeks. The official reason given was "economic necessity and heritage preservation".'

Stephanie raised an eyebrow before looking at Olivia. 'Preserving it by demolishing it?'

'Essentially,' Fiona replied. 'They planned to convert some of it into luxury flats and demolish the rest.'

'Surprised they weren't planning to burn it to the ground,' Olivia interjected loudly.

'What?' Fiona asked, her confusion mirrored on the faces of her colleagues.

'Never mind,' Olivia said, dismissing the comment. 'So, that means he was involved in some underhand dealings with brown envelopes, and then someone found out about it.'

'Or they knew enough to send threats,' Devon suggested, tapping the page. 'And knew enough to threaten to go public. Either he thought paying them off would resolve the issue, or...'

'Or he panicked,' Stephanie finished. She looked back at the board, at Nigel's smiling face. 'He was being threatened. He was in over his head. But if he took his own life, why do it in such a remote place?'

No one answered.

'It doesn't feel like suicide,' she added, shaking her head. 'Feels like someone is sending a message, making the death as messy as possible so that his body is barely recognisable.'

'We need to find out if anyone followed him or if he met someone there,' Noah said.

Stephanie turned to Fiona. 'Get in touch with the local council. I want to know everyone involved in that church development. Names, contact details, everything.'

'Will do.'

'Devon, track down those bank transfers. I want to know who received the payments, how, and when. If there's a shell company involved, we'll track that too. We need to determine who knew Nigel's secrets and who wanted him silenced.'

She returned to the incident board, pinning the threatening messages in red ink beneath Nigel's photo.

She turned back to Devon.

'We need a name and number linked to those text messages. Whatever it is, whoever is behind it, is likely the reason Nigel either took his own life or was silenced. I want to know what he was being blackmailed for and who was responsible.'

CHAPTER
NINETEEN

Stephanie shut the fridge door carefully and sauntered towards the sofa, a fresh apple in hand. She settled into her corner, which had become worn down under her weight, and tucked her legs into her chest.

The television was on, playing a repeat of a David Attenborough nature programme. Images of savannahs and wildfires flickered across the screen, with orangey-red flames licking up the trunks of ancient trees.

She blinked. Swallowed.

Took a bite of her apple.

The flavour barely registered. The sound of the fire crawled under her skin. Her pulse fluttered in her throat. She forced herself to look at the screen. The flames, the ash, the smoke.

That was one of the coping mechanisms Elias had advised her on: exposure therapy. Except it wasn't quite the same. The fire was on the other side of the television screen. Still, she felt the room getting hotter, clammy, stuffy.

She lowered the apple, stared at it for a moment, then set it down on the coffee table, unfinished. Standing up, she wiped her hands against her joggers and turned off the television.

Silence, save for the pounding of her heartbeat in her ears. She backed away from the screen and caught her reflection. Her father's face appeared, holding a lighter to his cheek. A small flame sparked and flickered back at her, illuminating his features.

And then she felt the heat crawling up her back.

The faintest scent of burning.

She sniffed hard. The smell intensified. She scanned the living room but saw no sign of smoke, flames, or heat. It was all in her mind, the fire crawling out of the television like a scene from *Poltergeist*. It was all in her mind, but her body didn't know that. Something prohibited the message from reaching her brain, and she clawed at the bottom of her T-shirt, pulling it off in one motion. Next, she stepped out of her jogging bottoms. Her skin felt wrong, uncomfortable. Prickly, like it was on fire, like someone was brushing her with a fiery paintbrush. Smothering her, even though she was now half-naked in the middle of the living room.

Her father's face stared back at her intently, his gaze unrelenting. The fire on the screen swelled ferociously.

She bolted upstairs to the bathroom.

The shower squealed to life, and she stepped beneath the spray before it had time to adjust, letting the icy water hit her with full force. She gasped but didn't move. Stayed perfectly still. Held her breath as the water streamed over her shoulders and down her back, plastering her hair to her face.

It's not real, she told herself. It's not real. It's not real.

The fire wasn't there, just as *his* face wasn't really there.

After a few minutes, a numbing sensation took over her body, and the panic began to wash away with the water down the drain. Stephanie reached for the tap and turned off the water. The flat was silent again. Stepping out, she reached for a towel and dried herself in a daze before getting dressed and returning to the living room. Her damp hair dripped over her shoulders and down her back. She changed into her top and jogging bottoms before returning to the sofa. The apple was still on the coffee table. Then she summoned the strength to glance at the television screen.

Mercifully, her father's face had disappeared, and all she saw was black and her fuzzy reflection as the scene changed to an image of an animal escaping the blaze.

CHAPTER
TWENTY

Olivia swore under her breath as she yanked her umbrella open and slammed the car door shut with her hip. A low fog, heavy with rain, had descended on Surrey, and it was all she had. She'd been in such a rush to leave the house that morning that she'd forgotten her raincoat. And the boys had forgotten theirs too. Not to mention, Josh had forgotten his sports kit for the third time in a row. It was clear that the previous night's meeting with his form tutor had made absolutely no difference to his attitude or willingness to change. Olivia had been forced to listen to Mr Kapoor explain his concerns about her son's behaviour while all she could think about was how she would punish him.

The punishment hadn't come yet. But it would. When he least expected it.

Umbrella in hand, she approached the small row of police cars that had pulled over on the side of the road. Nigel Hadlow's Jaguar had been found earlier that morning. A handful of reports, along with information from the manufacturer's tracking system, indicated that it had been discarded on the side of a quiet country lane, not far from the barn.

As she approached, she realised the car had suffered the same fate as Nigel. What had once been a sleek, modern Jaguar was now little more than a white carcass, wrecked by a savage fire. The roof had caved slightly inward from the heat, warping the frame. The paint had disappeared, stripped down to its metal. The tyres had burst. The windows had exploded, leaving shards of glass scattered on the side of the road and the wet grass. The faint outline of the number plate confirmed it was Nigel's car.

A pair of crime scene investigators were photographing the wreckage. Standing behind them was Elias, arms folded, observing their every move. Olivia's bad mood, which had begun to ease at the sight of the burnt-out Jaguar, dissolved entirely when she spotted him.

There was just something about a man in uniform.

When he turned and caught sight of her, something knotted in her stomach. He gave the smallest nod in greeting. No smile. Firm. Assured. Grounding.

She stepped around the debris, coming to his side. 'Morning,' she said, introducing herself.

'Detective.' He gestured towards the wreck. 'As you can see, we've got another mess on our hands.'

He spoke, but she paid little attention. Her gaze dropped, catching sight of the scars on his neck and right hand, which disappeared into the cuff of his jacket.

There was something about a man in uniform with the wounds to back it up.

She swallowed. 'Looks like it was torched pretty good.'

'Burnt from the inside out,' Elias explained. 'Fire originated somewhere in the front passenger footwell. Could've been an accelerant or an improvised incendiary device, but I won't know for sure until we've had a chance to examine it in detail.'

Olivia frowned, scanning the scorched shell. 'Anything forensic...?'

'If there was DNA, prints, blood, or fibres, they're ash now. Same with electronics. The vehicle's onboard computer was melted beyond comprehension. It could well have been burning for half a day, maybe longer.'

Olivia turned slowly, surveying the surroundings. The road was little more than a single-track lane, shielded by tree cover, with no houses in sight.

'Any evidence it was moved after it finished burning?'

Elias shook his head. 'Nah. She was burnt in situ. You can see where the tyres have melted into the tarmac.'

Olivia pulled out her notebook, flipping to a clean page. 'How far away's the barn from here?'

'Just under a quarter mile.'

'So why dump it here?' she murmured.

Elias let out a dry laugh. 'That's your job to find out. I just tell you the facts.'

CHAPTER
TWENTY-ONE

'Still think it might be a suicide, ma'am?'

It wasn't the question itself that irked her; it was the intonation, the *tone* behind it. As if the answer were obvious and she was stupid for suggesting they keep an open mind.

'Like I've said time and time again, we keep an open mind until we have concrete evidence to suggest that Nigel was killed,' she replied, glowering at Giles. 'Do I think it's strange that Nigel's car was found a quarter of a mile from where he died? Yes. Do I find it strange that both have been destroyed by fire? Yes. But there's nothing to suggest he didn't park the car, set it alight, and then wander off to the barn to do the same to himself.'

'But why would he set fire to the car and then do himself in shortly afterwards?'

She shrugged. 'Sadly, the only person who knows for certain exactly what happened is Nigel himself. And since his body is nothing more than a burnt crisp, we don't have the luxury of asking him. Sure, is it possible that someone stopped him on the side of the road, interacted with him, burnt the car, and then transported him to the barn? Of course it is; that's a very real possibility, but until we gather evidence to substantiate either theory, we can't know what happened. That's why I want us to pursue both avenues so nothing gets overlooked.'

The atmosphere in the room fell a few notches as Stephanie folded her arms across her chest. Giles sank lower in his seat, returning his attention to his screen.

'In other news...'

The voice came from Devon. He spun around in his chair and looked up at Stephanie with hope and optimism on his face.

'Yes?'

'Do you want the good news or the good news?'

She scowled at him, unimpressed.

'Just tell me, please, Devon. What is it?'

'I think I've found the person who sent the messages and emails to Nigel before he died.'

She relaxed her arms across her chest slightly. 'Go on.'

Devon turned fully in his chair, legs spread wide, fingers twitching as he grabbed a printed sheet from the desk.

'So, I ran a few advanced traces on the email metadata. The account sending the messages was encrypted and bounced through several international servers. At first, I found nothing. But then I thought, what if this person isn't quite as clever as they think? So I looked at the account setup of the email address itself, and when I compared it against historical contact data in Nigel's phone, I discovered a burner number that matched one of his deleted call logs. That number was registered to a PAYG SIM, purchased last month from a newsagent in Woking.'

He held up the printout like it was a trophy.

'And?' Stephanie prompted.

Devon's grin widened. 'And that same number was once linked to a temporary social media profile that tagged a development protest last autumn. I dug into the metadata of that post, with a little help from Facebook, and traced it to an IP address.'

Stephanie raised an eyebrow. 'Where?'

'Somewhere in Woking. Belonging to a Miss Tina Keel. Who, funnily enough, works for Woking Council, in the housing and development department.'

Stephanie paused, taking a moment to consider the implications. 'Very good,' she said.

'And to make things more interesting, her name was on the list at the conference Nigel attended. I called the organisers, and they confirmed she was registered through her council email address.'

'Nice work. And you did all this yourself?'

He chuckled, as if holding back something. 'Not quite. I had a bit of help from the digital forensics teams. But I helped put in the requests and chased things through.'

'What would we do without you?' She smirked. 'All right, I think it's time we paid a visit to Miss Keel.'

'So long as you're back in time for the pub after work,' Fiona called.

'Pub?'

'The place you go to forget about all your worries and strife. A few of us fancied drinks.'

Stephanie glanced down at Devon in front of her. He offered her a comforting nod. 'I'll be there too,' he said. 'Life and soul of the party.' Then he gave her a look that said, *don't worry about me, I'll be fine*.

CHAPTER
TWENTY-TWO

When she'd first met Devon at the start of a serial killer investigation, she'd found him abhorrent and a bit of a bully. However, now that she'd got to know him, and now that she'd seen a different side of him – a pained, emotionally torn, and vulnerable side that had recently relied heavily upon drink – she'd developed sympathy for him. She regarded him as an equal, as a friend. She had seen him in the middle of an alcohol-filled hole, and she'd been the one to help pull him out. Which was why she felt she was best qualified to voice her concerns.

Stephanie glanced at him in the driver's seat. 'Are you sure about the pub tonight?'

Devon kept his eyes on the road. 'You sound like my therapist.'

'I'm being serious,' she said. 'I just don't think it's the best idea. Especially in a place like that.'

He nodded slowly. 'I get it. And I appreciate the concern, I really do. But I've been doing all right. Haven't touched a drop in...' – he paused as if checking an internal clock – 'three and a half weeks.'

'That's good,' she said, meaning it. 'Really good.'

'Helps that I've been seeing more of Finn lately,' he added, his voice softer now. 'Weekends, some evenings. Even managed a school run last

Thursday. Makes things feel a bit more normal. Like I've got something to lose again.'

Stephanie gave a small grunt. 'Just be careful, Devon. That's all I'm saying.'

'Always, ma'am.'

The satnav chimed as they turned into the car park of Woking Borough Council.

Twenty minutes later, Tina Keel was finally ready to see them.

A woman in her late sixties stood in the doorway, blinking at them through thick glasses. Her thinning white-blonde hair was styled into a low bun, and she wore a wool cardigan over a floral blouse that strained slightly across her middle.

She turned to her assistant, confused, as if she had just sniffed a bad smell.

'Janie, what's this? This isn't my three o'clock.'

Janie, the receptionist whom Stephanie and Devon had bothered for the last twenty minutes, turned to face them. She opened her mouth to speak, but Stephanie beat her to it.

'We're with Surrey Police, Ms Keel. We wondered if we could ask you some questions.'

'Police? Whatever for?'

'Might we have this conversation inside?' Stephanie gestured towards the office.

'I... Yes.'

Stephanie and Devon thanked Janie, then followed Tina into her office. The space was modest, with all the essentials. On the table sat a full cup of peppermint tea, the smell of which lingered in the air. A framed print of a Woking skyline hung above her desk, though the glass was cracked in one corner. Tina lowered herself slowly into a squeaky office chair and offered them the seats opposite.

'I wasn't expecting the police to be here,' she said.

'People rarely do,' Stephanie retorted, as she pulled out a chair opposite.

'What's this about? A planning issue?'

'We're here in connection with Nigel Hadlow.'

Tina's expression froze. 'Oh. Right. Why?'

'He's dead,' Stephanie answered bluntly.

Tina's face widened with shock while the rest of her body remained frozen, even the rise and fall of her chest. 'Dead?'

'Unfortunately.'

'How?'

'His body was discovered after a fire.'

She audibly gasped. 'But what...? Why do...?' She chuckled awkwardly as she suddenly came alive and shifted in her seat, avoiding their gaze. 'What does that have to do with me? I mean, why are you here?'

Stephanie leaned back, giving Devon the floor to continue. 'We understand the two of you have had some previous run-ins with one another, would that be fair to say?'

Tina traced her finger over her ear, pushing strands of hair back. 'I don't... I don't know what you're referring to.'

Stephanie opened the folder and withdrew a stapled sheaf of printed messages. She laid them on the desk.

'Did you send these?'

Tina squinted down at them. Her cheeks flushed a deeper shade of pink. She leaned closer.

'Yes,' she said after a pause. 'Yes, all right. I did. But it's not what it looks like. I wasn't *threatening* him, not really. I just... I just wanted him to stop.'

'Stop what?' Devon asked.

'Being so... *corrupt*. Half of the buildings you see in the skyline nowadays are from his company. And all of them have been dodgy deals made with back handers and brown envelopes. I know about the conversations he had with some of the department heads in this place and others. His name was lauded about like he's some sort of Brad Pitt, and he thought he could get away with it.' She shook her head in disgust. 'When I found out about it on the church site, St Clement's, I tried to intervene, but by that point it was too late.'

'That didn't stop you threatening him over it.'

Tina ignored the insinuation. 'I tried to raise it internally, but nobody listened. Which isn't a surprise when the people I report to are the ones whose wheels are being greased. I just don't think what he and his company were doing was right. And then... and then I discovered there's another church on their roster. St. Mary's in Shalford. It's been there for decades, just collecting dust, and so I messaged him about it anonymously. I thought if I scared him a little, made him sweat, maybe he'd back off from that church site. Maybe he'd confess. It must have worked because I haven't seen any news or development on it since.'

The issue that had been causing Nigel Hadlow sleepless nights. The issue that had pulled him back into his smoking habit.

Stephanie studied Tina a moment longer. 'You weren't at all involved in what happened to him?'

Tina looked up, her eyes shining with grief and innocence. 'Absolutely not. I didn't want him dead. I wanted him held to account. There's a difference.'

'We understand you attended the conference in Farnborough?' Devon continued.

'That's right. As soon as it finished, I went home. Had dinner. Watched telly with my husband and the dog. I swear on it, I had nothing to do with what happened to him.'

Stephanie exchanged a look with Devon, then gave a small nod. 'All right. Thank you, Ms Keel. We'll need a list of anyone you spoke to about this. And I may need to call you again.'

'Of course. Anything I can do to help.'

As they stood to leave, Tina added, 'He was a bad person. But he didn't deserve what happened to him.'

CHAPTER
TWENTY-THREE

The Weyside pub buzzed with midweek chatter, warm and noisy, providing a snug refuge from the early winter drizzle outside. The scent of roasted meat and gravy wafted from the kitchen, mingling with the familiar tang of beer and alcohol. Stephanie leaned back in the booth near the window, her coat piled beside her and a half-drunk Guinness in front of her. She'd chosen a spot with a clear view of the pub, her eyes frequently darting to Devon, seated a few chairs away, cradling a pint glass filled with Diet Coke. The ice cubes clinked quietly as he took a sip.

Across from them, Giles and Noah were in full swing, halfway through telling a story they'd already shared twice since she joined the team.

'No, no, listen,' Giles said, gesturing wildly with his hands. 'We've just finished this visit, right? House full of cats. I mean *full*. I walk in, and this little ginger menace just launches itself off the fridge at my head. Like a missile.'

'You screamed,' Noah said, grinning.

'I shouted. There's a difference.'

'Mate, you *squealed* like a toddler at soft play.'

Laughter erupted around the table.

As they launched into a new story, quickly captivating the rest of the group, Fiona tapped Stephanie on the shoulder.

Setting her glass of wine on the table, she said, 'I meant to tell you earlier, but it slipped my mind.'

Stephanie shifted her attention, half-turning in her seat.

'Go on.'

Fiona lowered her voice. 'I reached out to Nigel Hadlow's mum about that photo found at the crime scene, the one of the young boy?'

Stephanie's stomach tensed. 'Yeah?'

'She hasn't got a clue who he is. Says it's not Nigel, not anyone from the family. No nephews, cousins, or neighbours. She was quite firm about it. Said she'd never seen the boy before in her life.'

Stephanie set her glass down with a quiet clink and stared across the room for a moment, her thoughts racing. The warmth in her chest dissipated, replaced by a slow, sinking cold.

'What do you mean she doesn't know who it is?'

Fiona shrugged. 'Says it's nobody she recognises.'

Stephanie's gaze fell on the table. 'Then who the bloody hell is it?'

CHAPTER
TWENTY-FOUR

A pain, immeasurable and overwhelming, welled in his head. Flashes of white exploded across his vision every time he moved his eyes, illuminating nothing in the darkness surrounding him. Christ, his head hurt. He'd never felt anything like it. He was forced to keep his eyes closed, left to rely on his other senses while nausea bounced about in his skull.

He knew he was on a solid surface, a hard floor. That his shoulder, elbow, hip, and ankles – the points of contact with the ground – throbbed with a deep, dull pulse, as if he had been there for days. He tried to move, but quickly realised there was nowhere to go. The pads of his fingers scraped against a wooden surface, smooth and sanded down. His breath caught in his throat. He stretched his fingers out farther, reaching in all directions. A wall. And another. And another. Above his head. Behind him. To his side. He stretched out his legs, but came to a sudden stop before he reached full length. Another wall.

His pulse began to race. No... no, no, no.

Panic rushed in, fast and wild. He twisted his body, his knees knocking against something hard. His head bumped against the lid, just a few inches above his face. He reached up again, running his hands across the top. Wood. Edges. Corners. Nails.

He was in a box.

Trapped.

He opened his eyes in the vain hope of waking from the nightmare, from the hellish dream, but all he saw was deep, cavernous black.

He pounded his palms on the roof of the box. Bolts of pain shot down his wrists and into his elbows.

'Hello!' he shouted hoarsely, the sound bouncing back at him like a cruel echo, mocking him. 'Hello? Somebody! Help! Is anybody there?'

He held his breath, listening. No voices. No footsteps. No chance of rescue. Just the sound of his own rising panic, his heavy breathing. A bead of sweat trickled down the side of his face, and he clenched his jaw tight. After a few seconds, his eyes began to adjust to the light. Somewhere in the roof was a small gap, a hole carved into the wood. A breathing hole, nothing more. Soon, he saw the vague outline of his hands, his T-shirt, and his cramped body curled inside the box.

Then he heard it. A sound. Faint. A footstep? A cough? The sound of life! Maybe someone was coming to rescue him.

But then another sound registered, and he realised how wrong he was. A low crackling. Like paper being scrunched slowly. Distant, but getting louder.

And then came the smell. Something thick, cloying. Smoke.

Before long, it made its way into the box. He was breathing it in, suffocating on it. Coughing, convulsing. His body jerked with each pained movement, his shoulder and forehead banging against the confines of the box.

Smoke continued to seep through the hole, thick and unrelenting.

Regaining his composure, he slammed his palms against the lid.

'Please! Somebody help! Let me out!'

He stared through the hole, willing someone to appear – a hero, a rescuer. Then a shadow moved beyond it, brief and flickering. It passed quickly across what little light there was, then vanished into the gloom.

'Wait! Come back. Stop! Hello? Please, don't leave me in here!'

He rammed his shoulders against the lid. Kicked at the walls with his heels. The box didn't budge. Whoever had built it had made it to last.

He quickly wore himself out and panted, pausing to catch his breath. It made no difference. The smoke was coming in fast now, heavier and denser. And then came the glow. In the hole. At the edges. Bleeding through the gaps in the wood.

Fire.

All-encompassing, consuming. Burning around him. The crackling sound became amplified, like a subwoofer in the background. Slowly, he began to feel the heat. The fire was rapidly closing in, the smoke suffocating him. The air inside the box was thick and syrupy, and every breath became harder than the last. His lungs screamed for oxygen, but all they found was poison. Acrid smoke clawed down his throat and into his chest, choking him from the inside out.

He twisted violently, scrabbling at the lid, the walls, the corners. His fingernails caught on the grain and tore, one by one, blood slicking the wood. He kicked and shoved with all the strength he had left, but there was nowhere to go. Every surface pushed back against him. The walls felt closer. Tighter. As if the box itself was shrinking around him.

'Please...' he rasped. 'Don't do this.'

His voice was broken now. He could barely hear it over the roar of the flames.

A sudden jolt of heat surged through the base of the box. The soles of his feet blistered. He screamed, curling his legs away, as if it might make a difference. The box creaked above him. Loud, threatening. The wood was giving way, changing shape under the strain.

He could hear it; the fire licking its way up the sides, hungry and ruthless.

Another flash of light passed over the breathing hole. He snapped his eyes toward it. Another shadow. Closer this time. It hovered. Watching.

'Please!' he sobbed. 'I'll do anything, just let me out!'

But the shadow disappeared again.

And then came a sound he hadn't expected: nails splitting. Wood cracking. The box was no longer just a prison. It was becoming his pyre. He shrieked as a line of searing orange spread across one wall. The inside began to glow. Tiny tongues of flame poked through the cracks, reaching for him.

The heat was unbearable now. Sweat poured from his face, sizzling on the timber.

He kicked again, a wild, last-ditch effort, but his legs met resistance. No give. No way out.

He was going to die in there.

Burn.

Alive.

He opened his mouth to scream again, but there was no air left to scream with.

Only smoke. Only fire.

And then darkness.

CHAPTER
TWENTY-FIVE

The Grade I listed Church of All Saints was located in Ockham, a small village on the east side of the A3, which connected Guildford to London and the M25. It was set back slightly from the road, bordered by a low wall and an iron gate, both now blackened from the heat, the gate's hinges warped and brittle. The building, originally squat and angular, now had a slate roof that sagged near the centre, visibly damaged by the inferno that had raged the night before. Surrounding the church, nearby gravestones were covered in ash, their inscriptions obscured, leaning away from the building as if trying to escape the fire.

Originally dating from the thirteenth century, the church had seen various extensions over the years, including the King Chapel on the north side. It was a place steeped in history, where generations had once come to worship and mourn. Now, however, on another grey and dreary November morning, it stood as nothing more than a blackened shell – silent, ruined, and thick with the stench of smoke.

Stephanie pulled up to the outer cordon and hopped out of the car. The middle of the road was occupied by two fire engines, with their crews packing away equipment after extinguishing the blaze. Stephanie paused at the sight of the building before her. She already knew what they would find inside: another body. The caller from Control hadn't mentioned it, but as soon as she heard the woman mention a fire, she recognised the grim truth. This was no casual arson. This was no accident. It was premeditated. And in her mind, if there was a body inside, this was no suicide.

Her body trembled softly as her eyes fell on the wreckage. She had tried to summon the courage to face the ruins during the drive over, but it made little impact. All she could see and think about was her father and the burn on her forearm that stung beneath her jumper.

Her heart went out to the building and its historical significance. A piece of history, like Notre Dame in Paris, burned to the ground and lost to the elements. Before she could move (not that she wanted to), she saw Elias approaching the fire engine. He spotted her and came over, glancing down at the small folder she'd picked up from the passenger seat.

'You got the resources I gave you then?' he asked, pointing at them.

'These? They're something else. But yes, I got them. Very kind of you, thank you.' She surveyed her surroundings and then lowered her voice. 'But you really didn't need to.'

'Have you used them yet?'

She hesitated before responding. 'I had a look last night after watching a documentary. I can already feel myself processing this place better than I would have done the other day.'

He raised an eyebrow, clearly sceptical of her statement. Even she didn't fully believe it.

'How long have you been standing there?' he asked.

'I just arrived.'

'Right. And can you put one foot in front of the other?'

She glanced down at her feet. 'Eventually.'

He huffed. 'Would you like me to tell you what happened, or would you prefer to see for yourself?'

Images of their last crime scene visit flooded her mind: the smell, the smoke, the charred remains, Nigel Hadlow's blackened and crumpled body. If she could avoid it, she would.

'I don't see any reason to waste a perfectly good set of PPE,' she replied candidly.

Elias chuckled dryly before gesturing for her to follow him a little farther from the outer cordon, away from the noise of the fire engines and attending crew.

'We were called just before five am,' he began, his voice low. 'A local resident woke up to the smell of smoke and saw the glow from their bedroom window. By the time the crews arrived, the place was already well alight. From what we've been able to assess, the blaze originated in the nave and spread quickly through the roof into the chancel. It took over an hour to bring it under control. What's left is... mostly rubble and mess.'

Stephanie nodded, her eyes fixed on a nearby tree. Elias continued.

'Fortunately, thanks to all the rain we've been having, it didn't spread to any of the nearby trees or fields, so it was contained.'

'Has anyone been inside?'

Elias nodded. 'Only for a quick security check.'

'And?'

Elias exhaled heavily and turned slightly, pointing through the soot-streaked windows. 'First responders from my team found a body.'

She paused for a moment of quiet contemplation.

'But this time they found it in a box.'

'A box?'

'What's left it that didn't burn. We found it in front of the altar, where the aisle meets the chancel, hidden beneath what's left of the lectern. The flames had already consumed it by the time the team got water on it.'

Stephanie turned to look at him. 'A coffin?'

'Not exactly.' He rubbed the back of his neck, his gaze clouded. 'I mean, it was roughly the same size – big enough for a fully grown adult – but it was just six pieces of wood put together, hand-built and nailed shut from the outside.'

'How bad is the body?'

Elias hesitated, which told her everything she needed to know. 'Same as your victim from the other day: charred beyond recognition. One hundred percent burns across one hundred percent of the body. We'll need dental records or DNA for identification. There was very little left… structurally.'

Stephanie inhaled slowly through her nose.

'From what we've been able to assess, it doesn't look like the fire was started in the box. It was set around it and burned inward.'

'Accelerant?'

'Potentially. We won't know until we run tests. We did find a single breathing hole in the corner of the lid, which suggests whoever was in there was conscious, or at least breathing, when the fire started.'

Stephanie felt her throat tighten. 'Any sign of who they were?'

Elias shook his head. 'Nothing. But we'll keep looking.'

Stephanie closed her eyes for a moment. Another body, burned alive. Boxed in. It felt symbolic. But why?

Before she could ponder that further, a member of the fire crew shuffled over. A man in his early thirties, fit and active like the rest of his team, hovered on the outskirts of the conversation, waiting for approval.

'What is it?' Elias asked.

'A car,' the man said. 'We've found a car that's in the same condition as the church.'

CHAPTER
TWENTY-SIX

'Where?' Elias asked, raising an eyebrow.

'About a hundred yards east of the church, in the field behind that row of trees. It looks like it was dumped and torched sometime last night. It was still warm when we got to it just now; wasn't hard to spot once the sun came up. Must have missed it while everything else was going on.'

Stephanie glanced at Elias. 'Make and model?'

The firefighter nodded. 'Looks like an Audi Q5.'

'Plates?'

'It's badly burnt, but the number plate is definitely visible.'

That was a relief. If they could get the plate, they could run it through the database and find the owner faster than it would take to request dental records.

'Let's go,' she said, already walking.

Elias fell into step beside her, guiding her through a narrow gap in the hedge that opened into a wide field of flattened grass and churned-up mud. The November sky pressed low above them, grey and brooding, and the smell hit her before she saw the wreck.

The car sat in a shallow dip, angled awkwardly in the field. The fire had gutted it completely. Its skeleton was blackened and blistered, the once-luxurious paintwork disintegrated to reveal warped panels and a scorched undercarriage. Every window had shattered, leaving jagged teeth in the frames. The tyres were nothing but melted rims, and the alloy wheels had buckled from the heat, sagging under their own weight. Stephanie peered into what had once been the driver's side. The leather seats were gone, and the dashboard had melted in streaks.

'Same as Nigel Hadlow's vehicle,' she muttered. 'Only this time, it's closer. We're within walking distance of the scene.'

'Less than a few minutes away,' Elias agreed, glancing back at the distant silhouette of the ruined church. 'Which means he either drove the car here himself and torched it, or someone else was responsible.'

Staring at the vehicle, she said with a smirk, 'I thought you only presented the facts? I don't think this is anything other than murder. Not if there were nails in the coffin. Someone had to have put them in there, and had to have placed his body in there first.' She surveyed the earth around her. 'We need to get this place sealed off and searched for footprints in the mud. We shouldn't be here.'

Elias carefully moved away from the vehicle, looking down at the ground. 'Do you think the victim was dragged here or conscious when they arrived?'

'My gut says they were dragged. I don't know.'

They slowly made their way back across the field, the wind picking up and tugging at Stephanie's coat. Rain began to fall again, thin, icy pellets that needled against her cheeks. The temperature had dropped to match the macabre surroundings.

As they emerged from behind the hedge and entered the churchyard, Stephanie noticed a handful of CSIs and fire investigators dotted around the perimeter of the building. A few were photographing scorch marks along the wall, while others were marking debris with yellow evidence markers.

Elias slowed beside her, brushing mud off his gloves. 'I suggest we get some drone shots of the side, to see if there are any tyre tracks in the field and determine where the car came from.'

'Good idea,' she replied.

Elias was about to respond when someone called out in the distance. 'Ma'am! Elias! Over here!'

They turned to see one of the fire examiners waving them down from the south-facing wall of the church. He was crouched by a shallow dip in the grass, just beneath a scorched window arch, gesturing urgently.

Stephanie picked up her pace, her feet squelching in the wet ground.

'What is it?' she asked as they arrived.

'Quickly. I think you'll want to see this...'

CHAPTER
TWENTY-SEVEN

Stephanie hurried the short distance to the edge of the building. As she approached, the smell intensified, hanging around the building like a bubble. She pushed the wreckage from her mind and focused solely on the fire examiner, who was dressed in full uniform and holding an object in his hands.

She recognised it immediately but didn't want to get her hopes up until she saw it properly... until she laid her eyes on the items inside. The fire examiner was a tall man, just over six feet, and rugged in appearance. His broad shoulders filled his coat, and a deep scar marked his chin. He looked at her expectantly as she came to a stop in front of him.

'I wasn't there at the last incident, but I heard about it,' he began, glancing down at the object.

Slowly, he opened his gloved hands to reveal a small metal tin, almost identical to the one that had been discovered at Nigel Hadlow's crime scene. Stephanie's breath caught as she looked down. The tin was the same size, scorched around the edges, the lid slightly warped from the heat, the hinges brittle and blackened, with flecks of soot still clinging to its surface like ash on skin. The fire examiner cradled it gently, as though the slightest wrong move might cause it to disintegrate.

Elias stepped closer behind her, silent.

'I found it tucked just beneath a ledge,' the examiner continued. 'It was hidden, wedged into a gap between two stones. Still warm.'

Stephanie crouched for a better look as he opened the lid slowly.

Inside was a photograph.

Just like there had been before. But now she was seeing it in the flesh, for real.

The image was faded, the edges curled, but mostly intact, protected by the tight seal of the tin. It showed the face of a boy around thirteen or fourteen, staring directly at the camera with a thin smile, as if wishing the photograph would be over with as quickly as possible. The background was indistinct at first glance, but as she leaned closer, she noticed a shape behind the boy's shoulder. A curved line. A shadowy outline. Possibly someone else's shoulder or arm, part of something larger. A bigger picture, perhaps, as though the photo had been cropped or torn from a group image. A missing piece of a puzzle.

She closed her eyes, trying to recall the photograph found at Nigel Hadlow's crime scene. Were they the same? Similar? Taken from the same larger image?

Her memory conjured it; the boy in the previous photo had stood in front of a background resembling the edge of a stage curtain. This one had the same lighting and the same shadow across the child's cheek. A sibling photo, or perhaps a different child entirely, snapped moments apart?

Stephanie opened her eyes and gestured to the fire examiner.

'Can you bag that? *Carefully*. We'll need a side-by-side comparison with the first one as soon as possible.'

The man nodded, handing it off to a nearby CSI.

'There's something else,' he said, still holding the tin. He turned it slightly so Stephanie could see the inner lid. Inscribed into the metal, in neat, precise writing, was:

For the LORD your God is a consuming fire, a jealous God —
Deuteronomy 4:24

Stephanie felt her stomach tighten and her mouth go dry. Another cryptic religious message.

She glanced at Elias. 'What are the chances we find two tins containing similar photographs and religious message at two similar crime scenes, and they're not related in some way?'

The question was rhetorical, but Elias answered anyway.

'If I was a gambling man, I'd say not very likely, ma'am.'

She nodded contemplatively, unable to pull her eyes from the lettering in the tin. The cogs in her mind began to whir, to process, to conjure up the next steps. The fire examiner closed the tin and handed it over to another CSI, who tucked it inside a sterile evidence bag.

A breeze stirred what remained of the ivy near the edge of the building, brushing soot into the air like falling snow.

She needed to find out who those boys were. Before another body appeared in a box.

CHAPTER
TWENTY-EIGHT

'Do you still reckon it's a suicide, ma'am?'

The question came from Giles again, and once more, there was that smug, *I told you so* intonation in his voice, which irked her.

She folded her arms across her chest and let out a hot puff of air before half-turning to the incident board behind her. By now, some snapshots of the second crime scene had been attached to the board, including the CSI's photographs of the boy and the tin.

'No, I do not,' she began, returning her attention to the team, who all looked up at her patiently. 'The modus operandi of Nigel Hadlow's death and this latest one are almost identical. The same cause of death. The same burnt-out car. The same tins containing similar photographs of the boys and the religious inscriptions. There's now enough evidence for us to assume that these two are connected, though there's still a lot of work to be done.' She pointed to the photograph of the second boy. 'Forensics will be working the scene as soon as they've been given the all-clear from the fire team. However, in the meantime, we need to confirm the victim's identity. Fortunately, this time, we've got a possible read on the number plate. I want that number tracked down and a name associated with it. That's our biggest priority. Also, keep an eye on missing persons reports coming through overnight, in case we get a repeat of Nigel Hadlow's disappearance.' She grabbed her mother's necklace and traced it around her neck, thinking of her. 'Now, nobody seems to recognise the boy in the first image, so whenever you're speaking with friends, family, or colleagues – of either victim – I want you to show them both photographs. They must recognise at least one of them.'

'Shall we go back to Nigel Hadlow's friends and family?' Devon asked.

'Hundred per cent,' she replied abruptly. 'You don't need to tell them what's happened, just that we've found another photo in our investigation and wondered if they could identify the child in it.' She cast another quick glance at the two photos side by side. 'Something tells me that these have been taken from the same image and that it's part of something larger.' She turned back to the team, lowering her voice. 'Something also tells me this is the start of something big. We need to be ahead of it before anybody else turns up. While we're waiting for confirmation on the victim's identity, I want CCTV unearthed of the vehicle and the surrounding area. Elias and the team suspect the fire took place in the middle of the night, possibly after midnight. It was found shortly before five in the morning. That's our window. Five hours to trace the victim's car as well as the potential killer's.'

'In the middle of the country lanes? Should be breezy,' Fiona retorted.

'Congratulations,' Stephanie said, shooting the constable a derisive look. 'You've just nominated yourself in charge of house-to-house enquiries for that comment. Well done.'

A small cheer and a round of applause from Devon rippled through the team. It was the most time-consuming and least enjoyable of the jobs, often yielding very little fruit, but it was also one of the most necessary and important. Because, on the one time out of ten you got a nugget of information, it was a golden nugget that could help unlock a door to the investigation.

'Thanks, ma'am. Understood.'

Stephanie replied with a facetious smile. 'Once we know the victim's identity, I want to know everything about their lives. Where they work, what time they go to sleep, when they wake up in the morning, what time they go to the toilet – and where. I also want connections...' She turned to the whiteboard, grabbed a red marker, and in thick ink, scribbled a line between the two photographs, going over it several times. 'I want to know what connects these two people. There's something; I can feel it in my bones. We just need to identify what. Any questions?'

Silence descended on the team. They all nodded politely at her, absorbing the information and processing what their next twelve hours would look like.

'Fantastic, then let's get to work.'

At once, they stepped out of their chairs and hurried back to their desks, moving with a sense of hesitant optimism. Stephanie hung back for a while, watching their movements before starting towards her desk. As she closed the door behind her, her mobile began ringing.

Unknown number.

She froze. Dread welled within her, starting in the pit of her stomach and quickly rising to her throat. Her first thought was that it was her half-brother, blindsiding her with a call from a number she didn't recognise.

She stared at the screen until it went to voicemail. If it was important, they'd leave a message.

A moment later, one appeared. Her finger hovered over the button for a moment longer than usual. She prodded it, then pressed play.

'Hi, Steph. It's me. Call me when you get this.'

CHAPTER
TWENTY-NINE

Why did people do that? Call and then ignore the return call immediately afterwards? As if they'd finished leaving their voicemail, and then quickly turned their phone off. Were they afraid of the person calling back?

'Doesn't make sense,' she muttered to herself as she moved about her office. Stopping by the window, she looked out at the field beyond. On the grass, a small team of six dog handlers huddled together, chatting, while their dogs roamed freely, sniffing about and enjoying their brief respite.

Just as she was about to launch a verbal tirade into the phone, the person on the other end answered.

'Louis,' she said. 'What have you been doing? I tried calling you back, and you ignored me.'

'I... I went to the toilet,' he replied defensively. 'Is that not allowed in your office? Here, people can use the bathroom as much as they want.'

'Glad to hear *Surrey Live's* still breaking new ground in workers' rights,' Stephanie said, smirking as she leaned her hip against the desk.

Louis snorted. 'We're trailblazers, what can I say?'

'You could start by telling me why you called.'

'Straight down to business? All right. We've heard some rumblings about another fire, this time at Ockham Church?'

She hesitated. 'What are you asking me here, Louis?'

'Whether it's true...'

'Might be. Depends on who your sources are.'

'Don't make me beg, Steph. You know how humiliating that is for a man in my position?'

'You mean standing in the toilets pretending you're not avoiding my calls?'

He chuckled. 'Touché. Look, I'm not trying to push. I can get one of my guys to go down and have a look for themselves, but petrol ain't cheap these days, and train tickets even less so.'

'So it's a cost-cutting exercise?'

'Just a tightening of the purse strings. Are the two related? What's happened?'

Stephanie sighed heavily, briefly explaining what they'd discovered that morning.

'Who's the second body belong to?' he asked.

'We're working on it.'

'Are the two connected? It's not every day people are set on fire, Steph. Unless it's a case of arson gone very, very wrong.'

'Sadly, I don't think that's what we're looking at.'

'Then I think you need to prepare yourself for this potentially going national. People are going to go crazy for this one. Engagement will be high, and before you know it, you'll have hordes of journalists and reporters outside the crime scenes.'

'You mean like your guys do sometimes?'

He grunted the question away. 'All I'm saying is I'd like to get ahead and get the facts from you before someone misquotes a rumour.'

There was a brief pause. Stephanie was reminded of the agreement they'd made when she first joined Surrey Police. She had wanted their relationship to be mutually beneficial, very much an "I scratch your back, you scratch mine" approach. He'd been fair to her in the past, especially during the Bogeyman case a few weeks earlier when he had refused to publish images of her that compromised her professionalism, proving that she could trust him.

'All right,' she said. 'But nothing goes live until we've made the ID. If you put anything out early, you'll be cleaning charcoal out of your mouth for weeks, understood?'

'Scout's honour,' he said, though she was fairly sure he'd never made it past Cubs.

She filled him in on the essentials: two victims, similar MO, bodies burnt to a crisp, and the matching tins with the cryptic inscriptions and photographs. He didn't interrupt, though she could hear the scribble of pen on paper.

'This is big,' he said finally.

'Tell me something I don't know.'

'No one's been stuffed in a burning box since the Middle Ages. And even then, they usually saved it for witches.'

'Thanks for the history lesson, Professor.'

'I'm thinking of adding a column to the platform: Louis's Little Lectures. What do you think?'

Stephanie smirked. 'You'd need someone to ghost write it. Your spelling's atrocious.'

'That's slander.'

'I've seen your emails. They're like code-breaker puzzles. Half the time I have to forward them to the team for translation. It's a wonder the magazine's doing so well.'

'Well, maybe I'll stop messaging you, then. See how you like that.'

'Tempting,' she said, dragging a finger down the side of her coffee mug. Her smile faded slightly as she glanced back at the whiteboard covered in case notes. 'Anyway, there's still a lot we don't know, and I've given you everything I can.'

Louis let out a long breath. 'You think it's the same killer?'

'Yes. I think it is. And I think they've only just started.'

A short silence followed, and when he spoke again, his voice had softened slightly. 'Well, you know how to reach me if you want to talk it through. Or, you know, just complain about my spelling again.'

She chuckled. 'I might take you up on that.'

'Keep me posted. And, Steph?'

'Yeah?'
'Try not to end up in the third box.'
'I'll do my best,' she said.

CHAPTER
THIRTY

A little over two hours later, they had a name.

The wreckage of the Audi Q5 belonged to a man named Carlos Vazquez.

Carlos was fifty-three, a long-time Surrey resident who'd spent most of his adult life working in construction. According to their preliminary background check, he specialised in high-end residential developments, overseeing groundwork and site management for a firm based in Croydon. He was married to a woman named Ana, his wife of twenty-two years, and they had a grown daughter living in Manchester. No previous convictions. A man who paid his taxes, kept himself to himself and, up until that morning, had never had any run-ins with the police. To all intents and purposes, he was a model citizen.

His name had surfaced shortly after the forensics team finished processing the burnt-out Audi. The number plate, though partially melted, had yielded enough characters for Noah and the team to run it through the DVLA. From there, they had landed on Carlos.

Less than half an hour later, Stephanie and Olivia stood outside a tired-looking brick building on the outskirts of Woking's town centre, arms folded against the growing wind. The sign above the entrance read: Cloverfield Dental Practice. Ana Vazquez's place of work. Patients came and went every few minutes, children rubbing their numbed jaws, wrapped in their mother's arms as they kept their heads low against the drizzle.

Stephanie hated this part. The polite confusion before the collapse into grief. It never got easier, but there was no point in delaying the inevitable.

'Let's go.'

They hurried towards the entrance. A woman at reception glanced up with a professional smile that faded as soon as they introduced themselves.

'Mrs Vazquez is in the office. I'll let her know you're here.'

They waited in the reception area for only a minute before a woman in her early fifties emerged. She was petite, with dark curly hair tied into a neat ponytail, and wore a navy-blue tunic beneath a white coat. She froze as soon as she spotted Stephanie and Olivia, her expression confirming in her mind the reason they were there. She held her hand to her mouth and inhaled sharply.

'Oh my God,' she said, her voice a whisper.

Stephanie stepped forward. 'Mrs Vazquez? I'm DI Broadbent; this is DC Willard. May we speak with you in private?'

Ana blinked rapidly, already shaking her head. 'Is it Carlos?' she asked, panic rising in her throat. 'Is he all right?'

Stephanie softened her tone. 'If we could just sit down for a moment.'

Tears welled instantly in Ana's eyes, but she nodded and turned stiffly on the spot, leading them down a short, narrow corridor past a line of treatment rooms. At the end was her small office. A framed photo of a teenage girl in graduation robes sat on the desk. Ana closed the door behind them, but she didn't sit. She hovered by her desk, arms folded across her chest as if trying to brace herself for what was about to come.

'What's happened?' she asked again, her voice thinner now. 'Please. Just tell me.'

'This morning, we found a car registered in your husband's name near All Saints Church in Ockham.'

Ana's eyes widened, saying nothing.

'The car had been burnt out and was hidden behind the church.'

She moved her hand to her mouth. Stephanie swallowed deeply.

'Your husband was not in the car... however, there was an incident *in* the church involving another fire. We have found a body. At this stage, we cannot confirm if it was your husband; however, the evidence is leading us to believe it is.'

For a moment, Ana didn't say anything. Her face contorted as if her brain was struggling to process the information, as if they had spoken to her in another language. Her legs gave out, and she sank into the chair behind her desk.

'No, no, no,' she muttered, the words tumbling out as she stared at the floor. 'It's him, isn't it? That's why he didn't come home last night. I've been going out of my mind trying to contact him, to reach out. I... How long until you know it's him?'

Olivia moved to her side, crouched down, and placed a comforting hand on Ana's shoulder.

'The body has been taken away for a post-mortem. It will take some time for them to identify him; however, what would really help is access to his dental records and also some DNA.'

Ana sniffed back a globule of snot. 'You're in the right place for it.' She pointed to a computer on the other side of the room. 'All of my family's records are on there.'

Stephanie glanced at the computer, then back to Ana. Olivia looked back at her, and Stephanie caught her eye, responding with a curt nod.

'Thank you for that,' Olivia continued. 'We'll take the evidence away. In the meantime, to help our investigation...' She reached behind her, fishing inside her back pocket. 'We were hoping you might be able to tell us what your husband was doing last night?'

'He was working,' Ana replied, sniffling repeatedly. 'He was working late. A couple of his team were on site, and he was in the office.'

'What time was he due home?'

'He didn't have a set time. He just messages whenever he leaves.'

'And did he message you last night?'

Ana shook her head. 'That's when I started to panic. It wasn't like him. It wasn't until nine or ten o'clock, when I hadn't heard from him, that I tried ringing his mobile.'

'What happened?'

'It went straight through to voicemail.'

It must have been switched off, Stephanie thought. Either he'd turned it off and driven to the church at night, or someone had turned it off for him.

Olivia pulled out a piece of paper that contained scans of the two photos found at the crime scenes. She passed the sheet across to Ana and let her have a look.

'We need to ask,' she said. 'Do you recognise either of the boys in these photos? Take as much time as you need.'

But Ana didn't need it. Immediately, she pointed to the image on the left, the one found at the first crime scene, at Nigel Hadlow's location.

'Who is that?' Olivia asked.

'That's Carlos,' she replied. 'That's my husband.'

Stephanie approached with apprehension. She took the sheet from Ana and pinched it between her fingers as if it were radioactive.

'You're sure this is your husband?'

'Of course I am. He looks exactly the same now. Hasn't changed in the thirty-odd years I've known him.'

While Ana reached for a tissue on the dentist chair, Stephanie paused in quiet reflection. The explanation was clear to her. The identity of the second victim had been found at the first crime scene. The killer had told them exactly who would be next. Which meant...

Her eyes fell on the second photo.

Which meant she was staring at the third victim.

CHAPTER
THIRTY-ONE

Devon had been listening to the ringing sound in his ear for so long that he found himself humming along to it.

Hmmph-hmmph.

Hmmph-hmmph.

The call cut out. Still no answer. He slammed the landline back into its cradle and tried again, this time calling Olivia's mobile.

He bounced his leg up and down impatiently as he waited. Come on, come on. Come on, come on, he thought in time with the trilling tone. What was taking them so long?

Just as he was about to hang up, the call was finally answered.

'Devon?'

'At long last! You're alive. I thought something bad had happened to you.'

Olivia chuckled. 'You're not half wrong. Steph did almost pull out in front of someone at a T-junction.'

'She's just as bad as the people she complains about.'

'Only because she was trying to answer your call.'

'Serves her right. She knows the rules. Since when did you start calling her Steph? When did you get *that* upgrade?'

'I've always done it. That's what you get for being nice to people.'

He leaned back in his chair. 'Yeah, yeah. Nice, shmice.'

'Are you calling just to wind me up, or did you have something specific in mind?'

As if suddenly remembering the reason for his call, Devon leaned forward in his chair and shook his cursor, waking up his computer screen.

'As much as I'd love to sit here and listen to your voice all day, I was just calling to let you know – well, let Steph know, actually – that I've got something I think might be worth checking out.'

'Clever. Well done.' There was a pause as Olivia pulled the phone away from her ear and switched the call to loudspeaker. The sounds of the car engine and traffic filtered through the microphone.

'You almost made me crash, Devon,' came Stephanie's distant voice, as if she were speaking from another dimension. 'It had better be important.'

'How does a connection between Nigel Hadlow and Carlos Vazquez sound?'

'That sounds like you have my attention.'

'I've been digging through Carlos's and Nigel's social media accounts, and I spotted the two of them looking pally at Pyrford Golf Course.'

'Excellent work. Thanks for letting us know. We'll head down there now.'

'No, you won't,' he retorted. 'I've already called ahead. They're expecting me in the next hour.'

It was a lie, but Stephanie didn't need to know that.

'Oh,' she replied.

'We can't have you two having all the fun now, can we? Gotta save some of the good stuff for the rest of us.'

CHAPTER
THIRTY-TWO

Devon turned off the main road and followed the narrow, winding drive that led into Pyrford Golf Club. Rain tapped steadily against the windscreen, falling from the uniform slab of grey above. The golf course looked pristine, with lush velvet greens that refused to be beaten by the miserable weather – much like the players currently making their way around the course. He pulled into one of the marked visitor bays and cut the engine. Devon had never been a fan of golf; he found it pretentious, conceited, and full of arseholes. It was an opinion he'd formed long ago, when he'd come across a suspect in an investigation who was a golf enthusiast and treated him with such contempt that Devon had felt a strong urge to arrest him, despite the man's obvious innocence. Ever since, he'd harboured a chip on his shoulder regarding the sport and its players, namely white, middle-aged men with more money than sense – a category he was quickly falling into, minus the money, of course.

He braced himself for the sort of pillock he might encounter, exhaling his discontent through his nostrils before shoving open the door. The wind caught it immediately, swinging it wide. He grabbed it and slammed it shut, hunching his shoulders against the gusts as he crossed the short distance to the clubhouse. Inside, a wall of warm air enveloped him, accompanied by the low murmur of quiet conversation. A couple of men in their sixties sat at a table near the window, scrolling on their phones with half-finished drinks beside them, their faces etched with discontent.

Devon approached the reception desk, where a young woman looked up from behind a computer screen.

'Good afternoon,' he said, flipping open his warrant card. 'I'm looking to speak with the owner or manager on duty. Shouldn't take long.'

The girl's eyes widened in blind panic. Her mouth opened and closed, unable to form words. She looked as if she'd never seen a police officer before.

'Right. The police? Erm...' She glanced around the reception, as if lost. 'Right. Um, that'll be Mr Walker. I'll just... Sorry. I'll give him a call. Wait, no I won't. I know where he is.' She turned from him, then spun back, hand raised. 'Sorry, I'm all over the place.'

'It's fine,' he replied, flashing her a comforting smile.

The receptionist disappeared behind a door. While he waited, Devon glanced out of the window at the tapestry of green in the distance, observing the group of men in gear determined to ensure nothing interrupted their hard-earned time away from their wives and families.

His attention was pulled away from the window a moment later, when a man who looked as if he'd fallen out of a Ralph Lauren catalogue emerged, dressed in a polo shirt that was tucked into a pair of white chinos.

'You must be Mr Walker,' Devon said.

'And you must be lost,' Mr Walker retorted. 'We haven't had any issues recently to warrant a visit from the police.'

Here we go, Devon thought. Another arsehole intent on winding me up.

He forced a smile. 'Lost? No. Though if you ever find me at one of these places on a personal visit, then yes, I am very much lost and recommend you call the police immediately.'

Mr Walker blinked, unamused. 'Charming.'

Devon replied in kind. 'Mind if we talk somewhere private?'

The man sniffed, then gestured stiffly for Devon to follow. He led him past the reception and through a short corridor lined with framed club photographs of players holding cups and trophies. The hallway opened into a small office that reeked of leather polish, featuring a worn Chesterfield in the corner and more golf memorabilia mounted on the walls.

Mr Walker motioned to a chair. Devon remained standing.

'I wanted to ask you about two of your members – Carlos Vazquez and Nigel Hadlow. Either of those names ring a bell?'

Walker's eyes narrowed in thought. 'They don't sound familiar.'

Devon pulled a folded sheet from his coat pocket and laid it flat on the desk. It displayed a photo taken from Carlos's social media profile of both him and Nigel Hadlow on the golf green, clubs in hand.

Walker leaned forward for a better look. As soon as his gaze landed on the photo, a flicker of recognition crossed his face.

'Ah. Them. Yeah, now I know who you mean. They come in about once a week, sometimes more in the summer. Usually mid-morning tee-offs, weekdays mostly.'

'Do they come together?'

'Always. They're golfing buddies.'

'Anyone else usually with them?' Devon asked.

Mr Walker nodded. 'There is someone else you should probably speak to. They always played as a three, occasionally a four if they brought a guest.' He turned towards the corner of the office and tapped at the keyboard of a high-tech iMac computer. The CCTV feed popped up – a live split-screen of the grounds, car park, and bar area.

Devon was just about to ask for the name of the third player when Walker pointed at the screen. 'Speak of the devil.'

A silver BMW X5 pulled into the car park, the tyres splashing through shallow puddles. The driver's door opened, and out stepped a man in his late fifties, hair neatly combed, dressed in waterproofs with golf shoes already on his feet.

Devon raised his eyebrows, then checked his watch. It was the middle of the day in the middle of the week. Is nobody in this bloody country employed? he thought.

'What's his name?' he asked.

'Terry Houghton. One of our more regular regulars. Used to run his own recruitment firm. Sold it a few years back. Retired early, but still pretends he works part time.'

Devon smirked. 'Perfect. I'll have a word with him.'

＃ CHAPTER
THIRTY-THREE

Terry Houghton was the kind of man who filled a room before he even stepped through the door. Tall, broad, and built like an overfed Labrador, he had the lumbering presence of someone who had once been athletic but had long since succumbed to the comforts of age, drink, and a well-stocked fridge. His stomach pressed tightly against the zip of his waterproof coat, as if it might burst free if he laughed too hard, and a set of thick jowls rested beneath tanned skin that suggested he had spent too many sessions on a sun bed or enjoyed frequent trips to the Mediterranean.

He was in the middle of removing his golf bag from his boot when Devon stepped beside him. The man grunted with displeasure, eyeing him suspiciously.

'Can I help you?'

'Mr Houghton?'

'Yes...'

Devon flashed his warrant card in the man's face. 'Might I have a word with you somewhere? Preferably away from the rain.'

The man's expression revealed nothing, as if this wasn't the first time he had encountered someone in Devon's position. Either that, or he was an excellent poker player.

'The car's big enough,' Terry replied.

'Excellent. Are you driving?'

Terry shot him a look of disdain before dropping the golf bag back into the boot and slamming it shut. Devon moved to the passenger seat and climbed in, noticing the expensive watch and bracelets dangling from Terry's wrist. When Terry eventually joined him, the car sagged a few centimetres beneath his weight.

'I can't say I've ever had a meeting with a police officer like this before,' he said.

'But you have had a meeting with us?'

'A few, yes,' Terry replied, yanking off his gloves and tossing them into the centre console. 'Nothing worth writing home about.'

Devon leaned back in the seat, unbothered by the man's ego. 'Let's keep it simple then. I'm looking into two men – Nigel Hadlow and Carlos Vazquez. You knew them?'

Terry snorted, reaching into the armrest for a cigar tin. 'You could say that. Played a few rounds with them now and again. Once a week, give or take, when our schedules aligned. Not exactly best mates, but I knew them better than I know most of the men who come here.' He cracked the tin open and paused. 'Mind if I smoke?'

'Yes,' Devon said flatly. 'I'm trying to quit,' he lied.

Terry grunted and closed the tin. 'Didn't think coppers could afford to be precious these days.'

Devon smiled without humour. 'We save it for special occasions. Like when two men are burned alive.'

That did it. A flicker of discomfort crossed Terry's face. 'I heard something about that on the news.'

'They were the victims.'

Terry exhaled through his nose, his eyes drifting to the drizzle. 'Christ.'

'As I'm sure you can imagine, Mr Houghton, we've been doing some research into Nigel's and Carlos's lives.'

'Which is why you're here.'

'Which is why I'm here.'

Terry turned back slowly, his eyes narrowing. 'Is that your theory, then? You think it's something to do with me?'

'No,' Devon replied, short and sharp. 'Not unless you give me a reason to think so.'

Terry let out a hollow laugh. 'I've got better things to do.'

'Tell me about them. Any idea why someone would want them dead? Did you notice anything strange recently? Did either of them mention being followed, or someone coming into their lives that they didn't necessarily want hanging around?'

Terry didn't think for long. 'Nigel was a worrier, the anxious sort. Mostly because of his work. He couldn't switch off. Was always checking his phone. Carlos, on the other hand, was quiet, a bit dull, really. But we all got on. And neither of them mentioned anything to me. It's golf, Detective. Not a book club. We don't stand around talking about our thoughts and feelings. We come here to switch off, get away from life for a little while, and, more importantly, improve our game.'

'And yet someone went to extreme lengths to make sure they suffered,' Devon said. 'If you had to guess – debts, arguments, dodgy deals... anything come to mind?'

Terry scratched the edge of his jaw. 'Nigel... he mentioned something a few months ago. Said he was short.'

'Short?'

'Money.'

'Short for what?'

'Said he needed some money to help something he was working on get over the line.'

The deal with the council.

Devon raised a brow. 'And you helped him out?'

Terry shifted in his seat. 'Just some cash. Fifty grand. Interest-free. Didn't see the harm. He said he'd pay me back by Christmas.'

Devon studied him. 'You tell anyone else about this loan?'

'I told the taxman, if that's what you mean. Whether Nigel did or not is up to him.'

Devon nodded, the cogs in his brain beginning to turn over. 'And Carlos, did he know about the loan?'

'Doubt it. Like I said, we played golf. That was it.'

Devon reached for the door handle. 'Appreciate your time, Mr Houghton. If you think of anything else, let me know.'

Terry grunted again.

As Devon stepped back out into the rain, he muttered to himself, 'No one seems to work anymore, but they've all got fifty grand to throw around.'

CHAPTER
THIRTY-FOUR

Stephanie bounced her leg up and down repeatedly, turning her thoughts over in her mind.

The photograph of the young boy found at the first crime scene had been the second victim.

She couldn't believe it. The killer was playing with them. Telling them who would be next to burn alive.

She stared at the computer screen, at the image that had been discovered at the second crime scene – the unnamed boy in the photo – until the pixels seemed to merge into one. She was convinced they had been taken from the same larger photo. That the two men, Carlos and Nigel, were connected by something more tangible, more historic than a golf membership. Otherwise, why else would the killer use photos from their childhood? To make it harder to identify them? To stay one step ahead?

She closed her eyes. Her head was beginning to throb, and for the first time in weeks, her taste buds tingled with the craving for something fatty and greasy. A kebab. Chicken shish, specifically. With charred edges, slathered in garlic sauce, wrapped in warm pitta, and loaded with crunchy salad. She could almost feel the oil dripping on her fingertips, taste the vinegar-soaked tang of pickled chillies on her tongue...

She exhaled sharply through her nose and sat back, forcing the thought away. Her stomach growled gently, the echo of her cravings ringing in her ears. *Not now. Not today.* She focused again on the photo on the screen, pushing her hunger down, away from the part of her that needed to think.

The background of the image still nagged at her. That shape. Something in her mind scratched at the edge of it. A banner? A gym rope? A school display board?

Her leg stopped bouncing.

She stood abruptly, the chair scraping across the floor.

A moment later, she found Olivia at her desk, headphones in, eyes flicking between two screens filled with the victims' financial statements. She looked up as Stephanie approached, pulling one earbud free.

'Can you run something for me?' Stephanie asked.

'Always.'

'Carlos Vazquez and Nigel Hadlow... I want to know if they attended the same school. Somewhere local, probably. Secondary or maybe primary. Late 1980s to early 1990s. See what comes up.'

Olivia raised an eyebrow but didn't ask questions. 'Give me a sec...'

Stephanie watched over her shoulder, her fingers twitching at her sides. Her heartbeat had started to quicken again; not with anxiety this time, but with anticipation.

After less than a minute, Olivia sat back. 'Boom. Both listed on the register for St Jude's School in Oxshott. Same year group, even. From 1981–1986.'

Stephanie let out a long breath.

There it is.

'They knew each other,' she said. 'Long before golf. Long before now.'

Olivia frowned. 'So what connects them to the killer?'

'I don't know. But I reckon that's a good place to start.'

CHAPTER
THIRTY-FIVE

St Jude's School, a private school for boys aged eleven to nineteen, in Oxshott sat tucked behind a narrow row of oak trees. Walls of ivy covered the Victorian mansion which doubled as the main building. Great gravel paths led to the entrance, flanked by meticulously manicured lawns maintained by a dedicated team of grounds staff. In the background was a small woodland, where the melody of birdsong fought with the distant hum of a lawnmower. Despite the oppressive grey clouds looming above, the place seemed full of colour and hope, as if the kids' tuition fees paid for a brighter colour paint or superior grass.

As they arrived, Stephanie felt a familiar pang of recognition. The building looked a lot like her old school, where, as a troubled teenager from a broken home, she had wandered the corridors during class, hiding from teachers and slipping into empty classrooms whenever she could. It reminded her of leaving the school premises whenever she felt like it to visit Kimberley's junior school, watching her classes through the window. It reminded her of a time of hurt, of pain, of suffering, of crying out for attention in the only way she knew how – and resenting everyone who offered it.

Those had been troubled years. Years where she'd thought, for a long time, that she might have gone down the same path as her father. Into a life of crime. Drugs. Drink. Living off a broken and battered system. But then something had changed. She couldn't quite remember what. A conversation. An argument. Something she'd seen or something she'd witnessed. There had been a turning point – a stark, noticeable moment in her life – when everything flipped, leading her to fight for her education and career.

Stephanie stepped out of the car and gazed at the school's crest, carved into the sandstone arch above the entrance. Two stags reared on either side of a shield, their antlers entwined with laurel. Beneath it, in Latin: Virtus per Scientiam. Strength Through Knowledge. She scoffed under her breath; it was the kind of crap designed to make wealthy parents feel better about buying their sons' futures.

Olivia joined her side, her eyes surveying the grounds. 'My school had more teenage pregnancies than this place has students.'

Stephanie chuckled as they ascended the stone steps and entered the main building. Inside, the hallway was wide and lofty, echoing faint footsteps. Old photographs of boys in cricket whites, school plays, and a future fencing champion adorned the wood-panelled walls. In the distance, a bell rang.

A secretary with silver hair and a navy cardigan greeted them from a narrow desk. 'You're here to see Mr Forester?'

Stephanie nodded. 'DI Broadbent and DC Willard.'

The woman didn't ask for identification. She pushed herself away from her desk, and led them down a corridor lined with closed classroom doors. A few curious students peered through narrow glass panels, but no one spoke.

The headteacher's office was behind a heavy oak door at the end of the hallway. The secretary knocked once, waited, then let them in. Mr Forester stood as they entered. A tall, lean man in his early sixties, he wore a dark grey suit with the collar open. A pair of glasses rested halfway down his nose, and he peered over them to greet them. He checked his watch.

'If nothing else, I love it when people are punctual,' he said, his voice slow and deliberate. 'It's a core part of what we teach here.'

'If you're not early, you're late,' Stephanie replied coolly.

Mr Forester's face warmed. 'A woman after my own heart.'

'Not quite. I heard it from someone who heard it from someone else.'

The smile faded almost as quickly as it had appeared. 'Ah. Well. Never mind. Still, please, take a seat, take a seat!' He gestured to two armchairs facing his desk, upholstered in a stiff, forest-green fabric that crackled faintly as Stephanie sat. The wooden arms bore decades of elbow wear. The desk, made of solid mahogany, gleamed beneath the yellow glow of an antique library lamp, with leather-bound books stacked in one corner. Stephanie felt as if she had stepped into a room from Hogwarts.

Forester settled into his own high-backed chair, clasping his hands before him.

'Now,' he said, adjusting his glasses. 'My wife mentioned you're here regarding a very troubling matter. Two former pupils, yes?'

Stephanie nodded. 'Carlos Vazquez and Nigel Hadlow. They were students here in the eighties. Does that ring any bells?'

Forester's brow furrowed in thought. He shook his head slowly. 'I'm afraid not. I've only been head here for the last eleven years.'

'We believe they were students here together.'

'We see quite a few friendships forged at St Jude's – lifelong bonds. The alumni network is extensive, and many remain close. We take pride in that, actually.'

Stephanie wasn't interested in being pitched to. Alumni this. Career prospects that.

'Would we be able to take a look at some of the old yearbooks or student records?' Stephanie asked.

'But of course.' Forester stood. 'Follow me. We keep archives dating back to the late nineteenth century. I can't guarantee they'll have the answers you're looking for, but you're welcome to look. We just ask that you return everything to its place and handle some of the older artefacts with care.'

He led them out of the office, down a back staircase, and through a short corridor that opened into a small, low-ceilinged room at the far end of the building. The musty smell of mildew was intense down there.

Wooden cabinets lined the walls, and at the centre of the room was a long table scattered with binders and photo albums.

Forester moved to one of the cabinets and pulled open a drawer with a grunt. 'Here we are. Years 1980 to 2005. Help yourselves. I'll leave you to it, unless you need assistance?'

'We'll shout if we get lost,' Olivia said, already reaching for the nearest album.

Forester nodded and left them to it, his footsteps echoing off the stone floor as he disappeared down the corridor.

Stephanie pulled out a thick binder marked 1983 and set it on the central table. She opened the leather book carefully. The centre spread held a panoramic black-and-white photograph of the entire year group arranged in rows on the front steps of the school. Boys in blazers and ties, some smirking, others squinting against the sun, while teachers stood at either end, hands clasped in front of them.

'There,' Olivia said, tapping her nail against a face near the middle of the second row. 'That's Hadlow.'

Stephanie leaned closer, scanning the students beside him.

'Carlos,' she murmured.

Vazquez stood to Nigel's left, looking younger than in the photograph left at the crime scene. His hair was thicker, his features rounder, but it was undeniably him. The same dark eyes, the same posture. The two boys were shoulder to shoulder.

'Okay, so we've got *them*,' Stephanie said. 'Now we just need every name from the rest of the year group.'

They spent the next half an hour flipping through the rest of the yearbook, scanning the individual portraits of each student, noting down the names listed beneath them, and taking photographs on their phones for reference.

Then they turned to the teachers' section.

'Most of these guys look like they were born in the Stone Age,' Olivia muttered.

Stephanie snorted. 'You're not wrong. Look at this one. Mr Harrow, Head of Latin. That moustache could suffocate a child.'

'Bet that was a nightmare during sex.'

Stephanie shot her colleague an unimpressed look before returning to the task. Over the next ten minutes, they scanned through the staff list, jotting down names worth cross-referencing. A separate binder held recent alumni updates, detailing retirements, obituaries, and the occasional commendation.

'Deceased, deceased, moved to Spain, deceased,' Olivia said, skimming a section. 'Looks like there aren't many left to ask.'

Stephanie sighed and leaned back in the chair, her eyes gritty from scanning too many names, too many faces.

Just then, the door creaked open, and Forester appeared, adjusting his cufflinks.

'Any luck?' he asked, stepping into the room.

'Some,' Stephanie replied. 'We've confirmed they were classmates.'

'I'm glad we could be of some assistance.' He placed his hands behind his back. 'I did some checking of my own and thought this might be relevant. One of the students from that same year group, the class of '83, is actually a teacher here now.'

Stephanie straightened. 'Really? What's his name?'

Forester paused, then smiled as if revealing a secret. 'Matthew Kynaston. Teaches chemistry. Shall I call him up for you?'

Stephanie met Olivia's eyes. 'Please do.'

CHAPTER
THIRTY-SIX

Matthew Kynaston entered the archive room with the cautious unease of someone unaccustomed to being summoned. He was in his early fifties, the same age as Carlos and Nigel, with a narrow frame wrapped in a tweed jacket that had seen better decades. His tie was loosely knotted, and the cuff of his jumper that protruded from the jacket was grimy.

'You wanted to see me?' he asked, his voice soft yet precise.

Stephanie turned from the table, closing the binder in front of her. 'Mr Kynaston? I'm Detective Inspector Broadbent. This is DC Willard. Thank you for coming.'

He nodded once, stepping closer while keeping his hands in his pockets. 'You can call me Matthew,' he said. 'Headmaster Forester mentioned it was about some of my old... peers. I'm assuming this isn't a reunion?'

A faint smile touched his lips, but Stephanie didn't return it. 'Carlos Vazquez and Nigel Hadlow. Both in your year, from eighty-one to eighty-six. Do you remember them?'

The names seemed to stir something behind Kynaston's eyes. He took a moment to glance down at the yearbook still open on the table, leaning slightly over it as if afraid of the memories conjured by the faces before him.

'Yes... I remember them,' he said quietly this time, his voice barely more than a whisper.

Stephanie waited, observing the subtle shift in his posture. Tension crept into his shoulders and upper back, and his fists clenched.

'And?' she prompted gently, aware from his expression that some sort of trauma was beginning to bubble beneath the surface.

Matthew exhaled through his nose and straightened up. In that moment, he looked older, the lines on his face deeper and more prominent. 'They were bullies,' he said plainly. 'Carlos and Nigel. Not just to me. There were a handful of us they singled out. Anyone smaller, quieter. Anyone who didn't fit into their world.'

Olivia glanced at Stephanie, then stepped forward. 'What did they do?'

Matthew hesitated, his eyes flicking back down to the grainy black-and-white image in the yearbook. 'What didn't they do? The usual cruelty, I guess you could call it. They took the piss a lot, gave out nasty nicknames. They used to take my glasses and pass them around like they were playing basketball. Once, I found them glued to the underside of my desk. The only way I could get them to stop was by wearing contact lenses. Another time they filled my locker with mud. And then they humiliated me by pulling my pants down in the changing rooms.'

Stephanie's stomach tightened. She hadn't been a victim of bullying in school – her abuse had been confined to the home – but she had seen it, and she had witnessed the impact it had on those affected, how they couldn't trust anyone, how they were angry at the world, often channelling that anger at the wrong people, and how they lost belief and confidence in themselves.

They were victims, just as much as she had been.

'Did you report it?' she asked.

Matthew laughed softly. 'To who? Back then it was a different time. Half the teachers thought a bit of bullying was good for you. That it built character, made you tougher and more prepared for the world. The others were either getting drunk or sleeping with each other. And besides, Carlos was the son of someone who donated regularly to the school, and Nigel's father was high up in politics somewhere, so those kids were basically untouchable. Nothing would've come of it.'

'What were the names of the other boys they targeted?' Olivia asked.

'There were a few. A boy named Tom Latchford. And David Reece. And Jonathan Hale. Christ, I haven't thought of them for years, but their names stick with you, you know.'

'Did they receive the same sort of abuse, or was it worse?'

'It was *all* bad, Detective. No one considers themselves lucky that they got let off what *you* might call "lightly".'

'Right,' Stephanie said, feeling the need to apologise. What was worse for one person might have been nothing for another. 'Do you know what they're doing now?'

Matthew pursed his lips and shook his head. He placed his hands in his trouser pockets. 'Afraid not. We weren't exactly close. The only thing that connected us was what we went through, but we didn't have a group; we didn't talk about it. Otherwise, that would have just made things worse. They would have come for us harder.'

'Was there anyone else? Were Nigel and Carlos working as a duo, or were there more of them?' Olivia asked softly.

Matthew's eyes dropped to the floor as silence hung in the archive room. For a long moment, no one spoke. Then he said, 'They had a little gang. Four of them in total. Anthony Shore and Darren Fairhurst were the other two. They all seemed to follow Nigel around like his little disciples, his little minions.'

Matthew's voice was filled with disdain.

Stephanie scribbled the names into her notebook. 'And these boys, were they as bad as Nigel?'

'Worse, in some ways,' Matthew said, rubbing the back of his neck. 'Darren once locked a boy in the sports cupboard for half a day, and Anthony used to write vile things on bathroom walls; he was responsible for all the rumours that got spread around the school about me. They were as guilty as one another.'

Stephanie exchanged a glance with Olivia, then looked back at Matthew. 'Carlos and Nigel are both dead.'

Matthew's head jerked up. 'What?'

'They were killed in separate incidents within days of each other,' she said evenly. 'Burned alive. We believe their deaths are connected.'

Matthew's face drained of colour. 'Jesus Christ,' he muttered, blinking hard. 'I-I didn't know. I mean, I saw something about a fire in the news, but I didn't know it was them.'

Stephanie studied him carefully. The shock looked real. The disbelief. The horror.

'Do you know anyone who might have wanted to hurt them, or anyone who's capable of this?' Olivia asked.

Matthew didn't answer straight away. He chewed the inside of his cheek, his mind racing.

'I mean, anyone could have,' he said finally. 'If you'd asked me forty years ago, I'd have said all of us. But that was a lifetime ago. I-I don't know, Detective. I haven't spoken to any of them since I left school, so I couldn't possibly tell you.'

Stephanie nodded slowly. 'Fair enough. I have to ask, though... where were you on the nights of their deaths?'

Matthew's mouth parted in disbelief. 'You think *I* had something to do with this?'

'It's a routine question. Nothing more.'

He paused, processing. 'I was home. With my wife. And our daughter. She's seven weeks old.'

Stephanie did the calculation in her head. Matthew saw the confusion on her face because he added, 'My wife's a lot younger than I am.'

That was an understatement, Stephanie thought to herself but said nothing. In the end, Olivia jumped in by offering him congratulations on the newborn.

'Thanks,' he said, coyly. 'It's been a whirlwind. I just wish someone had told me from the start how little sleep you get.'

'If they did, then nobody would have them in the first place.' Olivia glanced down at her notebook. 'Would your wife be able to corroborate your whereabouts?'

Matthew replied with a single nod. 'Absolutely. We've barely left the house. And I've got pictures. Timestamped. We're documenting everything: her first smile, first bath, first poonami.'

Olivia grimaced. 'Don't. You're bringing it all back up for me. My boys were nightmares. I mean, they still are. But...' She shook her head in a grimace. 'I can still smell it now.'

Matthew chuckled softly, his face warming again.

Stephanie closed her notebook. 'That's all for now, Matthew. Thank you for your time. And for your honesty.'

He gave a small nod and started towards the door, then hesitated. 'Detective?'

'Yes?'

'Whoever did this... if it was someone from back then... I hope you find them. And I hope they get help. Because no one ever gave it to us.'

Then he left, the heavy door clicking shut behind him.

CHAPTER
THIRTY-SEVEN

Tom Latchford, one of the names Stephanie had given her as a victim of Nigel's and Carlos's bullying, worked in a phone shop on the high street. As Fiona stepped through the doors, a blast of warm air from the air conditioning unit above the entrance hit her face so forcefully that it nearly stole her breath. The inside of the phone shop, like much of the high street nowadays, was completely empty, save for an elderly woman trying to top up her phone, only to be informed that it had to be done over the phone.

Fiona surveyed the rest of the shop, counting five advisers to two customers. A wildly disproportionate ratio. But it was hardly surprising; nowadays, everything could be done from the comfort of your bed or sofa. She couldn't remember the last time she'd gone into a phone shop to upgrade her phone; she usually did it during her lunch break on the rare occasions it arose.

She pretended to browse the shelves for a short while, waiting to see if anyone would accost her like they usually did. But nobody came. The advisers stood behind the counter or sat at desks in the back, scrolling on their phones, lost in their own worlds. All were young, in their late teens or early twenties, and none of them looked like they wanted to be there; instead, they looked as if they had been dragged out of bed kicking and screaming by their parents.

Fiona felt like a mystery shopper, poised to give some appalling feedback to the company's head office. But before she could think about what she would say, a door at the back opened, and a man in his fifties emerged, his heavy footsteps stomping across the linoleum floor. Fiona immediately sensed he was the one in charge. Not from his age, but from the way he carried himself and the look of disgust that twisted his features as he cast his gaze around his employees. For a moment, he paused in the centre of the shop, hands on hips, surveying his team. Nobody acknowledged him.

Muttering something under his breath, he turned his attention to Fiona.

'Is there anything I can help you with today, miss?' he asked, adopting his best customer service voice.

Fiona chewed her fingernail briefly before responding. 'I was looking for Tom.'

His head tilted to the side. 'That's me.'

'I thought as much.' She lowered her voice. 'My name's DC Singleton. I'm with Surrey Police. I was wondering if there's somewhere I might be able to ask you a few questions?'

His face contorted with confusion, as if she'd got the wrong person.

'You are Tom Latchford, right?'

He nodded.

'Who went to St Jude's?'

Another nod, weaker than the first.

'Excellent. Then I'm in the right place.' She gestured towards the back of the shop. 'Shall we?'

Tom's expression glazed over. He turned around and headed towards the office. The employees remained glued to their phones as they passed by. The door at the back of the store led to a steep flight of stairs, lined with scuffed skirting boards. Inspirational messages adorned the walls, along with bar charts tracking their monthly sales progress. Fiona followed Tom up, the sound of her shoes thudding on the steps behind him.

At the top, he unlocked a door using a combination of passcode and key, ushering her into the upstairs office. The air there was warmer and muggy. A bank of dusty computers lined one wall beneath a tangle of cables and blinking routers. A battered filing cabinet sat in the corner, its drawers slightly ajar, and a metal safe nestled beside it, painted the same grey as the walls. Fiona pulled one of the spare office chairs into place and sat down, waiting until Tom had slumped into his own seat – one with a tear down the middle and squeaky wheels – before opening her notebook.

'There's no need to look so alarmed,' she began. 'You're not in trouble. I'm here in connection with two individuals we believe you may know.'

His eyes widened with panic, a thousand different thoughts flickering behind them. 'Okay.'

'Carlos Vazquez,' she stated plainly. 'And Nigel Hadlow. Do those names mean anything to you?'

Tom froze, his gaze fixed on the wall behind her, his hands clenched in his lap.

'I... yeah. Yeah, I know them. We went to school together. We were in the same year. Same boarding house for a time, even. They were...'

'Would you consider yourself friends?'

'Pah!' he exclaimed, filling the room. 'Absolutely not. The farthest thing in the world from friends. You couldn't pay me a million quid to say that.' He shook his head violently. 'They made my life hell.'

'How?'

'They used to call me "Latch-on" like I was a parasite. They took my books and soaked them in water. One time, they even pissed on them in the toilets. I had panic attacks every day before class. Couldn't look a teacher in the eye, let alone make friends. I felt so alone in that place. They ruined me pretty good. My parents thought I'd be some great academic; they even had dreams of me going to Oxford to study physics. Instead, I ended up here, flogging phone contracts to pensioners who can't hear me speak.'

His mouth twitched and his fists clenched, like he was about to cry or punch a wall. He did neither.

'They humiliated me,' he continued, grinding his jaw. 'They made me feel like I was nothing. And eventually... I became nothing.'

Fiona paused.

She scribbled a few notes. 'I'm sorry you went through that. I don't suppose you ever kept in touch?'

'Pah! Good one. Oh, you're being serious. No, of course we didn't. As soon as we graduated, I made it my mission to forget everything about that place.'

Another scribble in her notebook. 'I'm not sure if you've heard the news recently, but I wanted to inform you that they're both dead.'

Tom blinked and his jaw loosened, but his fists remained clenched. 'What?'

Fiona explained the circumstances surrounding their murders while chewing on her fingernails.

'Shit,' Tom replied.

'That's one word for it.'

'You think... you think someone from school...?'

'We don't know. That's why I'm asking you: where were you on the nights in question?'

He scratched his jaw, suddenly looking very small.

'I live alone,' he said eventually. 'Flat above the off-licence near the station. Haven't had a partner in years. Was probably watching telly or scrolling on my phone. I...' He shrugged. 'But I didn't have anything to do with what happened to them. I don't drive, so I couldn't have got to them...'

Fiona met his gaze. He didn't flinch.

'Can anyone confirm that?'

'Not unless my kettle's learned to testify.'

She gave a tight nod and jotted it down. 'I appreciate that. We're speaking to a lot of people. Routine, that type of thing.' She took another bite of her fingernail, realising she was in desperate need of a smoke, something she hadn't thought about for a long time. 'Did you ever keep in touch with other people from your school?'

Tom shook his head without hesitation. 'Like I said, once I was out of there, everyone else was out of my life. But I'll be honest, I can't blame whoever did this. They were disgusting, evil people. And I doubt they got better as they got older. Bullies stay bullies; they don't change. So it doesn't surprise me that something like this happened to them in the end.' A thin smile crept onto his lips. 'Justice is a bitch.' He pulled out a small cross necklace and rubbed it between his fingers.

Fiona let the silence linger for a moment, her eyes falling on the charm in his hand.

'You're religious, I take it?'

The question made him pause. He glanced down at the necklace and then hid it, as if it had just betrayed him.

'Yeah,' he said eventually. 'I am.'

'Always been?'

He shook his head. 'No. I found God later. After school. After... all of that.'

'Because of what happened?'

'In spite of it, maybe. I was in a bad way for a long time. Couldn't hold down a job. Drank more than I should've. Therapy helped a bit, but it was faith that gave me something solid.' He hesitated, then added, 'It gave me a reason to get up in the morning. And a reason to stop blaming myself.'

Fiona nodded slowly. She stopped chewing on a piece of nail. 'And what about them? Carlos and Nigel. Do you... forgive them?'

Tom's face stiffened.

'That's what I'm supposed to do, isn't it?' he said at last. 'Turn the other cheek. Leave judgement to the Lord. That's what it says.'

'But?' Fiona prompted gently.

'But I'm not there yet. I pray for strength, and I ask for peace, and most days I can go about my life just fine. But when I think about what they did to me... the way they took something from me that I've never got back... I struggle. I really do.' His voice cracked slightly. 'People always talk about forgiveness like it's a switch you flip. Like you just decide one day to stop hurting. But it's not. It's work. And I'm still in the middle of it. I pray every night. And I know it's wrong, but some nights... back then, I prayed they'd get what was coming to them.'

CHAPTER
THIRTY-EIGHT

The heat hit her first. Instant. Suffocating. A wall of it pressed against her chest, searing her skin and climbing down the back of her throat.

Stephanie stood at the end of the driveway, barefoot and dressed in her pyjamas, staring at the inferno that had once been her childhood home. Brilliant flames of orange and yellow licked the windowpanes, cracking the glass and melting plastic frames. Smoke poured from the roof, curling into the sky. The smell of charred material filled the air. Somewhere in the distance, she could hear sirens, but they were too far away. By the time they arrived, it would be too late.

Her mum and sister were in the window, trapped in the upstairs bedroom, banging on the glass, pounding their fists, both of them screaming for help. But she couldn't do anything; she was frozen to the spot, her legs refusing to move.

'Mum...' she called out. 'Kim!'

But her voice was weak, drowned out by the roar of the flames.

Then the front door burst open, and her father stumbled out, his entire body ablaze. Skin bubbling, clothes melting to his flesh. Like something out of a disaster movie. His screams echoed up and down the street. Her body flushed cold with fear. Her father staggered a few feet towards her, arms outstretched, but he made it no farther. He collapsed to the ground as the fire consumed him.

'*Stepphhyyyy... pleeaasseeee...*'

The sound of his voice – just on the cusp of death – sent a jolt through her spine. Her eyes stayed fixed on the smouldering body that had just moments ago been her father. He lay face down, his skin a patchwork of bubbling flesh and exposed bone. The fire still crackled under his torso, still consuming him. His arm twitched once. Then nothing. He was still.

And for a brief second, Stephanie felt nothing.

No grief.

No pity.

She remembered being eight years old, standing in the kitchen in that ugly green dressing gown with frogs on it. He'd told her she was weak, that she needed to toughen up. Then he'd taken the metal end of the lighter and pressed it to her forearm until she screamed.

Now, he was a victim of his own method of abuse.

'Stephanie!'

The scream snapped her out of it.

It came from upstairs. Her mum and Kimberley, still pounding on the glass, still in desperate need of rescue. The smoke in the room was rapidly covering their faces. Soon, she wouldn't be able to see them.

Soon, she wouldn't be able to hear them.

She turned to run, to do something, but her legs were made of stone, her lungs tight, her arms trembling. Then a blur of motion tore past her.

A figure. Male. She recognised him instantly. Jordan. Her half-brother. Sprinting towards the fire without a second thought, without a shred of concern for himself. The hero, coming to save the day and rescue the damsels in distress. Stephanie cried out after him, but it was too late. He was inside, swallowed by the smoke.

A knot twisted deep in Stephanie's gut.

No. No, he didn't get to be the one.

This was *her* family. *Her* mum. *Her* sister.

Not his.

He didn't get to swoop in and be the one they revered and

celebrated. He didn't get to be the one who pulled them to safety and rewrote history.

Stephanie took a step forward. The flames roared higher. The house groaned. And her mother's scream pierced the air again.

Yet, over that, she could still hear Jordan inside. Coughing. Calling out. Coming to the rescue.

Stephanie's throat tightened, her lungs burning even before the fire touched her. A voice in her head told her not to do it. Told her she'd die if she went in. But another voice shouted louder.

He doesn't get to be the one who saves them. You do.

She ran.

Straight towards the inferno.

But before she could reach the front door, her dad came alive and, with evil, demonic eyes and a snarl on his face, grabbed her by the ankle and pulled her to the ground.

And then blackness.

Stephanie bolted upright in bed. Her chest rose and fell in sharp, erratic bursts. Her hands trembled. Her face and hair were wet with sweat, and she felt hot, like she was burning, like she was in the flames of her nightmare.

She clawed at the sheets and flung them off, half expecting them to smoulder in her hands. Her skin prickled, every nerve ending screaming. She stumbled out of bed, bare feet slapping against the carpet, heart pounding like a siren. Breathing fast and shallow. Her lungs wouldn't fill. She couldn't think. Couldn't stop the rising panic.

It's still on me.

She crashed into the bathroom, turned the cold tap in the shower all the way, and stepped in without even removing her pyjamas.

The icy water hit her like a slap.

She gasped and staggered back but forced herself under it again. She braced her hands against the tiled wall, head bowed, as the water poured over her, drenching her hair, and soaking her clothes.

Please, stop burning...

She turned slowly, letting the water wash over every inch of her, half expecting to see smoke rise from her skin. She stayed there, shivering, her teeth starting to chatter. Eventually, she pressed her back against the tiled wall and slid down into a squat, arms wrapped tightly around her knees.

The dream had felt real. Too real.

And not just the fire.

The jealousy.

The hatred.

That need to be the one who saved them.

She squeezed her eyes shut.

What kind of person was she becoming?

What kind of person would rather burn alive than let someone else be the hero?

She wasn't sure.

But right now, soaked and shaking at the bottom of her shower, she wasn't sure she wanted to.

CHAPTER
THIRTY-NINE

The rain came down in waves; cold, stinging pellets slicing sideways through the trees. Stephanie pedalled harder, recklessly tearing along the forest trail. Mud splattered up her calves, streaking across her thighs. Her tyres carved deep grooves in the sodden path, sending debris and earth flying in every direction.

The wind howled through the branches overhead, tugging at her jacket and threatening to throw her off balance. But she leaned forward, refusing to give in. She pumped her legs harder, driven by the memories of the dream, the flames, and Jordan's face as he vanished into the fire.

Her lungs burned, but she welcomed the pain. It was real. Tangible. *Deserved.*

Leaves slapped against her cheeks, twigs scratched her forearms, and the bike jolted beneath her as she hit a knot of exposed roots. She gripped tighter, muscles locked. A steep incline loomed ahead, slick with mud and loose stones. She didn't slow; instead, she attacked it with venom, thighs screaming, back hunched low like a predator. The forest around her blurred as she breathed heavily against the cold, each exhale exploding in a cloud of steam.

No sirens.

No flames.

No screams.

Just the way she liked it.

Eventually, she reached the top of the incline and emerged onto a long stretch of flat land.

Then she slammed her fingers on the brakes, skidding the bike to a halt and kicking up a chunk of mud high into the air. Something in the distance caught her eye several hundred yards away; a small, black, scorched blemish across the ocean of lush, densely coloured green fields below. The barn where, just a few nights before, Nigel Hadlow had lost his life. Her body shivered with grief, and a lump formed in her throat. Images of what the blaze must have looked like – the fire, the heat, the immense and immeasurable pain – appeared in her mind. Had he been conscious before the flames took hold? Had he known what was coming? Had the killer been kind enough to make sure he didn't, or had they ensured he suffered the maximum amount of pain?

She suspected the latter. It was clear to her now that the killer had sought revenge against Nigel Hadlow and Carlos Vazquez, that they had a list of enemies they deemed worthy of justice. She was certain they had done everything in their power to ensure the victims were aware of their impending fate.

She was sure Nigel Hadlow and Carlos Vazquez had been awake, conscious, breathing, *aware* of the fire that would slowly consume them, right up to the moment it took their lives.

Rain continued to fall horizontally, blurring the barn in the distance. Thick raindrops trickled from her hair into her eyes. She tried to blink them away, but it made no difference.

Standing there, one leg planted on the ground while the other rested on the pedal, she swung her waterproof bag from her shoulder and pulled out her mobile. It was her day off. Supposed to be, anyway. Time she should have spent recovering, relaxing – mentally and physically. But, as usual, she had different ideas.

She unlocked the device and scrolled across to her address book, raindrops pelting the screen. She found Olivia's name and prodded it repeatedly. After several attempts, the call finally connected.

'Steph?'

'Morning.'

'What are you calling for? Isn't it supposed to be your day off?'

Before she could respond, a gust of wind battered her from the side.

'Where are you?' Olivia asked.

'Out and about. Seeing the countryside.'

'You sound like you're in the Drake Passage.'

Stephanie pretended to know what that meant and replied with a grunt. 'It's just a bit of wind. And rain. Lots and lots of rain.' She cupped her hand to her ear, trying to shield the phone from the elements. 'I just wanted to see what everyone's agenda was for the day.'

'Micromanaging?'

'What? It's not—! I'm not—!'

'Sounds like it to me, ma'am. Would you like regular updates on when we're going to the toilet as well? Would you like to know how many coffees we're having?'

'Wellard...'

'We've got it under control,' Olivia said. 'It's your day off. So just relax. If anything urgent comes in, we'll be the first to let you know. All right?'

'I just wanted to—'

'And we thank you for that, but we don't need it. Everything's being taken care of. I'd like for you to have an actual day off, please.'

Stephanie's gaze shifted from the barn in the distance to a small row of trees.

'Why do I feel like I'm being told off?'

'Because you are.'

'Is this how you talk to your kids?'

'Oh no. They usually get it much worse than this. You should be grateful; I'm being kind to you.'

Stephanie chuckled. 'I appreciate it.'

'Enjoy your day, ma'am. I don't expect to hear from you until tomorrow. Oh, and be safe out there. It's wet and muddy.'

The smile on Stephanie's face widened. 'Yes, *Mum*.'

As she hung up the phone, the wind and rain subsided, and a thin break in the clouds appeared. It was small, but Stephanie took it as a sign, a sign to take a step back and enjoy what little free time she had to herself.

First, she would need to turn her back on the barn and get out of there as quickly as possible. Feeling optimistic that the day might actually be a good one, and with a plan beginning to form in her mind, she pocketed her phone, placed both feet on the pedals, and pushed away, kicking up mud and filth.

CHAPTER
FORTY

Rain lashed against the windscreen as Olivia turned off the main road and followed the narrow, winding lane leading to the bungalow on the outskirts of Weybridge. The wipers were fighting a losing battle against the downpour, and the heater hummed quietly, warming her feet and thighs, but her thoughts were elsewhere, preoccupied with Stephanie and her inability to switch off.

The inspector worried her sometimes. It was unhealthy, the amount she worked, the way she consumed every waking moment of the day with the job. It wasn't good for her, nor did she believe it was good for her bulimia. Olivia recalled the moment she'd stumbled upon Stephanie's secret. The office had been empty; it was night, and everyone had left after a couple of rounds at the pub. Stephanie had been the only one remaining, and then Olivia had heard the retching sounds, the splashes in the bowl, followed by the flush of the toilet. They had agreed not to discuss it – Stephanie had assured her it was all under control – but concern for her senior still lingered in the back of her mind. The woman overworked herself, pushing her mind and body to their limits, and Olivia wondered how much longer she could sustain it. If she wasn't careful, something would give.

Either her sanity or her body.

Before she could let that thought garner any more weight, the automated voice on the satnav announced that she had reached her destination. David Reece lived in a squat, grey bungalow, the only one in a row of two-storey detached houses. The former student at St Jude's had come up as one of the names associated with Nigel Hadlow's and Carlos Vazquez's bullying victims, and after extensive research, she and Fiona had finally tracked him down.

Olivia pulled onto the drive and turned off the engine. Through the blurry pane of her driver's side window, she saw the glow of a monitor behind the living room curtain. She grabbed her coat from the passenger seat, shrugged it on, and dashed to the front door, skipping over the puddles.

She rang the bell and waited, pulling her hood down. A few moments passed before the door creaked open to reveal a man in his early fifties, pale and unshaven, wearing a checked shirt and chinos. He held a pair of headphones in his hands. The only reference she had for his appearance was the school yearbook image taken forty years earlier. His face had softened with time, and the angles of youth had rounded with age, but the resemblance was still there beneath the wear and tear of four hard decades. His hair had thinned; in the photo, it had been thick and dark, curling at the ends. The teenage version of him had worn an excitable, ebullient smile. The adult version didn't bother to smile at all.

'Yes…?' he said, blinking at her through the drizzle, his voice hoarse. 'Can I help you?'

Olivia held up her ID. 'I was hoping to speak to you about your time at St Jude's.'

His expression stiffened. For a moment, she thought he might close the door on her.

'Will it take long?'

'Only a few minutes.'

'I'm in the middle of work,' he said, half-apologetic, 'but I can spare a few.'

'Thank you,' Olivia replied, stepping over the threshold. She followed him into a lounge-turned-office, where two monitors displayed an email inbox and a PowerPoint presentation.

He motioned for her to take the armchair and sat on the edge of the sofa, twisting the headphones in his hands. 'So,' he said, sounding as if he was already done with the conversation, 'what's this about?'

'Carlos Vazquez and Nigel Hadlow.'

A faint hint of recognition flashed across his face. 'What about them?'

'They're both dead,' Olivia said gently. 'They were murdered.'

David blinked slowly. Once. Twice. Then he set the headphones down on the coffee table in front of him.

'Jesus.'

She let the silence linger for a moment before continuing. 'We've been looking into their pasts. Your name came up, along with a few others.' She reached into her coat pocket and retrieved her notebook. 'From what we've gathered, they weren't exactly model students.'

David leaned back, arms folded across his chest. 'You can say that again.'

Olivia nodded, pen poised. 'Can you tell me about your experience with them at St Jude's?'

He scoffed. 'I thought you said this would only take a few minutes.'

'The SparkNotes version, then.'

David let out a long breath, rubbed a hand over his jaw, and then massaged the rest of his face as if preparing to relive the trauma. He then proceeded to give her a condensed version of the abuse he had endured from Nigel, Carlos, and the other individuals responsible. As she listened, she thought he downplayed some of the trauma and his reaction to it. He gave the impression that it hadn't affected him, that he had been brave in the face of his abuse. However, there were inflections in his tone and twitches in his movements that suggested he'd been anything but.

'I'm sorry you went through that,' Olivia said once he'd finished. 'Kids can be arseholes.'

She was reminded of her own: of how difficult they'd become; how she worried every day about them suffering the same fate as David Reece, Tom Latchford, and Jonathan Hale.

And prayed that they hadn't chosen to wear the same shoes as Nigel Hadlow and Carlos Vazquez.

David shrugged. 'It is what it is. Can't do anything about it now.'

Olivia finished making a note in her book, double-clicking the pen at the end. 'And on the nights of the murders? Were you here?'

He gave a dry laugh. 'I was. Working late. I freelance. Design pitches, training decks. Mostly for firms that don't want to pay someone full time.' He gestured at the screen behind him. 'You can check the logins, time stamps, whatever you want. I didn't leave the house.'

'Appreciate that. We'll need to follow up, but it's helpful context.'

He gave a half-nod. 'You really think someone killed them because of what they did in school?'

'We're keeping an open mind. But you're not the only person we've spoken to who had a similar experience with them in school.'

'They made it their full-time job to ruin people.'

Olivia flipped to a fresh page. 'Have you kept in touch with anyone else from back then? Other students who might've had similar experiences?'

David shook his head. 'Not really. Something comes up now and then on Facebook, but I don't look at it. Can't be arsed to interact with them in any capacity.'

Olivia nodded, hesitated, then asked, 'What about Jonathan Hale? We've been trying to reach him but haven't had any luck. Do you know where he might be now?'

David's expression deepened. He looked away, his jaw shifting.

'What is it?'

He let out a slow breath. 'There's a reason for that: he killed himself. A few years after we finished college. Took a couple of pills, found a bridge, then decided to make sure the job was done.'

The air left the room.

Olivia opened and closed her mouth, lost for words. In the end, all she could say was, 'I'm sorry.'

David nodded, his face stony. 'They broke him. Just like they tried to break all of us. And if you ask me, they got what was coming to them. They all deserve to suffer.'

CHAPTER
FORTY-ONE

Instead of being tasked with speaking with more of Carlos's and Nigel's bullying victims, Devon had been sent to interview their accomplices, one of the individuals responsible for ruining childhoods. He had drawn the short straw. Literally. The team had written the names of victims, witnesses, and potential suspects on separate pieces of paper and tossed them into a pot. As a result, he was the only one to pick the name corresponding to one of Carlos and Nigel's co-conspirators.

Anthony Shore. A man who, after leaving St Jude's with uninspiring grades and what many of his peers and teachers described as an oversized ego, had fallen into car sales and quickly climbed the ranks until he ran his own car dealership in Addlestone, complete with garish flags and inflated prices. He lived in a new build with his second wife and rarely saw his children from his first marriage.

Devon had been sent partly to warn him and partly to question him.

He parked outside Shore Motors, the windscreen speckled with drizzle. Through the glass, he could see rows of shiny used cars, their bonnets angled to look appealing, their prices scrawled in thick marker on placards in the windshields. The showroom was lit from within, and Devon could just make out a slight man pacing behind the glass, phone pressed to his ear.

Devon killed the engine, stepped out, and pulled his hood up to shield his hair from the rain. As he reached the office door, he gave it a quick push and stepped inside. Warmth enveloped him immediately. The man behind the desk looked up and ended his call with a hasty, 'Yeah, yeah, I'll call you back. Just a sec.' He stood, smoothed the front of his cheap suit, and offered Devon a grin that was more rehearsed than a West End production.

Devon blinked. *This* was Anthony Shore?

He had expected someone broader, louder. The sort of man who oozed testosterone and smugness. But the figure before him was slight, wiry, and narrow-shouldered. His cheeks were ruddy and pockmarked, his hair a wispy comb-over of blond strands slicked across a pink scalp. Thick glasses magnified his pale blue eyes, giving him the appearance of someone who'd been on the receiving end of cruel jokes rather than the one dishing them out. He looked more like someone who'd been picked last in team sports, not someone who had ruled the playground.

'Afternoon,' Anthony said, his voice sharper than his appearance suggested. 'Here to look at anything in particular?'

Devon pulled out his ID. 'I was hoping to have a quick chat.'

Anthony's smile faltered. 'Police?'

'Just a few routine questions. About a couple of people you might've known. From school.'

Anthony's face twitched, then he gave an awkward chuckle and stepped aside, motioning towards the leather chairs in the corner of the office. 'That feels like a lifetime ago. What's this about?'

Devon sat. 'Carlos Vazquez and Nigel Hadlow. Ring a bell?'

That flicker returned, this time darker. 'Yeah. Sure. We were in the same year. Haven't heard those names in a while.'

'They're dead,' Devon said plainly. 'Murdered.'

Anthony paused mid-step on his way to the kettle. 'Both of them?'

Devon nodded.

Anthony let out a slow whistle. 'Bloody hell.'

'You don't seem particularly surprised.'

Anthony scratched the back of his neck. 'I mean... we weren't exactly lifelong mates or anything. Not since school. But that's still... Jesus. You say murdered?'

'We're investigating it. Right now we're looking into people who had ties to both victims. That includes old friends, classmates, enemies. Anyone with a possible connection.' Devon leaned forward slightly. 'That includes you, Mr Shore.'

Anthony gave a nervous chuckle. 'Right. Of course. I haven't seen either of them in years, though. Swear to God.'

'Still. I'll need to ask you a few questions.'

Anthony nodded, sat down behind his desk, and folded his hands together. Devon noticed a slight tremble in them. Whatever kind of bully he'd been back then, he wasn't that man now.

At least... not on the surface.

'What made you do it?'

'Sorry?'

'The bullying. What made you do it?'

Anthony played with his fingers. 'It was a long time ago. We... we were young. You know how it is. You get caught up in things.'

'Are you an intelligent man, Mr Shore?'

He looked confused by the question. 'Yes...'

'Do you know the difference between right and wrong?'

'Yes...'

'So you know that bullying people is bad.'

'I was a kid. I didn't think what we were doing would affect people so much.'

'So you're *not* an intelligent person.'

Anthony stopped playing with his fingers. Before he could respond, the door to the showroom opened. He climbed out of his chair, and called out to them, 'Sorry, but I've had to close for about half an hour or so. Would you mind coming back?'

The man grunted, paused, then headed back the way he'd come.

When Anthony turned his attention back to Devon, he said, 'Have you just come here to have a go at me, or ask me questions about Nigel and Carlos?'

'A bit of both, I should imagine. I don't like it when crimes go unpunished.'

'Being a bully isn't a crime.'

'It is when you're responsible for someone taking their life.'

Anthony froze. The colour drained from his cheeks, leaving his skin a sickly white. He blinked once, twice, then dropped into his chair as if his knees had given out. His mouth opened slightly, but no sound came. Just the soft patter of the rain against the windows.

Devon let the silence hang. He wasn't in a rush to save him from it.

When Anthony finally spoke, his voice was lower, hollowed out. 'Who?'

'Johnathan Hale.'

Anthony took a moment before responding. 'I didn't know. I mean...' He dropped his head into his hands. 'I feel so terrible.'

Good. You should.

He had no time for bullies, no patience for people intent on making others' lives more difficult than they already were. He thought of his own school days. Of the stolen lunches, locker doors slammed shut on his fingers, and the "harmless" nicknames that stuck long after they had stopped being funny. He'd never told anyone the worst of it, not even his mum.

'I...' Anthony continued. 'I don't know what to say. I... I'm in shock. And Nigel and Carlos, too... What's going on?'

'We think someone from the school is targeting them.'

'By "them", you mean me as well?'

Devon didn't answer. Instead, he pulled out a photo from his inside pocket – one of the old school yearbook pages Olivia had dug up. Anthony, Carlos, and Nigel, along with a group of other boys, smiled and posed like best mates.

He slid it across the desk. 'You still speak to anyone from this photo?'

Anthony stared at it, his eyes scanning each familiar face. He shook his head slowly. 'Not really. We kept in touch for a bit, but they all went off to university, and I was the only one who went into the working world.' Anthony inhaled deeply, then began playing with his fingers again. As he opened his mouth, the showroom door opened yet again. This time, he ignored it.

'Detective, you don't think I'm next, do you?'

Devon swallowed. Hard. 'You haven't seen anything suspicious recently, have you? Old faces, old friends?'

Anthony shook his head, though he didn't appear convinced.

Devon reached into his pocket and produced the photo of the boy that had been found at Carlos's crime scene.

'And you don't recognise the boy in this photo either?'

Anthony studied the photo, then shook his head. 'Not really, no. He looks familiar, but I couldn't tell you his name.'

'Then I'm sure you'll be fine,' Devon said, reaching into another pocket to produce a business card. 'Here are my details. If you see or hear anything, give me a call.' He glanced over at the customer who had just entered the shop. 'You have someone waiting for you. You've got a business to run. I'll be on my way. Thanks for your help.'

CHAPTER
FORTY-TWO

Stephanie waited at the door for what felt like an eternity, repeatedly checking her watch while her sister took her time to answer. She should have cut Kimberley some slack; after all, her sister was heavily pregnant, and mobility was becoming an issue for her. But still, Stephanie was eager to see her.

The smile remained on her face as Kimberley cautiously opened the front door a crack, revealing just a sliver of her face, as Stephanie had taught her to do, treating everyone with suspicion, especially when unexpected visitors arrived.

'Steph?'

Kimberley did a double-take, carefully opening the door as if someone were holding a gun to her head. If Stephanie didn't know her sister better, she would have thought she'd interrupted her from a nap.

'That's me.'

'What are you doing here?'

'Surprise!'

However, the surprise element of her unannounced visit didn't quite register on Kimberley's face. There was no widening of the eyes, no bewilderment or excitement from someone who hadn't seen a loved one in a few weeks. No warm embrace, just the cold, muted, and slightly confused stare of someone who had just woken up.

Stephanie pushed the door open and stepped inside.

'I had a day off, so I thought I'd come by and see how you are.'

'What?' Kimberley looked at her as if she were speaking a different language.

'I was told to relax by my team, so that's what I'm doing.'

'You should have called ahead. I... I would have tidied up. I would have prepared drinks. I would have cleaned.'

Stephanie stepped into the hallway, kicking off her shoes. 'Pfft. We shared a room together, Kim. I've seen every side of you... in more ways than one. I think I can handle a little uncleanliness.'

Kimberley shut the door behind her, wrapping a cardigan around her body. 'I could have called Jordan.'

'And that's exactly why I *didn't* tell you.' Stephanie pointed a finger at her sister. 'Because I knew you'd do something like that. I'm not interested in seeing him, Kim. I'm interested in seeing you, *my sister*.'

'Steph...'

'Kim... We can do this all day. But if you so much as think about calling him or messaging him to come over, I'm heading out of that door and leaving.'

Kimberley pulled her phone from her pocket, then quickly returned it. She let out a heavy sigh and moved into the kitchen, saying nothing. As Stephanie followed her in, she realised she had no idea what her sister had been talking about. Cleanliness was a word in both their dictionaries, but they had very different definitions. Kimberley was concerned about a spoon and mug left beside the sink, drying in the daylight that came through the window, while Stephanie's definition encompassed laundry on the floor, takeaway food boxes piled high on the kitchen counter, and evidence of a busy lifestyle scattered everywhere. To Stephanie, Kimberley's kitchen was spotless.

'Tea?' The disgust in Kimberley's voice was evident.

'If you're not going to spit in it, sure...'

Kimberley remained silent, brewing the tea with a series of grunts and heavy sighs. While the kettle boiled, she leaned against the counter, placing her hand on her baby bump. 'I just don't get it. *Still.*'

'Get what?'

'Why you don't want to see him.'

'We've been over this, Kim. I don't want to keep having the same argument. I thought I could come round, we could have a nice, civilised conversation, catch up on how things are going with you and the baby. I thought I could destress from work a little bit, but I guess that won't be possible. Please, can we not talk about Jordan for one minute? If and when I'm ready to see him, I will. But not a moment sooner. It has to be on my terms; otherwise, it won't ever happen. And I don't care if I'm being unreasonable. I think I've every right to behave like this. So, *please*, just drop it.'

Kimberley stirred the tea in silence, her face tense. She handed Stephanie a mug without a word, then shuffled over to the sofa, dropping onto it with the grace of a woman carrying far more than just a baby. Stephanie followed, clutching the mug between her palms, soaking in the warmth. The next hour passed in a kind of quiet truce. They talked about work (with Stephanie doing most of the talking) and about Jason, who, according to Kimberley, was now vetoing every baby name suggestion she came up with.

'He wants to call him "Dex",' Kimberley said with a theatrical eye-roll. 'Like, *Dexter*. Who names a baby Dexter unless you want him to grow up to be a serial killer?'

'I like the name,' Stephanie replied. 'It reminds me of Dennis for some reason. Dennis the Menace. Dexter the trickster.'

'The last thing I want is a little shit.'

Chuckling, Stephanie stood, took both empty mugs, and wandered into the kitchen to wash them. She turned on the tap and began scrubbing half-heartedly, letting the hot water stream over her hands, her eyes fixed on nothing in particular. Then headlights flashed across the kitchen tiles.

Her stomach flipped.

A car had pulled up at the end of the driveway.

Stephanie froze, fingers tightening around the sponge. She peered out through the blinds. A small red hatchback. She turned, heat rising quickly in her neck.

'You didn't.'

Kimberley appeared in the doorway, both hands resting protectively on her belly. 'What?'

'You didn't!' Stephanie snapped, the mug slipping from her hand into the sink with a loud crack. 'You invited him, didn't you?'

And then the doorbell rang. Stephanie's heart leapt into her mouth. She stormed out of the kitchen, grabbed her shoes, and headed to the door, ready to explode out of it.

'Steph, what are you talking about? I didn't—'

Kimberley opened the front door, cold air spilling into the hallway. But there was nothing there, just a small brown Amazon parcel. Kimberley struggled to pick it up, then shut the door behind her.

Stephanie felt a lump form in her throat.

'Idiot,' Kimberley said. 'It was just a delivery. I can't believe you thought I'd called him. When? When would I have done that? We've been talking for the past hour.'

Stephanie stared vacantly at the front door. 'When you went to the toilet.'

'My phone was on the sofa.' Kimberley groaned, shook her head, and returned to the kitchen, where she slammed the parcel on the counter.

'Kim...' She followed her sister into the kitchen. 'I'm sorry, I didn't mean to... I overreacted.'

Kimberley spun to face her, fire and fury etched into her expression. Her eyes blazed, and her chest rose and fell in short, shallow bursts.

'You need to sort it out,' she began. 'You need to get a grip.'

Stephanie opened her mouth, but no words came.

'I went to the hospital the other day. Thought something was wrong... really wrong.' Kimberley placed her hands on her bump. 'I tried you first. Called twice. Straight to voicemail. Jason didn't answer either.'

'Kim, I—'

'And then I called Jordan,' she said, quietly and simply. 'He was the only one who picked up.'

Stephanie closed her eyes for a moment. Shame crept up her spine like frostbite.

'He met me there. Sat in the waiting room with me. Didn't ask questions, didn't push anything, just... held my hand while I cried and thought something terrible was going to happen to the baby. He was there for me. I called, and he answered.'

Silence settled between them, heavy and awkward.

'You think I don't understand what he represents for you?' Kimberley said, her voice thickening. 'But he's still my brother. *Our* brother. And we've got the past thirty years of catching up to do. I'm not going to let what happened in the past ruin what can happen in the future. I'd love for you to be able to do the same.'

Stephanie couldn't look at her. Couldn't face the weight of those words. All she could think about was the nightmare she'd had the other night. The fire. The childhood home. Her mum and sister trapped in the bedroom window, burning to death. And then her hero half-brother running to their rescue, arriving at the last moment to save the day.

'I... I'm so sorry, Kim. I... I had no idea. You... you should have kept trying me, left a voicemail, something. You've got my work number if you can't ever reach me. But that's no excuse.' She reached out for Kimberley's hand. 'I should have been there for you, and I wasn't. For that, I'm sorry.'

CHAPTER
FORTY-THREE

Olivia's blood pressure was through the roof. Another issue at the school. Another incident involving Josh and his bad influence friend. This time, they had apparently thought it would be funny to lock a Year Seven pupil in the cleaning cupboard and leave him there during lunch. The poor kid had been found by a teaching assistant, crying and barely able to explain what had happened.

And now, for the second time in a month, Olivia had received a phone call from the deputy head, requesting a meeting to discuss behavioural expectations.

She gripped the steering wheel tighter as the satnav chirped instructions over the sound of the windscreen wipers. The road ahead was narrow and slick with afternoon rain. Her gaze flicked to the speedometer, then to the clock on the dashboard.

She couldn't stop thinking about it.

Josh. Her boy. Her sweet, sensitive little boy who used to sleep with the hallway light on and cried when his pet hamster died. The same boy who now muttered things under his breath, rolled his eyes when she asked about school, and stomped around the house like he owned it. Puberty was part of it, sure. She knew that. But there was something else, something more lurking beneath the surface. Anger? Insecurity? Influence?

She hated the friend he'd made. Alfie. She had never approved of the little pissant. Right from the start, right from their first exchange when he'd come round their house one weekend, she'd known he was bad news. The attitude. The way he spoke.

And now, here she was, on her way to speak with another one of the old bullies from St Jude's. Another grown man who had once taken pleasure in humiliating others.

She tried not to compare the two.

But as the wipers cleared the grey skies, her thoughts spiralled.

What if Josh turned out like the man she was about to meet? What if, twenty years from now, someone like her would be pulling up outside his business or home, asking questions about the kid he once bullied?

What if it was already too late?

She pulled over and killed the engine. The cottage was set back from the road, a squat brick building with a gravel path and peeling paint on the window frames. A battered Land Rover was parked out front. A wind chime tinkled in the breeze.

She took a moment to breathe. Then another.

Time to meet bully number four.

The door was opened by a man with thinning sandy hair and a tired face that seemed darker in the late afternoon gloom. He wore jeans and a hoodie with frayed cuffs and had a slight stoop to his shoulders.

'You the police officer?' he asked.

Olivia flashed her warrant card with a forced smile. 'That's me. May I come in?'

Reluctantly, Darren Fairhurst moved aside and let her through, as if she had just asked him to put the house on the market. The inside of the house was dim and cluttered. Shoes crowded the hallway, and the faint aroma of stale cigarettes lingered beneath the more recent smell of baked beans and toast. A small dog barked once from a room towards the back of the house, then fell silent.

'Through here,' Darren muttered, leading her into a narrow living room that doubled as a dining space. An empty can of beer sat on the coffee table.

He gestured to the nearest armchair. 'Sit if you want. Sorry it's a bit of a mess.'

Olivia sat, pulling out her pen and notepad. 'As I mentioned on the phone earlier, we're investigating the murders of Nigel Hadlow and Carlos Vazquez.'

Darren nodded slowly, settling on the edge of the sofa as if unsure he was allowed to get comfortable.

Olivia clicked her pen. 'When was the last time you spoke to either of them?'

He rubbed his jaw, the scratch of stubble loud in the quiet. 'Uh... a few months back. Carlos messaged me out of the blue, inviting me to an afternoon of golf with them.'

'And you went?'

'Yeah. Thought, why not? We're not getting any younger.'

'And how was it? Catching up?'

Darren shrugged. 'It was all right. A bit weird at first. We hadn't spoken properly in decades. But once we got past the awkward stuff, it was like no time had passed. Carlos still had that smug laugh. Nigel still went on like he knew everything.'

'Did they mention anyone else from school? Anyone they'd been in contact with?'

He shook his head. 'Not really. They kept it light. Old stories, mostly. "Do you remember so-and-so?" That kind of thing. After golf, we went to the Red Fox, the pub down the road, had a few drinks. Nothing mad.'

'Did anyone else join you?'

'Nope. Just the three of us.'

'Did you notice anything strange at the pub? Anyone watching you? Anyone else from your school days hanging around?'

Darren paused, chewing the inside of his cheek. 'No one I recognised. The place was busy. Saturday afternoon footie crowd. Loud, full of people in football shirts and kids on iPads.'

Olivia tapped her pen against the page. 'And the conversation? Did anything unusual come up? Anything that stood out?'

Darren gave a small laugh, but there was no humour in it. 'It was mostly nonsense. Until Nigel brought up the school trip.'

That made her look up. 'Which trip?'

'Year Nine. Some outdoor adventure place in the New Forest. You know the kind: we're climbing the walls and going on the zip lines while the teachers are in waterproofs wishing they were in the Bahamas or the Maldives.'

Olivia nodded slowly. She didn't interrupt.

Darren shifted in his seat. 'We were bastards back then. Real bastards. And there was this one kid... Ray something. Roy? I don't know. His name began with R. Weird little religious kid. Anyway, we called him Mouse because he barely spoke.'

'What about him?' she asked carefully.

He let out a breath, long and heavy. 'It was supposed to be a joke. A test of bravery or some bollocks that Carlos had told him. One night, we snuck out of our cabins, grabbed him from his bunk, and took him with us into the woods, stripped him to his underwear, and tied him to a tree.'

'You did what?'

'We thought it was funny. We told him he had to stay there all night. That if he made it until morning, he could join our group. Be part of the gang.' Darren rubbed his face. 'He pissed himself. Cried. Screamed. We left him there anyway.'

Olivia stared at him. 'And what happened?'

'One of the teachers, I think, found him just after dawn. Still tied up, covered in bites, shaking so hard they thought he was having a seizure. They said it was hypothermia. Nearly killed him.'

A long silence fell between them.

'You didn't get in trouble?'

'We pretended like we had nothing to do with it. And he didn't grass us up – which we were absolutely astounded by – so nothing ever came of it. And then his parents pulled him out of the school a few weeks later anyway, so we had nothing to worry about.'

Olivia's mind raced. A half-naked thirteen-year-old child tied to a tree in the middle of the woods, left to freeze to death while his tormentors slept comfortably in their bunks. It wasn't just bullying. It was cruelty. Ritualistic and humiliating. And now, two of the perpetrators were dead. Burned.

'What was his full name?' she asked.

Darren frowned, digging through old memories. 'Raymond... something weird. Not English. Maybe Czech or Polish? Radoslav? Radan? I don't know.'

Olivia wrote the nickname down slowly.

'You don't think it's him, do you?' Darren asked. 'Coming back for us after all these years?'

She didn't answer right away. But the thought had already taken root in her mind.

'I think whoever's doing this knows what happened to that boy,' she said. 'And I think you need to be very careful, Mr Fairhurst.'

CHAPTER
FORTY-FOUR

That evening, Darren Fairhurst stood over the stove, stirring a saucepan of pasta with the same stained wooden spoon he'd used for years, the television murmuring in the background. Some new quiz show that he wasn't really paying attention to, but it provided enough noise to make him feel comforted. Especially after his earlier conversation. He hadn't stopped thinking about what she'd said.

That copper – Olivia something – had unearthed memories he hadn't wanted to think about in years: the woods, the cold, the crying, and Mouse, whatever his name was. Small and shivering, tied up. A practical joke that, in hindsight, hadn't been very funny. Darren hadn't seen it that way back then; none of them had. But now, with two of the old gang turned to ash, it was impossible not to reflect on it.

He shook his head and turned off the hob.

It was nothing to be scared of, he reassured himself. Just a strange, freakish coincidence. Nothing more.

He plated his meatballs and pasta, grabbed a beer from the fridge, and shuffled over to the dining table that overlooked his living room. His little dog, Max, yapped once in the corner before curling up again in his basket.

Then the doorbell rang.

Darren froze, halfway through sitting down.

One ring. Then silence.

He frowned and set down the plate, brushing his palms on his hoodie. No one visited this late, especially not in this weather. He glanced at the clock: 9:13 pm.

Max barked again, this time louder and more insistent.

'All right, all right,' Darren muttered as he headed down the hallway.

Through the frosted glass, he could see a vague silhouette – tall and unmoving.

Cautiously, he unlocked the door and cracked it open.

'Yeah?'

And then he saw it: the figure. A face he hadn't seen in years, a face that sent a surge of fear through him, smiling.

'What are...? You...?'

Before he could finish, something swung towards him. Fast.

Darren barely had time to raise an arm in defence before the blow connected with the side of his head. A sickening crack, like a cricket bat striking wet leather, echoed off the hallway walls. His legs gave way beneath him, his knees slamming into the floor.

His vision wobbled. The hallway stretched and warped. A high-pitched ringing filled his ears.

The figure stepped forward, swallowing what little light remained from the lounge. Gloved hands reached out, caught Darren by the collar, and yanked him fully inside before kicking the door shut behind them.

Darren tried to speak, tried to scream, but another sharp blow caught him across the jaw, and everything turned white.

Max barked furiously from the living room, claws scratching against the floorboards, but he didn't come closer. Useless dog.

The last thing Darren saw before the blackness enveloped him was that unmistakable smile, the same one a blast from the past used to wear.

CHAPTER
FORTY-FIVE

A deep sense of foreboding knotted in the pit of her stomach as Stephanie pulled up to Darren Fairhurst's house on the outskirts of Cranleigh.

Another fire. Another incident involving someone connected to Nigel Hadlow and Carlos Vazquez. There was no doubt in Stephanie's mind that they were linked, and the killer had chosen Darren Fairhurst as their next victim. The only problem was that Stephanie didn't know how close she could get to the crime scene.

Images of the fire involving her childhood home continued to plague her thoughts. Kimberley. Her mother. Screaming for their lives. She hadn't even arrived yet, and already she was envisioning them trapped inside, their cries echoing in her ears.

And then their faces were replaced by Darren's, a man she had never met. What had started as her sister's and mother's high-pitched screams transformed into deeper, more guttural cries as the flames engulfed him.

The noises were so overwhelming that she couldn't hear the radio presenter announcing the news.

This morning, another fire was reported in the Surrey area. This follows a string of fire-related incidents that the police are actively investigating.

Someone had already caught wind of it and passed the information upstream. The national press...

As she continued down the winding country lane, shielded by trees and hedges that appeared lifeless, her phone chimed on the dashboard. She glanced at the screen, hoping for a message from her sister. But, of course, it wasn't. Kimberley was too proud and stubborn to make the first move and apologise.

So was Stephanie.

Kimberley had placed her half-brother on a higher pedestal. Something she could not, – and would not, get over so easily.

Instead, the notification was an email. Unimportant. One for later.

Then Darren Fairhurst's house came into view: a Victorian cottage in the middle of nowhere, surrounded by a large, four-acre plot of land. The first thing Stephanie noticed was the smell. Thick and dense, it seeped through the air vents and lingered in the cabin. It intensified when she pulled over and climbed out. Something biological. Burnt skin. Burnt hair. Burnt body.

Her stomach lurched.

She forced herself to walk, though every step towards the house felt like wading through cement. The house loomed ahead, cracked and blistered from the fire. Dozens of reporters huddled by the outer cordon, cameras slung over shoulders, microphones pressed to lips. She ignored them, keeping her head down and moving with purpose. At the inner cordon, she signed in, changed into a forensic suit, and ducked beneath it.

And then she saw him.

Elias.

He stood beside the skeletal remains of what had once been a garden trellis, his fire-retardant gear shielding him from the gusting wind. His scarred face was turned towards the wreckage, but he glanced at her as she approached. Stephanie kept her eyes low, trying to avoid looking at the exterior of the house.

Her sister's screams echoed in her mind. The thought of her sister losing her life, losing the baby in the fire that had never happened...

Her vision blurred.

Her knees buckled slightly.

The ground swayed beneath her.

'Stephanie...?' Elias was at her side in an instant, strong arms catching her before her legs gave way. 'Whoa, whoa. Sit down. You're okay. Everything's okay.'

She didn't argue. Couldn't. She hadn't eaten anything in nearly twenty-four hours; her entire body felt weak. Elias guided her to a low garden wall that had survived the blaze and eased her down onto it. The cold stone grounded her slightly, and the fresh air hit her lungs in jagged bursts.

He crouched in front of her. 'Breathe in for four. Hold it for four. Out for four. It's called box breathing.'

She nodded, barely, and tried to match his count. One. Two. Three. Four...

It wasn't immediate, but the thudding in her chest began to ease. The sweat at the nape of her neck started to cool. Her throat, which had felt like it was clamping shut, loosened enough for a few clearer breaths.

Elias remained where he was, his eyes fixed on her.

'You all right?' he asked.

'No,' she rasped. 'But I will be.'

'Are you all right to have a look at what we've found?'

She hesitated.

'You're clearly not. That's fine. We can stay here.' Elias joined her side. 'We found a body in the kitchen. Same as before, so I'll spare you the grisly details. But it looks like he might have been cooking dinner when the fire started.'

'Could it be accidental?'

'Possibly. But, given everything else that's happened, my instinct says no.'

Stephanie stared at the pavement. By now, her breathing was under control, and the fog in her mind had dissipated. She climbed to her feet. As she brushed down her suit, a member of the crime scene investigation team hurried over.

'Ma'am,' she said. 'Sorry to interrupt, but I thought you should see this. It's another tin.'

Stephanie turned to the CSI. 'Another tin?'

'It was in the fireplace, tucked right up in the chimney. Still intact.'

Stephanie's legs became firmer. More reliable. 'What was inside?'

The CSI held the evidence bag open slightly so Stephanie could peer in.

Inside was another small, faded photograph of a young boy, grinning at the camera. The same age as all the others. The same style. Taken from the same larger photograph.

And beneath the photo, scratched into the tin, were the words:

As you sow, so shall you reap. – Galatians 6:7

Stephanie stared at it, her mouth dry. Another religious note. This time about justice, getting what one deserved. She recalled what Olivia had briefly mentioned the day before: the victims had been involved in an incident concerning a young boy and a tree.

Was *he* the killer? Was he making sure those boys paid for what they did, one by one?

She stared back at the ruined house, her voice dropping to a whisper.

'How many more are involved?'

CHAPTER
FORTY-SIX

The magnet attached to the whiteboard with an audible click. Stephanie's gaze lingered on the photo of the third boy before she turned away from it. A concerned hush had fallen over the office, and the team looked as troubled as she felt.

'It's happened again,' she said bluntly, releasing a heavy sigh through her nose. 'This photo was found at an address belonging to Darren Fairhurst.' She turned to Olivia. 'You were the last one to speak with him, Wellard. What can you tell us? What did he say?'

Olivia's eyes were red and puffy, as if she had been crying and beating herself up over something. 'I... I should have known this was going to happen.'

'What do you mean?'

'He asked me if I thought the killer would come for him. He asked if he had anything to worry about. And I just... I just didn't know what to say. I gave him some boilerplate excuse to watch out for himself. I didn't help him.'

Stephanie felt a pang of sympathy for the constable. A lot of work and responsibility had been placed on her in the past few days, alongside everything she was dealing with at home. It was clear that she was struggling to keep her head above water.

'You can't blame yourself,' Stephanie said. 'We didn't know for certain he would be next.'

'I did.'

'How?'

'The incident with the kid from school. The school trip. The person called Mouse, who they lured out of his room, tied to a tree, and left there overnight.'

Stephanie nodded. 'Do we know where this "Mouse" individual is now?'

A shake of the head. 'I didn't get a chance to look into it.'

'Fine. I want everything we can find on that person. I want to know where he lives, where he eats, where he works, including his name. And I want to bring him in to find out what he was doing last night and on the nights of the other deaths. This is serious. Three times this has happened now. We can't afford to let that number increase.'

'Surely there can't be that many more victims to come,' Giles interjected. 'How many bullies were there at this school?'

Before she could respond, Devon jumped in. 'Four. Anthony, who I spoke with yesterday, is the last one. He said he hasn't spoken to Nigel or Carlos in years.'

Stephanie turned to the board and searched for the man's name on the list. 'Regardless, he's going to be high on the list. So I want him secured and protected. I want someone to go to his house or place of work, inform him of the severity of the situation, and advise him to be vigilant and report anything suspicious. In the meantime, let's see if we can station a car outside his house. Just in case.'

That would be an interesting conversation with DCI McGowan. However, if she believed there was a credible threat to life, and she could prove it, then he would have little to argue about. She turned her attention back to Olivia. A thought popped into her head. 'Wellard, when was the last time Darren Fairhurst met either Nigel or Carlos?'

'The other day, ma'am. They went golfing together.'

'When?'

'About six weeks ago.'

'That's not the other day then.'

Olivia lowered her head. 'Sorry. I just... I say that for everything. Two years ago. Six months. Yesterday.'

'Well don't. It's confusing. Be precise.'

She didn't mean to take it out on Olivia, especially after how much the constable had helped her, but she was tired, hungry, and irritable, and she could feel the weight of the investigation pressing down on her.

'Devon, when was the last time Anthony Shore saw Nigel and Carlos?' Stephanie asked.

'Years ago,' Devon replied. 'Like I just said.'

'Be specific. How many years?'

He shrugged. 'I don't know.'

'Find out. In the meantime, if Darren Fairhurst was with them at the golf club—'

'And the pub afterwards,' Olivia added.

'And at the pub afterwards, then we need to canvas everyone who was at either the club or the pub on that day. It's possible the killer saw them all together and that's what inspired this little rampage. And while you're at it, I want someone to find out the last time all the bullies were together, including Anthony. If the killer saw them recently, that might have been the catalyst for this.'

'Why now, ma'am? Why after so long?' Fiona asked.

She paused to think. 'Maybe they were all at the golf course and bumped into the killer. Perhaps it's someone they used to bully, one of the people whose lives they've influenced that we haven't spoken with yet or don't know about. Maybe the killer was working as one of the servers and they didn't recognise him, or maybe they did and continued to treat him like shit, still, after all this time. Bullying sticks with people. They harbour deep-seated resentment. Something – a proverbial straw – must have broken the killer's back, and now they're seeking revenge on our victims. We need to find Mouse and get him in as soon as possible. In the meantime, let's gather CCTV footage and conduct house-to-house enquiries. I know his neighbours are half a mile down the road, but someone might have seen something. Also, put together a timeline of his murder. What time did the fire start? Did anyone see anything beforehand or after? Check ANPR. All the usual stuff, the nitty-gritty boring bits that will help us find this killer.' She paused, surveying their faces. 'Any questions?'

There were none.

'Good. Then get on with it.'

CHAPTER
FORTY-SEVEN

DS Noah Mackenzie sat uncomfortably in a floral-patterned armchair. The cushion had all but disappeared after decades of use, causing him to sink into the wooden frame, which pressed uncomfortably against his muscles. The front room was filled with the musty smell of old carpet, mingled with a hint of freshly baked ginger cake cooling on the table between them. Mrs Fairhurst, frail and birdlike, moved slowly and with great care. Her cardigan hung loosely on her shoulders, and her hands trembled visibly as she set down a mug of tea on the side table.

'It's ginger cake,' she said, her voice faint. 'Darren always liked it. I made some in preparation for his visit this weekend.'

Mr Fairhurst, bald with sunken cheeks and cloudy eyes, sat in a recliner opposite. His breathing was shallow and laboured, and his hands were veined and liver-spotted.

'Thank you,' Noah said gently, accepting the tea but setting it aside untouched. He cleared his throat and placed his notepad on his lap. 'I appreciate you seeing me today. I know this isn't easy, and I'm very sorry for your loss. I'd rather not have to deliver this kind of news at all, let alone in person, but... it's necessary.'

Neither of them responded.

'Your son, Darren, was found this morning at his property near

Cranleigh. His house was destroyed in a fire. I'm afraid... he didn't survive.'

Mrs Fairhurst lifted a hand to her mouth, while Mr Fairhurst blinked hard but said nothing. Only the tick of the grandfather clock in the corner broke the silence.

'We're treating the fire as suspicious,' Noah continued. 'There are... elements that connect it to two other recent deaths. A Mr Nigel Hadlow and a Mr Carlos Vazquez. Do those names mean anything to either of you?'

'They ring a bell,' Mrs Fairhurst said. 'But I can't place why.'

Noah explained the connection. 'They were all schoolmates who attended St Jude's together in the eighties.'

Mr Fairhurst gave a slow nod.

'We found something at one of the earlier crime scenes. A photograph,' Noah said. He opened a plastic sleeve and carefully withdrew a printout of the photo found at Carlos Vazquez's crime scene. The second boy, which, if the first was anything to go by, would belong to Darren Fairhurst.

He handed it to Mrs Fairhurst, who adjusted her reading glasses and peered at it, her lips moving as she studied the image. Then she passed it shakily to her husband.

'That's Darren,' she said, her voice thin. 'That's definitely him.'

'Are you sure?'

Mr Fairhurst squinted. 'You can tell by the ears.'

'Do you know when or where this photo might have been taken?'

Mr Fairhurst shook his head softly. 'It doesn't look like it was at school.'

'No,' Mrs Fairhurst said. 'Definitely not school.'

'Maybe a school trip?' Noah suggested.

But Mrs Fairhurst shook her head. 'I doubt it.'

Noah retrieved a second photo from his folder. 'This was found at the scene of Darren's death. Same format. Same style. Do you recognise the individual in this photograph?'

He passed it to them. Both Fairhursts stared.

Then Mr Fairhurst grunted softly. 'No idea. It was such a long time ago. I scarcely remember what his friends look like nowadays, let alone the ones from back then.'

'Could it be someone from school?' Noah pressed.

Mrs Fairhurst took the photo for a closer inspection, then returned it. 'I honestly have no idea. I'm sorry.'

'And the names Mouse or Ray? Do they mean anything to either of you?'

Mrs Fairhurst flinched slightly but only frowned. 'Mouse? Like the animal?'

'It was a nickname that's come up a few times in our enquiries.'

They both shook their heads.

Noah leaned forward slightly, letting a stream of hot, defeated air escape his nostrils.

'Do you think the boy in that photograph might have been the person who took our son from us?'

Noah returned the photo to its sleeve. 'The opposite. We believe it's the killer's next victim. Which is why we need to identify him as quickly as possible. I will leave this here with you in case it jogs your memory. I realise this is difficult, but if anything at all comes to mind, anything unusual from Darren's school days, any particular trips he mentioned, or incidents, or people he might not have got on with, please let us know. Even the smallest detail could help us get justice for him.'

Mrs Fairhurst's voice cracked as she said, 'He was a difficult boy, Inspector. But he was still our boy.'

Noah nodded solemnly. 'I understand. Thank you.'

As he left, the tea and ginger cake remained untouched on the table.

CHAPTER
FORTY-EIGHT

All the boys were starting to look the same. They had the same eyes, same nose, same boyish, pubescent features, same thin, uninterested smile, and same washed-out look that suggested none of them wanted to be there. Not to mention they almost all had the same style of haircut. Occasionally, a curveball would be thrown in with someone sporting a mullet or quiff, but for the most part, it felt like searching for a particular tree in a dense forest. Before long, Giles lost track of where he was. How many pages of the St Jude's 1983 school yearbook had he skipped past since his eyes had glazed over? How many potential victims had he overlooked?

A heavy yawn escaped his lips as he reached for the coffee on his desk. A latte. The kind that left you with coffee breath and meant you had to give everyone a wide berth when speaking to others. He had been tasked with identifying the fourth boy in the yearbook and had been at it for over an hour. So far, he had sifted through three years' worth of yearbook photos, starting from year seven and moving into year nine. With another two years to go before all the boys in the class of '86 graduated and either went off to college or entered the wider world of work, time was ticking.

In Giles's opinion, the boys in the photographs looked no older than thirteen, year nine. That meant, if the boy appeared in any of the yearbooks, Giles should have already located him and put a name to the face. But in his fatigued state, he had found nothing. Either he was too tired, or the boy simply wasn't present in the photos. Of course, the next victim could have missed the yearbook photo day, and Giles couldn't blame him for that. He remembered the pain of his own photo days: his mother meticulously doing his hair, only for it to be ruined by the time his photoshoot came after lunch; teachers ensuring his uniform was immaculate before he went in, only for it to become loose the moment he hopped onto the seat. The only good part of that experience was standing in the queue for ten to fifteen minutes, missing some of class. As an added bonus, if he remembered correctly, it was always during his least favourite lesson: science.

He turned another page.

More rows of identical boys. Stiff poses, blank expressions, and a brown blur of forgettable haircuts. Giles rubbed his eyes, then blinked hard, trying to focus. He leaned closer, squinting at one boy's chin, then another's ears, then another's jawline – searching for something, anything, that matched the face in the tin.

Nothing.

He sighed and flipped to the next spread.

More group shots. Football team. Science club. Drama society. He paused on one – a blurry picture from a trip to the Lake District. Boys perched on rocks, squinting into the sunlight. It looked vaguely like it could belong to the right era. Giles tilted his head, eyeing each face in turn. Still no match. Still nothing.

He ran a hand through his hair. 'This is impossible,' he muttered.

'How's it going?'

Giles turned to see Stephanie, arms crossed loosely, her face pale under the harsh fluorescent light, standing beside him.

'You don't look that much older than them,' she said, nodding at the open page in front of him. 'Some of them even have a bigger beard than you.'

Giles self-consciously massaged the stubble on his face that stubbornly refused to grow past its current state. 'You joke,' he said, pushing his chair back slightly, 'but I'm halfway to applying for a GCSE in maths again.'

Stephanie smiled faintly. 'Anything?'

He shook his head. 'Not a thing.'

'No? Keep looking. He's got to be there somewhere.' She hesitated, then laid a hand on the back of his chair. 'Take a break if you need to. We can't afford for your eyes to fall out now.'

'You saying I'm useful?' he asked, mock offended.

'Don't push it, Giles.'

She moved off, and Giles cracked his knuckles, turned another page, and kept going.

CHAPTER
FORTY-NINE

Stephanie stood outside Clive McGowan's office, her hand hovering just above the handle. The light behind the frosted glass was on, and she could hear the faint scratch of a pen or highlighter moving across paper.

She knocked quietly.

'Come in,' came the voice, edged with authority.

She pushed the door open and stepped inside. The office was cramped but tidy. The walls were lined with filing cabinets and laminated maps of Surrey pinned up with magnets. A whiteboard behind the desk displayed a yearly calendar filled with a mix of professional and personal appointments scribbled in the boxes.

The chief inspector, dressed in full uniform, looked up from the documents in front of him. He held a highlighter in one hand and a mug in the other. His eyes narrowed slightly as he set both items down.

'Close the door, Stephanie. Sit.'

She complied, sinking into the chair opposite him.

He studied her for a moment, the silence stretching long enough to make her stomach twist. He had summoned her via an email that had appeared unexpectedly in her inbox. She had no idea what the meeting was about.

'How are you feeling?' he eventually asked.

'Fine, sir,' she replied quickly. 'Working hard.'

He let out a small scoff and leaned back in his chair. 'That's funny. Because "fine" people don't nearly collapse at crime scenes.'

Stephanie said nothing, instead fiddling with the necklace wrapped tightly around her neck. 'I didn't collapse, sir.'

He scrutinised her. 'Would you like to tell me what happened?'

'It's not as bad as it sounds, sir. Honest. Where did you even hear about it?'

'A call from Louis, who got a call from one of his reporters. Fortunately, nobody else has caught wind of it, and he promised to keep it out of print. Seems he's looking out for you,' Clive explained. 'And I'm glad he did; otherwise, I doubt you would have come forward, would you?'

She looked at him blankly. When she said nothing, he widened his eyes, as if waiting for a response.

'I thought that was rhetorical, sir. Of course I would have come forward. It's my duty.'

'Right, and it's my duty to make sure my staff are fit and healthy and have access to all the resources they need.' He knitted his fingers together and breathed in deeply. 'I'll ask again: what happened?'

'I got a bit light-headed and just needed to sit down for a moment, that was all.'

'Light-headed? Had you...?' He paused, contemplating how best to frame the question on his lips.

Stephanie knew exactly what he wanted to ask. It was tricky ground, so she decided to assist him.

'It's not *that*,' she lied, releasing her grip on the necklace. 'I've been good. Keeping it under control.'

She didn't want to mention that she'd missed a meal or two because she'd been working so late.

'I'm glad to hear it. I just... had to ask. But don't think I haven't noticed how much you've been working these past few months. You've been through a lot, and it's understandable that it's catching up with you. But if something's going on, I need to know.'

Stephanie hesitated, her fingers curling tightly together in her lap.

'It's nothing like that. I know what I'm doing. I can handle myself. Hopefully, I've proven that. Besides, I've been through a lot worse.' She hesitated. 'It was... fire.'

He frowned. 'What do you mean?'

'It seems I have a fear of fire, and the fire at Fairhurst's place... it triggered something. It's not the first time. It's just been getting progressively worse as this investigation has gone on.'

The chief inspector nodded slowly, his expression softening as he leaned back in his chair. He exhaled through his nose and rubbed a hand over his chin, the rasp of stubble loud in the quiet office.

'All right,' he said. 'Thanks for telling me. That's not easy, and I appreciate it.'

Stephanie gave a small, almost imperceptible shrug, as if it didn't matter.

'Have you ever tried grounding techniques?' he asked after a moment. 'Breathing exercises? Five-sense check-ins?'

Stephanie blinked. 'What?'

'It's basic stuff. When something triggers you, find five things you can see, four you can touch, three you can hear... you get the idea. It slows everything down and brings you back to the moment.'

She raised an eyebrow. 'Didn't take you for the mindfulness type, sir.'

He gave a dry smirk. 'I'm not. But I did some trauma training about fifteen years ago, and I guess some of it stuck. It might be worth looking into. It won't fix everything overnight, but it gives you something to hold onto when things begin to get out of control.'

Stephanie nodded faintly, neither committing to the idea nor dismissing it.

Clive drummed his fingers once against the desk. 'What about professional help?'

Stephanie reached for her necklace again and gave him a wary look. 'You're starting to sound like Elias.'

'Elias?'

'The watch manager helping us with this operation.'

McGowan grinned. 'Sounds like a smart man.'

She sighed and rubbed her hands over her face. 'I don't want to be taken off this case.'

'You won't be. Not unless you give me a solid reason to. Are you still fit to run this investigation?'

'Yes.'

'Then that's all I needed to hear. As long as you don't burn out on me, we're all good.'

She smirked. 'Pardon the pun.'

'Unintentional, I swear.'

Stephanie allowed herself a brief smile, but it faded almost as quickly as it appeared. Her shoulders remained tense beneath her shirt.

'Look,' Clive said, his tone lowering into something almost fatherly. It was a tone she hadn't heard in years, nor had she believed she would hear it again. 'I've been doing this long enough to know when someone's walking a tightrope. You don't need to be a hero, Steph.'

She nodded, swallowing the tightness in her throat. 'Noted.'

'Good. Now go take a break before you throw yourself into another inferno, literal or otherwise.'

She stood, brushing imaginary creases from her trousers. 'I'm fine, sir.'

'If you say that often enough, maybe one of these days I'll actually believe it.'

Stephanie turned for the door, her hand on the handle, then paused. 'Thanks for not making this... a bigger deal than it is.'

Clive waved a hand. 'Like I said, don't be a hero. And, Steph?'

She looked over her shoulder.

'Talk to the therapist. Or anyone, really. I promise you it'll do more good than you think.'

Stephanie nodded once more. 'I'll think about it.'

Then she stepped out, pulling the door closed behind her.

CHAPTER
FIFTY

Stephanie hadn't even returned to her desk when Fiona intercepted her in the corridor outside the incident room, clutching a folder against her chest and wearing an expression that made Stephanie's stomach tighten.

'Steph,' Fiona said hurriedly. 'You got a second?'

Stephanie slowed down, exhaled sharply through her nose, and turned to face her. 'What is it?'

'We can't find him.'

Stephanie blinked. 'Who?'

'Mouse. Ray... Whatever his name is.'

Stephanie narrowed her eyes. 'What do you mean you can't find him?'

'We've only got a *partial* name. A nickname. It's not enough to go on. We've gone through the school records from St Jude's, cross-referenced them with trip registers, parental consents, and even gone off the beaten track with nickname guesses. We've checked census data, NHS logs, police databases. Nothing. No one fits the criteria.'

Stephanie rubbed a hand over her brow, tension flaring behind her eyes. 'So you're telling me this person doesn't exist?'

'I'm saying either we've been given the wrong name, or someone went to great lengths to disappear after that trip.'

Stephanie looked past her into the incident room, where Giles was hunched over his laptop and Noah's empty chair sat beside a ring-stained desk.

Stephanie's jaw tightened. She took a steadying breath, then turned back to Fiona. 'Right. Get everyone in the MIR. Now.'

Fiona didn't hesitate. She peeled away and disappeared through the door, her voice rising above the conversations inside. 'Team briefing. Five minutes.'

They were gathered around the section of the office designated for major investigations a few minutes later. Stephanie paced from side to side, as if she were on a mission.

'Right,' she said bluntly, placing her hands on her hips. 'Where are we?'

Nobody responded. They all looked at one another, avoiding responsibility. Finally, Stephanie nominated Giles to go first. The constable cleared his throat and smoothed his tie before beginning.

'I... Well, there's not much to report, really, ma'am. I've spoken with a handful of the neighbours around Darren Fairhurst's neighbourhood, and nobody reported seeing anything. They're all in their sixties and seventies. Most of them couldn't believe anything like this could happen down their street. A couple of them had hearing problems, so that was a non-starter.'

'CCTV?'

Giles responded with a light shrug. Some have got doorbell cameras and some more advanced security systems, but a lot of them have been set up incorrectly or are only pointed directly at the front doors or their driveways, meaning most of the road and surrounding area is cut off.' Giles paused as if remembering something, then hurried to his desk. He logged into his computer, pressed a few buttons, and then sprinted to the printer. He returned with a sheet in hand, sticking it to the incident board. 'I managed to look through one neighbour's security footage – a couple in their seventies whose son had installed it for them – and I found this still of a car going past at around the time the house fire might have started.'

'Do we know when it started?'

Giles nodded. 'It was in Elias's report. He reckons it was somewhere between five in the evening and midnight. The only problem is...' Giles pointed to the blur in the top right corner of the image. 'I can't make head nor tail of what make and model it is. So, yes, we have *something*. It's just that this something is worth less than the paper it's printed on.'

Stephanie thanked him, then called him back over.

'See if you can find anything matching that... *shape* on CCTV in the surrounding area,' she instructed the constable. 'And also check if it appears at either of the previous crime scenes.' Stephanie slowly scanned the room to select her next target. She pointed at Devon. 'What have you got for me?'

Devon stopped slouching in his chair and shifted himself higher. Folding one leg over the other, he said, 'Since this morning, I've been going through Fairhurst's financial records, and I haven't seen anything that might have been a cause for concern. I thought there might be a connection between Darren, Nigel Hadlow, and the man who gave Nigel money, Terry Houghton.'

'Why?' she snapped.

'Just in case the school route doesn't work out, ma'am. I thought we needed to keep our options open.'

She didn't like the idea of wasting time, but she understood where he was coming from and conceded that it made sense. If they focused all their time, energy, and effort on the bullying victims and it came to nothing with no backup plan, they would be back to square one – a place she didn't want to be.

'Very well,' she said with a curt nod. 'Any other instances where our victims might be linked?'

Devon looked at her blankly, like a rabbit caught in headlights. 'Not that I've noticed so far. But... I'll keep looking.'

'Great.' She turned to Giles again. 'What about the boy in the photograph?'

'I've tried, ma'am, but I have absolutely no idea who this kid is.'

'Still nothing?'

'The photo's poor quality, it's forty years old; the person in it could look completely different now.'

'I don't want to hear excuses,' she retorted, her patience wearing thin. 'Have you shown the photo to Anthony Shore or his parents to see if *he's* the person in the photograph? Noah is still out on surveillance, and we'll have a team watching him overnight. All of this will have been a waste of time and money if he isn't the boy in the photograph.'

Giles's face widened with disbelief, as if he'd just discovered fire.

'I hadn't thought of that. Sounds delicious!'

'Doing your job for you,' she said. 'In the meantime, we need to find Mouse as a priority. Fiona, I know you've been working on it, but I want Olivia to chip in, and I want you to do everything you can to find this individual. Speak with anyone and everyone. So far, he's our biggest suspect.'

CHAPTER
FIFTY-ONE

After several hours of researching, calling, hanging up, waiting, crossing names off her list, and contacting people through various means, Fiona finally discovered the name of someone who'd attended the boys' school trip to the New Forest.

A teaching assistant named Michael Glover had been brought in at the last minute after another staff member dropped out, resulting in his name being omitted from several documents. In the end, Fiona had to rely on a former student's hazy and faded memory to get his name.

Of all the staff members who'd been sent on the trip, Michael was the only one still alive. Now in his sixties, he was one of the youngest attendees, having been fresh out of university when he returned to the place where it all began for him: St Jude's.

Michael Glover's house was a squat, two-storey cottage with a sloping moss-covered roof and ivy creeping up the brickwork. Its name was barely legible on a wooden sign covered in lichen and leaves. One of the upstairs windowpanes had a hairline crack running through it like a vein, and the paint on the sills was peeling. Nettles and weeds had overtaken most of the flowerbeds in the front garden, and an overturned terracotta pot lay beside a cracked gnome whose colours had long since faded.

Fiona stood just inside the living room, trying not to breathe too deeply. The air was heavy with the stench of stale tobacco that clung to the back of her throat. The carpet beneath her feet was the colour of weak tea, and she could see where the furniture had carved permanent grooves into it. The place bore all the hallmarks of someone who had lived there alone, with no evidence of a spouse or partner, not even someone who visited frequently.

Michael lowered himself into the armchair with the ease of someone who had spent a lifetime moving and taking cod liver oil tablets.

'Lovely place you have here,' she said.

'It was my parents'. I inherited it when they passed. Nicer than the place I was living in, so I thought I'd move in.'

That explained the furniture. Fiona reached into her bag and pulled out some documents.

'It took me a while to find you, but I understand you taught at St Jude's, is that right?'

'I never taught. I was a teaching assistant. My dad was the teacher there. He got me the job.'

So you were a nepo baby.

The term referred to someone whose career success was attributed to famous or well-connected parents. In Michael's case, it was his father who had secured him the position at the school, perhaps to the detriment of other, more qualified candidates.

'How long were you at the school for?' she asked.

'About ten years.'

'And you remained an assistant during that time?'

He nodded. 'Never saw the need to change. I made good money, didn't have much stress, and the headteacher liked me.'

Of course he did. Otherwise, Daddy might have had something to say about it.

'What did you do after you left the school?'

'Dad decided to retire, and I decided I didn't want to be there anymore without him, so I went to work in an office in the city.'

Fiona made a note. 'What can you tell me about your time at the school?'

Michael cleared his throat. 'It was a good laugh most of the time. I was only a few years older than some of the boys, so they saw me as an older brother. A couple of times they asked me to get them cigarettes and alcohol when they were underage. Most of the time I refused, but there were a couple of occasions when I helped them out, only because I knew they would only go and get themselves into trouble by stealing them if I didn't.'

Fiona said nothing, just listened and waited for him to continue.

'Rest of the time, we were just having a lot of banter. I think I helped bridge the gap between them and the teachers in a way. A lot of them trusted me with personal things, secrets, that sort of thing.'

Fiona shifted her weight slightly. 'Did any of those secrets have to do with the trip to the New Forest?'

Michael hesitated. She noticed the change in his breathing. Shallower. His fingers curled tighter around the mug in his lap.

'Which trip?' he eventually asked.

'The one in 1983. You were called in at the last minute to help supervise.'

Another silence, this one longer.

'I remember it,' he said. 'Bloody awful weather that week. Rained every night. The tents collapsed twice. One of the boys got bitten by something on his ankle and wouldn't stop crying for hours.'

'What about the incident involving a gang of boys and someone called Mouse?'

Michael didn't flinch at the name, but she saw his nostrils flare ever so slightly. He looked past her, out of the window.

'You heard about that, did you?'

'Yes. And I'd like your version of that night, please. What was his name?'

'Rami Krüger. Second-generation immigrant from Germany. Weird little kid,' Michael said at last. 'Always on his own. Always scribbling in a notebook or talking to himself. Bit of a loner. Bit of a freak, if I'm honest. But he always used to hang around with those kids. Stuck to them like glue. Tried to, anyway. I think he wanted to be part of their gang so badly that he was willing to do anything. So one night, they took him out, tied him to a tree, stripped him down to his briefs, and left him.

Nigel, Carlos, Darren, and Anthony – the kids responsible – they thought it was hilarious. They said it was a prank. A joke. Something the rest of us were supposed to laugh at too. But when I got out there the following morning on a run and saw him...'

Michael trailed off, his mouth twisting slightly, as if the memory had an unpleasant taste.

'He was shivering. Arms above his head, wrists tied with rope they'd stolen from one of our activities earlier that day. Eyes all wide and watery. Mouth smeared with dirt. Like an animal caught in a trap. When I found him, he was crying his eyes out.'

Fiona's throat tightened. She waited.

Michael leaned back in the chair, sighing. 'I untied him. Told him everything was going to be all right. That I'd take him back to the camp and get him warm.'

'How did you know Nigel and his friends were responsible?'

'Rami told me. But only because I forced it out of him.'

'According to others we've spoken with, nobody was ever held accountable for the incident. The boys were allowed to walk free. Why?'

Michael pretended to look at something stuck in his nails. 'There are two reasons for that,' he said. 'The first is... well, Rami begged me not to say anything to anyone. He said he wanted to get in with Nigel and the rest of them so much that he was willing to take it to the grave. And the other reason, I'm not so proud of.' He paused. 'Deep down I thought it was hilarious. Boys being boys. A bit of hazing. Nothing serious.'

'You don't think that kind of humiliation might've stuck with him?' Fiona asked quietly. Her voice was even, but her hands had clenched into fists at her sides. 'Might've shaped him?'

Michael finally looked up at her, more sharply now.

'I've no idea what happened to him after that,' he said. 'He left St Jude's, and I never saw him again.'

Fiona made a note. Now they had a confirmed name, they might have more luck tracing Rami Krüger's whereabouts. She reached into her bag and produced the photograph that had been found at Darren Fairhurst's crime scene. She passed it across.

'Do you recognise the boy in this image?'

Michael studied the boy's features for a considerable time, taking in every pixel. Fiona watched him, analysing his reaction for the faintest hint of recognition. But there was none. In the end, he shook his head and returned the image to her.

'It doesn't look familiar,' he said. 'When was that taken?'

'We don't know. But we suspect it's from a similar time to when Darren, Nigel and Carlos were at school together.'

Michael folded his arms. 'Doesn't ring any bells. Sorry.'

Fiona packed up her bag to leave, then something occurred to her.

'I'm sorry to report,' she started, 'but Nigel, Darren, and Carlos are dead. At each of their crime scenes, we've discovered tins containing religious messages inscribed inside. Now, as I understand it, St Jude's wasn't a particularly religious school, was it?'

Michael shook his head. 'I don't know what it's like now, but it wasn't while I was there.'

'Were any of the kids religious?'

A shrug of the shoulders. 'Sure. They had all different faiths.'

'Do you know what Danny, Carlos, and Nigel believed, if anything?'

Michael considered for a long moment, then shook his head. 'I never heard anything explicitly mentioned. It wasn't the type of thing we discussed.' He snapped his fingers. 'Except for little Rami. He was always reading things from the Bible or talking about it. He knew these long passages of it verbatim, and would always find a way to bring any topic of conversation back to God and Jesus. Most of the time, I ignored him, but I know that he spent a lot of time going to church.'

CHAPTER
FIFTY-TWO

Noah wasn't particularly enthusiastic about the new idea that Devon had introduced to the team. The idea of assigning tasks based on chance by drawing straws. It didn't exactly thrill him, especially since he had drawn the second shortest straw of the day. As a result, he found himself parked opposite Anthony Shore's modest semi-detached house in Addlestone like a guardian angel, surveying the property and street to ensure the man remained safe from potential harm. A guardian angel that was only there for a short while longer before the shift change took place and he would be replaced by a uniformed officer tasked with the night shift. For the past three hours, he had been sentenced to the confines of the pool car, accompanied only by a couple of bottles of water, a handful of snacks, and a notebook. Aside from the occasional pigeon waddling across the road, there had been absolutely nothing to report. Anthony had been home all afternoon, with no one venturing near the property. Outside, it had long been dark, and the only light he had to fend off the darkness was the weak glow of a streetlight halfway down the road.

Noah checked his watch for the fifth time in less than a minute, and each time he was as disappointed as the last to see it was still 6:55 pm.

'Bugger it,' he muttered, stretching his arms in a yawn as far as he could within the cramped vehicle. 'Dinner time.'

He reached for the last half of a KitKat on the passenger seat and stuffed it into his mouth. The dinner of champions.

Then his phone buzzed.

Rachel. His wife.

He smiled faintly and answered. 'Hey.'

'Hey, you busy?'

He glanced towards the house. 'Rushed off my feet. A bird's just landed on the roof, so I need to keep a close eye on it, just in case it shits on the patio.'

Rachel chuckled gently. 'The girls want to say goodnight. You've got thirty seconds before they explode.'

Noah's heart softened. 'Put them on.'

He heard the rustle as the phone shifted.

'Daaaad!' two tiny voices chorused through the speaker.

'Hey, my monsters,' he said, his voice full of warmth. 'You brushing your teeth? Or are you sneaking chocolate under your pillows again?'

More giggles followed.

'Mum says you're fighting fires,' said the older one, Amelia.

'Not fighting them. Just watching houses to make sure they don't catch fire.'

'Is ours going to catch fire, Daddy?'

'No, sweetheart. I've already checked our house to make sure it doesn't.'

'When are you coming home?' asked Trinity.

'Soon, bubba. You'll be asleep, but I'll see you in the morning.'

The girls groaned with disappointment, then Rachel stepped in, instructing them to finish brushing their teeth and wait for her in the bedroom. They screamed goodbye before disappearing.

'I'll let you know when I'm coming home,' he told Rachel before ending the call.

As he placed the phone on his lap, a pair of headlights swept across his windscreen. An unmarked car had pulled up behind him, with a uniformed officer at the wheel.

Finally.

PC Grace Patel climbed out and waddled over to his window.

'Quiet one?' she asked.

'As dry as the Sahara,' Noah replied, deadpan.

'Lucky you. Though it beats being stuck in traffic near Guildford with a dog that wouldn't stop vomiting earlier.'

'You win. And on that note, I'm out of here. He's all yours. Enjoy.'

'Thanks.'

As Patel wandered back to her car, Noah turned on the engine and pulled away. Glancing back at the house one last time, unease prickled along the back of his neck.

Anthony might be safe for now.

But for how long?

CHAPTER
FIFTY-THREE

Stephanie sat at the kitchen table, one leg tucked beneath her and the other bouncing restlessly against the chair leg, the blue light from her laptop screen casting a soft glow across the half-empty wine glass beside it.

She had already read the email three times, drafted a response several more, and quickly deleted each one.

Dear Ms Broadbent,

We are writing to inform you of a delay in the sale of your late father's property. During final checks, it came to light that the original deed includes a restrictive covenant dating back to 1973, limiting certain uses of the land. The buyers' solicitors have raised this as a concern, and as a result, the conveyancing process has been paused until we can either negotiate a deed of variation or obtain legal indemnity insurance.

We understand how frustrating this may be, particularly at this stage, but we are working to resolve the issue as swiftly as possible.

Kind regards,

HG & Sons

Stephanie's jaw clenched.

Restrictive covenant. She barely knew what it meant, but it sounded like bollocks designed to stall things and keep her trapped in limbo. The house should've been sold by now. She and Kimberley had emptied the rooms, dealt with the ghost of their dad, and put it on the market. It was the estate agents' problem now. The sale was meant to draw a line under her father and everything associated with him. Closure. Yet here he was, finding a way to make things difficult for her, wedging himself into her life somehow. Some dusty line in a decades-old deed was now holding her life to ransom.

She let out a bitter laugh and reached for the wine.

'You'd love this, wouldn't you?' she muttered to the silence. 'Still managing to screw things up from the grave.'

Her stomach growled, a familiar and unwelcome sensation beginning to well at the back of her mind. She recognised the warning signs and the triggers.

And she wouldn't give in to them. She needed air; she needed space.

Stephanie glared at the laptop for another second before slamming it shut and pushing it away.

It was time to get out.

She quickly changed into her leggings, sports bra, T-shirt, and hoodie. Her trainers were already by the door, muddy from the last jog she had attempted and abandoned. She tied her hair up, plugged her earphones in, and left the house without looking back.

Outside, the air was thin, and cooler than she had expected. But she ignored it and ran without thinking, letting muscle memory guide her as she headed towards the University of Surrey campus. She didn't know why, but something had pulled her back there. To the place where her return to Surrey Police had begun. To the place where four female students had lost their lives.

The campus was quiet at this hour. The beginnings of winter had settled over the field and in the streets, convincing students it was better to stay indoors than brave the discomfort of a night out. Her shoes slapped rhythmically against the tarmac as she cut through the southern entrance, past the library, and veered right towards the lake.

It hit her near the steps of the student union building.

Maya Corcoran. The third victim of her father's master plan for revenge, the voodoo doll found in a box placed on her back.

Stephanie's breath caught in her throat, and for a moment, she slowed to a walk. She glanced at the pool of water where Maya's body had been found. Only a few hours before she'd been found, Stephanie had been wrestling with her on the floor during their jiujitsu training. Since then, she hadn't returned to the sport, as if it had been tarnished with the memory of what had happened to Maya.

With thoughts of that night swirling in her mind, Stephanie pushed on, crossing the concourse and jogging past the locations where the other bodies had been discovered – stabbed, suffocated, burnt alive. Four victims on the campus alone. Four families shattered. And her father, the man who had raised her, had orchestrated it all from his care home armchair.

Stephanie stopped running. She bent forward, hands on her knees, her breath sharp and ragged. Sweat pricked at her neck.

She wasn't just running to clear her head anymore. She was running because some part of her had brought her back here. Not for fitness. Not for distraction. But for reckoning.

Even after everything, her father still had her circling the same ground, caught in the gravitational pull of the horror he had left behind, unable to forgive herself for the trauma and trouble he had caused.

She straightened slowly, rolling her shoulders back and wiping her sleeve across her forehead.

But she had had enough. For too long, he had clung to her thoughts like a disease. But not anymore. She was finished with him.

'I'm not yours,' she whispered to the dark campus around her. 'Not anymore.'

Then she took off again, her pace steadier this time, heading towards the back gate and away from the heart of the university.

Something had pulled her back there that night.

But that would be the last time.

CHAPTER
FIFTY-FOUR

She didn't want to be there. Not only was she increasingly tired and worn out from sleep deprivation and the stresses of the investigation, but she also believed she had no reason to be there. However, she had promised Clive she would go. Promised him only in order to appease him and get him off her back.

Therapy had always been a taboo subject in her world. The stigma surrounding it made her feel weak, as though she were a lesser human being, so she had avoided it at all costs. She knew she had issues – of course she did; she wasn't stupid – but she'd had her own methods for dealing with and processing them. While those methods may not have been ideal, they had mostly worked for her.

What was the saying? *If it ain't broke...*

She shifted in her chair, tugging at the sleeve of her jumper as if the thin fabric could shield her from the room itself. She felt uncomfortable, even claustrophobic, as though the walls were closing in around her and the stuffy atmosphere was sucking the oxygen from her lungs. She glanced down at her lap and fidgeted with her fingers, waiting. She didn't want to survey the rest of the room; she was content with the debilitating thoughts rattling around in her mind as she waited for a stranger to pick apart her past like a vulture stripping a carcass; what was left of it, anyway.

Any minute now, the therapist would come in, and she'd have to look up, make polite noises, and perhaps even answer a question or two.

Then the talking would begin. The reliving of her childhood.

She would be forced to sit there and listen to the therapist's advice, hearing things she already knew.

Stephanie could already feel heat prickling at the back of her neck. Not from the radiator behind her, but from the memories, the angst, the anxiety, the paranoia, the sensation she'd felt in her dream.

The faint scar on her forearm, where her dad had held a lighter to it, suddenly flared with searing pain, spreading over her body. Her stomach twisted faintly, and her breathing quickened. She ignored it, pinching the skin on her thighs to distract herself from the sensation.

Just a little longer, and this would be over.

Then the door opened with a soft click.

A woman stepped inside, mid-fifties, sensible cardigan, her hair neatly done. She smiled and crossed the room as if she had all the time in the world.

'Stephanie?' she said, her voice gentle, almost tentative.

Stephanie looked up, forcing her face into a semblance of neutrality. 'That's me.'

'Thank you for coming in.'

Stephanie gave a quick, almost imperceptible nod. 'I'm only here for Clive. He said it would be good to chat some things through.' She cleared her throat and straightened her back. 'Right, shall we get this over with? I've got a busy day to get back to.'

CHAPTER
FIFTY-FIVE

There was no better feeling than experiencing a breakthrough, especially when you were the one responsible for it. The immense pride, the adulation, and the sense of satisfaction that washed over you as you made the discovery before your colleagues; it was unparalleled and a feeling she was not accustomed to.

Olivia wasn't quite sure how she had managed it, but after several failed attempts, she had located the man she believed to be Mouse. The man who, following his ordeal in the New Forest with the gang of boys, had left St Jude's, fled Surrey with his family, and changed his name. The only issue was that he was now living in Norfolk, a three-hour drive away. A journey that meant she would be away from home for a long time, and potentially overnight.

She raised her hand to knock on Stephanie's door but paused when she heard voices inside. After they stopped, she knocked.

'Come in...' Stephanie's voice was low, almost distracted.

Olivia carefully opened the door and stepped inside.

'I've found him.'

Stephanie looked up from her desk, confused. 'Found who?'

'Rami Krüger. Mouse.' Olivia stepped farther into the room, leaving the door open. 'Except his name's now Felix Krüger. He changed it by deed poll years ago. He lives in a village outside Norwich. I've triple-checked and triple-checked again – it's him, it's definitely him. One hundred percent.'

Stephanie straightened, the cogs in her brain beginning to turn. 'You're sure?'

'I'm *sure*.'

'Fantastic. Well, get yourself ready, we're going down there now.' Stephanie started to rise from her chair.

'I can't go,' Olivia replied quickly. 'I can't leave the boys. It's too far, and I can't afford to leave them alone overnight. God knows what they'll do to the place.'

Stephanie bit her lip, already turning over possibilities in her head. 'You're right. Forgive me, I should have remembered. Someone else...' She glanced towards the Venetian blinds that blocked the light from outside. 'Fiona?'

'Somebody called?'

Both women turned to see Fiona standing in the doorway, her hair slightly windswept, one eyebrow raised as if she had been listening longer than they realised.

Stephanie let out a faint laugh. 'Speak of the devil.'

Fiona smirked, stepping inside. 'And she shall appear. Now, who are we chasing to Norfolk?'

'Have you been there this entire time?'

'I'm a woman. I was born with very good hearing.'

Fiona had opted to drive, saying she didn't get a chance to do it often and loved long-distance car journeys.

'My dad was a big petrol head,' she shared as they slipped off the A3 and onto the M25. 'He had about fifteen different cars when I was growing up: BMWs, Audis, Mercedes, Alfa Romeos, that sort of thing. He bought most of them second-hand, beat-up, and then worked on them in his garage. Proper boy racer, always going to illegal meets and racing around the streets.'

'In Surrey? Really? I didn't think the driving scene was that big around here. I always thought it was more about showing off who's got the biggest shotgun and who can catch the most at the local fox hunt.'

Fiona let out a small snort.

'We had a lot of issues back in Essex with that sort of thing,' Stephanie said. 'Every other month or so, there were dispersal orders in place for people blocking the roads. Especially down Southend way.'

'My dad would've been a part of that,' she said. 'Knowing him, he was probably the one organising it. I don't know what it was about them, but he just loved cars. I remember we would always watch *Top Gear* together on a Sunday.' Her face warmed with the hint of a memory. 'My brother wasn't interested; he was always busy doing his own thing on the PlayStation.'

'You were close with your dad, I take it?'

The speedometer ticked over seventy miles an hour.

'Best friends,' Fiona replied. 'Inseparable. I learned a lot about cars with him. Money was always tight, and we couldn't always go away. He could never afford to take time off, so I just spent the school holidays with him, learning what the different parts did, how it all worked and went together, and then we'd go out for a drive afterwards.'

'I bet you blitzed the driver training at Hendon,' Stephanie joked.

'Without blowing smoke up my arse, yeah. I did all right.'

And it showed. Usually, Stephanie felt uncomfortable doing anything more than sixty, at a push sixty-five, without breaking into a sweat. Yet here they were, exceeding the national speed limit, and she felt oddly calm, relaxed, and safe. It was counterintuitive, but she sensed that Fiona was an excellent driver; she had been in the car with Giles and Olivia already and had feared for her life with both of them. But not with Fiona. With Fiona, she felt secure. Like they could reach a hundred miles an hour and her heartbeat would remain steady.

She glanced over at the constable, her gaze falling over Fiona's thin, slightly tanned arms, her muscular thighs, and her short, bitten fingernails.

'I must admit, I never had you down as a car enthusiast,' Stephanie said.

'You mean because of my athletic physique? Don't let appearances fool you, Steph. I'm just as useless at sport as I am at parallel parking.'

A brief moment of silence settled upon them as they sped past a car in the middle lane.

'Were you close with your dad?' Fiona asked, then realised her mistake immediately. 'Sorry. I don't know why I asked that... I wasn't thinking properly. Sorry. I should've known...'

Stephanie laughed about it. 'It's fine. I mean maybe there were a few days when I was a baby that I don't remember, but for the most part, no.'

'How have you been holding up?'

'Good days. Bad days. Mostly I'm just glad he's out of my life so I can finally move on with it.'

Thoughts of the email she'd received the night before and her earlier conversation with the therapist echoed in her head, and she realised that he would never be entirely out of her life, that she would always have to live with it, but she would have to come to terms with it in a different way.

'I'm... I'm pleased,' Fiona replied, clearly finding the conversation awkward.

Stephanie smiled politely, then turned her attention back to the speedometer: eighty miles an hour.

'At this rate, we'll be there by lunchtime.'

'That's the plan. Then back in time for *The Chase* at five.'

Before Stephanie could respond, her phone vibrated in her pocket. She pulled it out and stared at the screen. Elias. She answered the call.

'Can you talk?' he asked.

'Currently on the M25, fearing for my life, so I might not have long left. Go for it.'

'My team and I have completed the report for Darren Fairhurst's crime scene,' Elias explained, his voice seeming deeper, more mysterious than usual. 'In short, there's not much to say. Just that the fire originated in the kitchen and quickly spread, as I originally thought. Darren's body was found in the same room, in a similar position to the rest of the victims. Though we did notice there was what looked like a plate full of food on the dining table.'

Stephanie chewed on that a moment.

'Did it look staged?' she asked.

'I don't know,' he said, noncommittal. 'All I know are the facts, and that's what we've worked out so far.'

'I appreciate it. Thanks.'

A pause.

'How are you feeling after the other day?'

'Fine.'

'You know, there's a firewalk you could try.'

Her breath caught. 'Are you mad?'

'It'll help. It helped me face my fear a long time ago,' he said. 'It's really not as bad as you might think either. It's all about what goes on upstairs rather than down on your feet. Once you've controlled what goes on in your mind, you'll be fine.'

She chuckled. 'If I could do that, Elias, I wouldn't need to walk across fire in the first place.'

'Fair point. But the offer still stands. If you're interested, let me know, and I'll see if we can arrange something at the station.'

'Under expert supervision, I'd hope.'

'I'll make sure someone else is in charge.'

'That's one less awkward conversation for me to have.'

She thanked him for the update, then hung up. As she set the phone on her lap, Fiona glanced at her.

'Elias? Again? Calling you directly on your mobile?'

Stephanie knew where the conversation was headed.

'Don't even start. There is nothing going on between us, nor will there be. Now pay attention to the road and get us there in one piece, *please*.'

CHAPTER
FIFTY-SIX

Thanks to some unconventional, and probably illegal, driving from Fiona, they arrived at Felix Krüger's house in Norfolk after two and a half hours; thirty minutes quicker than planned.

'I didn't know it was possible to shave off as much time as you did,' Stephanie said as she climbed out of the car, adrenaline surging through her and making her knees weak.

A gust of wind battered into her, almost knocking her off balance and blowing thick strands of hair into her face.

'But did you die though?'

Stephanie touched her chest and abdomen jokingly, then tied her hair into a ponytail. 'If my heart rate's anything to go by, I don't think I'll be around for much longer.'

Felix Krüger lived in a small cottage on the coast of Norfolk, the kind that looked as though it would appear in a rom-com starring Jude Law and Kate Winslet. Its brick walls, covered with lichen, appeared to have been there for hundreds of years, surviving the elements. The air smelled of seaweed, sharp enough to sting the nose, and somewhere beyond the dunes came the muffled boom of waves hitting the shore, carrying with them messages from the other side of the North Sea. A gull circled overhead, letting out a long, complaining cry before disappearing into the grey pillow of cloud. Fiona glanced up and sniffed the air.

'Smells like we're about to get soaked,' she muttered.

Stephanie rang the bell, its faint chime sounding from deep inside the cottage, quickly swallowed by the sound of the sea.

A few moments later, the door opened a crack before swinging wider, revealing a man in his early fifties with neat, thinning hair and glasses that caught the light. He wore a mauve cardigan zipped to the neck and an endearing smile. He was short and looked anything but a serial killer.

'You're here quickly,' he said, his voice gentle. He opened the door wider.

'The traffic was surprisingly light,' Stephanie said, glancing quickly at Fiona.

Felix gestured for them to enter. The inside of the house was neat and bare, with a place for everything and everything in its place. Stephanie got the impression Felix believed that a tidy home equated to a tidy mind, and vice versa. He pointed to his living room at the end of the corridor, then offered tea and coffee.

Stephanie stepped into the living room and had to blink, surprised by how bright it felt for a November afternoon. A patterned rug stretched across the polished floorboards, sitting beneath a pair of cream armchairs angled towards a small fireplace where a single log burned quietly. A low oak coffee table stood between them, stacked neatly with books. The air smelled faintly of the sea and salt from the coast. On the wall, a clock ticked, and a watercolour painting of a lighthouse hung above the mantelpiece.

Stephanie's gaze skimmed a bookshelf in the corner. Books, books, and more books. A cornucopia of religious studies, textbooks, crime, fantasy, and romance. Evidence of a life lived in solitude. Stephanie imagined herself sitting there on a winter's afternoon, enjoying the heat from the fire and a good book, ignoring the battering wind pounding against the windows. Then she realised how unlikely it was, how improbable it would be for her mind to finally stop working and allow her to switch off.

'Beautiful home,' she said as Felix returned from the kitchen. He handed out the drinks, then pulled out a small footstool and sat on it.

'You'd be surprised how much work goes into a little place like this. I've had it for years, and I couldn't see myself living anywhere else,' he explained.

Stephanie and Fiona lowered themselves into the chairs, sinking deeply into the worn cushions.

'How long have you lived here?' Stephanie asked.

Before responding, Felix slapped himself on the forehead with the back of his hand. 'How silly of me – cake! I forgot to offer you some cake and biscuits. Would you like some?'

'No, that won't be necessary.'

'Nonsense.' He propelled himself out of his chair. 'It's lunchtime and you've come a long way. I have lemon cake, red velvet, chocolate, and some cookies. All homemade, except for the cookies; they're store-bought.'

Stephanie and Fiona shared a glance. The offer was tempting, but the thought of eating unhealthy food sent the connections in Stephanie's brain into overdrive. However, she was too polite to decline the offer. They gave him their requests, and he returned a few moments later, shuffling across the floor, wearing a proud host's grin.

'Why do you have so many cakes lying around the place?' Fiona asked, already chewing on a mouthful of her red velvet cake. 'Don't get me wrong, I'm not complaining. I just can't remember the last time I baked *one* cake, let alone three.'

'I get a lot of visitors,' he explained. 'I find that cake usually helps people talk about their problems.'

'What problems are those typically?' Stephanie asked.

Felix straightened his back and placed his hands on his lap. He watched them eat like a proud mother waiting for her children to open their gifts at Christmas. 'Oh, you know, just their issues with life, relationships, work.'

'You're a therapist?'

'Oh, heavens no. I'm a priest. I pass on God's message to them, advising that everything is going to be all right in the end.'

'A priest?' Stephanie repeated, lowering her slice of chocolate cake to her plate. She hadn't eaten any of it yet.

'Yes. You should have quite a few of them in Surrey.' He chuckled.

Stephanie took a moment to absorb that. A killer priest, burning people alive as acts of retribution and justice. Was it possible? A large seed of doubt crept into her mind, beginning to sprout its roots deeper and deeper.

'How long have you been one?' Fiona asked.

Felix pursed his lips, tilting his head slightly as though counting backward. 'Thirty-two years, give or take. I started young, in a small parish in Cambridgeshire. Thought I'd be there my whole life, but God' – he gave a small, almost secretive smile – 'God has a way of moving you about like pieces on a chessboard. I ended up here, and I've been here ever since.'

'And when you say you "pass on God's message",' Stephanie said, still holding her fork, 'how exactly does that work? I mean... how do you hear Him?'

'Oh, I don't hear Him the way you'd hear a friend in the next room,' Felix replied. 'It's more of a... presence. A sense. I'll be reading the Bible or walking along the beach, and a thought will settle in my mind. That's when I know it's Him. My job is to listen, and then to help others listen for themselves.'

'So it's never like' – Fiona waved her fork vaguely in the air – 'a booming voice from the clouds?'

He laughed, shaking his head. 'If it were, half the congregation would run for the hills.'

Stephanie took a slow breath. The cake remained untouched in front of her. 'We appreciate you taking the time to speak with us,' she said slowly. 'Did my colleague explain the purpose of our visit?'

Felix's expression dropped slightly. 'Some old... *friends* of mine.'

'You'd call them friends?'

'Not exactly. Acquaintances, then.'

A gust of wind clattered into the window as he said it. The grey clouds took on a darker shade, and the room became enveloped in it.

'We have spoken with several former friends and school peers of yours, and we understand Nigel, Darren, and Carlos were... very good at making sure they didn't have many friends outside their own group,' Stephanie said.

'That's one way of putting it.'

'And we understand there was an incident involving yourself and the boys in question. An incident involving you and a school trip.'

Felix's gaze dropped for a moment to the carpet, and when he looked back up, the watery hazel of his eyes seemed sharper. 'That's correct. What would you like to know?'

'Your version of events.'

And so he told them of how they'd knocked on his door in the middle of the night, how they'd convinced him to let them tie him to the tree, and how they'd promised he'd be a part of the group once he survived the night.

'I'm sorry you went through that,' Fiona said. 'How did that make you feel towards them?'

'Angry at first. Bitter. Like I wanted to get back at them. But then I spoke to God, and He helped me heal and forgive them.'

'You moved shortly after the incident...'

'That was my mother's doing. She didn't want me in a place where I was going to be bullied every time I went away from home.'

'You changed your name...'

'That one was my doing. When I was of age, I decided to ramp up my faith and become a priest, but I felt like my old name was holding me back. So I decided to change it, to put that part of my past behind me. Plus, it's my grandfather's name, so it's a little homage to him.'

Fiona licked her plate clean of cake crumbs, then leaned forward slightly, resting her elbows on her knees. 'When was the last time you saw Darren, Nigel, or Carlos?'

Felix's brow furrowed as if the question was akin to trying to remember the name of a neighbour's cat from childhood. 'Oh... a very long time ago. Years. Decades, really. I couldn't possibly say when exactly. I believe it was when I left the school.'

Stephanie exchanged a glance with Fiona, then reached into her bag and withdrew a printout of a photograph. It was the image of the fourth boy found at Darren's crime scene, the one whose identity had stubbornly refused to come to light. She laid it gently on the coffee table between them.

'Do you recognise him?' Fiona asked.

Felix reached for a pair of glasses on the coffee table and peered at the image, holding it at arm's length. His lips pressed together, then parted in a small sigh. 'No... I'm sorry. I have no idea who that is.' He sounded genuinely regretful, though Stephanie couldn't tell if it was for the boy or for being unable to help.

She nodded, sliding the photo back into her folder. Then she produced another: a sheet containing high-resolution images of the religious messages that had been left inside the tins discovered at the crime scenes.

She pushed it towards him. 'These were found at the scenes. We're interested in your interpretation.'

Felix didn't touch the paper at first. He sat very still, as though weighing whether he should. Then, finally, he reached forward, his pale fingers brushing the edge of the sheet. His eyes moved across the words slowly, like a man reading a sacred text.

'These are... disturbing,' he murmured. 'I recognise them. They speak of retribution and troubled times. And... whoever wrote them is intent on seeking justice, and I pray for that little boy in the photograph – who I presume is now a fully grown adult with a life and future – that they don't get it.'

So do we, Stephanie thought.

'Were you aware of any religious beliefs amongst Darren, Nigel, and Carlos?' she asked.

Felix thought on that a moment. 'I always sensed those guys were *somewhat* religious. That they had an understanding of the Bible, but not that they necessarily knew as much about it as I did, if you know what I mean? But I definitely got the impression they were religious, but not devout. It was the same with a lot of the boys who went to that school.'

CHAPTER
FIFTY-SEVEN

Kimberley clenched the phone so tightly that she feared she might break it. In that moment, she wanted nothing more than to snap it in two, throw it against the wall, and stamp on the shards until they splintered into a hundred pieces.

Stephanie wasn't answering again; her calls went straight to voicemail. Her sister, the one who had promised to be there for every call and every urgent situation, was nowhere to be found. Kimberley had wanted to believe her, had wanted to give Stephanie the benefit of the doubt. She understood that her sister had a demanding job that required long hours and frequent travel. But this was the second time Stephanie had let her down, and Kimberley wasn't sure how many more chances she was willing to give.

Part of her still resented Stephanie for lying about their parents and childhood, while another part understood and appreciated her justifications. She was locked in an internal struggle, the two opinions battling for dominance. Right now, she had no idea which side was going to win.

To make matters worse, Jordan wasn't answering his phone either.

And there was little point in trying to reach her husband. He was in the city, at work. By the time he eventually answered the call or read her messages and then made the journey home, she would have already seen the doctor.

Could she trust no one in her family anymore? Had they all decided to betray her and create a secret life among themselves?

She released her grip on the phone, unlocked it, and opened the Find My app. Navigating to the friends section at the bottom of the screen, she saw a map of the country with profile pictures of Stephanie, Jordan, and Jason. First, she tapped on Stephanie's face, which revealed that she was in Norfolk.

'What's she doing over there? She never mentioned anything about going to Norfolk...'

Work. She put it down to work. Either that or she'd lost her phone, or perhaps she'd been kidnapped, or was meeting another family member Kimberley didn't know about.

Before she could work herself up any further, she pressed on her half-brother's picture.

He was also in an unusual location: Salisbury.

Again, there had been no mention or reason for his presence there.

And then she checked her husband's location, which was the most concerning. That morning, he had told her he was in Watford for a client meeting that would last all day. Yet, when she looked, his icon showed Romford, Essex.

'That lying b—'

Before she could finish her thought, a sharp pain flared in her abdomen. She clutched it with one hand and gripped the hospital chair with the other, suppressing a groan that threatened to escape her lips. All around her was a small army of ill and injured people, each preoccupied with their own pain and situation, oblivious to her distress.

There had been blood again. More blood than last time.

The sudden pain disappeared almost as quickly as it had come. She had no idea what was happening to her body, to her baby, or why her family had abandoned her in her time of need.

Abandoned her, except for one.

For a long moment, she stared at the screen. Was she really going to do this? Could she?

Her eyes lingered on the Phone icon on the home screen. Tentatively, as if doing it too quickly might cause the device to explode, she prodded the app and navigated to her voicemail. There, dominating the list, were several messages from her dad, spanning before, during, and after his dementia. He had regularly maintained contact, calling her at all times of the day for a chat. She remembered those calls with great fondness; they had discussed work, school, Jason, and even Stephanie. He had been sweet and pleasant.

Before everything had gone wrong.

Her dad had been the only man who hadn't let her down – at least, in their relationship. They had shared a bond, and for a time, it had felt genuine. But of course, it had all been a lie, a façade.

And despite that, her memories of him were warm, sweet, and happy.

And that was what she needed right now.

Pushing thoughts of her sister and what she would undoubtedly say to the back of her mind, Kimberley pressed the first entry in the voicemail log.

'All right, Kimbo? It's me, your dear old dad. Sorry to have missed you. I expect you're probably at work or something, so no need to give me a call back.' A pause. 'It's been raining buckets out here. But it's good because the grass needs it, even if it was only for about thirty-two seconds. I'll have to cut it in the next couple of days once it's grown a bit. Anyway, catch you later. Love you, kiddo.'

Kimberley's body swelled with warmth and the image of her dad staring at the window, looking out at the grass in the back garden. Some of the tension in her shoulders fell away.

She listened to another message. And another. And another.

With each one, she recalled the moment she'd first played the message, the emotions she had felt, knowing that one day, after the dementia had taken hold of him for good, she would never again hear his voice.

Before she knew it, thirty minutes had passed. She didn't even hear the nurse calling her name from across the waiting room.

'Kimberley Taylor? The doctor's ready for you. If you'd like to follow me.'

With a grunt, Kimberley struggled out of the chair and waddled behind the nurse, holding her belly with one hand and the phone in the other, a wide grin on her face.

CHAPTER
FIFTY-EIGHT

Anthony Shore's mother, Carole, lived a few miles south of her son in East Clandon. Now in her eighties, she required a Zimmer frame to help her move around the house. But despite her physical ailments, Giles quickly realised she was as sharp as a tack and still possessed the charm and quick wit she had had throughout her life.

He closed the dining room door behind him and assisted her into a seat.

'You didn't need to do that,' she said. 'But I'm not going to say no to a nice strapping lad like you.'

Giles chuckled awkwardly. 'Careful, Mrs Shore, keep talking like that and I'll be here every day doing the heavy lifting.'

She gave him a sideways glance, her lips twitching into a smirk. 'You'd get bored of me in a week. I'd have you scrubbing the skirting boards and polishing the silver in no time.'

'Imagine what the neighbours would think,' Giles joked, pulling out his notepad. 'But for today, I'm afraid I'm not here for cleaning duty. I wanted to talk about your son, Anthony.

'Anthony? What's he done now?'

'Have you spoken to your son recently?'

'Not for a couple of weeks. Why?'

'He hasn't mentioned anything to you about a situation involving some of his former school friends?'

She shook her head. 'We're not the sharing type. He got that from his father, and his father got it from his father before him. But... why? What's going on?'

'We've currently got your son under surveillance because we believe there's a credible threat against his life.'

'Pardon?'

'A credible threat. It means—'

'Yes, yes. I know what it means. What the bloody hell does it have to do with my son?'

'There have been a string of murders we believe may be connected to Anthony. Do the names Nigel Hadlow, Carlos Vazquez, and Darren Fairhurst mean anything to you?'

It didn't take long for the names to register. 'From St Jude's?'

Giles nodded.

'They were in his friendship group,' she continued. 'They were all very close. They used to go around each other's houses after school and on weekends. What's happened to them?'

Giles explained how they'd died and the potential connection between them. Carole's reaction was one of horror, for several reasons.

'What do you mean my son was a bully?' she asked. 'What do you mean he did those horrible things to those poor people? And what do you mean someone's now killing the people in his friendship group?'

Giles opened his mouth to respond, but Carole let out a high-pitched wail. 'Forgive me. I...' She began panting heavily, clutching her chest. 'This is a lot for me to take in. I...'

'Can I get you a drink?'

'Water,' she wheezed.

Giles slid out from beneath the table and rushed into the kitchen. Inside, he scrambled through several cupboards, throwing them open before eventually finding a glass. As he filled it with water, dread washed over him; the last thing he wanted was for this poor woman's heart to give out right in front of him.

Once the glass was full, he hurried back into the dining room and handed it to her. She thanked him and took a delicate sip.

'Should've asked for something stronger,' she said, some life returning to her voice. 'There's some vodka that's been sitting in a cabinet for the past twenty years.'

'Single or double?'

Carole chuckled, which then turned into a coughing fit as she held the glass to her lips, sipping.

Giles gave her a few moments, allowing the colour to return to her cheeks. When she seemed steady enough, he reached into his inside pocket and pulled out the small envelope he'd brought. 'I know this is a lot to process right now, but we're protecting your son. We can make sure nothing happens to him. But first, we need to confirm that he is under genuine threat.'

'Genuine threat. What does that mean? I thought you—'

'I'd like you to take a look at this photograph.'

He slid the image across the table.

'Do you recognise the boy in this photograph?'

'It's Nigel Hadlow,' she said without hesitation.

'Are you sure?'

'Yes. I recognise him from when they were at school. Nigel was always over, playing out in the garden with Ant.'

Giles slid another photograph across to her.

'What about this one?'

'Carlos Vazquez.'

Two for two.

Another photograph.

'And this one?'

'Darren.'

Now it was time for the fourth photograph. The one they suspected belonged to her son. The one that confirmed who the next victim would be.

He slid the photograph across the table with the same care and attention he had given the rest of them. This time, Carole peered at it over the rim of her glasses. Her expression didn't shift right away, but Giles noticed the faint narrowing of her eyes and the tilt of her head.

'Do you recognise the boy in *this* photo?' Giles asked, his heart pounding and palms clammy.

She lifted her gaze and then shook her head. 'No.'

The words felt like a punch in the gut.

'No?' he asked, suddenly as breathless as she'd been moments before. 'Are you... are you sure?'

'I know what my son looks like, Detective. He hasn't changed since he was a baby. And that most certainly is not him.'

CHAPTER
FIFTY-NINE

What had been a quick, if not terrifying drive up was the complete opposite on the way back. An accident on the A12, followed by a four-mile-long tailback on the M25 at the Dartford Crossing due to a broken-down lorry, had dashed their hopes of a speedy return. By the time they arrived back at the office, it was just after seven o'clock, and Stephanie felt exhausted, ready for bed and a restful night's sleep beneath her freshly washed duvet with her teddy bear, Bart, for comfort.

But there was no time for that.

Giles had delivered a bombshell update she'd spent the entire journey trying to process. Their next victim, the person she and the rest of the team believed was about to die in a fiery inferno – based on the evidence they'd gathered so far – was in fact wrong. Anthony Shore, the car dealer from Addlestone, was not the boy in the photo.

If it wasn't him, then who was it?

Stephanie was the first to enter the office, closely followed by Fiona. At that hour, the office was quiet; only Giles and Devon remained, their eyes glued to the computer screen, sitting in silence. As they burst through the doors, both men jolted at the sound, panic evident on their faces.

'Christ on a bike!' Devon exclaimed, clutching his chest. 'Almost gave me a heart attack.'

'I think a little bit of poo just came out,' added Giles.

Stephanie didn't laugh. Without saying a word, she dropped her things in her office and stormed towards the incident room. She summoned the team by snapping her fingers and gesturing for them to come over.

As if evacuating their homes, the team hurried over, grabbing what they could, spilling pens onto their desks and sheets of paper onto the floor.

When they were finally settled, Stephanie pointed at Giles.

'I need your conversation with Carole Shore. Verbatim.'

'Verbatim?'

'It means word for word.'

'I... I know what it means. I just don't have it word for word.'

'Then as close as you can. If Anthony Shore isn't our guy, we need to be absolutely, one hundred per cent, unequivocally sure. What did she say?'

Giles plugged a tab of gum in his mouth, as if trying to settle his nerves. 'The boy in the photograph wasn't her son. She recognised all the other boys like *that*.' He snapped his fingers. 'Without hesitation. But when it came to identifying her own son, nothing. She didn't recognise him.'

'And you're sure?'

Giles nodded, offering a perplexed expression, as if she'd just asked a stupid question. 'Bearing in mind she recognised complete strangers from forty years ago with incredible accuracy, I'd be a little bit worried if she couldn't recognise her own son. So, yes, I'm certain.'

Stephanie didn't like his tone but conceded that he was right.

'Did she give any indication as to who it might be?'

Giles stopped chewing on his gum, pursed his lips, and shook his head. 'She couldn't place him.'

'Crap.' Stephanie placed her hands on her hips and turned to the incident board. For the first time in a long time she felt lost, out of her depth. She reached for the nearest chair and flopped into it, exasperated, staring up at the board. Letters, photographs, newspaper reports, and maps looked back at her. The culmination of their entire investigation so far. And she was certain there was a link in there, a connection they had missed, something that connected all four boys. But it eluded her, hiding away from view, nestled amongst the details.

So far, the killer had always been one step ahead: calculated, organised, selecting their victims and planning their actions and escape in advance.

Stephanie's eyes fell on a small section of the noticeboard containing the childhood photos of the victims. Three photographs, three victims – with a fourth to come. A list that existed inside the killer's head, known only to them, detailing how many more victims there might be. Meanwhile, they could only play catch-up, following the breadcrumbs left behind at each crime scene.

Was it possible to leapfrog somehow? Get one step ahead? She didn't think so.

'We need to find the next victim,' she said bluntly. 'And we need to do it before the killer gets to him. Looking at the pattern, the killer has struck every couple of days, which means we do not have long at all.' She checked her watch. 'In fact, we have absolutely no time at all.' She propelled herself from the chair. 'Trawl through everything we have. Look for further connections between Nigel, Carlos, and Darren. Have we missed anyone from school? Someone who may have slipped through the net? Someone from the golf club? Someone from Nigel's work or the council? Anyone you think might have had something to do with all three of them? Dig, dig, and then dig some more. We need to uncover every aspect of these men's lives before it's too late.'

CHAPTER
SIXTY

Olivia sat cross-legged on the sofa, the coffee table in front of her buried under ring binders, printouts, and loose sheets piled in untidy stacks beside several cans of Diet Coke. She'd been scanning the same page for the past two minutes, but the words swam before her, refusing to stay together and make sense. From upstairs came the rise and fall of her sons' voices – one laughing so hard he let out a wheezing gasp, the other shouting something about "camping the spawn point". It was a familiar chorus she'd grown accustomed to in the evenings, the thumping of footsteps above her head and the occasional muffled burst of digital gunfire filtering through from their consoles. She loved this time of night, when they were happy, occupied, indoors, and, for once, not at war with each other.

For the next few hours, she had peace. Or at least, some semblance of it.

She reached for the next sheet of paper at the top of her pile. It contained the religious messages found at the crime scenes. The borders of the pages were filled with annotations taken from the internet, notes, and scribbles of her thoughts and ideas. They had been quietly nagging at her for days, like an itch at the back of her mind that she hadn't been able to scratch, thanks to everything else that had been going on. On the surface, the messages appeared to be simple statements about sin, justice, and retribution. But there was something else, something more than just a nod to the victims' past misdemeanours for their bullying and atrocious behaviour.

She didn't believe the killer had anything to do with Nigel Hadlow's property deal, nor that they were affiliated with the golf course in any way.

It was something about the religious notes.

She pulled her laptop from beneath the pile, logged in, and opened HOLMES 2. Her domain. She had been responsible for its upkeep since joining the team, so she knew the software like the back of her hand. At times, she felt she understood its ins and outs better than she did her boys.

On the system, she found an entry from Fiona: the transcript and notes from her and Stephanie's discussion with Felix Krüger, the priest. Olivia opened it and read, skimming over the polite preamble until her eyes landed on a single line buried towards the end:

'I always sensed those guys were somewhat religious. That they had an understanding of the Bible, but not that they necessarily knew as much about it as I did. I got the impression they were religious, but not devout.'

She rolled the phrase over in her head. *Somewhat religious*. She clicked away from the file, ran a quick search, and pulled up an older transcript she hadn't encountered before.

This one was from the interview with Carlos Vazquez's mother conducted by Noah. She scrolled down, past the basic biographical information and into the conversational section of the notes.

There it was.

'Oh, Carlos used to go to Sunday school. Every week for years. St Joseph's. Though he stopped going when he was about fourteen, when girls and football got in the way.'

Olivia felt a prickle at the back of her neck. She moved to the entries that had been uploaded from St Jude's. Amidst the deluge of school reports, sick notes, exam results, and everything else the school had kept on file for their students, Olivia found it: mention of a Sunday school in all three boys' personal profiles. At one point in time, their parents had deemed it important enough to mention to their teachers, who had then recorded it.

Olivia sat back, letting the connection settle, her sons' laughter and banter from upstairs drowning out the noise inside her head.

This wasn't just about their behaviour at school. This was about their behaviour in front of God. And their killings served as a reminder of a past misdeed, a former betrayal. And someone out there hadn't forgotten what had happened.

CHAPTER
SIXTY-ONE

When Stephanie woke up the following morning, she felt a combination of emotions: relief, doubt, and delight.

Relief that there had been no overnight reports of another fire, another inferno, another victim.

Doubt that the killer was still out there, waiting for the next victim to emerge.

Delight at Olivia for unearthing a new, tangible connection between the three boys. A connection that tied them to the religious messages.

'I could have kissed you when I saw your email this morning,' Stephanie said as she wandered across the church car park.

'I love you and everything, ma'am,' Olivia replied, slamming her car door shut. 'But that might be a step too far.'

They met in the middle of the car park with leaves scattered across the tarmac, sodden and heavy from the persistent overnight rain. Overhead, a blanket of grey dampened the mood. Before them stood St Joseph's Church in Guildford. Its original structure was erected in 1860, but the most recent development had been in place since the eighties, perched atop concrete pillars that made it look as if it were floating above the car park.

They climbed the steps and approached the entrance, pushing open the heavy wooden door that groaned in protest. The air inside was cooler and smelled faintly of candlewax. Rows of empty pews stretched before them, their wood polished smooth by decades of wear. Natural light filtered through triangular windows, while a few candles and lights illuminated the darker corners the beams failed to reach.

As they made their way up the central aisle, their footsteps echoed around the hall. As they strolled towards the altar, a door to the side of the chancel opened, and a man emerged, tall and slightly stooped, his black clerical shirt and dog collar stark against his grey tweed jacket. His thinning hair was neatly brushed back, and he carried a set of keys in one hand and a slim folder tucked under his other arm. He froze as soon as he spotted them. Stephanie placed him in his late sixties, but his athletic build and wide frame suggested he might be a few years younger.

'Can I help you?'

'Forgive us for disturbing you,' Stephanie said, offering her warrant card. 'This is my colleague, Olivia. We're here to follow up on a matter involving some individuals we believe were part of this church at one point in the past.'

'I... Of course.' He set the items down on a nearby surface, knitted his fingers together, and let his hands rest by his front. 'Whatever you need, I will be more than happy to help.'

'And your name is?'

'Reverend John Ellery,' he replied coolly.

'Father,' Stephanie began, 'we're looking into three individuals: Darren Fairhurst, Nigel Hadlow, and Carlos Vazquez. From what we've pieced together, they attended Sunday school here when they were boys. We were hoping you could tell us more about that.'

The priest's brow furrowed. 'Sunday school...' He shifted his weight slightly, his polished shoes squeaking against the flagstones. 'When was this?'

'Early- to mid-eighties,' Olivia said. 'Around 1983 to 1985 potentially.'

A faint smile of polite apology touched his lips. 'That would have been before my time here. I came to St Joseph's in the early nineties, so I'm afraid I wouldn't have known them personally if they did attend.'

Olivia shot Stephanie a glance, the flicker of disappointment evident on her face.

'Is this related to the business with the fires?' he asked.

Olivia nodded.

'Oh dear. Terrible. Simply terrible. I've been praying for them.'

'Why?' Stephanie leaned forward. 'What made you say that?'

'It was the only thing I could think of that might explain why you're here. We've seen it a lot on the news recently. I, and the rest of the community, have been moved by their tragic deaths.' His gaze was earnest, and his voice softened by genuine sympathy, which slightly eased Stephanie's suspicions.

'Do you have any sort of archival records for that period?' Olivia asked. 'Membership lists, Sunday school registers, photographs?'

'We do,' Father Ellery replied. 'But not much. It's all pen and paper here. We haven't quite moved into the digital age yet, so a lot of it might have faded over the years. But if you've got the time, I'd be happy to show you to the records room. It's not far, just through here.'

He led them through a narrow side corridor, their footsteps echoing faintly on the stones. The walls were lined with faded photographs of past parish events – jumble sales, harvest festivals, the odd blurry wedding party – all framed in different shades of wood.

The records room was a modest space at the rear of the church. A small window cast a thin stream of light over a wall of steel filing cabinets, each labelled in fading marker pen. The reverend unlocked one and began rifling through the folders, setting a few bulging files on the desk for them to look through.

Stephanie and Olivia wasted no time in scanning the contents: attendance sheets, sermon notes, baptism certificates, and old newsletters, faded from years of obscurity. But they found nothing relevant or tied to the case. No sign of the three boys, no photo of a Sunday school group from the period they were investigating.

'Looks like there's a gap,' Olivia murmured under her breath. 'Records jump straight from '83 to '87.'

'That happens sometimes,' Ellery said, not unkindly. 'Paperwork goes missing. Volunteers come and go. Not to mention some of it might have been lost in the numerous clear-outs we've had over the years. We do our best to keep things in order, but it's hard to keep track of *everything*.'

Stephanie shut the last folder a little harder than necessary. 'Do you know who looked after this place before you took over, Father?'

'Absolutely. I worked under his tutelage for years, and we keep in touch.'

'Is he still with us?'

'Yes,' Ellery replied. 'However, you might struggle. He's currently in a care home, suffering from dementia.'

CHAPTER
SIXTY-TWO

Her body trembled at the prospect of entering another care home, and she hadn't even left the church yet.

As they made their way back towards the church doors, something caught her eye: a small corkboard mounted on the wall near the entrance. One item in particular stopped her – a modern photograph of a dozen grinning children mid-bounce on a brightly coloured inflatable castle, their hair flying.

She stepped closer. 'What's this?' she asked, tapping the glass over the photo.

The reverend followed her gaze. 'Ah, that's from our weekday after-school club. We've run it for... oh, close to fifty years now. One of the longest in the country, if memory serves me correctly. Tuesdays and Thursdays for the under-thirteens, Wednesdays for the under-elevens. It's just a place for the kids to let off steam after school: games, snacks, crafts, and more recently, video games. Keeps them from hanging around the streets.'

'It's run by the church?'

He nodded. 'By volunteers, mostly. Parents, parishioners. We use the church hall, and sometimes the garden out back in summer, when the weather plays nicely.'

Stephanie's brow furrowed. 'And is it open to anyone, or just families from the church?'

'Open to everyone,' the reverend replied without hesitation. 'Always has been, and always will be. People in the community view it as a good thing.'

Stephanie looked at the photograph again. The faces meant nothing to her, frozen in that split second of joy, but she couldn't help picturing Darren, Nigel, and Carlos there, tumbling and laughing in the same space.

She wondered if that was the sort of wider photograph from which their faces had been cut out.

She felt the same emotions again.

Delight, that they'd got a further lead at the care home, even if it meant confronting her demons head-on, and doubt that this revelation had only widened their potential net, moving them farther and farther from the truth. If the killer was a member of the under thirteen's social nights but had no affiliation with the church and was just a general member of the public, they would be firmly back to square one again.

CHAPTER
SIXTY-THREE

They arrived, and every fibre of Stephanie's being wished they hadn't, wished they were elsewhere. Jumping into a snake-infested swimming pool. Anything.

Her entire body tensed. Her stomach was a tight knot. She told herself to breathe slowly and smoothly, to practise the box breathing Elias had taught her, but the rhythm wouldn't come. Instead, her breaths were short, sharp, and jagged. The smell already filled her head. The smell of decay, death, and the slow march of time. A stench that no disinfectant or air freshener could mask.

She hadn't set foot in a place like this since the incident involving her father, and she hoped she never would again. But life had a funny way of doing things you didn't want. It had an even funnier way of kicking you while you were down.

Stephanie sat there for a moment, reliving the events of that day with her father: the discovery of the voodoo doll, the scuffle with Wayne, his care worker, the chase and sudden apprehension on the driveway, the horrifying realisation that her father had masterminded a series of brutal murders, followed by the dreadful understanding that he had escaped.

She blinked hard and gripped the steering wheel tighter, her knuckles whitening.

Olivia glanced across from the passenger seat. 'You okay?'

Stephanie gave the smallest nod, her throat too tight to speak.

'Want me to lead this one?'

'Makes sense,' Stephanie replied. 'Good experience for you.'

Olivia smirked knowingly, then climbed out of the car. Carefully, Stephanie followed her to the care home, her legs feeling like lead. The front doors slid open as they approached, releasing a waft of thick, warm air. They bumped into some visitors who stepped aside to let them through. Inside, the hum of a vacuum cleaner mingled with the clatter of cups and conversation somewhere down a corridor. Stephanie's chest constricted, and her body flushed cold. She gasped for air.

A panic attack. Sudden and all-consuming.

But it was over as quickly as it had begun when Olivia placed a hand on her arm, pulling her from her thoughts.

'You sure you're good?'

'Yeah. Never better.'

Another lie. But it helped her get through.

He's not here, she told herself. He never will be. He's gone.

Before they could step farther into the building, a woman in her fifties emerged from behind the reception desk. Her uniform, a pale lilac top and navy trousers ,was spotless, though her tired eyes suggested she'd been on her feet for ages. A badge on her breast pocket read Sharon Gallagher.

'Can I help you?' she asked, offering a polite but practised smile.

Olivia returned the gesture and explained who they were and who they were there to see.

'He hasn't done what I think he's done, has he?' the receptionist asked.

'Like what?'

She glanced down the corridor. 'Well, you know... you hear stories about priests and young boys all the time. I just assumed...'

'No,' Olivia replied, shutting the conversation down. 'Nothing like that. We're just hoping he might be able to remember a few faces for us, that's all.'

Sharon scoffed. 'You're joking right? He has pretty advanced dementia. He's barely talking. I don't think you're going to get much out of him.'

'We won't know unless we try,' Stephanie said, already starting off in the direction of the corridor. She didn't appreciate the woman's attitude.

'We'll take our chances,' Olivia added more politely.

'You're going the wrong way, by the way. He's down here.'

Stephanie stopped, swivelled on the balls of her feet, and then followed Sharon in the opposite direction, down an empty corridor. They passed open doors, catching glimpses of neatly made beds, walkers parked beside armchairs, and the hunched shapes of residents dozing under blankets. Somewhere, a TV blared a daytime travel show.

Sharon stopped outside a half-open door. She knocked lightly, though she didn't wait for an answer before pushing it open.

'George? You've got some visitors.'

The man inside sat in an armchair by the window, staring out at the skeletal branches swaying in the wind. His hands rested loosely in his lap, long fingers twitching now and then, as if playing a tune against his leg. His face was blank, expression vacant, as if it had been like that for years.

Stephanie felt something shift deep in her stomach. He was sitting the way her father had pretended to, the way he'd convinced her and her sister that he was ill, that he had every right to be there. She was convinced the man in front of her was putting on the same act, and that he would come to life any moment.

'George, this is the police. They've come to ask you some questions. Are you going to help them, George?'

No response. Not even the faintest flicker of recognition on his face.

'Does he know we're here?' Olivia asked.

Sharon shrugged. 'Some days, yes. Some days, like today, not really.'

'Can he talk?'

'Again, some days, yes. Some days, no.'

Stephanie had heard enough. She thanked Sharon for her time and asked her to leave. As soon as the woman shut the door behind her, they crouched down on either side of the man. Olivia produced the photographs of the boys while Stephanie studied George Grant. His body was frail, malnourished, his clothes hanging off him as if he were a child wearing adult clothing. He looked as though he hadn't eaten a proper meal in months. The skin on his face and arms sagged, and a thin sheen of tears hung low in his eyes, reflecting the last few rays of life.

'Hi, George,' Olivia began. 'My name's Olivia. And this is my friend Stephanie. You don't know us, but we work for the police. We're going to show you some photos now, and we wondered if you could tell us who they might be. A little bit like guess who.'

Stephanie raised an eyebrow at Olivia; the woman shrugged, as if to say, it was all I could think of.

'Do you understand, George?' Olivia asked.

The man lifted his head a fraction, a hint of something flashing behind his eyes. Stephanie took that as a promising sign. 'Go on, get this over with. Show him the first one.'

'This is the first photo,' Olivia said as she placed the document in George's line of view. 'Do you recognise the boy in this photo?'

No response.

'His name's Nigel Hadlow. We believe he went to the same church as you in the eighties. It was a long time ago now, but do you remember him?' Olivia showed George a recent photo of Hadlow. 'This was him a couple of weeks ago. This is what he looks like now.'

They waited and waited as George's vacant eyes glazed over the photographs, with nothing to show for it. In the end, Olivia removed the photographs and placed images of Carlos Vazquez on his lap.

'What about this one? Does this boy look familiar to you? His first name was Carlos...'

Still nothing.

Stephanie let out a quiet sigh through her nose. She could feel the minutes bleeding away into nothing, each second turning into a waste of time.

'Let's try the third,' Olivia said, her voice still gentle. She placed the photo of Darren Fairhurst on top of the others. 'This one. Darren. Do you remember him?'

George's fingers twitched against his leg, but his gaze didn't sharpen. He just stared straight ahead, eyes fixed on some point in the photo.

Olivia tried again. 'He would've been about twelve or thirteen back then. Same as all the other boys.'

Nothing. Not even the smallest flicker of recognition.

Stephanie turned to the door. 'Come on. This is pointless. We're not going to get—'

But before she could finish, Olivia said, 'One more.'

Stephanie stopped halfway to the door but didn't turn around. She heard the soft rasp of paper as Olivia slid the final photo into George's line of sight – the grainy image of the fourth boy.

George's breathing changed. Just slightly. A sharp inhale, followed by a slow exhale.

And then he said it.

A name.

It was so soft that Stephanie almost thought she'd imagined it. She turned round to see Olivia's eyes flick up to hers, wide with surprise.

'What did you say, George?' Olivia asked gently, leaning in.

His lips trembled, the sound barely audible. 'Kenny...'

Stephanie froze. The name felt like a shard of ice sliding down her spine. Kenny. Kenny. Who the bloody hell was Kenny?

Her mind raced, the sound of her own heartbeat thundering in her ears. She stepped forward, suddenly back in the room. 'What was his last name, George?' she demanded, unable to keep the urgency out of her voice. 'Kenny who?'

But it was too late. Whatever window had been open in George's mind was gone. His eyes clouded again, and his gaze fell on his lap, expression as blank as the reverse of the paper Olivia had placed in front of him.

They'd lost him.

CHAPTER
SIXTY-FOUR

The moment they stepped into the incident room, Stephanie snatched the marker pen from the edge of the whiteboard and scrawled the name "KENNY" in thick black letters. She underlined it once, twice, and then a third time, the squeak of the pen echoing in the stillness.

Within seconds, the team had gathered around her.

'Who killed Kenny?' Devon asked, the corner of his mouth twitching.

Stephanie shot him a look that could cut glass. Ignoring the reference to *South Park*, she said, 'Not the time, Giles.' He raised both hands in surrender, but she could see the others smirking behind him. 'Yeah, laugh it up, but if we don't find out who this Kenny is' – she prodded the name with the marker – 'then Kenny might very well end up dead, and we'll still be none the wiser about who killed him.'

'Is this our fourth victim?' Fiona asked.

'We believe so.'

'How did you find him?'

Stephanie quickly glanced at Olivia. 'It's tenuous, but a former priest in his eighties with dementia gave it to us.'

Devon snorted. 'Brilliant. Rock-solid source, then. Shall we ask Mystic Meg next?'

Stephanie capped the pen with a snap. 'This is all we've got. So unless any of you have a magic wand hidden away, we're going to squeeze every drop out of it.'

The smirks faded, then the team quickly filed out to return to their desks. Stephanie remained in front of the board, staring at the name as if it were a crystal ball.

'Search through the school reports at St Jude's,' she called to the team. 'Look for anyone past or present with that name. Speak with teachers or pupils at the school. If that doesn't work, talk to the victims' parents, see if they remember their sons hanging out with anyone called Kenny. Turn over every rock, every lead. If someone once walked a dog named Kenny past a victim's house, I want to know.'

Olivia was already pulling files from a stack. 'We'll need to check if there's anyone in Darren's, Nigel's, or Carlos's lives now called Kenny. Anyone from the golf club, for example.'

'Good,' Stephanie said, her eyes still fixed on the black scrawl. 'Until we know who he is, we can't protect him. And if we can't protect him...'

She didn't need to finish the sentence. Everyone in the room knew how it ended.

Stephanie closed the door behind her, leaning against it and letting the air escape her lungs. The quiet of her office wrapped around her, comforting, like a warm embrace. She could still see George Grant's vacant, slack face, but it wasn't his features that lingered; it was her father's. The same posture, the same glassy eyes pretending to be empty when, in reality, something was ticking away behind them. Calculating. Waiting.

Her fingers curled into fists before she realised she was doing it. She took a seat at her desk, rubbed at the ache in her temples, and told herself to stop replaying the scene.

Just then, her mobile phone rang, making her jump. She stared at it for a moment before answering.

'Hello?'

'Hey. It's me.'

Elias.

'To what do I owe the pleasure?' she asked.

'Where have you been? I've tried calling you at the office a couple of times.'

'Doing my job,' she replied.

'Have you checked your emails?'

'Not yet. What do you want?'

'I've sent you the details of the firewalk I told you about.'

Stephanie's body flushed with heat. 'Firewalk?'

'Don't play dumb now, Steph. I spoke to a couple of the guys here, and they were happy to organise it for you.'

She swallowed, hesitated, and began tapping her finger on the table. 'Do I have a choice?'

'Of course you do. One of the guys has invited his wife along, as she's always wanted to do it, so it won't be a complete waste if you don't turn up.'

A sense of relief washed over her. Just as she was about to respond, her phone chimed, illuminating the screen. A text from her sister. She read the message before the preview cut off.

I need to speak to you. Are you free to come over this eve...

'Steph, you there?' Elias asked.

'Sorry. What were you saying?'

'I was just wondering if you're going to be able to make it?'

Stephanie glanced at the screen again.

'I... I... Can I get back to you on that one? Something else has just come in.'

CHAPTER
SIXTY-FIVE

For the past thirty-six years, Stephanie had prioritised her sister above everything else. Or at least as much as she possibly could.

The last few weeks had been a blip in their story. But for the most part, Stephanie considered herself a good sister. She'd cared for Kimberley, provided for her during their time in foster care, defended her, made sure Kimberley had everything she needed, even at the expense of her own desires. She had sacrificed everything to give her sister a semblance of a normal life.

She hated it when they argued. She hated the silence that followed or the way they shut each other out. Sure, they had fought as teenagers, with Stephanie acting like a concerned and overprotective mother, but nothing had compared to this rift. Their family felt fractured, and Stephanie didn't know how to piece it back together. She'd always been the fixer, the one who held the glue and pressed the cracks closed until they vanished. But now, with Jordan in their lives, it felt as though the pieces no longer fit together.

She wanted it to be just the two of them. To rewind, to go back to the days when they'd curl up in their bedroom with a blanket, watch rubbish TV, and discuss the adverts, munching on a bag of popcorn between them.

But as she wandered through Kimberley's hallway and into the living room, there was no sign of popcorn, no indication of a temporary armistice. The air in the room was frigid, despite the central heating struggling against the November chill.

Stephanie let out a heavy sigh of relief.

'What?' Kimberley asked as she settled onto the sofa.

'Nothing.'

'You thought he was going to be here, didn't you?'

Stephanie took a seat on the other sofa opposite to her sister. 'The thought had crossed my mind. Where's Jason?'

'Upstairs, working,' Kimberley replied with the resignation of someone tired of coming second place. 'Says he's got something important to finish up, and that he doesn't want to disturb us apparently.'

'Means we have more girl time. Drink?'

'Oh, yeah. What do you want? I'll get it.'

Kimberley started to rise from the sofa, but Stephanie gently held her back. 'I've got this. I know where everything is. I'm sure I can pour myself a drink.'

'A Coke for me, please. They're in the fridge.'

'Coming right up.'

Stephanie went to the kitchen, poured two glasses of Coke into large tumblers, then returned. Kimberley thanked her for the drink as Stephanie took her seat. A moment of tension settled over them, neither knowing what to say or wanting to be the first to break the silence.

'Do you hate me?' Kimberley asked suddenly.

'What?'

'Do you hate me?'

'How could you say that? You're my sister. I love you more than anything. I could never hate you.'

'Sometimes it feels like you do.'

Where was this coming from?

'That's what being sisters is about,' Stephanie said. 'We're supposed to fight and argue, but at the end of it all, we'll always have each other.'

Kimberley couldn't meet her gaze, spinning her glass with her fingers.

'Do you hate me for wanting a relationship with Jordan?'

Stephanie opened her mouth but paused, reconsidering her response. 'No. I... I think... If you believe it's right for you, then I'm not going to interfere. I just... I'd just like you to respect my boundaries, just as I'm doing for you. I'm not forcing you to stop seeing him, so I'd appreciate it if you could stop trying to force a relationship between him and me.'

Kimberley lowered her head into what Stephanie assumed was a nod.

'I went to the hospital again the other night.'

The words sent shards of glass piercing through Stephanie's insides. 'When...?' Stephanie's eyes fell on the baby.

'When you were in Norfolk. I tried calling you, but then I saw where you were.'

Stephanie moved across the living room to sit beside her sister, placing a hand on her stomach.

'Were you alone?'

Tears welled in Kimberley's eyes. 'Jason was away for work, and Jordan was somewhere in Salisbury.'

'Oh, Kim. I didn't have a signal, and I didn't see any of the missed calls come through. Otherwise, you know I would have called you back... What did you do? Did you get to the hospital all right?'

A nod. More tears. 'I drove myself and sat there alone. I... I listened to Dad's voice.'

'How?'

'Voicemails. I've got some from when he was in the home. I... I just needed to hear someone familiar. I needed him next to me as a last resort.'

Stephanie removed her hand from her sister's stomach. The movement was only slight, minuscule, but Kimberley picked up on it.

'You *do* hate me.'

To prevent her sister from bursting into tears, Stephanie wrapped her arms around her, pulling her close against her chest. But it was no use; the floodgates opened. Stephanie consoled her with empty words and platitudes, while inside she seethed at her sister for relying on their father as a last resort. How could she invoke the memory of that man while she was going through an ordeal such as that?

Before Stephanie could ask what the verdict from the hospital had been, the doorbell rang.

'I'll get it,' Stephanie said instinctively, standing from the sofa.

She strode across the carpet, along the wooden flooring of the hallway, and opened the front door. She froze, her grip tightening on the handle. Standing before her in a smart shirt and trousers was Jordan.

But all she could see was her dad. His eyes, his cheeks, his nose. As if Jordan had torn their father's face from his body and wore it as a mask.

'What are *you* doing here?' Stephanie asked, her voice low.

And then it hit her.

Do you hate me?

Of course, the question had been loaded. Of course it had been more than just a request for approval regarding Kimberley's relationship with Jordan.

'Hey, sis,' he said with a half-hearted wave.

'You don't get to call me that.' Stephanie slammed the door in his face, turned her back on him, then put on her shoes. Grabbing her coat and bag, she flung the door open and barged past him.

'Steph, wait...'

'Don't talk to me,' she hissed as she made for her car at the end of the driveway.

Jordan chased after her, and just as she was about to close the car door, he grabbed hold of it. Stephanie's nostrils flared, and her body tensed with adrenaline.

'Get your hands off my door. Now!'

'I just want to explain myself, Steph. *Please*, I—'

Clenching her jaw, she said, 'I'm giving you three seconds to get your hand off my door. Otherwise, I'm going to put you on the floor. I don't care if you're supposedly my half-brother or just a stranger. I do not know you, and I do not want to know you. I will do it all the same. Now, three...'

Jordan's face contorted with indecision.

'Two...'

Just as she reached one, he let go. Stephanie turned the engine on, slid the car into first gear, and sped away, tyres squealing and engine roaring. She didn't glance back at him in the rear-view mirror, standing there like a lost child.

CHAPTER
SIXTY-SIX

Stephanie barely remembered the drive. The headlights of other cars, streetlights, and the sounds of their horns passed by like a mirage, as if she were sitting on a fast-moving train. She was going so fast that she hadn't even seen the car coming round the roundabout; the one she had nearly crashed into as she entered one of the Surrey Fire Service's training centres. Elias had texted her the location earlier that afternoon, hoping it would persuade her to attend. He stood at the far end of the car park, waiting for her. Looming behind him was a large structure – the skeleton of a long-forgotten warehouse, its metal frame scorched and warped in places from repeated fires. To the left, a double-decker bus sat in the shadow of the main building, its windows shattered and paint peeling away in large, flaked clumps. A ladder leaned against its side, and a faint smell of char clung to its exterior. Beside it, two other vehicles – a transit van and a saloon car – were propped on concrete blocks, their doors hanging open as if left in the aftermath of a crash. Farther back, past the fence line, the tail of an old passenger jet protruded from a separate training area, now riddled with scorch marks and dents. It looked as though it had been plucked from the wreckage of some disaster and placed there to be relived over and over again.

And then, in the centre of it all, was Elias's little setup: a strip of glowing embers, heat visibly shimmering above it.

'You look like you just outran the police,' he said as she approached.

'The way I'm feeling, I'm ready to.'

Stephanie's eyes fell on the glowing embers, her gaze becoming unfocused as it got lost in the charcoal and smoke. Despite herself, despite her recent reactions to fire, she didn't feel afraid; she didn't feel frightened. She was so furious and pumped up that she felt like she could run through one of the training exercises instead.

Kimberley and Jordan...

Jordan and Kimberley...

Do you hate me?

The question rang in her mind.

As did the answer: yes. Yes, she did.

'Where's the other person who was supposed to be here?' she asked.

'They had to pull out,' he said, unconvincingly. 'Some family emergency.'

She slowly turned to him, a smirk growing on her face. In the low light, the shadows from his scars cast a different look on his face. 'There never was another person, was there?'

He looked down, then shook his head. 'I thought if you knew someone else was coming, you'd feel more comfortable.'

'That's quite a gamble.'

'It's paid off, hasn't it?'

Was he trying something here? Was this his way of flirting, and she'd misread the signals entirely? She'd been out of the game for so long – so long that she'd never been in it to start with – that she'd forgotten what flirting and courting were like nowadays. Was she even interested?

'You're going to have to show me what to do,' she said.

'*Show* you?'

'You're a leader. People look up to you. So you should be leading by example.'

'Do as I do, not as I say... that sort of thing?'

'Bingo,' she said, as a small gust of wind lifted the heat from the coals, warming her cheeks and chin.

She watched in silent apprehension as Elias shuffled towards the edge of the path, stepped out of his shoes, and rolled his jeans up to his shins, revealing a set of deeper, more harrowing scars on his legs. In a perverse and oddly sexual way, she wondered what the rest of his body looked like. How damaged and broken it was.

How his wounds were on the outside, and how hers were on the inside.

'Take your shoes off,' he said, 'otherwise it sort of defeats the whole purpose of the exercise. Roll your trousers up, and then stand with your feet together.'

He placed his hands by his hips, puffed out his chest, and looked out at the horizon.

'It's all in the mind,' he said, pointing to his head. 'Keep your head up, your breathing calm, and your mind clear. And then walk...'

Without another word, Elias stepped forward. One bare foot, then the other, pressing down into the glowing trail. The embers hissed and shifted under his weight, little bursts of orange flaring brighter around his steps. He didn't rush. Each pace was deliberate and steady, as if he had nowhere to be but there, in that moment. When he reached the end, he turned back to her, his expression calm.

'That's it,' he said simply. 'You keep your mind where it needs to be, and your feet will follow.'

Now it was her turn. Her turn to confront her fear and touch fire for the first time since it had been forced upon her by her father.

Tentatively, a knot forming in her stomach and a thin film of sweat coating her forearms and lower back, she approached the path, standing in the same space Elias had occupied moments before. She pulled off her shoes and socks, set them down beside her, then rested her arms by her side. Here, the heat was intense; she could feel it around her feet, singeing the hairs on her toes, before slowly moving up her legs to the rest of her body.

'Remember, clear your mind,' he called from the other end of the path. 'If you need to stop, just take one big step either side of you. I'll be ready with some water if you need it.'

But she wouldn't need it, she told herself. As he spoke, something in her mind clicked. If Elias could do it – with all of his scars, the history of his wounds and pain carved into his skin – and look fire in the face the way he did daily, then she could too. It was all in her head. Mind over matter.

Besides, she'd been through worse than stepping through a strip of burning coals.

Much worse.

She stepped forward.

The first touch of ember was a shock, a sharp sting followed by a rush of heat. She ignored it, focusing on her breathing – slow, steady, one, two, three, four – keeping her gaze fixed ahead.

Another step. And another.

The pain was there, unmistakable and unavoidable, but she ignored it, willing herself to stay strong.

Do you hate me? rang her sister's words. Instead of adding fuel to the literal fire beneath her feet, it fuelled her determination, guiding her across the coals.

Before she knew it, she reached the other side, her pulse pounding in her ears.

As soon as she felt the cold earth beneath her, she leapt up and down, shouting excitedly.

'I did it! I did it!'

'Congratulations,' Elias said as he approached. 'Now all you have to do is jump into a fire and you'll be cured completely,' he added sarcastically.

CHAPTER
SIXTY-SEVEN

Her body tingled with euphoria on the drive home. She felt unstoppable. Like she could run a marathon. Like she could climb a mountain. And the best part? Her feet didn't even hurt; she couldn't feel anything at all. The darkness and mirage she'd experienced on the drive down had melted away, and the world took on a new light, a new glow. Every traffic light seemed brighter, every sound sharper. She could hear the melody of the tyres on the tarmac as if it were a song.

Stephanie caught her reflection in the rear-view mirror. Her cheeks were flushed, her eyes wide and alive. The adrenaline made her foot heavier on the accelerator, and she had to consciously ease off, forcing herself to breathe. The doubts, the fears, the shadow of her father – all of it disappeared. She didn't know what she'd been afraid of all this time.

For too long, she had let her fear control and consume her. Not anymore.

However, her sky-high elation was brought crashing back down to earth when she pulled onto her driveway.

She spotted the car a few feet down the road and recognised the number plate immediately. She wished it wasn't him. Wished that she could be faster getting out of the car and into the house than he could.

But it was too late. Jordan was fast approaching by the time she killed the engine and opened the car door.

'Steph, hey—'

'Get out of here,' she snapped. 'I don't want to talk to you.'

She slammed her car door shut and started across the driveway.

'Steph, I just want you—'

She stopped suddenly, spinning around, her face a mask of fury. 'What are you doing here, Jordan? This is my home. You can't just turn up at my home unannounced. You're not welcome here. You're not welcome anywhere. You're not welcome in this family. There's a reason your parents gave you up to Elliot. They didn't want you. And neither do I. So just... just go.'

Jordan froze like she'd slapped him.

For a moment, his mouth stayed half-open, as if the words he'd meant to say had been knocked out of him. The security light caught the side of his face, revealing the flicker of angst before he clenched his jaw so tightly she could see the muscle pulsing in his cheek.

'Right. Got it,' he said deeply. 'I thought we could have had a relationship. Something to make up for the past thirty years, but clearly that's not the case. For what it's worth, this hasn't been easy on me either, all right? I didn't ask for this, just as you didn't. I didn't ask to be born into a mess. I didn't ask to be passed around. But I thought' – his voice cracked – 'I thought maybe with you, it would be different. That we could take all the crap we've been through and... I don't know, build something out of it.' He shook his head, his eyes shining in the low light. 'But instead, you've made it clear you want nothing to do with me. I've been unwanted my whole life. I'm used to it. But I'm not a bad person. I'm not like either of them. I'm different. I'm me. And I thought I could prove that to you. I thought I could show you.'

'By harassing me? By sending me letters? By stalking me outside my house? That's not normal behaviour, Jordan. That is very much how *they* would have behaved, so I struggle to believe you when you tell me you're nothing like them. Because from the evidence I've seen so far, it simply isn't true. Now, I'm giving you thirty seconds to get off my driveway before I put you on it face first.'

Jordan turned abruptly, his shoes crunching against the tarmac, and strode back to his car without another word. The slam of the door reverberated through the quiet street, followed by the growl of his engine fading into the night.

Stephanie stood frozen on the driveway, the hint of a burning sensation beginning to warm beneath her soles.

CHAPTER
SIXTY-EIGHT

The tissues on the sofa beside her gradually increased until they'd formed a small mountain. She hadn't stopped crying since Stephanie's departure, sitting there on the sofa, sobbing into her chest while the television played in the background. Jason continued working upstairs, completely oblivious to the confrontation that had occurred at the front door.

He hadn't even come down to check on her or see what the fuss was about. He was probably just hiding up there, keeping as far away from the drama as possible. Sometimes, it felt like her life was an episode of *Real Housewives*, and she hated it. She hated Jason. She hated Stephanie. And she even hated Jordan.

How had he known Stephanie was there? They hadn't agreed to meet. He must have seen that Stephanie wasn't at home and come over on the off chance she was there. Now, Stephanie probably thought Kimberley had betrayed her, but that wasn't the case.

When did it all go so wrong in their family?

Before she went down that particular rabbit hole, she heard movement upstairs. The sound of footsteps on floorboards slowly made its way towards the stairs. Jason appeared at the bottom of the stairs a few seconds later, phone still in hand, his brow furrowed as he entered the living room.

'Kim? What's going on?' he asked, taking in the pile of tissues, the red blotches on her cheeks, and the way she had sunk deep into the sofa.

She sniffed, grabbing another tissue. 'We had an argument.'

'Is that what all that shouting was about?'

He settled on the cushion next to her, the cushion dipping under his weight.

'So you heard us?'

'Yeah.'

'But you didn't think to come down?'

'I was on the phone.' Jason rubbed the back of his neck, as if hiding something.

'Were you on the phone with the person you were meeting in Romford the other day?'

His eyes widened, though he tried to hide it with a look of disgust. 'Romford? What are you talking about?'

'Oh, don't play dumb,' she snapped. 'You were in Romford the other day. You lied to me.'

'Lied to you?'

'You said you had a meeting in Watford, but when I looked at your location, you were in Romford.'

His mouth opened and closed as he struggled to find the right words. 'You were stalking my location?'

'I was in the hospital, Jase. I needed you. I thought you might be able to come home and help, but then I saw where you were.' She slowed down to catch her breath, on the verge of hyperventilating. 'And then when I asked you how work was, you said it was fine. I even asked what Watford was like, and you said it was "all right". I thought maybe I'd made a mistake, but now I don't think so. What were you doing in Romford? Why were you there, and why didn't you tell me?'

'Why were you in the hospital?' he asked.

But she wasn't ready to talk about that. He didn't deserve to know what was going on with her body, what was happening with their child.

'Don't change the subject, Jason. Answer me. What were you doing in Romford?'

'It was... work. The meeting got rearranged to a different location.'

She didn't believe him. And from his tone, it was clear he didn't believe himself.

'You expect me to believe that?'

Jason's jaw tightened. 'I don't have to defend my every movement to you.'

'You lied to me, Jason. And now you're sitting there, looking me in the eye, and doing it again.'

'I'm not—'

'Don't,' she snapped, cutting him off. 'Don't even try to gaslight me into thinking I'm imagining things. I have the proof, Jase. Your location. The time. The day. You were in Romford.'

His nostrils flared. 'Maybe if you weren't tracking me like I'm some criminal, we wouldn't be having this conversation.'

'Oh, right,' Kimberley shot back, leaning forward, her eyes blazing. 'Because the problem here is me checking your location, not you lying about where you've been. Not you disappearing when I needed you. Not you hiding upstairs tonight while I was down here falling apart.'

Jason stood abruptly, the sofa cushion springing back in his absence. 'You always twist everything to make *me* the bad guy.'

'Maybe because you are,' she replied, her voice low and steady, each word deliberate.

Jason tightened his grip on his phone. 'I'm not doing this right now,' he muttered, turning towards the corridor. He strode to the dresser, snatched up his car keys, and didn't look back. The jangle of metal was followed by the sharp click of the front door unlocking, then a violent slam that made the picture frame above the sofa rattle on its hook.

Kimberley sat frozen for a moment, listening to the distant roar of his car starting and pulling away, before it faded into the distance, leaving her in the heavy, oppressive silence of the house.

She stood, wiping her face with the back of her sleeve.

Then she froze.

There was a warm, wet sensation spreading down her thighs.

She looked down.

Blood.

A dark, thick stream, running down her legs, dripping onto the pale carpet. The sight hit her harder than any of Jason's words. Instinctively, her hands went to her stomach, and her breath quickened in short, panicked bursts.

'Oh God. Oh God, no...'

Her phone was on the arm of the sofa. She snatched it up, her hands shaking so badly that she nearly dropped it, and pressed the call button for Jason's name.

The ringing in her ear felt like it lasted an eternity.

'Pick up... pick up!'

A click.

But it wasn't Jason's voice.

'Hello?'

She froze again. '*Jordan*?'

'Yeah... Kim? You called me.' His voice was wary, confused.

Her knees nearly buckled. 'I... Oh God, I didn't mean to... I was trying to call Jason.'

'Okay... well, you got me instead. What's going on?'

'There's blood, Jordan. A lot of blood. It's...' Her voice cracked. 'It's the baby!'

Silence. Then Jordan's voice became deeper and more urgent. 'Where are you right now?'

'In the house. Alone. Jason's gone.'

'Stay exactly where you are. I'm coming.'

CHAPTER
SIXTY-NINE

The remains of Kenny Musgrave's curry sat congealing in its foil tray on the coffee table. The sight of it made him want to throw up more than he already did. He turned his attention away from it and back to the television, continuing to flick through the channels. Football highlights. The news. A quiz show. Some American drama with people shouting in court. None of it was worth watching, none of it worth his time. Not to mention, he was struggling to concentrate after consuming such a copious amount of food.

His eyelids began to grow heavy as he slipped into a food coma. He slumped deeper into the sofa, one hand resting across his swollen stomach, the other clutching the remote. Just as he was about to give in to the drowsiness tugging at him, a knock came at the door.

A single, deliberate rap.

He jolted upright, the remote slipping from his hand and clattering onto the floor. His first thought was that it was a mistake, that he'd misheard it. But then something settled on him – a premonition, an awareness – that convinced him otherwise.

Another knock followed. This time unmistakable.

He leaned forward, straining his ears. Nothing but the hiss of the central heating and the rain against the windowpane.

Kenny cleared his throat. 'Who's there?'

No answer.

He stood slowly, his knees protesting. The floorboards creaked under his weight as he trudged towards the hallway, pausing halfway. He debated ignoring it, returning to the sofa, pretending it hadn't happened.

Then came a third knock. Louder. Harder.

Kenny's chest tightened. He rubbed his face, wishing he hadn't eaten so much, wishing his body didn't feel so heavy and sluggish. He hovered by the living room doorway, peering through the hallway to the front door, when a vibration rattled against the arm of the sofa behind him. A short, sharp buzz sliced through the stillness.

Kenny froze, then turned his head. His phone lay where he'd left it, screen lit. He shuffled back, picked it up, thumb smearing the glass as he swiped across the notification.

A new message from an unknown number.

It's Bovo – need you outside, mate. Don't make me wait!

Kenny frowned, his tongue stuck to the roof of his mouth. What did Bovo want at this time of night? And why hadn't he called instead of texting?

Another buzz.

Hurry up, mate, it's pissing it down out here.

Kenny sighed. 'All right, all right, I'm coming. Calm your tits!'

He made for the front door without giving it a second thought. He twisted the handle and pulled. The door creaked open an inch, then wider, letting in a rush of damp night air that made him shiver. The man outside was on him before he could react. A tall, imposing figure, much more athletic than him, who looked as if he hadn't just eaten a takeaway for two.

The next thing Kenny knew, he was on the floor, dazed, staring up at the ceiling, trying to comprehend what had just happened.

Then the figure straddled him, sitting on his stomach, which felt like it was about to burst.

Kenny groaned in pain, but as soon as he recognised the man in front of him, he caught himself. In that moment, nothing else mattered. There was no pain, no discomfort. Just shock and pure, abject fear.

'Hello, Kenny old friend,' the man snarled down at him. He pinched Kenny's cheeks and shook them from side to side. 'Looks like you've put on some weight since I last saw you. I wonder what that will smell like when you start to burn.'

CHAPTER
SEVENTY

Stephanie's feet pounded against the floor as she sprinted through the corridors of Royal Surrey University Hospital. Her body shook with adrenaline and panic. Overwhelming. All-consuming. Her breathing came in heavy, rasping gasps, and her heart raced in her chest. She had received the call from Jordan on Kimberley's phone, notifying her of the situation, and had immediately dropped everything.

Her eyes darted from room to room, hospital bed to hospital bed, searching for her sister. Eventually, she found the designated room where Kimberley had been placed. She burst in, the door swinging open violently. There, in the centre of the room, curled into a foetal position on the bed with her back to Stephanie, was Kimberley. Sitting in a chair beside her, phone in hand, was Jordan.

'Kim...' Stephanie said softly, her voice breaking.

Ignoring Jordan, she hurried to her sister's side. She reached the bed and crouched down so she could see her sister's face. Kimberley turned her head slightly, slow and reluctant. Kimberley's eyes were swollen, the skin around them raw from crying and rubbing. But there were no tears left now. Her complexion was the colour of chalk, her lips pale and dry, as if the colour, the life, and the vitality had all been drained from her.

Stephanie reached for Kimberley's hand. It was cold, limp in her own.

'Oh, Kim. I'm so sorry,' she said, tears beginning to form in her eyes. 'I'm so sorry. I wish I had been there. I should have been by your side.'

Kimberley said nothing, continuing to stare into blank space as if she were looking at something far away that no one else could see. Stephanie tightened her grip on her sister's hand, knowing her words were no consolation. Nothing anyone could say would make up for the pain and hurt Kimberley was going through. But she felt the need to keep talking.

'You're going to get through this,' she said as a tear streamed down her face. 'Everything's going to be okay. You...'

Her voice trailed off as her thoughts turned to their mum. She imagined what their mother would have said in this situation, how she would have properly consoled Kimberley and made everything all right.

But their mum wasn't there. For the past thirty years, Stephanie had been playing the roles of both mother and sister, intertwined like two pieces of metal fused together. Now it was time to do it again.

Releasing Kimberley's hand, she pulled back the sheet and climbed into the bed with her, resting her sister's head on her chest. But Kimberley didn't move, didn't flinch, didn't draw closer. Right now, she was just existing.

Stephanie began stroking her sister's hair, just as she had when they hid in the wardrobe or under the bed from their dad, soothing her, calming her down, telling her to ignore the noises.

'Do you remember,' she murmured, her voice low, as if speaking to a child, 'that time Mum found us hiding in the airing cupboard after Dad kicked off and stormed out? We thought we were being so clever, whispering to each other in the dark. And then the door swung open, and there she was with that ridiculous feather duster, pretending to be some sort of witch coming to put a curse on us.' She let out a soft laugh through the lump in her throat. 'You screamed, and then I screamed, and Mum just... she started laughing so hard she couldn't stand up straight. And she said...' Stephanie's voice wobbled, but she pressed on. 'She said, "If the world sometimes feels scary, laugh at it. That way it can't hurt you".'

Her fingers threaded gently through Kimberley's hair, combing out a tangle of knots. 'She was good at protecting us, making sure we were safe.

I know that she's watching over us, watching over *you*, making sure that you're safe, that I'm safe. That we're all safe, and that we're going to be okay.'

Kimberley didn't respond. Her head remained heavy on Stephanie's chest.

Jordan shifted in the chair. The sound was small but sharp in the quiet room, taking Stephanie by surprise. She glanced at his uncomfortable expression; he seemed smaller somehow, as if the news had drained the life from all three of them.

'Where's Jason?'

Waving his phone in the air, Jordan said, 'He's not responding. I've been trying relentlessly, but he's gone AWOL.'

'AWOL? Why?'

'We had a fight,' Kimberley said, her voice barely more than a whisper.

'A fight?' Stephanie repeated.

'I accused him of lying to me, he didn't deny it, and then he stormed out. And then... then it happened.' Kimberley swallowed dryly.

'Does he *know*?'

Jordan shook his head.

'I don't want him to know. I don't care about him. He's responsible for this. He's the reason I've lost my baby.'

<h1 style="text-align:center">CHAPTER
SEVENTY-ONE</h1>

Stephanie woke to a stubborn stiffness in her neck and shoulders, the result of having been folded into an awkward position for far too long. She was only vaguely aware of Kimberley still draped across her, her chest rising and falling softly, her head heavy against Stephanie's arm. She briefly remembered falling asleep shortly after arriving, the stresses and turmoil of the evening having exhausted everyone. Gently, Stephanie stroked her sister's back as she turned her attention to her half-brother.

Jordan was slumped in the chair beside her, his body contorted over the armrests, legs sprawled at odd angles. An uncomfortable night's sleep for all of them. But Stephanie wouldn't have had it any other way; she was happy to forgo the comfort of a bed and warm winter duvet for Kimberley.

Eventually, Stephanie shifted to ease the dull ache in her lower back and let her gaze wander, partly to take in the room and partly to warm up her neck muscles, which were causing her significant discomfort. The room was barren, the walls plain, the furnishings sterile. Stephanie knew they were designed that way, but would it have hurt to include a picture or a fake plant, anything to make the space feel less like a visit to Leanna Moore's office?

And then her eyes fell on the door. No sign of Jason. Had he somehow found out and was refusing to tend to his suffering wife? Or was he still missing in action?

Before she could dwell on it, her phone began to vibrate.

Olivia.

She silenced the vibration before it could wake the others, glancing down at Kimberley. Her skin looked almost translucent in the thin light. For a moment, Stephanie's hand lingered against her sister's back, feeling the faint warmth there. Then, gently, she slid her arm free from under Kimberley's head. The movement caused her sister to shift and mumble something incoherent, but she didn't wake. Stephanie then eased her the last few inches onto the pillow, arranging the blanket to cover her properly.

Jordan's snore broke the silence, and Stephanie watched him for a moment, noting the angle of his head that would pain him later.

She stood slowly, her joints complaining, and stretched her arms above her head, her spine popping loudly. Then she stepped around the bed and exited the room without looking back, letting the door shut slowly behind her.

Just as she was about to answer the call, it cut off. She dialled Olivia, and the constable answered immediately.

'Ma'am,' she said. 'Sorry it's early, but I've just got off the phone with Control. They've got another one. There's been another fire.'

Stephanie held her breath, her lethargic and tired mind beginning to race.

'I can't,' she said, slowly turning to the door. 'I... I have a family emergency. I'm not going to be able to come in. You or someone else will have to attend. I'm sorry.'

Olivia didn't reply immediately. 'Is everything okay?'

'Not really. My sister's just lost her baby. I need to be here right now.'

'If you need anything, you know where we are.'

Stephanie thanked her and added, 'Don't be afraid to keep me in the loop. I'll have a read of any emails if and when I can.'

'Of course, ma'am. Understood. Leave it with me.'

Stephanie hung up and was about to return to the room when someone called her name.

'Steph!'

Jason was hurtling towards her. He looked like he hadn't slept or changed clothes in the last twenty-four hours.

'Steph, what the bloody hell is going on?' He slowed to a stop beside her. 'I've had all these missed calls from Jordan and Kim. What's this about the baby?'

'Where have you been?' Stephanie asked.

'I was... at a friend's.'

'Why didn't you answer your phone?'

'I was... I was drinking. I passed out.'

Stephanie didn't believe a word of it.

'Tell me what's happened. What's happened to Kim? The baby?'

Stephanie didn't respond; her reaction said everything.

Jason's face went slack.

'No...' The word came out hoarse, almost soundless. He staggered back a step until his hand hit the wall behind him, fingers splayed against the white paint. For a heartbeat, he stayed there, swaying slightly, and then his knees gave way. He crouched, palms pressed flat to the wall to steady himself, a raw, guttural sound breaking out of him. He buried his face in the crook of his arm, shoulders jerking with each sob, the sound echoing down the quiet corridor.

Stephanie stood rigid, the phone still clutched in her hand.

Before she could console him, the door opened, and Jordan emerged, tired and confused, rubbing his neck.

'What's going on?'

Jason wasted no time. He pushed Jordan aside and rushed into the room.

Kimberley startled awake, blinking against the harsh light. Her head lifted groggily from the pillow, eyes squinting in confusion until they landed on Jason. For a split second, she just stared as though she couldn't quite place him, and then her expression fell.

'Kim...' Jason's voice cracked. He was already at her side, falling to his knees beside the bed, reaching for her hands. 'I'm so sorry. I wasn't there. I should've been there. Please...'

She recoiled slightly at first, as if the sound of his voice was too much. Then she broke, fresh tears spilling down her cheeks.

Stephanie stood frozen in the doorway, Jordan just behind her. She could feel the heat of his presence at her shoulder, both of them outsiders in this moment between husband and wife.

Then Kimberley's head turned, facing them both.

'Can you... can you both leave us?' she rasped, her voice breaking on the last word. 'We need some time alone.'

Stephanie nodded. Without speaking, she reached for Jordan's arm and guided him back into the corridor. She closed the door softly behind them, but the muffled sound of Jason's grief still seeped through.

CHAPTER
SEVENTY-TWO

Kenny Musgrave lived in a small village called Dunsfold, home to the Dunsfold Aerodrome, made famous by the BBC programme *Top Gear*. Throughout the journey with Devon, Olivia couldn't shake her thoughts of Stephanie. Her maternal instincts were firing on all cylinders, and her concern for the inspector was at an all-time high. Not because of the trauma surrounding Stephanie's family – which was significant enough on its own – but the potential impact it might have on Stephanie's bulimia. Olivia had been quietly observing Stephanie in recent weeks and after everything she had been through, she was pleased to see the inspector looking better. Happier, less tired, more present, and, as far as Olivia could make out, eating properly. Stephanie had got the demons under control.

At least for the time being.

Olivia's thoughts were interrupted as they arrived at the crime scene. Another blackened building, scorched and burnt to a crisp, stood in stark contrast to its neighbours. Their fourth crime scene in less than two weeks. This was getting serious. And Olivia was beginning to feel the pressure. Officially, she wasn't the SIO, but with the level of responsibility and extra work she had been given, the burden of catching the killer felt heavy on her shoulders.

Failure was not an option.

Devon cut the engine, and they both stepped out into the cold air. The house was a hollow shell, its roof partially collapsed. A flurry of uniforms, hi-vis fire jackets, and white forensic suits moved in and out of the property. Crime scene tape flapped in the wind, cordoning off the road where neighbours and a small army of press stood in clusters, whispering among themselves.

Olivia scanned the scene from outside the cordon, searching for Elias. Nothing.

She turned to Devon. 'Where's Elias?'

He shrugged. 'Fighting fires elsewhere, maybe?'

Before she could respond, a man in overalls approached, helmet tucked under his arm. His beard was flecked with grey, and soot was smeared across one cheek. 'You guys with MIT?'

'Yeah,' they answered in unison.

'I'm Trevor Hart.' He offered a brief nod. 'The watch manager for this crime scene.'

'Where's Elias?'

'Been pulled to another incident, so you've got me instead.'

'Have you been briefed on what's been happening recently?' Olivia asked, feeling defensive about who she was speaking with.

'I've been at every one,' Trevor replied.

She swallowed hard. 'All right. Good enough for me. What have we got?'

Trevor quickly turned to the crime scene before looking back at Olivia and Devon. 'The house belongs to a man named Kenny Musgrave. We received reports of the fire at about ten o'clock last night. We managed to extinguish it within an hour or so. Sadly, we found a body on the sofa. We had to wait until daylight before we could begin our search.'

Olivia took a moment to process that. Kenny Musgrave. The boy in the fourth photograph.

'Any sign of forced entry?' Devon asked when Olivia said nothing.

'Not yet. The front door's toast, *literally,* so we can't say for certain. However, the back doors look intact, but their hinges have warped from the heat, so it's difficult to tell.'

Olivia caught Devon's eye before turning back to Trevor. None of that was important right now. There was something much more pressing.

'Have you found another tin?'

His expression fell. He nodded. 'First thing we spotted.'

Olivia's chest tightened. 'Where is it?'

'Over here.' He motioned for them to follow. They stepped into crime scene suits, ducked under the tape, and carefully navigated past hoses and scattered equipment to a folding table set up on the driveway. Trevor reached for an evidence bag lying to one side.

Inside, soot-smudged but otherwise intact, was a small, dented metal tin. Trevor set it down carefully on the table and unzipped the bag.

'I was just about to open it when you guys turned up,' he said, flipping the lid back with a gloved hand.

Olivia leaned in. Nestled inside was the same style of photograph she'd seen three times already. Except this time it was different. This time it contained the portrait photos of two boys' faces instead of one. Both boys smiled thinly back at her, their expressions innocent and in stark contrast to the circumstances in which they'd found the photo. The boys had the same hair – a popular haircut of its time – but that was as far as the similarities went. It was clear to her that these boys were not brothers, as she had first expected. When her sons had been born, she hadn't seen the comparison between them, but as they'd grown older, she realised how uncannily similar they looked. She didn't get the same impression with these boys.

'Two of them?' Devon asked, leaning in to inspect the photo. 'Why are there two of them?'

'That was a rhetorical question, right?' Olivia replied.

Devon pretended it wasn't. 'I know what it means, but just explain what you think it means.'

She smirked. 'If we don't put an end to this, we're going to have two dead bodies the next time we come to one of these things.'

CHAPTER
SEVENTY-THREE

Olivia paced back and forth, gradually circling the car. The trilling tone rang in her ears, amplified by the nerves and anxiety that were quickly taking hold of her stomach.

No answer.

She tried again, this time moving counter-clockwise around the car, as if it would make a difference.

This was bad. The killer was constantly proving to be one step ahead of them. The day before, following the clue gleaned from the priest, George Grant – where he'd only given them a single name: Kenny – Olivia and the team had uncovered Kenny's identity. Kenny Musgrave had attended the same church and weekday social gatherings with Nigel, Darren and Carlos in the eighties. The only problem was that they hadn't been able to track him down.

Until now, when the killer had shown them where to find him.

As she reached the driver's side door, Stephanie answered the call, her voice taking Olivia by surprise and causing her to bump into the wing mirror.

'Bollocks!'

'Everything all right?' Stephanie asked, sounding unamused.

Olivia rubbed her hip. A painful one that would likely bruise and be sore for the rest of the day.

'Fine. Sorry... sorry to interrupt you again, ma'am—'

'Is it important, Olivia? I'm still at the hospital. I need to be with my sister and can't afford to spend too much time away from her.'

'No. Of course not. I understand. I...'

This was a mistake. She shouldn't have called. She should have trusted herself and Devon to handle it.

She glanced back at the crime scene, where Devon and Trevor were discussing the incident amongst themselves.

'We found another tin,' she said finally.

Silence. For a moment, Olivia thought the call had disconnected.

Then, a sigh echoed through the microphone.

'I'd be lying if I said I was surprised,' Stephanie replied.

'You will be when I tell you there were two photographs instead of one.'

A pause. A sharp inhalation.

'*Two*?'

'Two boys in the same photograph, arms wrapped around one another.'

Another pause, this one longer and more telling.

'Thanks for letting me know,' she said eventually, a hint of resignation in her tone. 'I'd love to be there, but I can't leave my sister. You... you, Devon, and the rest of the team are going to have to manage until I get back.'

'When will—'

'I don't know. But soon. Maybe tomorrow. You and the team will have to handle this one without me.'

'Okay...' Now it was Olivia's turn to sound resigned.

'Start by identifying the boys in the photograph. Speak with everyone we've already interviewed, especially Anthony Shore's mother and George Grant at the care home. They might recognise the boys and provide us with some names. Failing that, look into the church and the after-school club. Find a connection between the victims. Determine the link between the two potential victims. Why are they in the same photograph? It must have been done for a reason. Find out why, and do it as quickly as you can. You have everything you need. But call me if you need anything. I'll help where and when I can.'

'Thanks, Steph. We'll get right on it.'

Olivia hung up, pocketed her phone, inhaled deeply, and puffed her chest out, suddenly feeling a renewed sense of determination and confidence.

CHAPTER
SEVENTY-FOUR

The vending machine hummed to life, the coil rotated, and the packet of crisps edged forward, then jammed halfway, dangling just out of reach as if mocking her.

'Bloody thing,' she muttered under her breath, jabbing the enter button again.

Nothing.

She jabbed it repeatedly, hoping it would work, but it didn't. Next, she pounded her fist on the window. Still nothing. Then she banged the side of the machine with the heel of her hand. The packet of crisps remained firmly in place.

Crouching down, she peered into the narrow slot, as if glaring at it might scare it into releasing its hostage. Her stomach growled in response.

Another thump, harder this time. The machine rattled but refused to surrender. She hooked her fingers through the flap, stretching until her knuckles scraped the plastic guard. The packet was too far, just out of reach.

Behind her, a voice rasped, 'I got my hand caught in one of those things once.'

Stephanie straightened and spun around to see Jordan leaning in the doorway, his hair sticking up on one side.

'Super embarrassing,' he continued as he entered the room. 'The guys who owned the shop had to come and pull my hand out... with the help of the fire brigade and some lubricant. By the end of it, there was a massive crowd cheering me on.'

Stephanie raised an eyebrow. 'Sounds like the machine won.'

'It didn't win,' he said, mock offended. 'I got my packet of crisps in the end.'

'After humiliating yourself in front of half the town.'

'You win some, you lose some.' He came to stand beside her, peering into the machine. 'What are you even fighting for? Prawn cocktail? You know those are basically a war crime, right?'

'They're the only ones left that aren't cheese and onion,' she shot back, taking offence. 'And I'm starving. I'll eat anything right now.'

Jordan tutted, gestured for her to move aside, then placed both hands on either side of the machine. 'The trick is to give it a massive shake,' he said. 'Like you're taking it by surprise. This is where the finesse comes in.'

'That's what you call it?'

'All my years of experience have been leading up to this moment.'

With a grunt and a moan, he rocked the vending machine left and right, until it looked like it was almost ready to topple over. After a few swings, the packet of crisps, along with a small packet of Skittles abandoned by a previous shopper, fell down the hole.

Jordan reached into the tray and handed them to her.

'Rescued from the jaws of capitalism.'

Stephanie took them, though she made a point of not looking too impressed. 'You've peaked in life,' she said.

'It's as good as it gets for me. Good thing I came when I did, otherwise, you might have needed to call the fire brigade.'

A thin chuckle broke at the corner of her mouth, and she did her best to hide it. She had realised as soon as she'd seen him at the hospital that she would have to be nice, to be civil, to maintain an unspoken truce between them. She didn't need to speak to him, but when she did, it would be amicable and friendly. For Kimberley's sake.

Jordan leaned against the machine, hands in pockets, watching her closely, eager to say something. 'You know, Kimberley didn't mean to call me, by the way,' he said after a pause. 'It was an accident. She meant to call Jason, but she just pressed the first name she saw with a J, and it went through to me instead.'

Stephanie froze mid-crunch. She didn't know what she was expected to say to that. She appreciated his honesty, but her walls were up, and it would take much more than that to bring them down.

'I'm just glad she got through to one of us,' she said coldly. 'I can't begin to imagine what would have happened if she didn't.'

'Yeah. She was... well, you know. Not in a good way.' He glanced at the floor for a moment before looking back at her. 'But I know for a fact she would have preferred you there over me or Jason.'

Stephanie remained silent, swallowing the lump forming in her throat.

'But I wasn't,' she said. 'I let her down.'

'You could never let her down, Steph. She adores you. Worships you. She's always telling me how you've always been there for her. How she wouldn't have got through half the crap in her life without you.' His voice softened. 'She's proud of you, Steph. Always going on about the cases you've cracked, the hours you put in, the way you've got her back no matter what. You're basically her hero.'

Stephanie's throat swelled with an unexpected lump. She hadn't been expecting this reaction from him, nor had she anticipated it from herself. The walls were slowly beginning to come down.

She looked down at the crumpled crisp packet in her hands, suddenly unsure what to do with her fingers. 'She's my sister. I'd do anything for her. I just... I just wish she'd say some of this to me.'

'Maybe she thinks you already know,' Jordan said gently. 'It's always easier to say these things to other people than it is to the person directly. But I know that she means it.'

Stephanie let out a long breath. 'Maybe you're right. Thanks,' she said quietly, surprising herself with how much she meant it.

Jordan gave a little shrug, as if to say it was nothing. 'You had a right to know. I know things have been quite tumultuous between both of you recently.'

She hesitated, then turned to face him properly. 'Look... I know I've acted like a bitch these past few weeks, but... but it's been strange, tough. It hasn't been easy for me, knowing that we're somehow related. I didn't want to believe it's real – and a part of me still doesn't – but you've been there for Kimberley whenever I haven't, and for that I'm grateful. So I guess what I'm trying to say is that I'm sorry, and that I should maybe come to terms with the fact that you're a part of our family whether I like it or not. For Kimberley's sake, and my own.' She cleared her throat. 'I'm not very good at this soppy stuff, if you couldn't tell.'

'Had me fooled,' he replied with a chuckle.

Stephanie allowed herself the smallest of smiles. 'Don't get used to it.'

Jordan's grin softened into something quieter, warmer. 'I'm not looking for you to like me, Steph. Though maybe one day I hope you will. I just want Kimberley to have both of us in her life. That's all. She needs us right now. Both of us.'

Wasn't that the truth.

She met his gaze then, really met it, and for a long moment, neither of them spoke. There was no point pretending she didn't see the truth in his eyes.

She held out the packet of Skittles to him. 'Peace offering?'

His expression flickered with surprise before he took them. 'Guess I'll take what I can get. Thanks.'

CHAPTER
SEVENTY-FIVE

As Stephanie opened the front door to her home several hours later, she was welcomed by a suffocating silence and stillness. The place had been empty for more than twenty-four hours, yet the atmosphere felt different. It was as if a dense cloud of grief and guilt hung low over the building, seeping through the walls and permeating the air. With every step, Stephanie breathed it in.

She stood there for a few moments, having stepped out of her shoes and dropped her belongings onto the kitchen counter, before she headed straight for the upstairs bathroom. She hadn't washed; she felt sweaty, smelly, and needed to cleanse herself of the day's horrors.

Her mind running on autopilot, she switched on the shower, undressed, and stepped in.

The water hit her skin hot and relentless, pounding against her shoulders, a suitable punishment for what she felt she deserved. At first, she focused on the sensation – the steam curling around her face, the sting where the water hit too hard – anything to distract her from the thoughts beginning to well in her mind.

But they crept in anyway.

Images she hadn't wanted to picture before now came regardless: a newborn's tiny fist curling around her finger; Kimberley smiling in a way she hadn't seen in years; the pride of announcing that she was going to be an auntie.

And then the image shattered. A hollow ache formed in her gut, spreading heavier and heavier until she could no longer stand. Her hands slid down the tiled wall as she crouched there, letting the spray beat against her back. With her forehead pressed to her knees and her hair plastered to her cheeks, tears mingled with the water streaming off her.

For a while, she stayed like that, the sound of the water drowning out the ragged sound of her breathing. She thought of Kimberley in that hospital bed, pale and still. She reflected on all the things she should have said, the times she should have been there, and the moments she had let her sister down.

It wasn't just the loss of a child; it was the loss of what it meant for all of them. The birthdays that would never happen, the family photos that would never be taken, and the fracture in Kimberley's marriage that had emerged from it all.

She wanted to stay out of their relationship – what happened between them stayed between them – but it was impossible not to see the signs. The signs that had been brewing for weeks.

When she finally lifted her head, her skin was red and raw, yet she still felt unclean.

She turned off the tap and sat in the sudden silence, dripping and empty. Deep down, she knew she would have to get up, dry off, and face whatever the future brought. But for now, she just stayed there, allowing the last drops of water to trail down her spine and the final tears to dry on her cheeks.

CHAPTER
SEVENTY-SIX

Her feet were firmly rooted to the ground once more, as the fire raged in front of her, flames consuming the sides of the building. Smoke filled the air, thick and acrid. Intense waves of heat battered her face and arms, curling the ends of her hair.

Before long, the sound of screams reached her.

But this time, it was different. There was only one person screaming. And another noise – worse, shrill, far more devastating. The sound of a baby crying, wailing, begging for survival. Stephanie's head snapped upward, her eyes scanning the jagged shapes of shattered windows until she found the source of the noise.

Kimberley.

She was framed in the smoke, one arm cradling a bundle pressed desperately to her chest. Even from a distance, Stephanie could see the way her sister's lips moved, shouting something she couldn't hear over the roar of the fire.

Yet the baby's cries sliced through the chaos.

Stephanie's stomach twisted into knots. Her sister and nephew were inside, desperate and dying. It didn't matter that she had no formal training – a firewalk was hardly the same as jumping into a fire – but she knew that she had to move, to do something. To protect her sister the way she'd failed to do so many times in the recent past. Every instinct screamed at her to do something. Kick down a door, climb a drainpipe, anything to get them out before the flames closed in.

She was about to move when a figure came into view, rounding the side of their childhood home. The fraud. The intruder. The person who hadn't been part of their lives, the person who hadn't even entered their childhood home before. Jordan. He had no right to be near it. This was their home, their space. But that didn't stop him; his eyes locked on the same window she had, instantly zeroing in on Kimberley and the child. There was no hesitation, no pause.

'Stay back,' he barked over the noise, already moving towards the front door of the property.

But she paid him no heed. Fists clenched, her legs jerked into action, almost of their own volition. She sprinted across the driveway, surging past Jordan, and came to a stop by the front door.

She froze. Already she could feel the intensity and ferocity of the heat burning within.

You can do this. If you can walk on fire, you can run through it, she told herself.

Without thinking, she lifted her leg and kicked through the door. A backdraft blew in, exploding a fireball in her face and launching her backwards. All she could smell was her singed hair. She continued regardless, shielding her face with her arm as she entered the front door. The place glowed a deep, dark orange, the ceiling smothered in dense, black smoke. The intensity of the fire sucked the oxygen from her lungs. Immediately, she began to understand how Nigel Hadlow and the other victims had felt in their final moments as the fire and flames began to take hold of their bodies.

A series of screams from upstairs pulled her from her reverie. Access to the top floor was open. She raced towards the bottom step and began climbing, cautious not to touch the walls or banister, lest she burn the skin on her fingers.

To her surprise, the fire had not yet claimed the building's structural integrity, and she was able to climb the stairs with ease. For a moment, she even thought she heard the familiar sound of floorboards creaking beneath her feet.

When she reached the top step, everything became eerily silent, save for the sound of her breathing and the distant echo of Kimberley and her baby in their parents' bedroom. Stephanie approached. The door was locked.

Before, when she'd come across that room, something had held her back, prohibiting her from entering. This time, she didn't hesitate; she kicked the door open, just as she had downstairs moments before, and crouched down, anticipating the backdraft that blew in over her head.

Her forearm burning, she dived into the bedroom and made for her sister. She found Kimberley tucked in the corner, cradling her baby against her chest.

Stephanie grabbed Kimberley by the arm and dragged her out, arms draped over her sister as they went. Moments after they left their parents' bedroom – the place that had witnessed so many horrors over the years – the roof collapsed and imploded in a fireball.

They descended the stairs carefully, holding their breath and shielding their faces.

At the bottom of the steps, light began to bleed into the hallway, signalling their exit. Stephanie felt a renewed sense of determination grow within her. This was it. The final push.

She tore through the door, and they burst into the sunlight, coughing and spluttering, choking up the contents of their lungs onto the driveway. It was relentless. But as onlookers quickly began to surround them, Stephanie became aware that she could only hear noise coming from her sister.

The baby's crying had stopped.

Stephanie took the baby from her, but it felt heavy and limp in her arms.

She didn't need to unwrap it to know that it had died, that it had succumbed to the fire, that she hadn't been able to save it – in real life or even in a dream.

CHAPTER
SEVENTY-SEVEN

Stephanie made sure she was in first thing the following morning so that she could get a head start before the rest of the team arrived. They had sent their daily reports at various times throughout the evening before, and she had been skimming them since five o'clock, trying to distract herself from the nightmare that had kept her awake.

She was halfway through Devon's report when the first person entered the office.

Olivia.

'Morning, ma'am,' the detective constable called out, dropping her bags by her desk. 'I didn't think we'd see you in today. Is everything sorted with the hospital?'

'As sorted as it can be,' Stephanie replied, stepping out from her desk. She joined Olivia in the kitchen, where the coffee machine sputtered to life.

'When was the last time you slept?' Olivia asked.

'Properly? About 1995. Recently? A few days ago. Hospital beds aren't all they're cracked up to be.'

'I don't think anyone in the entire history of the universe has ever said they'd rather sleep in a hospital bed than their own.'

Stephanie chuckled as she pressed the latte button on the machine and waited for its gears to kick into action. Olivia hovered beside her, looking as if she wanted to say something.

'Was it...? Is it...? How is...? I'm so sorry, Steph,' Olivia eventually said, placing a firm hand on Stephanie's upper arm. It was a small gesture, but Stephanie appreciated it, nonetheless.

'We're fine. I'm fine. The best way to process it is to do what I do with everything: bury my head in the sand and immerse myself in work to forget about it.'

'That's not healthy.'

'Since when is anything I do healthy?'

Olivia had no response. The coffee machine finished brewing, and Stephanie took her cup back to the office. When she entered, everyone except Giles had arrived, dressed in raincoats, their hair damp from the persistent light rain that had been falling since she woke up.

'Morning, everyone,' she called. 'Good to see you all so early. I want an update on the state of play, so get yourselves settled and in the incident room in five minutes.'

A little over five minutes later, the team sat in front of her in the incident room. Giles had rushed in at the last minute, the only one without a hot drink to ward off the chill in the office.

'Apologies for throwing everything into disarray yesterday,' she began, 'but I appreciate you all having the professionalism to deal with everything in my absence.' She turned to the incident board, noticing that someone had added Kenny Musgrave's name, photograph, and location. Her eyes flicked to the latest photograph of the two boys. 'This is not going away, nor is it getting any better. And now we potentially have two more victims coming soon. But first: where are we with our fourth victim? What do we know about him?'

Devon was the first to speak. 'His name was Kenny Musgrave. Fifty-three years old, same as the other victims. He lived alone and worked as a financial auditor. He ran his own company, registered on Companies House, but it's just him.'

'We've spoken with his neighbours, and they described him as an amenable person,' Noah continued. 'Friendly. Never got on the wrong side of anyone and looked out for a couple of neighbours when they were going through some financial issues with their car.'

Stephanie nodded. 'What about anything helpful? Connections with Nigel Hadlow, Carlos Vazquez, and Darren Fairhurst?'

'I spoke with Musgrave's dad,' Fiona said, picking at her fingernails as she spoke. 'And, well, he wasn't much help, to be honest. Apparently, he wasn't present for much of Kenny's life, so he didn't recognise either of the boys in the latest photograph. He did, however, confirm that Kenny went to a different school than the other victims and attended the after-school church club on weekdays when he was growing up. He remembers that because he had to pick him up from there a couple of times.'

'So all four victims, and potentially the next two, are from the church's after-school group and not St Jude's?' Stephanie repeated for her own benefit. 'Was Kenny religious at all?'

'His mum was,' Fiona continued. 'That's why he went to the after-school club, and it was also part of the reason his parents separated. But his dad didn't say whether he attended church on the weekends. Like I said, they didn't see much of each other.'

'Is there anything connecting the four victims beyond the club?'

Silence filled the room, with blank faces staring back at her. She couldn't expect too much for one day.

'Very well,' she said. 'Devon and Noah, I want you working on that now. Look into message histories, phone and financial records. Anything that suggests the four of them might have met up in the past few months.' She turned to the other side of the room. 'Giles, Fiona and Olivia, I need you to find out who those two boys are. Are they brothers? Best friends? Or is one of them the killer and the other the next victim? This is the priority. We've been one step behind this bastard the entire investigation. We can't allow him to take two more lives. We—'

Suddenly, a door on the other side of the office opened. DCI McGowan appeared out of the corner of her eye, slow and methodical, cutting her off. She quickly lost her train of thought.

'Inspector,' he said smoothly. 'When you're finished, might I borrow you?'

He said it so calmly, so quietly, yet why did she feel like she was being summoned to the headteacher's office?

After he disappeared into his office, she turned back to the team. Stuttering and distracted, she said, 'You all know what you're doing. You all know where I am if you need me. Let it rip.'

CHAPTER
SEVENTY-EIGHT

Stephanie declined the offer of a seat.

'Sure?' McGowan asked.

'Positive, sir. I've been sitting for almost twenty-four hours. My lower back could do with a rest.'

Clive fiddled with some pieces of paper on his desk awkwardly. 'How... how is *everything*?' he asked finally.

'She lost the baby.'

Clive dropped the documents and stared at her blankly. For someone in a senior position with years of experience, he looked, for the first time since she'd known him, as if he didn't know what to say.

'That's horrible,' he replied. 'I'm so sorry to hear that. Please pass on my condolences to your sister. If they need anything, I'm sure... I'm sure we can help.'

'I appreciate that, sir. But right now, I don't think anything can fill the gaping hole currently lodged in their lives.'

And their marriage.

'Of course,' he said softly. 'The offer still stands.' He paused, returning his attention to the papers again. 'I'm sure this is a tough time for your family. And I'm sure it's tough for you also, Steph.'

Stephanie quickly reached for the door. 'We don't have to do this, I have—'

'And it would be remiss of me not to consider how you're feeling during all this. I have a duty of care to you, just as much as anyone else. Even though I see you putting on a brave face for everyone, I've seen it enough times and experienced it myself to know when someone's struggling.'

'Sir...'

He raised a hand to silence her. 'You don't have to pretend you're okay when you're not. If... if things are getting too much, with life and the investigation, then you need to let me know.'

'Sir,' she said with a huff. 'With all due respect, thanks but no thanks. I know what I'm like. I know how to deal with trauma. I've been through it enough times to have a degree in it. But honestly, I'm fine. All I need is to get my head back in the game and focus the team on this investigation. Too many people are dying on my watch, and we need to make sure nobody else does.'

He laced his fingers together and stared at her blankly. 'Do you need support?'

'No. I have full faith in my team, and I have full faith in this investigation.'

'What suspects do you have?'

She opened her mouth, expecting a different question that she could quickly deflect, but no words came out. She had no answer. There were no suspects. Just more and more children who'd grown up leading different lives, all connected to something from their past that was now coming back to haunt them.

'We're working on all active lines of enquiry,' she responded.

He let out a small scoff. 'You know who you're talking to, right? That line might work on members of the public, but sadly not with me. I wish it did; it would make my life a lot easier.'

She lowered her gaze to the floor. 'You're right. Sorry, sir. We don't currently have any suspects.'

'And the identities of the two boys in the latest photograph?'

'A top priority for us,' she admitted. 'I myself will personally be heading up some of the interviews with the necessary people.'

That seemed to appease him momentarily. She cut in before he could respond.

'With all due respect, sir. I appreciate your concern. But I don't have time for this. I'm fine, and I will continue to be fine. Right now, I need to get out there and do something because two lives depend on me.'

She opened the door and left the room without giving him the opportunity to reply.

CHAPTER
SEVENTY-NINE

This time, the care home didn't seem as imposing or terrifying. Instead, it looked smaller, dirtier, more like an abandoned building than a place for the dying. The last time she'd walked through those doors, her chest had tightened, her palms had been slick with sweat, and her mind had spiralled with torment. Now, as Stephanie parked and stepped out of the car, there was none of that. No heart palpitations. No difficulty breathing. No voice in her head urging her to turn back.

She strode purposefully across the gravel, her coat drawn tight around her and her hair blowing in the wind. She found the receptionist, Sharon Gallagher, behind the counter and introduced herself.

'Here for George Grant,' Stephanie explained as she signed in on the register.

Sharon wasted no time rounding the desk and leading her down the corridor. Instead of going their previous route, the receptionist took her down another long corridor. They passed bedrooms filled with the tinny sound of cheap televisions and the stench of antiseptic spray battling an overwhelming smell of urine.

The place reeked of death and decay. And Stephanie had seen enough of it in her lifetime to know she didn't want to end up in a place like that, wasting away to nothing but skin and bones. A quick and painless death was the way she wanted to go. As little suffering for her loved ones as possible.

A few moments later, they entered the communal living room. At the head of the room was a large television screen playing some innocuous daytime programme that helped drown out the silence. Around the perimeter was a row of high-back cushioned chairs. The space was predominantly occupied by women, outnumbering the men almost ten to one. Stephanie offered them all a warm smile, waving at each of them as they stared blankly, their minds trying to decipher who she was and whether they knew her. Despite the room's morbidity, the patients seemed to be in good spirits. Those who could talk – an ability not yet claimed by Alzheimer's – engaged in conversation, while those lucid enough to wave back did so.

At the back of the room, tucked into a corner, sat George Grant, hunched over and staring at the floor. A female patient was muttering something to him, but he ignored her. As they approached, he became more aware and lifted his head slightly.

'George, you have a visitor, my darling. Her name's Stephanie. She's got something to show you.'

George blinked slowly, his eyes rimmed with red and his cheeks sunken. He looked smaller and frailer than she remembered, as if the weight of his body was caving in on itself. Yet there was still something in his gaze, something hidden behind his eyes, that suggested he wasn't *nearly* as gone as the others.

Stephanie crouched a little to get on his level. The receptionist gave her a quick glance before retreating to the edge of the room, giving them privacy while still observing.

'Hello, George,' Stephanie said gently. 'Do you remember me?'

His lips twitched, but gave nothing away.

'I've got something I'd like you to look at.'

She slipped her hand into her coat pocket, her fingers brushing against the edge of a plastic sleeve. When she pulled it free, the photo inside caught the light. She held it up so he could see.

'Do you recognise the boys in this photo?' she asked, calm and controlled. She realised she needed to exert a certain level of patience, much easier said than done without Olivia there to do the job for her.

George's eyes flicked to the photograph. For a second, there was nothing. Just the same distant, clouded stare that he'd given them last time. But the longer he looked, the more his expression shifted. His pupils dilated, his eyes widened, and his lips trembled before curling upward.

'They're very pretty.'

At first, she didn't hear it. But when the woman beside George repeated it, she realised what had happened. The woman to George's right had leaned across him, reaching for the evidence bag.

'They're very cute little boys,' the woman repeated.

Before Stephanie could respond, George nodded. 'Yes,' he whispered, his voice rough and papery. 'Very pretty indeed. I always liked them at that age.'

Stephanie's skin crawled. The way he said it wasn't innocent. The light behind his eyes wasn't illuminating the thought of childhood choirs or parish games. There was something else there. Something darker.

She didn't let herself react, though every fibre in her body wanted to recoil. Instead, she kept her tone level, professional and detached. 'You liked them at that age?'

George's eyes never left the photograph. His breathing had grown shallow and uneven, as if the images had stirred him from the fog more than any medication ever could. 'So soft, so trusting,' he murmured. 'It was the best time. Before the world and puberty ruined them.'

Stephanie felt bile rise in her throat. She reached into her pocket again, pulling out a second sleeve. Another photograph. Another victim. She held it up, watching him carefully.

George's reaction was immediate. His lips curved upward again. 'Yes. Pretty. I liked him too.'

Another photo. Nigel Hadlow's. Again, the same words. 'Pretty. Just the right age.'

Her pulse hammered in her ears, but she pressed on, her hands steady though her insides churned. One by one, she laid the photos out on her knees, each image of a victim eliciting the same response from him.

And then she slid the last photo across. Kenny Musgrave.

For the first time, George's hand twitched, creeping forward, trembling as it pressed against the plastic. There was a light in his eyes now. A spark. His cracked lips parted, and his voice emerged with startling clarity.

'That one,' he said, the words almost reverent. His finger tapped the plastic. 'Kenny. That one was my favourite.'

The room seemed to tilt around Stephanie. She forced herself to breathe, to stay rooted, though every instinct screamed to snatch the photos back and leave. She swallowed hard, keeping her voice flat.

'Tell me why, George.'

He smiled and leaned back in his chair as though sinking into memory. 'Because he sang for me,' he whispered. 'He had the most beautiful voice. And mouth.'

CHAPTER
EIGHTY

The phone felt heavy in her hands, as if weighed down by the update Stephanie had just given her.

'What did she have to say?' Fiona asked.

A few seconds later, Olivia came to. 'She thinks there might be some sort of sexual connection between the boys.'

'They were sleeping with each other? They were thirteen!'

Olivia shook her head, realising her mistake. 'No, no, no. I meant with the boys and the priests at the after-school club. She showed the photos to George Grant, and he said they were pretty.'

'*Pretty?*'

Olivia nodded. 'But from the way she said it, it sounded...'

'Wrong?'

Another nod. 'You don't think they did things to the boys, do you?'

'A person of influence abusing their position of power and trust? A tale as old as time,' Fiona said, taking a large bite of her pinkie fingernail. 'But I don't see how that might relate to these killings. If one of the boys was molested, surely he'd be getting revenge on those who did it – namely, the priests – and not on the people he used to attend the club with?'

Olivia's gaze fell on the tarmac. Then she lifted it up to the church in front of them.

'Unless Nigel, Carlos and the others introduced the killer to the priests, and now he's getting revenge on *them* for that,' she suggested.

A moment of solemn silence fluttered between them, carried on the breeze. They exchanged awkward glances. As a mother of two teenage boys, Olivia felt the thought wrap around her chest like barbed wire. She'd always been vigilant about the dangers lurking in plain sight, particularly the risks of grooming and paedophilia. It was a concern that never left her, especially in her line of work.

'What do you think?' Fiona asked.

Olivia didn't know. But it certainly changed the colour of the conversation they were about to have.

With the weight on their shoulders suddenly feeling heavier, they crossed the car park towards St Joseph's Church. As Olivia pushed open the heavy wooden door, a chill rolled over them, cooler than the air outside. Inside, they found John Ellery carrying a stack of hymn books.

The sound alerted him, and he called over, 'Back so soon?'

'Sadly,' Olivia replied. 'Might we ask you some more questions about the matter we discussed previously, Father?'

'Of course, of course.' John set the books down and gestured for them to follow him into the records room. It was quieter there, more secluded and, Olivia thought cynically, away from God's prying ears.

'I saw there was another fire last night,' he said. 'Are you going to tell me the victim also belonged to the church?'

'Yes,' Fiona replied bluntly. 'Unfortunately. His name was Kenny Musgrave. We believe he was part of the same group of friends as the other victims my colleague brought to your attention the other day.' She reached into her pocket, pulled out her phone, and showed him a recent photograph of Kenny that had been taken from his social media profiles. 'Do you recognise him?'

Ellery glanced briefly at the image. 'Can't say I do. And I'm usually quite good with faces.'

Olivia leaned forward a little. 'You mentioned before that George Grant had been heavily involved with the children's groups. We've since spoken with him ourselves. When shown the same photographs we've shown you, he described them as "pretty".'

The priest's brow tightened, and he gave a dry chuckle. 'George is an old man. His mind isn't what it used to be. I wouldn't put much weight on the words of someone in his condition.'

'Perhaps,' Olivia said, her tone deliberately mild. 'But when we pressed further, he said he liked them "at that age" and that one of the boys had a beautiful mouth.'

The priest lifted his head at that. 'I'm sorry, Detective, but I must object. George has dedicated his life to this church. He's baptised children, buried their grandparents, and given counsel in times of crisis. He is a priest, a servant of God, and I won't stand by while his reputation is dragged through the mud by insinuation.'

'We're not insinuating,' Fiona interjected. 'We're investigating. And if there was ever an incident involving George and the boys, we need to know about it.'

Ellery shook his head firmly, as though trying to swat the suggestion away like a fly. 'There was no "incident", nor has there ever been one. Believe me, in the years I've served, I've heard rumours about other parishes, other priests. But not George. Never George. He was trusted, respected, loved. Whatever he may have said to you, you're twisting the words of a confused man. If you've come here hoping for me to confirm some scandal, I fear you'll leave disappointed. The boys you're asking about were no doubt good lads. George guided them. Encouraged them. He never harmed them. And if you're suggesting otherwise, then I can only assume desperation is clouding your judgement.'

Fiona folded her arms, allowing the silence to linger. Olivia studied him closely.

'We're not desperate, Father,' Olivia said finally. 'We're thorough. If there was nothing, then there was nothing. But if there was... it will come out.'

Ellery's lips pressed into a thin line. 'Then I suggest you look elsewhere. Because you won't find your answers here.'

Olivia took him up on the offer and surveyed the room. There were stacks of papers and files littering the table by the wall, next to a smattering of old photographs. On a side chair, boxes brimmed with parish newsletters and old sign-in sheets. One pile was bound with string, though a knot had come loose and a sheaf had spilled open, revealing faces of men, women, and children frozen mid-smile from two decades ago.

She tilted her head. 'You've been busy in here.'

Ellery followed her gaze. 'Yes, well,' he said, clearing his throat, 'after your visit the other day, it got me thinking. The history of the church, the young people we've worked with over the years... I thought it might be helpful to put things in order. Perhaps even find something useful for you.'

'A clear-up,' Olivia said, stepping closer to the desk. Her fingertips hovered near the photographs without touching them. 'That's thoughtful of you.'

'Yes,' he replied quickly. 'I want to help however I can. If these terrible fires are connected to the church, then I'd be failing in my duty if I didn't do something to aid your investigation.'

Olivia moved a couple of papers aside with her fingers. Her eyes skimmed newsletters, a typed rota of Sunday volunteers, and a hand-drawn poster for a parish fête. Then, halfway down the stack, she caught the edge of something different: newsprint, thicker, faded.

She drew it out carefully.

It was a double-page spread from the *Surrey Advertiser*. The headline, half-obscured by the fold, read: *Church Lauded by Weekly Youth Group Community Focus*. Below it ran a black-and-white photograph, stretched across the double-page spread. A dozen boys, barely teenagers, dressed in shirts and trousers, were standing in the church hall, every face beaming at the camera with awkward pride, a bouncy castle behind them. At the centre, their arms draped around each other, were the boys she recognised instantly: Nigel, Carlos, Darren... and Kenny.

Olivia's chest went cold as her eyes fell on the photo. It was the same photo from which the pictures had been cut and left behind at each of the crime scenes. Her hand hovered just above the page, as though afraid that touching it might smear it.

'Where did you get this?' Olivia asked, sharper than she intended.

Ellery shifted behind her, peering down. 'That's from the *Advertiser*.

They used to come down a lot during my early days, and presumably before, to run pieces on us, to show the community what we were doing. A bit of PR.'

She lifted the page free from the pile, but there was nothing else on the document. No names. No ages. No interviews with any of the boys in the photograph. Just the faces of those who had been burnt to death. And somewhere amongst them, Olivia thought, the killer.

CHAPTER
EIGHTY-ONE

The windscreen wipers thrashed violently from side to side, battling the relentless rain that had worsened as the morning progressed. Her phone vibrated in its holder on the dashboard. It was Olivia. Leaning forward in her seat, she pressed the button and answered the call.

'Can you talk?' Olivia asked, her voice almost breathless.

'I'm driving, but go for it.'

'I've just left St Joseph's, and we've found the photograph of the boys. The original.'

'The *original*?'

'It's from a photoshoot of the after-school club that the *Surrey Advertiser* did in eighty-three. Everyone's there: Nigel, Carlos, Darren, Kenny.'

Stephanie became distracted and missed the car braking in front of her. She slammed on the brakes, narrowly avoiding a collision.

'What about the two new victims?'

'They're there as well. At the back of the group.'

The sound of wind and rain rustled through the microphone.

'Anyone else?'

'A few more individuals,' Olivia explained. 'There are about a dozen boys in total, along with three adults.'

'Who are the adults?'

'We don't know. We suspect one of them is George, but Father Ellery didn't recognise the rest. He mentioned they could have been church members who volunteered, perhaps parents.'

'Is there any wording in the article?'

'There *is*,' Olivia said. 'But not on the version we found. All we have is the photograph.'

The car ahead pulled away, but Stephanie remained where she was, distracted. It wasn't until the car behind sounded its horn that she moved on.

'Ma'am, you still there?' Olivia asked.

'I'm here. I'm thinking.' She paused as she navigated a set of traffic lights. 'What was the outcome of the grooming angle?'

'Fiona and I have differing opinions on that,' Olivia replied.

'Go on.'

Olivia cleared her throat before continuing. 'She believes that if there were a grooming scandal, the killer would be targeting the groomers, not the boys. Whereas I disagree. I think all the groomers are likely long dead, with the exception of George, and now the killer is seeking revenge on the boys who introduced him to the grooming. That perhaps, the victims being burned alive are the kids who persuaded the killer into joining the club and subsequently being abused.'

Stephanie turned into a quiet residential area and pulled over to the side of the road. The temperature inside the car suddenly felt stuffy, so she lowered the window, the cogs in her brain turning rapidly. She mulled over the information, weighing the pros and cons of each argument. On one hand, it deepened the connection between the victims. If they had all been subjected to child grooming and molestation, their bonds would have been more profound than anything in life. But why would one of them suddenly turn on the others and kill them? Why wouldn't they channel their anger towards those responsible for the trauma and nightmares?

That didn't make sense to Stephanie.

And then a thought occurred to her: the fires.

She believed the manner of death, along with the religious quotes left at the crime scenes, was symbolic. Too obvious to ignore.

Was burning people to death a form of justice or retribution for being introduced to a gang of groomers and child molesters?

Her gut said no.

'Let's keep our options open,' she said. 'There might be another piece to this puzzle. Let me give Louis a call and see if he can help us with the article.'

Stephanie ended the call with Olivia and immediately scrolled through her contacts. Her thumb hovered for a moment, then she tapped the one for Louis Brown. The line rang twice before a brisk voice answered.

'Stephanie. Isn't this a treat? What can I do for Surrey Police on a fine Saturday morning?'

'Louis, I need your help. It's about this investigation. We found the original photo of all the boys that have been killed, and it's from a photoshoot in an old version of the *Surrey Advertiser*. It looks like it was part of a wider feature the paper ran at the time.'

Louis grunted. 'What about it?'

'We believe it's significant. We need access to your archives – original prints, articles, any of the accompanying editorial. We believe there might be names of the victims and also the other members of the group somewhere.'

'Of course,' Louis said. 'Yes, you can have access. We keep the physical archives in the basement, everything digitised from ninety-six onwards. But if it's mid-eighties, you'll need the hard copies. I'm not there today, but I can have someone meet you at reception.'

'Good. We'll be there this afternoon.'

CHAPTER
EIGHTY-TWO

Just after midday, Stephanie, Giles, Olivia, and Fiona were set up in a small room at the *Surrey Live* offices. The space was barely large enough for two people, let alone four, especially with the constant stream of boxes being brought in by the newspaper's junior staff and interns. The decades of Guildford's history were right in front of them, waiting to be peeled open. It took nearly twenty minutes to gather everything in one place, and after Stephanie returned from the local M&S with a selection of ready-made sandwiches, snacks, and drinks, they were ready to begin. They had everything they needed for the next few hours of tedious, mind-numbing exploration.

'This is going to be nothing short of fun,' Giles muttered, eyeing the towers of cardboard stacked against the wall. His gaze then fell on the food and drink. 'They didn't have anything stronger in the meal deal section?'

Stephanie stood at the head of the table, hands on her hips, surveying Giles with a raised eyebrow. 'Sadly not. That comes later, provided you find a breakthrough.'

'Challenge accepted.'

'Right,' she said. 'We're looking at eighty-three, but I want to cover a year either side as well. Nineteen eighty-two to eighty-four. We need anything that mentions the church, after-school clubs, or fires. Anything that connects back to the boys. Accidents, vandalism, you name it. We go through every line. We miss nothing.'

Fiona gave a low whistle, pulling out a stack and laying it across the table. 'This is thousands of pages.'

'Then we'd better get started,' Stephanie said sternly. She knew it was drudgery, but she also knew this was where the answers would be buried. Somewhere in the endless columns lay the thread they needed to pull.

Before long, the room settled into a rhythm: the sound of pages flipping, papers rustling, and pens scratching. Occasionally, one of them would huff or mutter something under their breath. Outside, the excitement and fervour of a local newspaper buzzed on the other side of the door.

'Sounds like they're having all the fun,' Giles commented. 'This is worse than my GCSE revision.'

'You didn't revise for your GCSEs,' Fiona shot back without looking up. 'Don't lie.'

Stephanie allowed herself a small smile, but her eyes never left the page in front of her. Local fêtes, council disputes, obituaries, flood warnings – nothing. She reached for another page.

The first half-hour passed in silence, save for the rustle of newsprint and the occasional crackle of a crisp packet. Stephanie had positioned herself by the door, cross-legged with a pile of issues from March 1983. Giles worked the opposite wall, while Olivia and Fiona had wedged themselves together by the window, daylight streaming across their shoulders as they bent over the pages.

'Here's one about a vicar running a summer fair,' Olivia said after a while. 'Eighty-three, July. Big raffle, jumble sale, kids' games. Doesn't say much else.'

'Not helpful,' Giles muttered.

Next, it was Fiona's turn to offer something. 'There's a lot about burglaries that year. Someone was targeting corner shops. Might not be relevant, though.'

'Stick a note on it,' Stephanie said. 'Anything that looks like unrest in that area could matter.'

'What about an arson attack at a warehouse in Woking, injuring three?' Fiona asked, scanning the small column. 'Doesn't look like anything to do with the church, though.'

'Keep it,' Stephanie said.

The next few hours blurred into a loop: find something, read aloud, shake heads, move on. Each time a headline looked promising, it dissolved into nothing more than petty crime or the occasional scandal over council budgets and some of the members. By two o'clock, with the remains of the sandwiches long gone, morale was low. All Stephanie had read was line after line of irrelevant text blurring together: car crashes, burglaries, and nearly half a dozen articles about the opening of a new Sainsbury's.

'Two-car collision on the A3. Three dead,' Giles announced.

Stephanie glanced up. 'Nope.'

A while later, Olivia frowned. 'This one's about a school firework display. Two kids burned, but nothing fatal.'

'Where?'

'Dorking.'

'Not it,' Stephanie said.

Silence returned, broken only by the steady turning of pages. Then Olivia's sharp intake of breath cut through the quiet.

'Steph... I think I've got it.'

They all turned as she carefully flattened the brittle sheet against the desk. *Surrey Advertiser*, April 19, 1983. Middle of the front page, below the fold.

TEENS ESCAPE GUILDFORD HOUSE BLAZE
After-School Club Friends Survive Late-Night Fire
A late-night fire in an abandoned house on the outskirts of Guildford left several children shaken but unhurt on Tuesday evening. The blaze, which broke out shortly after 9 pm, tore through the crumbling property where a group of friends from a local after-school club had gathered.

All the boys managed to escape before the building was fully consumed by flames. Some suffered minor smoke inhalation, but none required hospital treatment.

The cause of the fire is under investigation, though early reports suggest it may have been started accidentally after the children lit candles inside the derelict property.

'It was like something out of a nightmare,' said Mrs Anne Whittaker, a resident who lives nearby. 'The whole place went up so fast. I could hear the children screaming. They're lucky they all got out.'

Witnesses described frantic attempts to help. 'We smashed a window to get some of them out,' said Mr Peter Clarkson. 'The smoke was choking everyone. It could have been so much worse.'

Volunteer staff from the after-school club confirmed the group had met earlier that evening before heading to the house. 'They were inseparable,' said one volunteer. 'Always making people laugh. We're just relieved they're safe.'

Parents have since called for stronger measures to prevent children from accessing abandoned buildings in the area. Surrey Fire Service has confirmed that a full enquiry into the blaze is underway.

Stephanie forced herself to speak, her voice low but steady. She didn't want to get ahead of herself. 'Does it name any of the boys involved?'

Olivia continued reading, her eyes quickly scanning the page. She opened her mouth, then closed it again, as if the air had been sucked from her lungs. 'Nigel... Carlos... Darren... and Kenny Musgrave... they're all named because they gave interviews to the paper.'

'That's the connection,' Stephanie said finally. 'That's what this whole thing is about...'

CHAPTER
EIGHTY-THREE

Fire. That had been the link between the victims.

A traumatic experience that had bonded them. She could feel it in her bones. But her intuition told her there was something more to it than the four boys being involved in a house fire.

The problem was, all the people they wanted to ask, the people who knew the truth, were all dead.

Stephanie paced about the small room, though in the tight confines, it felt more like shifting her weight from one foot to the other.

'We need to find out who these two people are,' she said, chewing on her bottom lip. 'I think someone might have died in this fire, and the individuals who were there know exactly what happened. Nigel, Carlos, and Darren have already shown they can lie and keep secrets between them; look at what happened with Felix Krüger.' She turned to Olivia. 'Does the article mention anything else about the incident?'

The constable shook her head.

'Any other names mentioned?'

Another shake.

Stephanie turned to Giles and Fiona. 'Please look through the reports from the months following the date on Olivia's paper. If there was a police or fire investigation, their reports might have been published.'

Nodding, Giles and Fiona began their search, taking piles of papers and setting them on their laps. They browsed through them in silence, sifting through the information carefully, turning the pages with extra attention, as if they now carried new weight and meaning.

Meanwhile, Stephanie pulled out her phone and called the office. Noah answered after a few rings.

'Ground control to Major Tom,' he said flippantly. 'This is Noah speaking.'

'Do you always answer the phone like that?' she asked.

'Only when I know it's you, ma'am.'

'How could you have known?'

He hesitated. 'Lucky guess? Anyway, how can I assist you?'

'I need you to stop what you're doing,' she said, then proceeded to explain the fire connection between all the victims. 'We assume a police investigation was launched alongside the fire investigation. I need you to check if the boys were ever brought in for questioning. Also, look for key witness statements from anyone affiliated with the church and the after-school club. They might be our next victims, or one of them could be the killer.'

A few moments of silence passed.

'Noah?' she asked. 'Noah, are you there?'

'My bad. Forgive me, I was writing down what you said, and my male brain doesn't allow me to multitask.'

She wanted to laugh, but now wasn't the time. 'Also, look into missing persons reports from that period. Nobody was reported as perishing in the blaze, but that doesn't mean to say nobody else was there. They may have been reported missing after the event.'

'Aye, aye, captain. Your wish is my command. I'll get back to you shortly.'

CHAPTER
EIGHTY-FOUR

Isaac had convinced himself that Portsmouth was far enough away. That three days holed up in Sarah's narrow Victorian terrace, surviving on instant coffee and whatever tinned goods she'd left behind before her holiday, was a better compromise than staying at home, where it wasn't safe. He'd seen the reports on the news, monitored them from the beginning. Naively believed that it wasn't possible, that that part of their lives they had all tried to put to rest couldn't have come back to haunt them. But all his friends from that era – Nigel, Carlos, Darren, Kenny – were now dead, killed, murdered. It wasn't until he'd seen the news about Kenny's death that the realisation had settled heavily in his chest: he was next.

There was no doubt in his mind.

The killer was coming for *him*.

But it was impossible. It couldn't be...

Should he have gone to the police? Yes. But for some reason, the chemicals in his brain had told him to run, to run away and never look back. He was a man of simple means. He didn't need much – just a bed, some warmth, food, and water. The rest were luxuries he could afford to live without. Besides, how could he have helped the police identify a dead child that wasn't dead and had now grown into an adult? He wasn't safe, nor would he be until he got as far away from Surrey as possible.

Isaac was in the middle of ransacking his sister's empty kitchen cupboards when the knock came.

Three sharp raps against the front door. Isaac dropped the tin of beans, the metal can clattering against the kitchen tiles with a sound that seemed to echo through the entire house. His hands began to shake uncontrollably as he gripped the edge of the counter, his knuckles turning white against the surface.

It could be anyone. A postman. A neighbour. Someone looking for Sarah.

Or maybe he'd imagined it. Perhaps the stress had finally gotten to him, and his mind was playing tricks. The house settled around him, the old radiator clicking as it cooled. Seagulls cried in the distance, and somewhere down the street, a car door slammed.

The knocking came again. And Isaac knew with absolute certainty that his life on the run had just expired. He forced himself to breathe, counting the seconds between each exhale the way his therapist had taught him years ago. One Mississippi. Two Mississippi. But the technique that had once helped him through panic attacks felt useless now.

His pulse hammered in his ears as he crept towards the front window, careful not to make a sound as he neared the glass. Through a gap in the curtain, he could see a shadow on the doorstep.

'I know you're in there, Isaac.' The voice drifted through the pane, calm and conversational, as if they were old friends meeting for lunch.

The blood drained from Isaac's face. His legs turned to jelly as he backed away from the window, his mind racing through impossible escape routes. The back garden was tiny, hemmed in by high fences. The upstairs windows were too high to jump from without breaking his neck.

'Come now,' the voice continued, accompanied by the soft scrape of a shoe against concrete. 'We both know this was always going to end one way or another. The others have paid the price for their sins. Now it's your turn.'

Isaac pressed his back against the wall beside the window, his breath coming in short, desperate gasps. He closed his eyes and tried to think, but it was pointless over the sound of his thundering heartbeat.

Then his survival instinct kicked in.

Isaac bolted towards the back of the house. His feet pounded against the wooden floors as he crashed through the kitchen, sending chairs scraping across the tiles. Behind him, he heard the front door handle rattle, followed by a sharp crack as something heavy hit the wood.

The back door was locked. Of course it was locked. His fingers fumbled with the key wedged in the slot as footsteps thundered through the house behind him. The lock finally gave way with a metallic click, and Isaac burst into the narrow garden, the cold Portsmouth air hitting his face like a slap.

The garden was even smaller than he remembered. But there, in the far corner where Sarah kept her bins, he spotted a gap where one of the fence panels had rotted away near the bottom.

Isaac dropped to his hands and knees, forcing himself through the splintered opening just as he heard the back door crash open behind him. The gap was narrower than it had looked. Jagged wood tore at his shirt, catching the fabric. He pushed harder, desperation making him reckless, but his shoulders were too broad for the rotten opening.

He was stuck.

Panic flooded through him as he writhed against the splintered wood, feeling the pieces bite into his back. Behind him, footsteps approached across the grass.

'Tsk, tsk, Isaac.' The voice was closer now, just feet away. 'That looks rather uncomfortable.'

Strong hands seized his ankles, and Isaac felt himself being dragged backward through the gap. Wood scraped against his skin, the fence panel groaning as his body was pulled free. He twisted frantically, trying to kick out, but the grip was too strong.

He was hauled to his feet and spun around to face his pursuer for the first time.

'Hello, old friend.'

Isaac opened his mouth to speak, to plead, to beg for forgiveness, but the blow came swift and precise, switching off all the lights in the world.

CHAPTER
EIGHTY-FIVE

They had a name.

Two, in fact.

The first was the name of the young boy who, on the night of the fire, had been reported missing by his parents. Noah had found him in the system shortly after their phone call, and Giles and the team had discovered newspaper clippings about his disappearance, timestamped a few days after the fire. His name was Toby Ashworth, and the team was able to loosely confirm his identity by matching an image of him in the St Jude's school yearbook with the photo of the two boys found at the fourth crime scene. They had a match; they knew the identity of one of the boys. However, the only problem was that Toby Ashworth's body was never recovered, and the investigation into his disappearance had quickly stalled and eventually stopped. It remained unclear whether he was involved in the fire at the abandoned house, as all the boys present maintained that Toby had not been with them.

The second boy in the photograph was believed to be twelve-year-old Isaac Grove, who also attended the after-school club on weeknights with the boys but did not go to St Jude's. His name and picture had first appeared in a small section of editorial text following the event, where he'd given a brief statement about the fire, apologising for the mess and upset caused.

Confident he was a potential victim – or potentially the killer – the team had tracked Isaac Grove's location to a small three-bedroom house in Camberley, a town that was situated right on the fringes of Hampshire and Berkshire.

They turned off the main road into a network of narrow streets. Stephanie sat in the passenger seat, watching the houses blur past, her thoughts racing as fast as the smudges. The satnav announced the turnoff, and the car slowed. Giles flicked on his indicator, the engine rumbling as they coasted into a street lined with nearly identical houses.

'There,' Giles muttered, nodding at a house halfway along the curve.

The convoy rolled to a halt a few doors down. In front of them, uniformed officers piled out of the van before moving to the front door. At the back of the pack was a tall, broad-shouldered officer carrying a heavy battering ram. Giles cut the engine, and a heavy silence quickly filled the car. Stephanie's heart raced, nerves twisting in her stomach as she watched the officers assemble.

This was it.

Inside was either their killer or their next victim.

She hoped for the former, but so far the killer had been one step ahead of them at every turn, and she would be lying if she said she felt confident.

'Ready?' Giles asked, already reaching for the door handle.

Stephanie gave a tight nod. She followed him out, the late afternoon air cool against her face. The uniforms fanned out, moving quickly and with effortless precision. A pair positioned themselves at the back gate, while another two flanked the front door. The sergeant in charge gave a sharp nod.

The ram swung.

A hollow crack reverberated along the street as the lock gave way. The door jolted open, crashing back against the wall. The officers poured in, boots pounding against laminate flooring, voices raised.

'Police! Show yourself!'

'Police! Make yourself known!'

Stephanie stood at the edge of the driveway, pulse racing, her eyes locked on the shadows inside.

A beat later, the sergeant's voice echoed back: 'Clear!'

Then another call from upstairs: 'Clear up here too!'

She felt her shoulders drop as she moved forward, stepping over the splintered frame of the doorway into the house. Giles followed her, his hand brushing the doorframe as he scanned the hallway.

'He's not here,' one of the constables said as they entered.

'He can't have been gone long,' she replied automatically.

Giles tilted his head. 'How do you know?

'Look.'

She pointed towards the coat rack. Only one peg was empty. She moved farther into the house, taking in the scene of the living room: the place was neat and tidy, with everything in its place. In the kitchen, a loaf of bread rested on the side, it's packaging half-opened.

'Maybe he's gone on holiday,' Giles suggested.

'We'll have to check with the airlines,' she said, opening the fridge. Inside, was an opened carton of milk. 'But if you knew you were going on holiday for a while, you wouldn't leave these things open, not for them to go off by the time you get back.'

She shut the door and ventured upstairs to Isaac Grove's bedroom, which confirmed her belief: the wardrobe door was open, with several hangers discarded over the half-made duvet. And the final confirmation she needed was in the bathroom: his toothbrush and toothpaste were missing.

Her throat tightened.

'He's packed a bag,' she said, standing straighter. 'Clothes, toiletries... looks like he left in a rush.'

Giles leaned against the doorframe, arms folded. 'Running from us?'

'Or from someone else.'

CHAPTER
EIGHTY-SIX

Stephanie sat at her desk, her elbows resting on the wood, her eyes fixed on the photograph laid out before her. It was the same image she had been studying for the past hour, her gaze wandering over every pixel. Twelve boys, frozen in time, smiling at her. It was late afternoon, but the darkness outside made it feel like midnight. Her desk lamp did little to illuminate the rest of the room. A plastic container of pasta salad sat unopened beside her, the fork still wrapped in its napkin. She knew she should eat, but the thought made her stomach clench and threatened to make her vomit.

A sudden knock on the door broke her trance.

'Come in,' she said, startled.

The door eased open, and Devon stepped inside, clutching a thin sheaf of papers.

'Got a min?' he asked.

Stephanie leaned back, stretching her spine until it cracked. 'Depends. Is it good news?'

He let out a short breath. 'Depends on your outlook, I guess.' He shut the door behind him. 'I went down the molestation angle, just in case there was something else there... and it's a dead end.'

Stephanie frowned. 'Dead end how?'

'The police conducted a full investigation back in the early to late eighties. Two men from the church were implicated following a stream of complaints. Both were charged, convicted, and served their time. It's all on record.' He dropped the papers on her desk and tapped them once. 'But the people who reported it weren't our guys. Darren, Nigel, the rest of them... they were all interviewed, but they unequivocally claimed nothing had ever happened to them and denied having any knowledge of what went on.'

Stephanie rubbed her temple, feeling the onset of a dull headache behind her eyes. 'They were kids. They could have lied; they've already got a track record of that.'

'I know. But somehow I don't think they would have. The kids were promised anonymity, and according to the SIO's notes at the time, he said that gave four of the five claimants the confidence to step forward. I think mathematically, of the four that have died, I think at least one of them would have come forward if that's what this is about.'

She let the silence stretch, her eyes drawn back to the photo. Finally, she sighed. 'All right. Thanks, Devon. At least it's something we can cross off.'

He nodded, lingering a moment longer, as if unsure whether to say more, before retreating. The door closed behind him, leaving her alone once again with the photograph, the darkness, and the unopened food.

Stephanie exhaled through her nose. She had just finished writing a note on her pad when there was another knock on the door. Olivia appeared, dropping into the chair opposite her, a look of consternation and concern etched into every pore of her skin.

'I think I have something, ma'am,' she began, a crack in her voice. 'And I don't know if I'm going crazy or if what I'm seeing is true. I don't want to believe it either way.'

Stephanie straightened in her chair, the sudden seriousness in Olivia's tone capturing her attention. 'What have you got?'

Olivia opened the file, her fingers trembling slightly as she spread the pages out on the desk between them. 'I wanted to comb through the original fire investigation. The building blaze back in eighty-three. But...' She swallowed. 'The files are missing.'

Stephanie leaned forward, eyes narrowing. 'Missing?'

'Not just misfiled,' Olivia said, shaking her head. 'Deleted. Entire witness accounts. Cross-referenced interviews with some of the boys who made it out. And... it looks deliberate. I checked the digital access logs through the archives.' She tapped one sheet, where a list of entries had been printed in neat black ink. Each line contained a timestamp and username.

Stephanie scanned the column until her gaze caught on the entry Olivia had circled in red pen.

Accessed: 02:14 – fourteen days ago

User: E. Thorne.

Her stomach tightened. She sat back slowly, the air in the room suddenly feeling heavier. 'Elias.'

Olivia nodded slowly, her eyes wide with fear. 'He was the last one to access the file before the deletions.'

Stephanie stared at the name on the page. Her mind replayed the last conversations she'd had with Elias. His story about the fire. A car crash as a teenager. The scars on his face. The way his eyes lit up when he saw the fire or spoke about it. The way he hadn't let it consume him.

She looked back at Olivia. 'Are you certain?'

A weak nod. 'I cross-checked against IT. No one else has touched those files in years. It was him.'

For a moment, neither of them spoke. Her eyes fell on the photograph again, on the boy in the image she believed to be Toby Ashworth. For the first time since she had been looking at it, she saw a recognition there. She saw the face of Elias in those eyes, in those features.

Before the fire.

Before the scars.

Before the pain.

CHAPTER
EIGHTY-SEVEN

Isaac Grove's head felt like it had been stuffed with explosives. His ears rang, a dull throb pulsing behind his temples, as though every heartbeat pressed a hot nail deeper into his skull. The world around him was on its side, and when he tried to move, his body jerked against something rough. Rope. Biting into his wrists and chest, the coarse fibres already cutting through the thin fabric of his shirt.

He blinked hard. Once. Twice. His vision gradually cleared. The air smelled damp, heavy with mildew. He was in a church – he could deduce that much – but not one that had seen light or worship for months. The stained-glass windows were half-smashed, boarded up with cardboard and plywood. Pews had been overturned and shoved to the side, and dust motes floated in the half-dark; the church was stripped bare, prepared for demolition.

Then he heard a sound. A breath. The scrape of shoes on the stone floor.

Isaac's head turned sluggishly towards it.

A figure moved in the shadows, steady and deliberate.

Toby.

He carried himself with a strange calm, his shoulders relaxed. In his hand, a small metal canister swung loosely, glinting under the flicker of a portable lamp he had propped on the floor. Petrol. The sweet scent of it was unmistakable.

'Please... please, Toby. You don't need to—'

The man he knew only as Toby Ashworth stopped and leaned close enough for Isaac to see the scar tissue across his jaw. Elias's breath was steady, the epitome of calm.

'I haven't been called Toby in years. So long I almost forget that was once my name. Tonight, you'll burn,' Elias whispered. 'Just as you left me to all those years ago.'

He turned away again. Isaac pulled against the ropes, the chair legs scraping against the stone, but the bonds held fast. Panic rose, choking him, as his head pounded harder with every frantic tug.

'I saved you till last,' Elias continued, his voice louder this time, echoing off the walls. 'You and me... we were supposed to be blood brothers, ride or die. Do you remember that? We said we'd never leave the other behind. But when everyone else suggested the fire and to leave me in there, you went along with it. You didn't even look back.'

Isaac shook his head frantically, desperately.

'That's not true. I couldn't—'

Elias slammed the canister down on the nearest pew with a crack, petrol splashing across the wood. Isaac flinched at the sudden sound.

'Don't you dare lie to me! *You* started the fire, Isaac. And *you* left me to die.' His scarred hand twitched as he lifted his sleeve with the other, revealing the web of burns crawling up his arm. 'This is what your loyalty cost me.'

Isaac felt sick. 'Toby, we were kids. It was a mistake. We—'

'Don't you dare hide behind that,' Elias hissed, stepping closer, his face inches from Isaac's. His eyes glistened with fury. 'I crawled out of that inferno alone. Skin hanging off me like melted wax. They said I shouldn't have lived. And maybe I shouldn't have. Because what came after... the months in the hospital, the stares, the whispers...'

Elias drew in a staggered breath.

'We thought you'd died.'

'You lied to the newspapers. You told everyone I was never with you when the fire started. You lied to protect yourselves.'

'How did you…? How did you survive?'

'When I got out, I ran and I ran, until I couldn't anymore. And then someone found me, in the woods nearby. He took me in, looked after me. Got me the medical attention I needed, helped put me back together. But I knew I couldn't go back. At least, not as myself. I wasn't Toby Ashworth anymore. I was unrecognisable. Everyone believed I'd gone missing, and so I kept it that way. I stayed with him, recovered, changed my name, changed my identity. Left my mum and dad behind. Left my life behind. Years it took me to piece myself back together. Years of watching all of you walk free, pretending like the past didn't exist. Like you hadn't left me to die in that room.'

Isaac strained against the ropes again, his wrists raw now. Still, they wouldn't budge.

'Toby, listen to me. It was a mistake. There was a problem with the lock. We couldn't get it open. There was nothing we could do. If I'd known—'

'If you'd known?' Elias barked out a laugh, harsh and hollow. He leaned back, picking up the canister once more, swinging it casually at his side as though weighing it. 'If you'd known, you'd have still run. Because that's who you are, Isaac. That's who all of you were. Cowards. Bullies. Only looking out for yourselves.'

He crouched low so Isaac couldn't avoid his gaze. The lamp's flicker cast demonic shadows across the scars on his face and neck.

'But not this time. This time, you don't get to escape the fire.'

CHAPTER
EIGHTY-EIGHT

The office buzzed with frantic energy. Stephanie stood at the centre of it all, monitoring, observing, and thinking about Elias. About his smile. About how close he had been to the investigation from the start. How he'd been right under her nose, and she hadn't seen him.

She shoved her feelings for him into a locked box and forced herself to focus. Right now, she was a detective, and a life hung in the balance.

'Anything from Elias's house?' she demanded.

'Negative,' Giles called across the room, holding his mobile to his ear. 'The uniform there right now is reporting that his car's gone. There's no sign of him.'

'What about his phone?'

'Dead,' Devon replied. 'Switched off or destroyed.'

Stephanie clenched her jaw, pacing a line across the incident room. 'And Isaac?'

Olivia emerged from behind her monitor. 'We've tracked him to his sister Sarah's address in Portsmouth. Hampshire Police have gone round, but they're also saying there's nobody home. There's a car on the driveway, but no sign of anybody inside. Though the front door appears to have been damaged in some way. They spoke with a couple of the neighbours, and they reported hearing a struggle earlier that afternoon, before a car sped off. Could be them...'

A silence fell, heavy as lead.

'Run Elias's car through ANPR and CCTV,' Stephanie said. 'Find out where he's going and where he's been. And put a call out on his registration immediately. If someone sees it, they need to pull him over and arrest him.'

Fiona tapped furiously at her keyboard, taking on the responsibility. A moment later, her chair screeched back. 'Got a hit,' she said. 'About ten minutes ago. On the A3, heading back into Surrey. But that's it. Nothing else.'

Stephanie froze. Surrey. Why Surrey? Why come back here when every road could have been an escape route?

'The church!' Olivia cried suddenly.

Heads snapped up.

'St Mary's in Shalford!' Olivia continued breathlessly. 'The one that stalled after Nigel Hadlow received those messages.'

'Yes!' Devon exclaimed. 'That's right.' He snapped his fingers repeatedly, as if trying to pinch a memory. 'I looked into Hadlow's company finances, and guess who was the auditor on their last accounts to Companies House? Kenny. That's right. And guess whose construction company received money from Hadlow? That's right. Carlos's. They were all working on it together, greasing each other's wheels. The only person who wasn't affiliated with the church project was Darren Fairhurst, but by that point, if Elias really is Toby Ashworth, it wouldn't matter.'

Stephanie's blood surged with revelation. The church. The fire. A final chance at getting justice for those who'd left him to die before the building was demolished. 'That's where he's taking him,' she said. 'That's where they are.'

Her words cracked like a whip, snapping the team into action.

'Giles, get ARV units en route. Devon, coordinate with local uniform; we'll need roads blocked, traffic cleared. Olivia, pull the blueprints of the church. I want every entrance point mapped before we get there. And we need the fire service there as fast as humanly possible.'

The team scattered, driven by her urgency.

Stephanie planted her hands on the desk, the photo of Elias Thorne and Isaac Grove staring back at her. And then it occurred to her. The significance of both boys being in the photograph. So far, the pattern had determined that the boy in the photograph would be next to die.

She didn't think Elias would change that.

Which meant that he was going to end this journey of justice and sin that night.

That he was going to kill them both.

CHAPTER
EIGHTY-NINE

Neither of them had said anything for a few moments. The only sound echoing around the church was Isaac's heavy, exacerbated, and panicked breathing. Soon, he began to feel light-headed, the adrenaline of the situation getting to him.

He was going to die. This was it. There was nothing he could do about it.

He was going to die.

All because of a mistake made forty years ago. A joke. A part of his history that he deeply regretted and had lived with ever since.

A recurring nightmare that had now materialised and resurfaced after all this time.

It was supposed to have been a joke. A bit of banter. A friendly bit of hazing. It had been Nigel's idea, originally: lock Toby in the cupboard, then start the fire outside the door. But they weren't really going to lock the door. They weren't really going to leave him there; they would use their body weight to pin the door shut until the last minute. But the fire had spread faster, harder, and brighter than any of them had expected, and by the time they'd sprinted out of there, it had consumed the cupboard door, leaving Toby to burn inside. The boys had been lucky to make it out alive. They'd all assumed Toby had perished in the blaze. And in that moment, as they stood outside the house, catching their breath, they had all promised one another, sworn themselves to secrecy, that they would never tell the truth, that they would never tell anyone what had happened that night, including the police.

And they had kept to it.

They had continued with their lives, grown up, developed careers, had families, all with the burden of their secret hanging over them. Sure, it became easier and easier to forget about it, to move on from it, but he had never truly forgotten. The sounds of Toby's screams had echoed in his thoughts, his dreams, occasionally surfacing like wolf howls in the night.

And now the man was here. A ghost, come back from the dead.

And now it was time to hear the screams again. This time his own.

Elias moved with the calmness and precision of a man in control. Of a man who had planned this in his head for forty years, every meticulous aspect of it. Of a man who was at ease with his decision, at peace with what was about to happen.

He moved with the calmness and precision of a man who had done this four times already.

Elias's footsteps echoed across the stones as he began dragging pews out from the shadows. The old wood groaned, legs scraping like nails down slate as he heaved them into a large circle around Isaac's chair, angling them as if creating an audience. Then he stacked smaller wooden objects atop them: hymn book stands, kneelers, and a broken confessional screen dragged from the corner.

Isaac's breathing became laboured, short and shallow, sharp pains shooting across his chest with each breath.

'Toby... please. You don't have to do this...'

The scarred man didn't stop. He paused only to glance up, eyes gleaming with enjoyment, then reached for the canister. The sharp reek of petrol hit instantly, suffocating. Elias tipped the canister without hesitation, glug after glug of liquid spattering across the timber, darkening the wood, soaking into the fibres. The fumes filled Isaac's throat, making his head swim. The last of the petrol splashed onto the stone, trickling in thin rivulets across the floor toward Isaac's shoes. Elias tossed it aside, the clang echoing like a church bell.

Isaac shook violently in the chair, the ropes cutting deeper into his wrists. 'Please, Toby. I swear to you, we never meant for it to—'

'Be not deceived; God is not mocked,' Elias said, his voice low and deliberate, each word amplifying as it echoed about the space. He drew a matchbox from his pocket, turning it over slowly in his hand, gauging its weight.

Isaac's eyes widened, his whole body trembling as Elias opened it with a flick of his thumb.

'For whatsoever a man soweth, that shall he also reap.'

Elias crouched in front of him, close enough that Isaac could see the deep valleys and ridges of burn tissue across his face. Elias studied him with unsettling calm, then slid a single match from the box.

'For forty years you've walked free. Forty years of life, of laughter, of happiness. The wages of sin is death.'

He struck the match.

The flare bloomed, painting his face in orange light. Shadows leapt onto the walls of the church, like demons summoned by the flame. Elias held it steady, his expression unreadable as the light danced in his eyes.

Isaac whimpered, jerking against the ropes, his head shaking violently. 'No, Toby, no! Please—'

'Vengeance is mine; I will repay, saith the Lord.' Elias's eyes fixed on him, unblinking, transfixed by the small blaze trembling between his fingers.

The tiny flame wavered. Elias tilted it closer to the petrol-soaked wood.

Isaac's scream tore through the church, but Elias's voice cut through it, calm, steady, resolute.

'Tonight, Isaac, He has chosen me as His hand. And tonight, you will pay for your sins.'

Elias lowered the flame.

CHAPTER
NINETY

Stephanie gripped the door handle as the car swung around the final corner and came to a sudden halt in front of the church. In the darkness, smoke poured out of the broken windows, thick, black plumes curling into the evening sky.

The moment she opened her door the heat welcomed her like an embrace. Acrid smoke clawed at her throat, forcing her to cough, but she pulled the neck of her jumper over her mouth.

For a moment, she froze, paused, staring at it.

Her father and his lighter appeared. Followed by the burning sensation on her arm and the smell of singed hair.

And then it was replaced with the image of her childhood home ablaze, her sister and mum stuck inside, clawing at the windows.

The smell, the taste, the heat.

She blinked hard, forcing the image away, and fixed her eyes on the task ahead.

Uniformed officers hovered by the churchyard gates, the orange glow bouncing off the reflective strips on their jackets. None of them dared go inside, the fire too strong. A man's scream tore through the stillness, raw and savage, followed by a crashing thud from somewhere within the building.

The hairs on Stephanie's arms rose as she hurried over to the uniformed officers. 'What's going on?' she barked. 'Where are the fire crew? Why is nobody in there?'

Fiona hurried around the front of a car and joined her side, phone pressed against her ear. 'They're delayed, ma'am,' she said. 'Two of their engines were in a collision on the way here. Nearest backup is at least five minutes away.'

Five minutes? They didn't have five seconds.

Another scream erupted from inside, higher-pitched this time, ragged and desperate.

Stephanie's pulse thundered as she stared up at the building, eyes following the smoke as it climbed higher into the sky.

She thought of the dream, of the fire in her childhood home, of the time she'd rushed in and saved her sister.

She thought of the firewalk she'd completed under Elias's supervision. Of her realisation afterwards: it was all in her head. Her fear, her paranoia, her worry. It was all in her head.

There were two people in there, and they were going to die if nobody did anything about it.

If she could walk on fire, she could save them.

If she could enter a burning building in her dream, she could save them.

So without saying anything, without thinking on it any further, she started towards St Mary's, reminding herself that it was all in her head.

Stephanie pulled her rollneck up farther covering her mouth and nose, squatting low as she shoved through the splintered doors. Instantly the world swallowed her whole. Heat touched her skin, pressing in from all sides, suffocating, prickling her arms, her scalp. The smoke was thicker inside, a black storm that ravaged and clawed her lungs raw with every breath. Her eyes streamed with tears, distorting the shapes surrounding her.

She forced herself lower, onto her haunches, crawling through the church. The air was alive with the sound of timber bending and popping. And then she heard it, so close it pierced her chest.

Isaac.

Broken, hoarse wails. She pushed towards the sound, blinking through the haze until the outline of a chair came into focus. He was tied down, his head lolling, arms and chest bound to the chair. His eyes bulged wide when he saw her.

'Help!' His voice broke into a cough, his body jerking as flames snapped and bit at the pile of pews around him.

'Hold still!' she rasped, finding a gap in the pews to join his side. Her fingers scrabbled at the knots binding his wrists and chest, but the rope had been pulled taut, almost fused. Her nails bent and split, but it was no use. She swore, screamed, choked as she tugged harder, leaning her weight into it. The heat was unbearable now, baking her back, stinging her face and arms. Every breath was a fight, every swallow like glass. She could hear the fire climbing, rapidly consuming everything in its path.

Time was running out.

'Please, you have to help me!' Isaac begged.

Stephanie braced her knee against the chair, reached into her pocket for a penknife, and began cutting. Her muscles screamed as the fibres eventually gave, strand by strand, until suddenly the knot burst loose. Isaac's hands fell free, but she didn't wait. She did the same on the bindings around his chest, and freed him with a heavy scream. Then she hooked her arms under his armpits and dragged him up, the chair clattering backward into the flames. His legs buckled, barely carrying his weight.

'Move!' she shouted, though she wasn't sure if it was to him or herself. 'Otherwise we're both going to die in here!'

Isaac didn't need telling twice. Together they staggered through the thick smoke, each second stretching like an eternity. St Mary's groaned again above them, as if its namesake was screaming in pain.

A deafening crack exploded as part of the roof splintered and dropped somewhere behind, causing the flames to surge brighter, hungrier.

Stephanie bent her head low, eyes stinging, dragging Isaac through the haze in the vague direction of the door she'd come through.

One more step. One more. Don't stop. Don't you dare stop.

If you can walk into the fire, you can walk back out of it.

The clean night air hit her like a blessing as she stumbled out of the smoke, one arm locked under Isaac Grove's armpit. His weight was dead and awkward, his legs buckling beneath him with every dragging step.

'Keep moving...' she choked. 'A few more steps. Come on...'

They collapsed a few feet clear of the doorway, the damp grass beneath her palms providing some respite to her inflamed and scorched skin. The church behind them was alive with fire, bathing the surrounding area in a low orange glow that flickered off the car windows. Somewhere deep inside, the flames roared and crackled, the sound as terrifying as it was hypnotic.

Isaac heaved against the ground, coughing until it seemed like he might bring his lungs up onto the grass. His face was slick with sweat and soot, eyes streaming, hair plastered to his forehead. She pressed a hand to his shoulder to steady him.

'Isaac.' Her voice was hoarse, urgent. 'Where's Elias? Where's Toby? Where did he go?'

He shook his head weakly, the whites of his eyes glaring in the firelight. 'I don't know,' he rasped, barely audible over the roar of the blaze and the cries of her colleagues quickly surrounding them. 'I swear, I don't know. He just... he left the moment you came in.'

Before Stephanie could respond, the team arrived, manhandling her and Isaac farther away from the fire. They spoke to her, questioning if she was okay, but she couldn't hear them. Her mind was preoccupied with Elias. Of how he had escaped one fire as a child, and how he was set to do the same again.

But then she remembered the photograph. Of how they were both supposed to die in the flames. She didn't believe he would light the match and simply walk away. That wasn't how he wanted things to end.

Stephanie shrugged off her team's grip, then turned towards the fire.

The heat struck her full in the face, blistering, relentless. She shielded her eyes with a filthy sleeve and stumbled forward, ignoring the shouts behind her. Pieces of ash and debris rained down, burning holes into the fabric of her clothes

'Steph! Stop!' Giles cried as he tried to catch her. His hand snagged her jacket but she tore free, eyes locked on the fire.

'He's still in there!' she croaked, pointing into the blaze, her voice more animal than human. 'Elias is still inside.'

Another explosion cracked from deep within, the roof groaning under the weight of the fire. The team swore behind her, but none were brave – or stupid – enough to follow.

Stephanie pushed forward anyway. Her body screamed at her, but she forced her legs to move. As she crossed the threshold, a sudden blast of heat and smoke drove her to her knees. She pulled the neck of her sweat over her mouth and nose, forcing one more breath into her protesting lungs, and staggered deeper.

The church was an inferno. Pews blackened and toppled in waves of sparks. Smoke rolled above her head in thick, suffocating coils, consuming everything, starving the space of any light. Her eyes streamed. Every breath she took seared her throat worse than the last.

And then she heard it.

A scream.

Elias.

It came from deep within the nave, distorted by the crack and roar of burning wood. The raw, guttural cry of a man swallowed by the very element he had wielded as a weapon.

Stephanie staggered towards the sound, struggling for balance. Her legs felt heavy, and her body was ready to collapse. But she couldn't stop. Not now.

The heat from the fire pressed against her like hands trying to claim her. She couldn't see him, couldn't see anything. She coughed and doubled over, black spots flashing in her vision. Her knees buckled, the smoke slamming into her chest like a wall. She clawed at her throat, tried to force her body to take air, but nothing came.

Her ears rang with another scream. Longer, deeper. Elias, burning to death.

She tried to push forward again. But her body betrayed her. She couldn't see. She couldn't breathe. Her own scream came out as nothing, swallowed by the fire.

And then she felt it. Hands grabbing her from behind. Strong, gloved hands. She fought them at first, thinking Elias had somehow reached her and was going to claim her as his last victim. But then she caught the reflection of a visor, the shape of a helmet, and finally ceded control. The firefighter flung her body over his shoulder and carried her out of there effortlessly.

As they breached outside, the night air rushed into her lungs, and she collapsed once more onto the grass and damp earth, coughing until her whole body shook.

Surrounding her, the fire crew shouted orders, voices drowned out by the collapsing church. The roof gave a monstrous groan, then buckled, sparks blasting into the sky like fireworks.

Stephanie blinked through streaming eyes, trying to look back inside. Elias's screams had stopped. All that remained was fire.

And then, as she continued to fight for her breath, she closed her eyes and passed out, collapsing into the cold, wet blanket of grass.

CHAPTER
NINETY-ONE

The first thing she noticed when she opened her eyes and glimpsed through the darkness of her vision, was that her throat felt as if she'd swallowed hot coals succeeded by a handful of razor blades.

Then, after she blinked several times, Kimberley's face eventually came into focus beside her.

'What are you doing here?' Stephanie asked, her voice a whisper.

Kimberley let out a small gasp. She reached for Stephanie's hand and wrapped it in her own, squeezing tightly. 'I could say the same about you,' she hissed. 'What were you doing? What were you thinking? You ran into a burning building, Steph.'

Stephanie opened her mouth to respond but Kimberley wouldn't let her.

'I've already lost a baby. I can't lose my sister too.'

That hit home. Hard. And suddenly what she'd done dawned on her. She thought she'd been in a dream. That she could just wake up, respawn, and that everything would be fine, perfect, normal. But the reality had been different. She had put her life in jeopardy.

She squeezed her sister's hand and smiled as warmly as she could. 'I'm sorry, I...'

That was all she could manage before falling into a coughing fit. Daggers exploded in her lungs and throat as she spluttered.

'The doctors said you're lucky to be here, the amount of smoke you inhaled,' Kimberley explained. 'And they said you were even luckier to not get more serious burns than you did.'

It was then that Stephanie glanced down at her arms and took in the bandages for the first time. She felt no pain there, just the odd sensation of discomfort, like an itch she couldn't quite reach.

'I think Mum was watching out for you,' Kimberley continued. 'They said the worst you suffered was second degree on your fingers and palms. You very nearly singed your fingerprints off.'

'A life of crime awaits...' Stephanie croaked jokingly, before bursting into another coughing fit.

'Stop talking. Please. You're only going to make it worse.'

Stephanie did as she was told, and for a moment they sat there in silence. There was so much Stephanie wanted to say, apologise for. She wanted to pick up her sister, hug her and never let go.

'I love you,' she said eventually.

'I know,' Kim replied. 'I love you too. And... and...' She inhaled deeply. 'Jordan wanted to come,' she continued. 'But he didn't think it was a good idea, so he stayed at home.'

Kimberley reached down by her side and lifted a small bouquet of flowers. White. Pretty.

'He got you these.'

Stephanie smirked. 'They're beautiful. Tell him I said thank you.'

'You mean you don't want me to chuck them in the bin?'

Stephanie shook her head. 'I realised he's not that bad. I guess I could get to know him a little bit more. So long as he stops turning up at my house...'

Kimberley's eyes widened. 'Seriously?'

A weak nod.

'We can go for a coffee one time, maybe some lunch,' Stephanie answered. 'All of us.'

Before Kimberley could respond, a knock came from the door, and the elation on Kimberley's face slid away. The door opened, and DCI Clive McGowan stepped in, his presence filling the room in that quiet, immovable way of his.

'Apologies for interrupting,' he said, closing the door behind him. 'I came to check if you were awake.'

'Just about,' Stephanie joked. 'Could do with a nap though.'

Kimberley rose from her seat and started towards the exit. 'I'll let you two have a catch-up.'

Stephanie was about to protest, until her sister swiftly left the room, filling the room with an uncomfortable silence.

'Why do I feel like I'm about to be told off?'

Clive chuckled. 'Not yet. Once you've fully recovered. Maybe sooner.'

'I look forward to it.' She raised herself on the bed, wheezing, her lungs struggling for breath.

'You need to take it easy,' Clive said softly. 'You're lucky to be alive.'

'I've heard.'

'Everyone's worried about you. Especially Olivia. So they'll be pleased to know that you're very much awake and breathing – just about.'

Stephanie said nothing. She'd already said too much, and the pain in her chest and throat was becoming too severe.

'I thought I'd come by and fill you in, put your mind at rest somewhat.'

She held his gaze.

'The fire's been put out at St Mary's,' he said. 'This time the fire brigade recovered Elias's body. He didn't make it.'

Stephanie said nothing, allowed no emotion to show in her expression.

'They didn't find any more tins, nor any photographs or inscriptions,' he continued. 'Which leads me to believe that it's over. You found him.'

'And Isaac?'

'Also alive. Alive and breathing. Just about. His burns and levels of smoke inhalation were much more severe than yours, but he'll survive. Thanks to you, Steph. You saved his life.'

'I could have saved another.'

Clive inched closer, shaking his head. 'When they found Elias's body, they found he'd locked himself in a small room and swallowed the key. He was never going to come out of there alive. He made sure of it. There was nothing more you could have done.'

THE END

B ut not quite. The story continues with *Noughts & Crosses*, the next book in the series:

The game is simple. The consequences are fatal.

Bodies are appearing across Essex and Surrey with noughts and crosses carved into their skin. Each victim played an online game before they died. They all lost.

Detective Inspector Stephanie Broadbent leads the investigation into what connects the victims. But as she digs deeper into the twisted mind behind the game, the investigation takes a personal turn — one that threatens to drag her past into the present.

The game has only just begun.

Coming soon
Click here to pre-order now

ALSO BY JACK PROBYN

The DI Stephanie Broadbent Surrey Hiller Crime Thriller Series:

BOOK 1: THE VOODOO KILLER

She returned home to start again. Instead, she woke the darkness she thought she'd buried. Before she's even settled in, a university student is found dead in her halls of residence after a night out. What first appears to be an open and shut case takes a darker turn when a voodoo doll is found near the body. Stephanie is forced to confront the ghosts of her past—while racing to stop a killer whose next move is already taking shape in thread and cloth.

Read The Voodoo Killer on Kindle and Kindle Unlimited

BOOK 2: THE BOGEYMAN

Thirty years ago, the people of Guildford were haunted by a figure who crept into children's bedrooms and watched them sleep. When he left, he left behind a single party balloon. And then he vanished. The visits stopped. Now it's happening again.

Read The Bogeyman on Kindle and Kindle Unlimited

BOOK 3: THE BURNING MAN

When the charred remains of a body are found in the quaint Surrey Hills, the trauma of DI Stephanie Broadbent's past is reignited. When another body appears, Stephanie uncovers a connection that threatens to set the world — and more bodies — alight.

Read The Burning Man on Kindle and Kindle Unlimited

BOOK 4: NOUGHTS & CROSSES

Across Essex and Surrey, bodies are turning up with **noughts and crosses carved into their flesh.** Each victim played the same online game before they died. Each one lost.

Read Noughts & Crosses on Kindle and Kindle Unlimited

ALSO BY JACK PROBYN

The DS Tomek Bowen Murder Mystery Series:

BOOK 1: DEATH'S JUSTICE

Southend-on-Sea, Essex: Detective Sergeant Tomek Bowen — driven, dogged, and haunted by the death of his brother — is called to one of the most shocking crime scenes he has ever seen. A man has been ritualistically murdered and dumped in an allotment near the local airport. Early investigations indicate this was a man with a past. A past that earned him many enemies.

Download Death's Justice

BOOK 2: DEATH'S GRIP

Annabelle Lake thought she recognised the Ford Fiesta waiting outside her school, and the driver in it. She was wrong. Her body is discovered some time later, dangling from a swing in a local playground on Canvey Island.

Download Death's Grip

BOOK 3: DEATH'S TOUCH

When the fog clears one December morning in Essex, the body of a teenage girl is discovered lying face down in a field. As a result, the case quickly lands on DS Tomek Bowen's desk who, while trying to juggle his newfound life as a single parent to a thirteen-year-old daughter, must unearth the deadly sequence of events and bring the truth to light.

Download Death's Touch

BOOK 4: DEATH'S KISS

The darkest secrets never stay secret for long...

When the body of a homeless man is discovered on Southend seafront, wedged between the beach huts of Thorpe Bay, the people of Essex don't raise an eyebrow.

But when the post-mortem reveals the identity to be that of local MP, Herbert Tucker, the town begins to sit up.

Download Death's Kiss

BOOK 5: DEATH'S TASTE

Some secrets never wash away...

On a windy and blistering cold morning, Morgana Usyk, owner of Morgana's Café, visits Mulberry Harbour a little over a mile out to sea. A short while later, her body is found in the shallows, floating beside the harbour.

Download Death's Taste

MAKE AN AUTHOR'S DAY

Here we are. The end.

Well, I say "we"... I mean *you*. Thank you.

Thank you for getting this far and sticking with me as I conjure up these greatly wild and bizarre stories in my head, and then later translate them to paper (or rather, digital files).

Amazon is littered with millions of books (literally, and I don't use that term lightly), and so it's often difficult to find your next read. You just want to know which book to dive into next. But sometimes you don't have the time to sift through them all, so what do you do?

Look at the reviews, of course.

We use them in every aspect of our life. Restaurants. Films. Our next television set. Pair of headphones. Almost everything is governed by the thoughts of other people.

Crazy, isn't it?

But what happens when you come across a book with no reviews? You might shy away from it. It's difficult to trust the book.

Your time is precious. Your time is valuable. You don't want to be wasting it on disappointing stories. Nobody does. And I don't want that for you. Sometimes I worry the same thing might happen to this story. But there's a solution.

A review goes a long way. And it gives me the confidence to continue crafting the crazy thoughts in my head — one day of turning this dream into a full-time career.

So, to help new readers discover the books, and to you reading more of the same, you can leave a review at the below links:

Amazon US
Amazon UK
Amazon CA
Amazon AU

Thank you.
Your Friendly Author,
Jack Probyn

ABOUT THE AUTHOR

Jack Probyn is a British crime writer and the author of the Jake Tanner crime thriller series, set in London.

He currently lives in Surrey with his partner and cat, and is working on a new murder mystery series set in his hometown of Essex.

Don't want to sign up to yet another mailing list? Then you can keep up to date with Jack's new releases by following one of the below accounts. You'll get notified when I've got a new book coming out, without the hassle of having to join my mailing list.

Amazon Author Page "Follow":
    1. Click the link here: https://geni.us/AuthorProfile
    2. Beneath my profile picture is a button that says "Follow"
    3. Click that, and then Amazon will email you with new releases and promos.

BookBub Author Page "Follow":
    1. Similar to the Amazon one above, click the link here: https://www.bookbub.com/authors/jack-probyn
    2. Beside my profile picture is a button that says "Follow"
    3. Click that, and then BookBub will notify you when I have a new release

If you want more up to date information regarding new releases, my writing process, and everything else in between, the best place to be in the know is my Facebook Page. We've got a little community growing over there. Why not be a part of it?

Facebook: https://www.facebook.co.uk/jackprobynbooks